THE WILD SIDE: A FRIENDS-TO-LOVERS ROMANTIC COMEDY

A FRIENDS-TO-LOVERS ROMANTIC COMEDY

CASSIE-ANN L. MILLER

The Wild Side (A Small Town Friends-to-Lovers Romance)

Copyright © 2022 Cassie-Ann L. Miller

All rights reserved.

Photo credit: Wander Aguiar Photography
Model: Vinicious

18052022

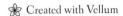 Created with Vellum

STORIES BY CASSIE-ANN L. MILLER

Lover Boy
Play Boy
Bad Boy
Hot Boy
Rich Boy
Dream Boy

The Dirty Suburbs Series

Dirty Neighbor
Dirty Player
Dirty Stranger
Dirty Favor
Dirty Lover
Dirty Farmer
Dirty Silver
Dirty Forever
Dirty Christmas

The Esquire Girls Series

Amber Nights (Amber – Books 1, 2, 3 & 4)

Madison's Story

For Madison, Always (Madison – Books 1, 2, 3 & 4)

Ruthie's Story

Ruthie's Desire (Ruthie – Books 1, 2, 3 & 4)

Hailey's story

Moments with Hailey (Hailey - Books 1, 2, 3 & 4)

Esquire HEAT Series

A Very Eager Intern

A Very Frustrated Attorney

Standalone Novels
Matteo

Beast

Happy New You

ONE

CASH

I PUSH BACK the cuff of my custom-tailored dress shirt and glare down at the face of my Patek Philippe watch.

Fuck, I'm running late. Very late.

Across the massive mahogany conference table, a bunch of disgruntled corporate executives slam around their whiskey glasses and grumble about having wasted their Wednesday afternoon.

Tough luck.

Today's negotiations were a complete bust but that's not my problem. If those assholes had approached this deal in good faith, we could have easily struck a mutually-beneficial agreement. Instead, they decided to be stingy.

So, no deal.

I know what my time is worth and I know what Westbrook Wealth Management brings to the table. I refuse to do business with a group of slick-haired swindlers trying to lowball me.

In one seamless movement, I briskly glide out of my executive chair and give them a curt nod. "Gentlemen." *And I use that term lightly.*

I'm unapologetic as I leave the men to their whining and exit the conference room. Nicky is hot on my heels, an iPad and a slim file folder neatly gripped in her manicured hands.

"Traffic is gonna be a mess at this time of day, and you still have to swing by the bakery," she reminds me as we hustle down the carpeted hallway back toward my corner office.

Through the gleaming floor-to-ceiling windows, I can see the sun diving behind the skyscrapers embellishing the Chicago skyline. The clouds are dark and thick.

That's not a good sign.

I throw her a scowl over my shoulder. "You're not helping."

She shrugs, struggling to keep pace with my long strides. "I told you I could have gone to the bakery for you."

"And I told *you* I'd handle it myself."

"The CFO of the city's fastest growing wealth management company fetching a birthday cake from a bakery halfway across town—on the company dime, no less. Yeah, that's fiscally efficient," she bites, unfazed by talking back to her boss.

"The icing gets smushed every single time you go to the bakery."

"That was *one* time."

"Every time, Nicky. Every time."

Agnes from Human Resources looks up from her fax machine and catches my eye. She gives me a grandmotherly smile. "Good luck tonight, Cash. If everything goes according to plan, next time I see you, you could be a married man!"

I crinkle my brow. *Uh...um, huh?*

Nicky snickers into her sleeve.

I turn my glare on her. "Do I even want to know what garbage the office rumor mill is spewing today?"

She flinches. "Probably not."

I shrug it off. I *so* don't have the time to deal with this.

"Were the balloons delivered?" I demand as we turn a corner down another long, busy hallway.

"For the seventeenth time, yes, the balloons were delivered. They're in your office." She pauses. "I still say you should go with roses. Red roses. Nothing says I'm here to collect my mail-order bride like red roses." The little devil smirks.

My younger sister has never shied away from pushing my buttons. I hired her as an intern here a few weeks back. More and more, I'm regretting that decision.

"She is not my mail-order bride."

"What do you want to call her?"

"She's my friend," I state as we enter my office.

And—whoa!—the balloons are here. A *lot* of them. I may have gone a bit overboard with my order. I have to twist my body like a contortionist just to get around my desk.

Nicky sets the tablet and folder on the edge of my neatly-organized wood and chrome tabletop. "Your friend who you promised you'd marry if she was still single at age thirty. Newsflash, boss—as of today, she's officially age thirty. Time to redeem your marriage pact," she sings.

"Jeez—that was a stupid joke Meghan and I made. A million years ago. You should quit spreading rumors about your superiors if you want to keep your job here. There is no marriage pact."

I check the time again. Shit. I should have hit the road hours ago.

"So I'm supposed to believe that you're driving the next six hours to deliver a birthday cake to a friend?"

"You can believe whatever you want to believe, Nicky," I deadpan, growing tired of this little chit chat, especially when I'm running so late.

"Admit it—at night, you lie awake thinking about wedded bliss with Meghan Hutchins."

"At night, I lie awake thinking about how much happier my life will be once I fire you."

My sister dramatically throws her head back and emits a heavy sigh. "You're twenty-nine years old, Cassius. You can admit to having a crush on a girl."

Sylvester from accounting pokes his head into my office, purple satin shirt gleaming and green polka dot tie swinging. He props a hip against the doorjamb and folds his arms across his chest. "Ooh! What'd I miss? Cash's off to do that whole arranged marriage thing? So fricking hot." He fans his cheeks and wiggles his narrow shoulders.

I telepathically shoot eye-daggers at his face.

He clams up and skitters off down the hallway.

Nicky titters under her breath. I snarl and narrow my eyes at her.

"Sorry," she mumbles.

She's not sorry.

Grabbing my dry cleaning and the balloons, I head for the door. On the way to the elevator, I nearly run head on into my father who's wandering out of the executive break room, dairy-loaded bagel in hand.

"Daddy, lay off the cream cheese, would you?" Nicky chides in a low voice. "Remember what the doctor said."

He looks like he might argue but we all know he's mush in Nicky's hands. Dad may be a hardass with my brothers and me, but my sister can get him to do practically anything she wants.

"Can't catch a break around this place," the old man

grouses. He takes one big bite out of his afternoon treat and dumps the rest into the recycling bin under someone's desk. He turns a grave expression toward me. "So the Blanchet Trust negotiations fell through this afternoon?"

"Yep." Avoiding eye contact, I stab the elevator button.

I can feel him staring at the side of my head. "Well, that's a shame..." he says carefully.

Nonchalant as fuck, I shrug. "You win some, you lose some."

The elevator arrives and thankfully, it's empty. But if I thought I'd get rid of my meddling family members so easily, I was wrong. My father and sister climb onto the lift right along with me and my three thousand helium-filled balloons.

"I reviewed the terms the company proposed," Dad says, craning his neck around the balloons to catch my eyes. "We could have made a few concessions. At least, for the sake of closing the deal."

I turn and stare at the elevator panel. I prod the 'ground floor' button half a dozen times. Can this thing move any slower?

"Those penny-pinching assholes were trying to under-value us, trying to cut down our portfolio management fees. I won't stand for it," I snarl. "I'm confident that we can quadruple their money in the next eighteen months. But I won't put in all that work for free. They have to make it worth my while."

I scowl at him. He scowls at me.

"Maybe you could have taken them out for drinks?" Nicky intervenes oh-so-helpfully, trying to play peace-maker. "You might have gotten them to loosen up a bit, y'know, in a more social setting."

My voice goes even rougher as my annoyance continues

to rise. "Our company's reputation speaks for itself. I don't have time to pander to time-wasters who aren't serious about what they want. I don't have to kiss anyone's ass."

I set up a firm, un-fuck-with-able boundary long ago—whoever has the nerve to demand even a moment of my precious time had better make it worth my while. I'm a busy man and there aren't enough hours in the day for bullshit.

"Jeez. Don't bite my head off." Nicky throws her palms up in surrender. "It was just a suggestion. Since the whole stubborn-grumpy-asshole vibe doesn't seem to be getting you anywhere." She turns to our father. "What's that Grammy always says about catching flies with honey instead of vinegar?"

Dad's face goes red and daggers of frustration shoot from his eyes. "You know how your brother is," he says to Nicky like I'm not standing right here. "Set in his ways. You can't convince him of anything." He stomps a foot.

Lately, my father and I have been arguing a lot. Mainly about strategies for growing the company. We hardly ever see eye to eye on the topic.

I should be in charge. He should be retired by now.

I square my shoulders, ready to go to war with him—as usual—but the hostility in the elevator dissipates when he sways a little on his feet. A slight frown ripples across his forehead. He lowers his face and pinches the bridge of his nose.

Nicky and I exchange a look. I open my mouth to say something, to tell Dad that he can't keep getting himself worked up this way. And beyond that, it's damn time for him to slow down. But my sister subtly shakes her head, reminding me that now isn't the time to get into it.

The elevator arrives on the ground floor. I wrestle my balloons out the door and try to hurry off with a quick goodbye, but my dad hustles on right alongside me, beating away the balloons that smack him in the forehead.

A teasing grin takes over his weathered face. "So...off to cash in your marriage voucher, huh?"

I groan. "Does everybody in this office just sit around gossiping about my non-existent love life?" With my free hand, I loosen the knot of my tie.

"Not everybody," Nicky quips. "You might find someone in the mailroom who doesn't—no, wait—don't they have that bet going on downstairs?"

Dad smirks. "Yeah, I put fifty bucks in the pot."

"Whaaaat?! I only put in a twenty!" Nicky groans. "The pay sucks around here. I'm gonna have to skip a couple lattes this week to up my bet."

I point a glare at her. "Your smug little attitude won't serve you well in the unemployment line, Nicky."

Dad throws an arm around my sister's shoulder. "Don't worry, honey. We'll get HR to check the box next to 'hurt Cash's feelings'. Then you can come work in my office, where you'll be appreciated."

"Aww, thanks, Dad!" The little brat beams and my own father high-fives her. "By the way, do I get a pay raise?"

Dad thoughtfully considers it.

"Nepotism will be the downfall of this place," I hiss under my breath.

Nicky ruefully shakes her head. "Y'see? There goes the pot calling the kettle black again."

That's where she's wrong. My rise in the ranks of this company has not been a free ride. My father may be the one who founded WWM but I've sure as hell paid my dues, working my ass off all the way up the ladder. And I plan to keep climbing. I have big goals for the firm's future. I just need to get Dad to see the vision I see.

That's a discussion for some other time, though. I snap out a gruff response instead of prolonging this pointless argument. "Stuff it. Both of you. Or I'm not coming back."

Stopped in the middle of the lobby, my father feigns shock, slapping his palms to both sides of his whiskered face. "Oh no! How ever will you find purpose and meaning in your life if you aren't chained to your desk eighteen hours a day, six days a week? Might you actually find a hobby or two to revolve your life around?"

Dad and Nicky throw their heads back with laughter.

I have no time for their bullshit. So I keep walking. Straight for the door.

Richard, the security guy, offers me a grave salute as I stroll past the front desk. "Good luck with all that arranged marriage stuff tonight, Cash."

Goddamn.

I don't stop shaking my head as I'm fleeing the building, desperate to get out of the city before the traffic holds me captive for the night. After a quick stop at the bakery, I hit the highway.

The worst part of the six-hour road trip is being left alone with my thoughts. Thoughts that keep creeping in, trying to hijack my lifelong friendship, and take it to places that terrify me. Thoughts I find myself battling to push aside for every one of the next five-hundred plus miles.

The further I drive from the safety of Chicago, the more tied up I get in my imagination. I've entertained the idea of marriage and kids, I guess. But it's always been something out there in the distant future. Far down the line. Something I could delay just a little bit longer. Something for some other day. But with each mile I drive, that landmark seems closer and closer on the horizon. Too close. It's terrifying.

I snap out of my introspection as I swerve onto my exit. Through the drizzle hitting my windshield, I glance up at a large, familiar highway sign looming above the roadway.

Welcome to Honey Hill, Iowa.

A strong gust of wind rattles the crooked sign as I drive past it, entering my sleepy hometown. I flick my indicator and make a quick right turn. I pull into the local gas station to fill my tank. A sense of nostalgia wraps around me. So many memories in this place.

In a hurry, I hop out and start fueling up. No fancy electric car for me. I drive a sleek luxury vehicle that demands premium gasoline every few hundred miles. Totally worth it.

While I'm pumping my gas, my phone beeps. It's a text message from my sister-in-law. Well, technically, my ex-sister-in-law but as far as I'm concerned, Alana is still family.

Alana: The weather's looking pretty bad and it's starting to get late. Are you sure you're coming?

I glance up at the darkened sky, inhaling the rain-scented air. I'm hoping to make it to my destination before it starts coming down for real, but my chances are looking slim.

Me: For the millionth time—yes, I'm coming

Alana: Ok

Alana: I'm getting nervous. I just don't want her to be disappointed

Me: I won't disappoint her

Never. She's my best friend in the world, dammit.

Me: Stop worrying

I hurry inside the gas station's convenience store, using

the restroom then browsing the sad-looking shelves and trying to decide whether I should grab anything else for Meghan.

I pause in the meager wine section and pick up a bottle of red that looks decent. I grab some soda, too, in case she's not in the mood to drink alcohol tonight. I march dutifully past the dozen different brands of condoms, willing myself not to even take a peak. But when I'm halfway down the aisle, something draws my eyes back to the condom display.

Heat throbs in my crotch. Damn. It's been a while.

Stop it, asshole.

Meghan is my friend, and I don't want to show up and make things weird with her tonight, especially on her thirtieth birthday.

I want to simply enjoy catching up. Hanging out together. Like always. Like friends.

It's just everyone else messing with my head, and making me lose my cool.

Have I ever imagined sex with Meghan? Sure. Yes. A time or two. Or twenty...thousand. I mean, Meghan's *hot.*

But I'm no fool. I'd never compromise our friendship just for a chance to get in her pants. Finding a woman to have meaningless sex with is relatively easy. If I really want to get laid, I don't have to try that hard. But a friendship like the one I have with Meghan? That's one in a billion. I could never put a price tag on it. And there's no way I'm doing anything to put it in jeopardy.

Giggles and shrieks from the front of the store grab my attention. As I approach the checkout, I see three girls in gas station uniforms eyeballing my Audi out the window.

Shit—the rain is already coming down heavier than when I walked in.

The girl with the short red ponytail winks at me as I set down my goods on the counter. "Nice ride, mister."

I scan the chocolate selection in front of the register, too distracted by my plans for tonight to pay this girl the attention she's so clearly seeking. "Thanks," I mutter, grabbing a bag of gas station brand peanut butter cups. Meghan's favorite.

A girl with mischievous eyes and straight black hair leans across the counter, exposing her cleavage. "Need some company tonight?" She smiles at me.

I don't bother to smile back.

The tallest of the girls walks up, slinging an arm over each of her friends. She attempts to sweeten the deal. "If they say three's a crowd, then *four* must be the magic number." She counts each of us in turn with subtle flicks of her chin.

Wow. Classy.

Thankfully, the suggestive comments come to a halt when their manager pops out of the back room holding a clip board. She rolls her eyes at her workers. "He has a girlfriend, you thirsty vultures." The woman turns a tired smile at me. "Hey, Cash."

"Hey." I recognize her as someone I went to high school with. For the life of me, I can never remember her name.

"You have a girlfriend?" The redhead pouts in my direction.

The manager answers for me. "Yes. Meghan. The cute vet technician who always comes in here. Everybody in town knows that."

Um…everybody in town knows that? Looks like the rumors about my love life extend well beyond the Chicago city limits.

Three pairs of eager eyes stare at me, waiting for my corroboration.

"Yeah," I confirm. Just to get these thirsty girls off my back. Meanwhile, inside my head I'm repeating my decade-old mantra. *Best friend, not girlfriend. Best friend.*

"Aww. That's too bad," the black-haired girl chirps with a fake pout. "Your girlfriend is so lucky." She looks ready to throw in the towel. Thank god.

"Well, don't keep her waiting." The redhead grins, shooing me toward the door. "Go! Go!"

I grumble a 'good night' and, on that, I rush out of the gas station into what is now a freaking downpour. The sky is black and the town has already gone quiet for the night. It's late as fuck.

My cheap plastic bags crinkle obnoxiously when I drop my haul onto my passenger seat. I yank open my glovebox and shove my receipt inside. Sure as hell I'm expensing this trip, whether the assholes in accounting like it or not.

As I'm shutting the glove compartment, an older, faded slip of paper flutters to the floor. I swallow and my throat knots hard as I pick it up. I let my eyes skim over the words jotted across the nine and a half year old scrap of paper, the signatures scribbled in sloppy, familiar handwriting.

On this twenty-fifth day of May, Cassius Westbrook and Meghan Hutchins hereby agree that if neither of them are married by the time they turn age thirty, they shall marry one another.

Putting the old receipt back where I found it, I forcibly shove those memories aside. I slam the box shut and pull out of the gas station with my wipers swishing rain left and right.

Just my friend. Meghan Hutchins is just my friend.

Although the whole world seems to be convinced otherwise.

TWO

MEGHAN

"Y'KNOW, TODAY ISN'T *THAT* BAD," I tighten my towel around my boobs and lift open the top of the washing machine. "Yes, it's my thirtieth birthday. And yes, I'm spending it doing my laundry—alone—but who am I to expect the world to stop spinning and throw me a pity party, y'know?"

I peer down into the hollow barrel of my washing machine. A full load of pink-tinted blouses stare back at me.

Those blouses used to be white.

Twenty-three minutes ago.

Shit—did I accidentally drop a red sock in there or something?

Rising onto my tiptoes, I lean down and dig through the damp laundry in search of the errant article of clothing responsible for ruining half my wardrobe. "What I'm saying is, life is all about choices. And I choose to be grateful," I declare as I pick the strawberry-patterned granny panties I wore to work this morning out of the load of discolored blouses. "I'm grateful for this house I bought all on my own. And for a job I love. And for you..."

Feeling a genuine flutter of happiness in my heart, I pause to tickle behind the ear of the five-pound ball of fur and bones curled up atop the dryer. Captain Ginger lazily opens one amber eye to squint vacantly at me.

"As far as birthdays go, this one isn't a *total* dud...right?"

The grumpy bastard lifts his little orange paw and smacks my hand away from his ear.

"Hey!" I chide softly. "Don't be mean to me. I'm going through a 'thing' right now. I could use some emotional support."

I pour in a bit of detergent and restart the washing machine, hoping to rinse the red dye out of my blouses. While the barrel fills with water, I turn around to scoop up the basket of tank tops, gym bras and yoga pants I just pulled out of the dryer. I find the haughty white Persian cat stretched out across the top of my clean clothes.

Well, no wonder I'm always covered in cat hair.

"Cotton Ball! You're not supposed to be there and you know it." I gently shoo her off and she hops down to her feet in that regal way of hers, cursing at me the whole time.

These two are a pair of entitled, little brats. Too bad they're so damn adorable. And I'm getting *way* more attached to them than I should.

With my phone clutched securely in my palm, I pad up the stairs, laundry basket tucked under my arm.

"As I was saying before I was so rudely interrupted, today hasn't been *entirely* lame. Alana took me out for lunch earlier, and she splurged on a huge piece of double chocolate cake. Isn't she sweet?" I grin at the thought of my lifelong bestie. "Anyway, we didn't come close to finishing the cake, so I've got at least one thing sitting in the fridge to look forward to later. Then, Emma and Ziggy promised to take me out this weekend, so I'll count that as another 'something' to look forward to."

I enter my bedroom, Captain Ginger and Cotton Ball tangling around my ankles.

These cats have been extra, extra clingy tonight. Which is a tad creepy, because the orange one usually stays hidden all day, only coming out to attack my socked feet while I get ready for bed.

But tonight, it's like they're rubbing up against my legs, mewling at me, and saying, "We understand you're thirty now and still all alone. Adopt us and we'll upgrade you from lonely bachelorette to crazy cat lady."

"I'm onto you," I murmur to them as I lower to the edge of my bed with a bottle of moisturizer in hand.

Most of my recent birthdays have been spent with my girlfriends, but this year, it seems that everyone has something more important to do. Alana, Ziggy, Emma—hell even the woman who birthed me—all had excuses for why they couldn't celebrate with me tonight.

I've been trying to brush it off, to not be offended, reminding myself that the girls all have their own lives to live with their own things happening. Especially on a week night.

But it sure doesn't help that what was promising to be a sunny spring day somehow rolled into a rainy and miserable night. I thought I could at least treat myself to a solo picnic on my back patio, but apparently the weather gods were like "Nope, we've got other plans, too."

I've been anticipating this day with mild to moderate levels of dread for pretty much the last three years. But now that it's here and has proven more uneventful than a trip to the eye doctor, I'm starting to wonder why I've been psyching myself out all this time.

My phone dings on the mattress next to me and I pounce on it. But disappointment sweeps over my body like a wave when I see it's just a few of the girls from Corri's hair salon, sending me a string of silly celebratory gifs.

Earlier, my friend Minka from Sin Valley sent me the most perfect birthday serenade featuring her rockstar husband, Declan, and their adorable babbling toddler, Melody. I smile to myself as I watch the video again.

Throughout the day, my phone's been buzzing with texts and calls from all my close friends and relatives, wishing me a happy day.

...Except for one person. Cash.

Which, for the life of me, doesn't make any sense. Cash has never, ever missed a single birthday. If we couldn't see each other in person, he's always called. The birthday calls have been the more frequent mode of celebration in recent years since he lives so far away. But this year? Nothing. Dead silence.

I'm surprised by how much that stings.

Yeah, I can gloss over all my other disappointments and make excuses for everyone else who has let me down today. But knowing that one of my closest friends completely forgot about me this year—on such a special birthday, too—that stings.

Right now, I feel anything but special.

After slathering my skin with lotion, I rise from the edge of my bed and drop the towel. I take in my reflection, examining what I'm workin' with.

"I'm kind of cute...right?" I mumble to my furry companions. "Totally. Yeah, definitely...Um, I think."

My hips are rounder than they were this time last year. I've gained a few pounds, for sure. But whatever. I have curves for days. And all the important stuff is still *relatively* tight and perky—for the most part—so I'm taking that as a good sign.

My blonde curls are a frizzy mess after my shower and without makeup on, I'd probably get carded at the liquor store. But what bothers me most is the flatness in my blue eyes tonight.

As much as it goes against my usual happy-go-lucky philosophy, the truth is, tonight, I'm sad. And I don't like it.

"It *could* be worse," I tell the cats who are now sprawled on my comforter. "I mean—I once heard this story about some poor woman who discovered a gray hair in her pubes *right before* she turned the big three-oh." I whisper, feeling a shudder of sympathy move through me. "Can you even imagine that?! At least I didn't find a grey hair in my bush today. There. Something else to be grateful for."

I'm searching for the silver lining. It's a full-blown search party over here.

I'm not entirely averse to aging or anything. I guess a part of me just hoped to have accomplished more by the time I hit this big milestone.

I would have loved to be married by now. And to have a bunch of kids running around the house, driving me crazy. Or at least to have a steady boyfriend to pop a bottle of cheap champagne with. With each passing birthday, it seems like Mom was right after all—the women in our family are cursed. We don't get happy endings.

Deciding not to feel sorry for myself, I dig through the basket of clean clothes and pull on some underwear along with my favorite yoga pants and a fresh tank top. I go down to the kitchen, rummage around in the fridge and put together a small dinner for me and my two foster cats.

I slap together a toasted sandwich for myself out of yesterday's grilled chicken and plop a couple cans of smoked salmon into the cats' dishes. My sandwich doesn't look too great, and I'm completely aware that the cats are feasting like royalty while I'm scraping together scraps from my fridge.

Getting out my leftover lunch cake, I flip it open and stab my fork through the frosting, deciding that it's *my* day. If I wanna eat my dessert before dinner, then to hell with societal rules.

I pour myself a glass of wine, not even bothering to open up the nice bottle. I just keep working on the bottle I opened last weekend. Seems like a waste to have *two* half empty bottles open at the same time on what's turning out to be a regular ol' Wednesday evening.

As I crunch into the mini chocolate chips hiding in the cake, my mind drifts back to one evening in particular. "Wanna hear something funny?" I ask Cotton Ball and Captain Ginger as I lean a hip against the kitchen counter. "Me and Cash made a marriage pact once. It was the night of his brother Davis's wedding to your aunt Alana. At the wedding reception, the guy I was dating started making out with some random stranger and left me standing there like a total fool. Cash, in an attempt to make me feel better about myself, swooped in to the rescue and promised that if I was still single on this very day—my thirtieth birthday—*he* would marry me." I chuckle wryly to myself. "It was all just a joke, though. I never *actually* expected him to just show up here and whisk me off to the altar."

Of course not.

Cash Westbrook is now the filthy rich CFO of one of the biggest financial firms in Chicago. He's gorgeous. He's brilliant. He has multiple degrees in business and finance from an ivy league institution and a list of accomplishments a mile long.

He's the perfect man, who has an unlimited pick from the most beautiful women in the country. *Of course* he's forgotten all about a silly promise he made to me nine and a half years ago. And on the off chance he didn't forget, it'd only be something he'd laugh about now. A funny story to tell his picture-perfect future wife someday.

I'd like to say I've completely forgotten about that marriage pact, too, but since that day, the contract scribbled onto the back of that gas station receipt has been there, dangling in the back of my mind like the lyrics to my favorite childhood song.

I take a small sip of my wine. "Cash is an incredible person. A bit of a grumpy jerk sometimes, but still an incredible person. And I'm so proud to call him my best friend. But that's all he'll ever be in my life."

A dark laugh escapes when I realize I'm having a full-blown conversation with my foster cats, only cementing my own looney future.

God, it's true. I'm officially the cat lady.

Okay, get yourself together, Megs. The world doesn't owe you anything. You've gotta just be grateful for what you have, right?

I'm not usually like this. I'm usually optimistic and upbeat. Here's the way I see it—there are two types of people in the world. Those who complain that they can't see the sunshine through the rainclouds. And those who choose to *be* the sunshine. Usually, I choose to be the sunshine. Usually. At the moment, I'm sort of struggling to wade my way through these rainclouds.

Dinner forgotten, I split up my unappealing sandwich and feed that to the cats, too. All the while, my phone is never far away. Though I know the day is over, and I've been long forgotten, I can't help but hold out hope for a call.

Stuffing the last bite of cake into my face, I drift to the darkened front window where sheets of rain fall and distort my view of the neighborhood.

My eyes catch on movement at the house across the street. Jasper and his friends are having another party over there. Well, at least *somebody's* having fun tonight.

Cash owns that house. He bought it years ago when my former neighbors left town and put it up for sale. When I questioned why in the world he'd buy a house in Honey Hill, when he never plans to move back home, he told me that you could never have too much real estate in your portfolio.

Spoken like a true business tycoon.

Except now, his freeloading younger brother Jasper is living there, turning the quiet home into his personal playboy bachelor pad, since Cash rarely comes home anymore.

The cats finish their multi-course meal, and we end up snuggling on the couch. I flip on the TV and browse my way to the National Geographic Channel.

I glance at my phone again. Still nothing. No missed calls. Not even a text.

It just doesn't make sense how after all these years that he'd forget.

Unless...

Unless he remembers *exactly* what today is and is freaked out that I'm going to hold him to our silly nuptial contract.

Oh my gosh—that's even more embarrassing. Does he really think I'm *that* pathetic? Now, all I want is to dig a hole in my back yard and hide out in it for the rest of my miserable days.

A documentary on tropical marine life plays as I distractedly pet the cats and scroll through my favorite clothing sites on my laptop.

I promised myself that I'd get my online shopping habit under control. But when I come across a T-shirt that says something about preferring to sleep next to a self-absorbed asshole that purrs instead of one who talks, I suddenly can't resist treating myself to a birthday gift tonight.

Within a few clicks, I'm handing over my credit card information. And then I'm staring at a confirmation email ensuring me that the quirky T-shirt is on its way to my address. To fill the gaping emptiness in my life.

Yes, I'm being dramatic. I know.

As the cats both purr their contentment, I struggle to accept my single cat lady status. If this is the best part of my whole day, what does that say about my future? Hell, I'm only thirty. If I'm around seventy more years, well...I'm not even willing to do the math. That's a lot of cats, and a lot of lonely nights.

A sudden strike of lightning and a crack of thunder sends the cats scampering off my lap and fleeing the room, desperate to save themselves.

Welp. That just confirms how much they care about their foster mom.

I might as well turn in for the night and stop the cats from shredding my bedding. But before I make it to the hall, a loud knock on my front door makes me jump. With a frown, I make my way across the living room and cautiously open the door.

I gasp.

A grumpy-faced Cash Westbrook is standing there,

soaked to the bone and out of breath, looking as though he just finished a triathlon in a freaking downpour. His expensive shirt is drenched and plastered to his broad, strong chest. He has an oversized bouquet of balloons, a dripping wet cake box and a bunch of soggy plastic bags clutched in one of his enclosed fists.

My mouth flops open and closed several times as I struggle for what to say.

He swipes at the clump of wet hair matted to his forehead. He thrusts his dripping wet offering at me with a scowl. "Happy birthday, Buttercup."

THREE

CASH

MEGHAN'S GOT a skip in her step as she ushers me inside and runs off to grab some towels.

"Can I make you some soup?" she offers brightly when she returns with a selection of fluffy, pastel-colored terrycloth stacked high in her arms. "Or some hot cocoa? To help you get warmed up?" She hands the towels to me. Before I can answer, her eyes dart to the room around us and embarrassment tinges her cheeks. "The place is a mess. Sorry. I wasn't expecting guests tonight."

She hustles around the living room, plumping the couch cushions and lighting some jar candles and making the place inviting for me. This is how Meghan gets when she's excited. But tonight, she's making me dizzy with the way she's energetically buzzing around. Especially with those two yowling cats tangling around her feet.

I'm sitting on the overstuffed suede couch, rubbing a large terrycloth towel over my soaked hair. "The place is not a mess," I tell her. "And I've got all the snacks we need right here." I jerk my chin toward the small dark wood coffee table where I emptied my gas station goodies the second I walked in.

I don't care about the state the house is in and I'm definitely not expecting her to offer me a four-course meal. I just want her to come hang out.

But at the moment, she's hunched over the coffee table, rearranging a pile of magazines. And I'm forcing my eyes to stay off her ass. Because I'm not a creep. Or at least, I'm trying not to be.

Her forehead crinkles as she pauses to stare pointedly at me over her shoulder. "I'm talking about *real* food, Cash. Aren't you hungry? You must be starving. You've been driving for hours." She straightens and turns hastily toward the kitchen. "I'm sure I have a fajita kit somewhere in the pantry. Oh, wait—I might be out of salsa. But I have this awesome new honey-mustard sauce so I could definitely marinate some chicken and—"

I snatch her by the hip and gently nudge her toward me. I stare up at her from my seat. "It's your birthday, woman. I did not come here for you to bust out your Martha Stewart skills in the dead of night. I'm here to spoil you. Now, get over here and sit down."

The overwhelming softness of my best friend's curves under my hands and the unexpectedly sweet smell of her skin catch me off-guard when we're this close. A prickle runs up the back of my neck.

Something passes between us. It's weird. It's tense. Heavy.

Are we...are we having a 'moment'?

As if sensing the weirdness, too, Meghan wiggles out of my hold. She stares at me from beneath her golden eyelashes. "I...I'm making you a sandwich," she declares conclusively, adding a sprinkle of awkward laughter. Probably an effort to diffuse the strange current crackling between us. *What the fuck is that, though?*

"Fine," I mutter, slumping backward against the cushions, hoping the space will help me catch my breath. "Hurry back."

I'm an asshole for checking her out the way I do as she scurries toward the kitchen—but damn—Meghan looks better than ever. The tank top, the messy hair, the yoga pants.

The. Fucking. Yoga. Pants.

They're plastered to her curves, making my imagination go wild. Meghan's body has always been incredible. But since the last time I saw her, her curves have filled out in ways I hadn't expected. It's a struggle to stop checking her out.

I don't know what the hell is up with me right now but I decide that appreciating her beauty is fine. Just as long as I don't let myself end up doing anything stupid. I didn't come here to make the girl uncomfortable in her own house, on her birthday. I came to be a friend.

I get off my ass, head for the washroom and peel off my soaked button-down shirt, before changing into a freshly dry-cleaned one. I'm back in the living room before Meghan is done with whatever she's whipping up in the kitchen. So I drop down in front of the fireplace and grab a couple logs.

"You mind if I get a fire going?" I call out to her.

"That would be great, actually," I hear her reply from the other room. Even from this distance, I can hear the smile in her voice.

My lips curl, too, and I try to remember the last time I smiled. It's been a while. But just mere minutes after arriving at Meghan's home, I can already feel the stress of my life in Chicago quickly dissipating. That's the way it is every time I hang out with her. With Meghan, it's like time slows down. She's always been my favorite person to hang out with. So easygoing. So chill. She's practically the only person who takes me to this zen place.

There's no way I'm letting my horny vibes fuck this up tonight.

My thoughts veer back to the safety and familiarity of the friend zone as I strike a match. I work on building the fire under the watchful eye of a sour-looking orange tabby cat staring at me from his perch on a five-foot cactus-shaped scratching post near the window. He doesn't utter a peep but the slash between his cat eyebrows says, "Make one wrong move with my cat mom, asshole, and I'll fuck you up."

Duly noted.

I have a blazing fire in front of me in no time. And thankfully, I've got myself under control.

Meghan emerges with a plate of leftovers and a bottle of beer. She smiles that cheerful, dimpled smile at me and it slams me like a brick to the chest.

Whoa—she's pretty.

I mean, of course she's pretty. She always has been. That's the thing that had me tongue-tied around her when we first met back at age sixteen. But it's like she's getting prettier as the years go by. Every time I see her, she's more gorgeous. Isn't it supposed to work the opposite way around?

She sets the food down in front of me and it suddenly hits me how hungry I am. I make myself at home on her couch as I scarf down my late night dinner.

"Look at you devouring that sandwich." She laughs from where she's sitting at the other end of the couch. "And you said you weren't hungry."

I lift a shoulder unapologetically. "Hey, what can I say? I like your cooking."

She knows without question that I'm always starving. It started back in high school and hasn't let up since. Meghan has never disappointed, always whipping a meal together whenever we hung out back then. I guess that hasn't changed.

"It's a sandwich, Cassius." Her head tilts to the side.

"Made by you. And it's fucking delicious."

That earns me an eyeroll accompanied by a poorly-concealed smile. She gets busy pouring herself a glass of wine.

I jut my chin toward all the gifts I dragged in and set on the faded Persian-style rug at the foot of the coffee table. "Open up your gifts. Chop, chop."

"Gosh," she hisses under her breath. "Do you have to always be such a bossy bastard? Even when you're being nice?" Her lips pucker into a pretty pink pout.

"Open the gifts." I deadpan, suppressing the grin that makes my nostrils twitch and the corners of my lips threaten to curl up.

She glares at me.

"Do it," I insist.

Despite her attempt at being sassy, her curiosity wins out—like I knew it would—and her hand dives into the first soggy gift bag.

She pulls each item one by one, painstakingly slow, out of the falling apart paper bag.

I sit back on my end of the couch, watching her in amusement as she opens everything. There's a little of everything in that bag. Some weird stuff. Some nostalgic stuff. Some big. Some small.

But her favorites tell me everything I need to know

about the person she is. She's a softie to the core and she places the greatest value on the sentimental gifts, not the ones that carry the biggest price tag.

"Oh my gosh!" She squeals and hugs the picture frame that houses a photo of us from high school. It's a snap of me frowning my ass off while she grins wide at the camera and makes bunny-ears with her fingers above my head. "I remember when we took this picture."

I remember that day, too. It was one of the many, many Saturdays my oldest brother, Davis, and his girlfriend at the time, Alana, spent dragging Meghan and me around town, forcing us to bear witness to their over the top PDA.

That particular Saturday, we were hanging out down by the dock. Meghan was snapping away with one of those disposable cameras she would carry around all the time. It was the last place I wanted to be and it was written all over my face. I still remember her sneak attack; the way she took me by surprise, tucking her tiny self under my arm, making a silly face at the camera and capturing this very picture.

Back then, we weren't even that close. Being around her would always make me nervous as hell. Because she was so damn hot and friendly and no matter how hard I scowled or how much I gave one-word answers to all her questions, she was always there, sweet as sprinkles, with that bright, happy personality of hers, trying to break down my walls. Eventually, she won me over. I couldn't shut her out even though I tried.

Sitting next to me on the couch tonight, she continues digging through her presents. I can't stop my eyes from momentarily straying down to her chest. The neckline of her tank top is mighty low, making her full chest look amazing. I'm kind of in love with it.

She would probably nut-punch me if she caught me

objectifying her like this. I'd deserve it. So I force my stare back up to her face.

When she comes across the diamond stud earrings in the jewelry box, she eyeballs them like they might bite her.

"These look...expensive," she comments.

I ignore the cautious look she gives me. "Try them on," I prod her, wiping my fingers on a napkin and setting my empty plate next to the lamp on the side table.

She hesitates before she carefully pulls the first earring out of the cushioned jewelry box and slips it into her ear. She repeats the action with the second earring. When her hair tangles around the stud, I reach out and tenderly brush her wild golden curls back.

"How do I look?" She smiles at me and it's like a magic trick. Just the sight of that dimpled smile, and the vexation I've been feeling all day disappears like a puff of smoke.

"Beautiful," I declare earnestly, my chest filling with pride and purpose, knowing I put that twinkling smile on my best friend's lips.

She gets this bashful look on her face that twists my gut, and I don't miss the way her eyes mist up right before she throws her arms around me and squeezes tight. "Thank you, Cash," she whispers into the collar of my shirt. "You made my day."

I feel an instant reaction at my crotch as my cock stirs to life. Meghan's body feels incredible against mine. Her skin is soft and creamy, and smells like some potent, fruity body wash. I love the way her tits feel, squished against my ribs. I can barely resist the urge to rub my hands up her back and under the hem of her tank top.

She's hugged me a million times over the course of our friendship. Why does it feel different tonight?

The memory of our ridiculous marriage pact stabs me in

the ribs. *Take one wild guess why things feel different tonight, dumbass.*

I smother the little voice with a reminder that the marriage pact was just a joke. Neither of us ever expected to go through with it.

Meghan pulls back. Too soon. *Way* too soon.

She turns her attention toward the coffee table and tears into the bag of peanut butter cups. She takes a huge bite out of one and emits a contented sigh. She speaks with her mouth full. "How did you know I was out?"

She still asks me that question every single time. I huff. "You're always out of peanut butter cups. Hell, I'd bet that you'll be out again before bedtime."

She rewards me with a wry smile. "That is one bet I will not be taking." Then she quickly folds the wrapper shut. "Oh my gosh, Cash. I'm thirty now. I can't be eating like this anymore."

I resist the urge to roll my eyes. Leaning forward, I wipe peanut butter from the corner of her lips with my knuckle. "Bullshit, Megs. You're hotter than ever."

She pauses. Her eyebrows lift high up her forehead in surprise at my words.

I don't care. I'm not backtracking. It's not like I'm hitting on her. But she deserves to know how attractive she is. "Your body is bangin', Buttercup."

She laughs nervously, her gaze dropping to the couch cushions. She picks an errant cat hair out of the fabric. "You trying to boost my ego, Cassius Westbrook? Patronizing me wins you zero brownie points. You know that, right?"

"Just giving credit where credit is due. You're gorgeous."

Our eyes hold again, and I feel that heat from earlier tickling up my spine. Her irises are pale blue like the sky and they shimmer like the diamonds in her ears.

Diamond blue.

That's the best way to describe Meghan's eyes. Why does it feel like that diamond blue stare is cracking me wide open right now?

Again—what the hell is going on between us?

Two mangy looking cats sniff around me, wandering back and forth around my legs. They've been getting closer and closer since I walked through the front door. I tried nudging them away at first, but I think I'm growing just as curious as they are. Now, in the heavy silence, they're the perfect distraction.

"Where'd you get these annoying furballs?" I change the subject when the mean-faced orange tabby sniffs at my socks.

Meghan's laugh chimes in the room. "I'm just fostering them."

"Fostering? How does that work?"

"They'll stay with me until they're adopted. Then I'll return them to the shelter when that happens, so they can go home to their forever family."

Jeez. I didn't even know that was a thing for animals. "That's nice of you. Though I'm sure it sucks, too."

She sighs sadly and reaches down to pet the fluffy white one that rubs against her leg. "Yeah. I'm going to miss them when the time comes. Anyway..." she pivots on the couch, facing me. "Speaking of people I've missed, I've missed you! And it's so great to see you."

I feel myself smirk. "I got you good tonight, didn't I?"

"Yes, you got me good," she confesses, laughing.

"Good." I feel a sense of victory.

I think back to the stressful day I had, and all the shit I went through trying to get here in time. But now that I'm sitting on this couch with my best friend, it was all worth it.

Her expression grows sad when she adds, "I'm really glad you're here, even if you're a butthead. It's been a quiet evening, and I was actually feeling pretty lousy that all the girls ditched me tonight. Can you believe those bitch-es?!" She snorts softly, no venom in her words.

I flinch and scratch the back of my neck. Whoops. "Yeah—about that..."

Her head tilts to the side, causing the tips of her hair to brush over her breasts. "Cash—what did you do?"

"I kind of, sort of bribed all your friends into not making plans with you."

"What? Why?!"

Of their own volition, my eyes momentarily travel down to her puckered nipples. "Because I wanted to monopolize you tonight."

Meghan's confused-looking eyes blink at me, and the static in the air shifts.

I hurry to clarify my statement. "I mean, I wanted to monopolize your night."

Words are exiting my mouth in my feeble attempt to explain my actions, but nothing I say is making this any better.

Meghan holds her breath as the sexual tension nearly chokes me. Shit. Why's this so hard tonight? I speak all day in front of corporate schmoozers, yet I can't hold a conversation with my best friend.

I try again. "I mean...I just wanted to surprise you. For your birthday," I fumble like a hopeless idiot, desperate to dispel this weird tension between us.

"Right. Of course." She shakes her head subtly. "Con-gratulations, then. I'd say you were successful." She's trying to sound casual. But I notice the shift in her body language.

She's feeling this tension, too. "How long are you staying in town?" she asks.

"I'm leaving first thing in the morning."

Her brows crinkle in displeasure. "So soon?"

"Yeah," I deadpan. "I've got this thing I do. It's called work." I lean forward and snatch my beer off the table. I take a long swallow.

Meghan rolls her eyes. "Yeah, I know all about work. I do it, too, you know. But I'll tell you, I definitely wouldn't do it if I were as rich as you, Mr. Money Bags."

"So, you're telling me that if you won the lottery tomorrow, you'd quit the veterinary clinic and abandon all those adorable little puppies and kittens and bunny rabbits who need you?"

I see the wheels spinning as Meghan contemplates my hypothetical situation. "Okay, fine. Maybe I wouldn't quit... but I'd scale back. I definitely wouldn't let my work schedule dictate my life."

"My work doesn't dictate my life," I argue unconvincingly. "I just...I like it."

Meghan laughs, but it only highlights her sarcasm. "Oh, yeah? Because it fills that cobwebby cave in your chest where your heart is supposed to be?"

My shoulders lift and fall, ambivalent to the topic. "If that's how you want to put it."

"Don't make that frowny face," she implores me. "I worry about you."

"Don't." I undo the buttons at my cuffs then roll my sleeves back to my elbows.

Her eyes follow my movements. I notice how they linger on my hands before traveling up my biceps and across my chest. The color in her cheeks deepens.

There's a subtle flicker in her eyes when they rise back to mine. She looks guilty.

Wait—did Meghan just check me out? I...I think she did.

She takes a moment to shake her shoulders loose, like she's hitting the reset button on her thoughts. Her goodnatured smile returns. "You're my best friend. How could I not worry about you?"

I track my fingers through my still-wet hair. "Honestly, it's not like I have much time for a personal life."

She's the one who frowns this time. "But you date... don't you?"

"Here and there. I don't want to sound like a dickhead, but when you're a guy like me, it's hard to take anyone seriously."

"What does that mean?" Meghan kicks off her pink fuzzy slippers and pulls her feet up onto the couch, settling in. The rain may be coming down hard outside but with the candles flickering and the fire crackling, the mood sure is cozy in here.

I shrug, considering how to best explain it. "Everyone who shows up for a date seems to have some ulterior motive. We hang out for a bit. We start getting to know each other. The sex is okay. Then—bam!—they ask me for a loan to send their sister to fashion design school, or to pay for their mom's swimming pool upgrade, or for a boob-job."

Her head reels back, eyes wide. "A straight-up boob-job?"

"A straight-up boob-job..." I confirm, with a slow nod.

"Wow. I just...I can't even...That's bold."

"In any case, I don't need a relationship." I take another swallow of my beer.

"Of course you don't. You have your fancy career and

your bags of money to keep you warm," Meghan teases. "What else could you possibly need?"

"I'm serious," I tell her, leaning forward to drop my elbows onto my knees. There's a sensation of excitement in my blood as I speak. "I have my sights set on a goal. Westbrook Wealth Management is close to the billion-dollar mark, Megs. So close."

I shouldn't be telling her this. This is confidential information. Not many people inside or outside of the company know that we've surpassed our financial projections over the past few weeks. But I see the way her eyes widen when I utter the news to her. The way her body shifts closer. The way she subtly holds her breath. It's like she's hanging onto my every word.

She's listening. And she *cares.*

That's what I fucking love about being around her. So I can't *not* tell her. In fact, she's the only person I'd trust with this information.

"I'm so proud of you, Cash." She briefly squeezes my hand.

"The company has grown by leaps and bounds over the past quarter," I continue. "I know I'm running against the clock but if I just put in the work, I know we can close the gap by the time our next earnings report comes out. And then..."

"And then...?" she questions.

My mouth snaps shut. This is the part where I shut down. This is the part I can't say out loud. Not even to Meghan. Because it sounds so damn stupid in my head.

I lean back against the cushions and exhale. "All I'm saying is, I have goals I'm working toward. I can't allow myself to be distracted by a woman. A relationship." I purposely don't look at her when I say that. Instead, my eyes shift out the rainy front window and fixate on my house across the street where my brother's middle-of-the-week party rages on. "I'll leave all the partying and women and drama to Jasper."

Meghan follows my gaze. She laughs. "Yeah, Jasper's definitely got it covered."

I turn the conversation toward her. "What about that guy you were dating a few weeks ago?" I not so subtly change the subject.

I wasn't a fan of the loser she mentioned the last time we spoke. Some dude who went to high school with one of my brothers. But I imagine the dating pool is shrinking for her here in this small town. There's only so much you can dig back into these hometown waters.

Honey Hill is a quiet five-thousand person town in the backwoods of Iowa. It's claim to fame is being the serene oasis where tourists come to recover after getting wild and shit-faced in Sin Valley. There's not a varied selection of eligible bachelors for single women to choose from around here.

"Things were going okay. Good, even. But then I mentioned my birthday was coming up, and honestly...the whole relationship quickly fizzled after that." I expect to see a hint of sadness to go along with her words but Meghan just yawns, looking disinterested. Like she's become accustomed to this kind of behavior. "I don't think I've ever had a boyfriend during the holidays or over my birthday. I'm... sensing a pattern."

"What pattern?"

She meets my inquisitive stare and then shrugs. "I guess they just don't want to buy birthday gifts..."

The fuck? "What kind of cheap asshole bails on a relationship just because he doesn't want to spend money on a gift?"

The kind who pisses me off, apparently. Why does Meghan go for jerks like this?

Her stare fixes blankly on the cluster of balloons floating in the corner of the room. "I don't think it was necessarily that he didn't want to spend the money. It was probably more of what it represents."

"Okay, then. What does it represent?"

"I don't know. Commitment?"

Huh. I quirk a brow, eyeballing all the gifts she just unwrapped. "If buying a birthday present for the girl he was spending time with was too much of a commitment for that douche, then he didn't deserve one second of your time. You hear me?"

A look of defeat shadows her beautiful face, and I feel bad for making her feel bad. But I need her to start understanding her worth. She deserves better than some loser making her question herself.

"Look, Cash, I'm thirty years old now. I went on my first date at fifteen. Which means that I've officially been dating for half my life. And it's been the same pattern over and over and over again. Maybe it's time for me to accept the cold hard truth."

"The cold, hard truth?"

"Maybe I...Maybe I'm just not commitment material," her words spill out.

Quickly leaning forward, I set down my beer on the coffee table with a loud clatter. Her eyes grow wide when I grip both her shoulders. "Look at me, Buttercup." I wait until I see the crystalline glints in her huge, blue eyes. "Listen. All of those guys you've dated are idiots. All of them. You are definitely commitment material. And it's just a matter of time before you meet the lucky man who'll appreciate that."

Our old marriage pact keeps knocking on the door, begging to spring free, begging to surface. But I steadfastly ignore it, keeping that door firmly shut.

I'm not looking for a relationship. My sole focus right now is getting Westbrook Wealth Management to the next level. Yes, Meghan is the perfect woman but she deserves someone who'd be completely devoted to her. And right now, the only thing I can devote myself to is my work.

Besides, my friendship with her is sacred. When I'm with Meghan, that's virtually the only time I can ever let my guard down. She's my safe place. I can't compromise that.

"Okay. If you say so, Bossy Pants."

"Damn right I do," I smugly lean back and enjoy the small smile that's teasing her lips.

"Well, in the meantime, I—like you—do not need a relationship at the moment." She yawns into her wine glass and says something under her breath. "I'd kill for a good orgasm or two, though..."

My groin tingles. "What?" I question.

Her eyes widen when she realizes she said that out loud. "Um...nothing. I just...nothing."

We shift into lighter topics, spending most the night talking and laughing, as she rambles on about the latest Honey Hill gossip and a wildlife documentary plays on the TV. I don't know why I was such a nervous idiot when I showed up earlier. A few hours in Meghan's easy company, and it instantly feels just like old times.

She hides another yawn behind her palm and I realize that I'm growing tired, too.

I shake my head. "I hope you know that I'm crashing on

your couch tonight. My brother has turned my house into a brothel."

She screws up her nose at me. "Sorry—you're sitting in Captain Ginger's spot and my cats don't like house guests."

I tilt my head at her. *Seriously?*

Her pretty laughter fills the room again. "Just kidding. Of course you can stay here. You don't even have to ask." A brief moment of silence settles over the room. "So you're leaving in the morning, huh?"

I nod. "Yup."

There's this stupid, hopeful feeling in my chest. There's this part of me wishing she'll ask me to stay longer.

But she doesn't. And I'm not quite sure how I feel about that.

At some point, her head ends up on the edge of my lap. We reminisce until we fall asleep in front of the fireplace.

FOUR

CASH

"DUDE, how many espressos is that now?" I say through a yawn, watching Davis refill his cup from the coffee machine. Yet again. "That can't be healthy."

My oldest brother grumbles wearily and throws the caffeine back like a shot. "Not enough. Never enough."

He drags his feet across the floor, rejoining me at the prep counter where I'm cracking eggs into a mixing bowl the size of a swimming pool.

Davis is chief deputy sheriff here in Honey Hill. That means he's the number two guy in the police department. If he's walking around like a zombie at the moment, I can only assume that last night was a long night of fighting crime in the cruel streets of Honey Hill. Or not. Nothing major ever happens in this boring ass town.

Our youngest brother, Harry, nimbly slides half a dozen trays of sourdough loaves into the industrial oven across the room. "I told you, bro—you should let me make you my kickass protein shake. You'll have so much energy, you won't even know what to do with yourself." He chugs exuberantly from his gallon-sized water bottle that's filled with some sort of workout mix. It's been years since I've seen him without that damn bottle.

At the table by the front window overlooking the quiet street, our cousin, Mason, has his sleeves pushed back to his elbows. He's listlessly kneading up a batch of our grandmother's ribbon-winning pie crust. "Be careful with that stuff. Last time I drank one of Harry's miracle energy drinks, I was running circles around my staff at the clinic and I nearly levitated out of a patient appointment." He chuckles tiredly.

Davis, Mason, Harry and I are all here helping to get the bakery up and running for the morning. Jasper's supposed to be here, too, but it's almost six o'clock and he's yet to show his smug face.

I'd been trying to be discreet about my quick trip home to see Meghan on her birthday. But somehow—I'm guessing Nicky ratted me out—the guys got word that I was in town and demanded that I show up here at the crack of dawn for a little brotherly reunion. Now, here those assholes are in all their tussled haired, scruffy-chinned, unshowered glory, giving me shit.

Just like old times.

A pair of early morning runners with neon raincoats and too-short spandex pants slow their stride to gape and make dreamy eyes at my cousin through the rainy front window. Accustomed to the attention, Mason throws the women a wink while sprinkling a dash of poppy seeds over his dough.

I'm sure to any sane person passing by at this ungodly, dark hour, rolling past the rainy front windows, we make for one ridiculous sight. Four big, burly guys kneading dough, whisking eggs, and cooking up pies. But when it comes to the women of Honey Hill, it's hard to be sure where they fall on the sanity spectrum.

Not to sound conceited but the ladies around here act like the Westbrook boys are some sort of demi-gods. I could care less about the attention but my brothers and cousin eat that shit up.

Our grandmother opened the Wildberry Bakery nearly fifty years ago and it is hands down the most popular bakery in Honey Hill. Harry says it's because of the delicious fresh-baked bread. Davis says it's because of the damn good coffee. Personally, I believe it's because of the worktable positioned in front of the floor-to-ceiling window over-looking Main Street.

Maude Westbrook may come across as any other sweet, pie-baking senior citizen but she is more than just the matri-arch of our family. She's a hustler. She's strong-willed, resourceful and definitely a shrewd business woman. She knows exactly what she's doing, parading her grandsons in front of this window like show ponies to draw crowds of drooling women from far and wide.

Jasper finally saunters in through the side door in a black *Jasper Auto Body* T-shirt and low-hanging, beat-up jeans paired with his oil-stained workboots. "I don't think I'll ever get over how ridiculous you assholes look wearing aprons." His eyes twinkle with amusement as he takes me in. "Espe-cially you." He tsks and gives me a vigorous back slap.

Elbowing him in the chest, I glance down at the faded pink Wildberry Bakery apron covering my striped tie, button-down shirt and charcoal grey pants. I do look kind of ridiculous. But how else am I supposed to keep flour and egg off my clothes? I didn't exactly bring along a plethora of wardrobe choices when I drove into town last night.

"I'm not even supposed to be here right now." I check the clock on the wall. *I should be on the road back to Chicago already.* "I'm heading straight to the office once I'm back in the city."

If I leave here within the next half-hour, I could be at Westbrook Wealth Management right on schedule for the marketing department's weekly briefing.

Harry readjusts the ball cap that's backwards on his head. "I can't believe you're leaving town without visiting Mom." His expression does nothing to hide his displeasure.

I feel a stab of guilt but I shrug it off, pretending I don't feel bad. "I'm busy. She'll understand. Won't she?"

Jasper gulps from a monster-sized can of some heart attack-inducing energy drink. "She'll understand that you're an asshole," he spits out under his breath before going to rummage around in one of the supply pantries.

These guys don't understand what it's like to be me. They don't understand my ambition. They don't understand my goals.

...And more importantly, they don't understand the knot that forms in my gut every time I see the pain in our mother's eyes.

I think I was the only one who ever noticed the way her eyes would bleed with disappointment every time our dad broke a promise or let her down. And today, I feel like whenever Mom looks at me, she only sees the son who abandoned her to walk in her ex-husband's footsteps. So my brothers can go ahead making their snide comments about my relationship with our mom all they want. They just don't understand it.

Our oldest brother shoots Jasper a nasty look. "You're late as fuck, asshole," Davis grumbles. "It's Thursday. Today was supposed to be *your* day to work. Yet *we* all got our butts out of bed before the crack of dawn. Where the hell were you, Casanova?"

It's a family tradition that at least one of us come in and help Grams prep for the early shift each morning. My cousins—Mason's sisters—help out in the afternoon.

I check the clock again. *I really need to get out of here.*

"The party last night was crazy, bro." Jasper grabs a packet of mini chocolate chips and hops up to sit his ass on one of the counters. "I don't even know where to start."

I'm surprised Jasper is here at all. His party kept going long after Meghan and I crashed in her living room in the wee hours of the morning.

Meghan. Just the thought of her is like a jolt to my insides. I don't want to think about that weird tingle that rippled down my spine every time she got too close last night and I don't want to think about how I had to beg my cock not to get hard when she laid her head on my lap and fell asleep. But apparently, my self-control isn't taking orders from my brain today. I can't stop thinking about the girl.

"If you weren't partying all night, man, you could get out of bed like an adult," Davis says, aggressively smacking his pile of dough with a rolling pin.

"Adulting is overrated." Jasper chuckles. "You're all just jealous 'cause you're all old men and I'm out here living my best life. And the ladies love it."

"Speak for yourself." Harry's lips swing into a cocky half-smile. "I'm getting more action than I can handle these days." My baby brother flexes his muscles but the rest of us just roll our eyes. None of us are buying his playboy act.

Harry is the romantic of the family. Which is deeply ironic since he probably gets more panties flung at him than even Jasper does. He was recently drafted by the Sin Valley

Paragons football team and everybody knows how women go crazy over professional athletes. But deep down, good old Harry is probably just aching to find a princess stuck in a tower so he can save her and ride off into the sunset with her.

Poor kid. He's in for a rude awakening.

Jasper barks a loud laugh as his energy drink starts to kick in. "You talk a big game but you're not fooling anybody, Harry. Did you even manage to get rid of your V-card yet?"

Harry turns a shade of crimson that's painful to watch. He stutters without getting a meaningful sentence out.

"Yeah, well, some of us don't want to catch that Sin Valley itch and have our dicks fall off," Mason says, in Harry's defence, causing me to bark a laugh. Mason turns his gaze to Davis. "We need to hurry up and get you elected mayor. So you can make some new law about getting Jasper a curfew or something, before he parties himself to death."

Jasper flips Mason the bird.

Davis cracks a smile for the first time since I've been here. "Heaven knows Jasper needs a curfew. But unfortunately, that's not exactly how small town government works."

For years, it's been a running joke in our family that Davis will eventually become mayor. Why the heck not? He's well-respected in the community. Everybody around town loves him. Well, maybe everybody except for his ex-wife. Not that Alana would ever get in the way of Davis's career ambitions. Still, my brother won't even entertain the idea. For the life of me, I can't figure out why.

"Then what good is it to have your cousin run for mayor?" Mason grumbles. "If you can't make any new laws..."

"You can't get me out of my parking tickets..." Harry throws in.

"It hasn't helped me pick up ladies yet..." Jasper gets in on the action.

"Oh, shoot." Davis snaps his fingers. "I forgot I'm supposed to run for public office and get elected to a position I don't even want just to help you losers get your lives in order."

"You're finally starting to understand what's expected of you." Jasper bobs his head encouragingly.

We're all joking, of course. We love to yank each other's chains.

"On a serious note, though," I say, "Who do I need to talk to about getting that sign over by the highway ramp fixed? The thing nearly collapsed on top of me when I drove past it last night."

Davis cranes his head from side to side and rubs his neck. "Come to the next council meeting, and we can put it on the agenda."

Jasper clucks his tongue. "Don't fall into the whole city council meeting trap. They get nothing done at those meetings. The last time, I showed up with an *entire* proposal for having one of those bottle spout drinking fountains installed at town square. It's been months. Still nothing." His expression drops in disappointment.

"You know there's such a thing as alcohol poisoning, right?" Harry deadpans.

"You know that all that exercise you do is probably shrinking your dick, right?" Jasper fires back.

Harry tsks. "Don't worry about my dick. With all the dickage I've got, heaven knows I have a couple inches to spare."

"Boys, boys, boys," Davis admonishes. "Why don't we

focus on what really matters today? The fact that the Prodigal Westbrook has graced us with his glowing presence this morning."

"Hey, leave me out of this." I roar out a yawn and scrub a hand down my face. Man, last night was a long one. But totally worth it.

I woke up slumped in an awkward position on Meghan's couch this morning. Her head was still on my lap and she was curled into an adorable, little ball. I had to use my best ninja maneuvers to slip out from beneath her. I pulled a quilt up to her shoulders and left a note on her coffee table before sneaking out the front door.

Just thinking about her now causes a dull ache to echo in my chest. I know this trip was only supposed to be overnight but it feels like I didn't get enough time with her. That sucks.

Jasper smirks at me. "Yeah, bro. You drive six hours to see a girl, but you can't even make time for your brothers?"

"What are you assholes talking about," I grouse, feeling put on the spot. "I make time for you." Sort of.

Mason raises an eyebrow at me. "I tried calling you three times last week. You didn't even pick up."

"And when my team was in Chicago a few weeks ago, you left halfway through the game." Harry genuinely looks hurt when he says that.

I scratch my forehead. "You all know I've been busy. I'm trying to bring in new business to the company. Client acquisition is not for the faint of heart. I practically live at the office these days." I try lamely to defend myself.

"Yeah, yeah. Busy, busy. We get it." Davis harrumphs, his voice heavy with sarcasm. "*Yet* you made time to come visit Meghan. What are we to make of that, brother?"

"We all know what that means, don't we?" Jasper's eyes

sweep around at the guys. He makes a lewd hip-thrusting motion causing the table he's sitting on to groan.

"Cash and Meghan, sitting in a tree. K-I-S-S-I-N-G." Harry starts singing and doing his most ridiculous dance moves.

I throw a clump of pie dough at his face.

But he's a professional wide receiver. The bastard catches it with an easy chuckle. And throws it right back at me.

Unfortunately for me, I'm tired as shit and my reflexes are on vacation. The dough smacks me in the cheek.

Harry laughs some more. *Dickwad.*

My thoughts flit back to my friendship with Meghan and the teenage years we spent together. Sure, our odd relationship confused most people and cost me more than a few dates back in the day, but I wouldn't change that for the world.

Meghan brings this...something to my life. I can't quite put a finger on it. It's this light. This glitter. This softness.

It's sunlight.

So yes, I'm protective when it comes to her. Our friendship is my most valuable possession. Because what she gives me, money can't buy.

"Come on," Harry berates me. "We all know you have the hots for Meghan. Are we gonna have to wait till you're in a nursing home before you're man enough to just admit it?"

Jasper jabs a thumb in my direction and laughs. "Poor guy. He knows he doesn't have a chance with that girl. She's out of his league."

"I see her at the medical center every day. Sweet girl," Mason says. "She's hot *and* she's smart. Plus she's too damn nice for her own good." My cousin looks genuinely skeptical that Meghan would give me the time of day. "Yeah, you actually think you can snag a girl like her?"

Mason may be our cousin—our uncle Eric's son—but we took him into our fold a long time ago. To save him from his house full of nutty sisters. I've always considered him a brother in every way that counts.

But if he doesn't shut up right now, I'm about to disown him.

Jasper crinkles his nose. "No offence Cash, but she'd never settle for you."

I swear, if I could burn off his eyebrows with just a glare, I would.

"But don't you guys have that marriage deal or whatever?" Harry asks, frown lines snaking across his forehead.

"How do you even know about that?" I ask, my jaw hanging open.

"Nicky!" all the guys say in unison. Then they glance around at each other and burst into laughter.

I should have known. My little sister can't keep her mouth shut to save her life.

"So what's up with that?" Davis is not letting this go. There's a concerned look on his face. "All joking aside—the two of you are an item now?"

"That's never gonna happen." Jaspers snorts through his nose. "Not if Cash can't even grow the balls to ask her out." My brother smirks in challenge.

Harry persists. "So you *really* aren't going to explore things with her?"

"What's there to explore?" I say, trying to stay aloof. "Meghan and I are friends. I wouldn't expect any of you to understand what that's like."

"Enlighten me, oh celibate one," Jasper says in some accent he just made up.

I drop my eyes and stare deep into the dough. "She's more than just some chick. She's someone I can go to with my problems. Someone I can laugh with. Someone who's always willing to take care of me and go out of her way for me. Why complicate that?"

Harry slowly angles his head to the side. "Sounds like a pretty good deal to me. Those are qualities I'd definitely want in a girlfriend."

From all his nodding, it's clear that Mason agrees. "A relationship is like all that good stuff you just described *and* you get to have sex with her, too. Sounds like a pretty sweet deal to me."

Davis's eyes sweep over all of us like he thinks we're a bunch of naive assholes. "Relationships are more complicated than that."

"How?" Harry asks cluelessly.

"What if they're not compatible?" Davis explains. "What if they don't agree on the little things. Like whether the toothpaste should be squeezed from the bottom of the tube or the middle? What if she acts like she's okay with him squeezing the toothpaste from the middle and all the while she's building up resentment on the inside? And then three years into it, all that resentment explodes on him in the middle of the grocery store or something like that? Then not only does he lose the sex. He also loses his best friend." He shudders perceptibly. "Not worth it, man." From the way his jaw ticks and his eyes go hard, I suspect he's speaking from personal experience.

Harry pipes up. "I don't know...It sounds like a risk. But some risks are worth taking. Right?"

"Not this one," I say adamantly. I'd never risk the easy connection that Meghan and I share.

The guys keep giving me shit and I pretend not to be

affected. All this talk of Meghan and the pact is really getting to me. Especially after the way things went down last night. I slept like a baby with her curled up next to me. Even in my king sized bed with my imported sheets, I usually struggle to get a good night's rest, but last night, it was so easy to fall asleep on that lumpy couch with her head on my lap.

I don't let the guys in on the thoughts haunting me. I just let them keep running their stupid mouths. Until we hear the bakery's back door open which means that Grammy must have just showed up to open up the shop.

"Okay, okay." I throw my hands up, keeping my voice low. "You're all idiots. Meghan is a gorgeous girl, but we're just friends. And don't let Grams hear," I add. "I don't want her getting any ideas."

"Don't let Grams hear what?!" I freeze when I hear my grandma's voice calling from the hallway. A second later, she appears in the kitchen entrance like a feisty apparition, eyeballing each of us one by one, waiting to see who will break first.

"Um...don't let Grams hear how beautiful she is," I pipe up before my brothers and Mason can rat me out. "It goes straight to her head."

Grammy rolls her eyes, not believing a word I say. She comes up and wraps her arms around me. "It's good to see you, my boy. You get more handsome every time you come to town."

I put a kiss on the woman's head where it's tucked against my chest. "All this beauty of mine pales in comparison to you, Grammy. It's like you're aging in reverse."

"Suck-up," I hear Jasper grumbling in the background.

Hater.

What can I say? Grams is my weak spot. She's the

reason we're all living and breathing, the matriarch who built the Westbrook family by the sweat of her brow.

She chuckles, beaming as she pulls away from me. "Keep the flattery coming, Cassius. Keep it coming. And don't think I haven't noticed you changed the topic." Right now, she's standing in front of me with a stack of money in her hands. "But I'll let you off the hook if you do me a favour."

"Anything you need," I declare.

"Can you help me open up the cash register, darling? We're running late, and I still have so much to do before we open."

Before I can answer, I catch Mason and Davis locking eyes, then trading a strange look with Harry and Jasper. What the heck is that about? What's so wrong with Grams asking for help? It's what we're here for, for crying out loud. Either they're all dipshits, or they know something I don't.

I don't stew about it too long. I dust my hands down over the front of my apron, trying to get some of the flour off.

"Sure, Grams. I got ya," I answer, glaring at the guys, desperate to escape their CIA interrogation.

"Thank you, darling." She glances at the rest of her grandsons. "Jasper, get off that counter. Come here and finish whisking these eggs for Cash," she orders, before handing over the money to me. She turns a sweet smile on me.

I only wish I were around more for her, but I know my three brothers and my cousin will pick up my slack when I'm out of town.

"All right, Grams. Let's get you richer." I follow her to the front of the shop and key in the code for the cash register, relieved for an excuse to get away from the guys and the shit-talk they're flinging my way.

But as I'm helping my grandmother open the cash register, Harry's words replay in my head.

It sounds like a risk. But some risks are worth taking. Right?

I hate to entertain the possibility that he might be right. But I can't help myself. Maybe I should spend more time with Meghan. Maybe I should at least examine the way I feel about her.

I'm more confused than ever. I check the clock again. But by the time I'm done counting out the nickels, dimes and quarters in the cash register, something is very, very clear to me.

I'm not ready to leave Honey Hill. Not yet.

FIVE

MEGHAN

I'M at the front desk, catching up on entering patient records into our database for all the animals we've seen today, when movement by the front door catches my attention.

I glance up and watch two young girls leave the pediatric clinic across the hall with their stone-faced mother. There's zero hint of the laughter or smiles that you'd expect from two little sisters. Instead, they stiffly walk out of the clinic, staring straight ahead.

Before they make it out of the second set of doors, the smaller girl—the one clutching a stuffed rabbit to her chest —turns, meets my stare, and gives me a tentative smile. Her blonde ringlets peek out from beneath the hood of her yellow raincoat to bounce around her twinkling blue eyes.

My heart gives a painful throb. I return her smile before they disappear.

This veterinary clinic, the town's optometrist, and a few other local doctors all share the same small medical center on Hanson Street. There's one main entrance before the doors branch off into our own separate offices.

It's confusing, but convenient. I can't tell you how many little old ladies have waltzed into this vet clinic demanding to get their nether regions examined, only to find out they made a wrong turn on their way to the gynecologist.

I don't judge them. I mean, I myself have occasionally let my legs get hairy enough to be seen here at the veterinary clinic...but unfortunately, pets are the only patients we take in this medical practice.

I snap out of my thoughts when my coworkers blow through the main door, shaking out their umbrellas as they return from lunch.

"Hey, girlie." Maxine, the receptionist, grins at me as she strolls across the waiting room, leaving a trail of rainwater behind her. "I wish you would have joined us at the cafe today."

Alana shrugs out of her brown tweed jacket and comes around the back of my desk to hang it on the hook. "We brought back your favorite yogurt," my bestie sing-songs.

I side-eye the container and the plastic spoon she sets down next to me. "Meh. You guys are going to have to do better than that."

Barbara, an older veterinary assistant, slumps against the front desk, demoralized. "My god—what a hardass you are." She pouts. "What's it going to take to break you?"

All morning, the girls have been showering me with apologies over having played along with Cash's sketchy birthday master plan. And all morning, I've been trying to give them the silent treatment. But my coworkers know all my soft spots, so it hasn't been working out too great for me.

I shrug a shoulder, feeling justified. "Making a girl think that no one cared about her on her birthday. That's low. Super low," I lay it on thick, giving the girls shit.

"It's not our fault!" Maxine protests.

Alana nods in agreement as she swaps her soggy rain boots for dry running shoes. "Yeah, we were under the strictest orders from Cash to stay out of his way last night. And you know Cash—what that man wants, he gets."

Maxine fans her cheeks as she comes around behind the desk to reclaim her seat. "Besides, we thought you'd prefer it that way. We figured he was going to sweep you off your feet with a swoonworthy romantic gesture." My colleague waggles her brows.

My heart gives an energetic thump when I think back to last night. I see Cash sitting there in my living room, his big shoulders and his massive presence taking up three-quarters of my tiny couch. I hear his deep, rough voice in my head. "*I wanted to monopolize you tonight.*"

Heat explodes in the pit of my stomach.

Goddamn. *He didn't mean it* that *way, Meghan.*

"Well. No romantic gestures over here. It's not like that between me and Cash." I'm starting to sound like a broken record. I've been repeating these same words since high school. Why's this so hard for people to believe? "We're just friends."

I slide out of the swivelling chair so the receptionist can get back to work. "Thanks for thinking of me over lunch," I tell the girls, waggling my peace offering yogurt in the air.

"Does that mean you forgive us?" Barbara grins.

"I'm strongly considering it," I say with a laugh.

They're already forgiven. But they don't need to know that just yet. Holding a grudge has never been my strong suit.

I head into the back to enjoy my snack lunch while I make some headway on the inventory.

Naturally, Alana follows me. "So...did he mention the pact?" my bestie questions when we're alone.

Again, my heart thumps.

"Of course he didn't mention the pact." I groan. "There *is* no pact. He never really intended to marry me. It was just a silly thing he said to cheer me up on a night when I was feeling shitty about myself."

I'll admit that the energy was a little weird when he showed up at my house yesterday, and for one crazy second, I found myself sort of wanting something to happen between us. But the atmosphere quickly smoothed out. Then Cash and me went back to being Cash and me. The same old friends we've always been.

"Maybe," she hedges. "But there's definitely chemistry between the two of you. Everyone can see it."

"You're just projecting. Everyone sees what they want to see. Sometimes, a girl and a guy are just friends and nothing more," I argue. I rip open the yogurt lid and dive in, as I drop into a plastic chair at the tiny circular break table. I look up to find Alana watching me. "At this point, I just accept that girls like me don't get chosen. We may be fun for a fling, but we just don't get picked for the long run."

Alana tosses her head back. "Oh my god, Meghan. I can't believe you're still telling that old story."

"What old story?"

"That one! Those aren't even your own words. It's just something your mom told you when she was in a really bad place. And now you've taken it on as your identity. You need to let it go."

She's wrong. I mean, *yes*, my mother said it, but it perfectly sums up everything I've ever experienced. "I've been dating all these years, and it's never led anywhere. I've never had a serious, committed, grown-up relationship. Never. And unless I expand my dating pool to start going after eighteen year olds, I'm running low on options."

Alana drops into the folding chair across from mine, shaking her head. "Have you really been dating, though? Because it doesn't count if you step into every new relationship with a helmet and a life vest and one hand on the emergency exit. You've never really thrown yourself into love, Meghan. You've never really—" She stops herself midsentence and a rueful look covers her face. She chews on the corner of her lip. "Y'know what? I'm the last person who should be giving anyone dating advice. We all know how love turned out for me."

I reach across the table and squeeze her hand. "Hey. Don't say that. Stop being mean to my best friend."

Alana met her Prince Charming back when we still had ten o'clock curfews and school dance chaperones. She and Davis were a dream couple, marrying at the tender age of twenty-one. But it didn't last.

These days, the two of them try to keep things cordial when they run into each other around town, and the rest of the Westbrooks still love her. But I can tell that my friend carries regrets to this day, even though she would never admit it to herself. Instead, she's thrown herself into work and keeps her social circle confined to our group of girlfriends.

"I just don't want you closing yourself off from love," she tells me.

"It's brutal out there, Al. The men in the dating pool are savages." I shudder. "You wouldn't want to *throw yourself* into anything with those jerks. It's called self-preservation."

To be honest, I'm so damn tired of the same old disappointment that comes from getting my hopes up over some new guy, only to find out a short while later that I'm in the deep end all alone. I'm done. Over it.

Alana shakes her head. "Well, that's just the thing.

Cash Westbrook might be sort of grumpy, but deep down, he isn't a jerk. And you know it. So if he really is interested in a shot with you, what other excuse are you gonna come up with to keep him at arm's length?"

"Cash never said he was interested in a shot with me," I retort.

She laughs wryly. "Cash's feelings for you are written in black and white on a gas station receipt with his signature at the bottom. Remember? You have a snapshot of it at the very back of your underwear drawer. I saw it that time you lost that earring of yours and we were tearing up your bedroom searching for it. Don't make me remind you. Because I will." She jabs a finger into my shoulder.

That was just a joke... The words die in my knotted throat before they can even make it out my mouth.

With a parting shrug, Alana gets up. "Patients are coming in soon. Gotta go grab my files," she says, squeezing my shoulder. On that, she walks out of the back room.

I pull a breath deep down into the bottom of my soul, trying to sweep out this shaky feeling inside me. I'd be lying if I said things didn't feel different between Cash and me last night. He called me beautiful more than a few times. And I swear I felt him staring at my ass when I was cleaning up my coffee table. And at certain points, he kept getting all stuttery while we were speaking.

My stomach fizzes when I think about it all. *I'm reading way too much into this.* Of course he doesn't think of me that way.

Cash and I have been super close for years. I understand him better than almost anyone. He keeps most people at a distance—even his family—people generally think he's nothing but a grumpy asshole with no heart. But I know better.

Over our friendship, I've learned how to twist and contort my way past the electric fence he's constructed around his emotions. It took years of patience and persistence. But it's been worth it. Every time Cash gives me a sneak peek into the deep, hidden parts of him, it's always worth it.

Eyeballing the clock on the wall, I scrape my yogurt container until it's empty. I wish I had more time to stew over Alana's comments, but she's right. The next patient will be here in ten, and I still need to prep the exam room.

I rise from my seat but before I can toss my trash into the bin, my phone rings.

My stomach fizzes all over again when I see who it is. "Cash. Hey." I tuck the phone between my shoulder and my cheek. "I'm just getting ready to head to—"

"Hey, Buttercup," he says, that commanding voice of his sinking into my cells and freezing me in place. "I'll be quick. Don't make plans tonight."

"Uh, why?"

"Because I said so," he declares matter-of-factly. Like he's the boss of me.

I swear he must hear me rolling my eyes.

He emits a gravelly sound that's probably supposed to be a laugh. But judging by my exaggerated visceral reaction, it's clear that my silly, horny, undersexed body interprets the sound as a mating call or something.

"Because I'm taking you out tonight. To properly celebrate your birthday," he informs me.

"You are?" I feel my forehead crinkle up. "I thought you'd be on the road by now. On the way back to Chicago."

When I woke up this morning, I was on the couch all alone. There was a quilt pulled up to my shoulders and a hand-scribbled note sitting on the coffee table. Cash wished me a nice day and promised to call me once he arrived back in Chicago. It was pretty clear from his note that he planned to leave town this morning.

"Nah, the weather is crap. Honestly, I'm not in the mood to deal with all that rain. I'll just wait it out in town for another day."

I glance out the back window, not knowing what to say. It *is* raining, but is the weather bad enough to justify Cash postponing his trip?

"Meghan, you still there?"

"Um, yeah. Yes. I just..." I clear my clogged throat. "I'm surprised you're not running back to the city. Weren't you going on and on last night about your big important job?"

He spits out a flat laugh. "And weren't you going on and on about me needing to take a damn break?"

"Yes, but since when do you listen to me?" I tease.

"You wanna go out tonight or not, Meghan?" he challenges in a no-nonsense rasp.

There's something about the impatience in his tone. It gets to me.

"Fine," I respond dumbly, my heart thudding.

He huffs through his nose. "So damn hard to please, you are."

"Stop complaining before I change my mind," I say, trying to sound annoyed.

"Be ready at six." Gosh, that man loves to order me around. Why is he so damn bossy?!

Before I can get sassy, he says his goodbyes, leaving me feeling even more tied up in my thoughts, frustrated with Alana and the girls for filling my head with craziness.

But maybe...maybe my friends see something I don't. Perhaps Cash has romantic feelings for me after all?

Cut it out, Meghan. You're being weird. Of course he

doesn't have romantic feelings for me. Pfft. We're just friends. As always.

My foggy brain vaguely registers the front office door chime as someone walks into the clinic. I hurry out of the break room.

Crap. Now my head's a mess *and* I'm running late.

SIX

MEGHAN

I TRY NOT to bounce around excitedly on my toes as I'm walking beside Cash, my hand in the crook of his elbow.

My heels clack against the concrete and my cute blue dress with gold details flutters around my knees. I dressed up a little nicer than usual tonight, under the silly assumption we were headed to the next town over to enjoy some high-romance, five-star dining. But my fantasies dissipate when Cash guides me around a puddle on the sidewalk leading to the Hot Sauce local bar and grill.

I hate to say it but all afternoon, I entertained the silly thought that Cash might make a move on me tonight. I mean, he *did* spontaneously extend his stay in Honey Hill, didn't he? And he made a super big deal, insisting on taking me out tonight. So, my imagination got a little carried away. But clearly, I was wrong.

Still I shouldn't be disappointed. I have no right to be picky, especially when my friend is going out of his way to hang out with me. Honestly, a burger and onion rings are more my speed anyway. And the Hot Sauce is Honey Hill's go-to drinking spot.

The small old time tavern in the heart of town is a favorite among the locals. With its exposed brick walls, its grouping of pool tables and the cozy dim atmosphere, it's always my first choice for a laidback evening of fun.

I just wouldn't have forced my achy feet into these Cinderella slippers had I known our true destination.

He flashes me a killer smile, holding the door open for me to step inside. One look at that smile and I nearly trip over my feet.

I've come to expect that smiles from Cash are a rarity. And this one isn't any old smile. It's a perfect set of straight, white teeth and twinkling soul-deep grey eyes crinkled at the corners. All that megawatt-age has me seriously off-kilter.

It's a major distraction.

And the moment I'm inside the restaurant lobby, I'm bombarded with shouting and blinding camera flashes.

"SURPRISE!"

"HAPPY BIRTHDAY!"

Once my eyes readjust and my heart climbs back inside my chest, I take in the sight before me.

Everyone's here. All my friends. My co-workers. Cash's family. Heck, even my mom.

For a second, my hopes for a romantic soiree between Cash and me deflate. I feel foolish for ever having considered that romance could be on the menu for tonight.

Cash is my friend—my best friend—I know that's what's for the best. All my crazy girlfriends need to just get with the program and stop filling my head with silly fantasies.

Once I've recovered from my momentary heartbreak, a sense of appreciation hits me. "You threw me a surprise birthday party?" I'm virtually on the verge of tears. No one has ever done that for me before. Not even when I was a kid.

"No big deal." One of Cash's broad shoulders casually pops up then falls.

"Of course it's a big deal." I sniffle.

He rented out this entire restaurant. He most likely shelled out a crap ton of money and somehow managed to get half the town here, all without me suspecting a thing. Plus, he did all that work and all that planning sometime between this morning and now.

Okay, fine—he's not secretly pining away for me. But this means something. It's a different kind of love. Not romantic love but love nonetheless. And it's sacred to me.

"Thank you," I lean in and say by his ear, squeezing his hand. "This is incredible."

He taps my nose with his finger, still wearing a ghost of a smile. "You deserve the best, Buttercup."

We make our way through the crowd. I can't help but notice the attention Cash gets from every woman we pass. And even though we're only friends, I get a sort of thrill being the girl on his arm.

At some point, we get split up. Music is pumping, trays of food are being carried around and the bartenders are pouring drinks. People are reaching for refills so quickly I have to assume that Cash is footing the bill for the liquor, too.

As I'm passing the bar, I stop just long enough to chat with my mom and her sister, Jane.

"You look gorgeous, honey." My mother slides an arm around my shoulders and kisses my cheek.

"Thank you, Mom. I love that you let your hair down tonight." I touch her glossy blonde curls.

Like everyone else, she apologizes for going along with

Cash's birthday shenanigans yesterday. I accept her apology with a laugh.

"Happy birthday, Meggie," my aunt calls from behind the bar where she's mixing me a boozy bourbon lemonade, my favorite. "And can I say that you look damn good on Cash Westbrook's arm. You two make such a cute couple."

"We're not a couple," I say and for some reason she looks shocked.

"You're not? I'd just assumed..." Jane blinks. "You're thirty now. And you're single. And the marriage pact says..."

I roll my eyes. "The marriage pact isn't a legally binding contract. It's a joke. It always was."

Jane's eyes wander to where Cash is standing across the room, arms folded stiffly across his chest as he watches Jasper and his mechanic friends play a game of pool. Her shoulders rise and fall sharply. "Now, don't take this as legal advice, but I say, marriage pact or not, you should fuck the shit out of that man."

My aunt has a half-finished law degree. For that reason, she feels the need to add a legal disclaimer to nearly everything she says.

"Auntie!" I shriek-laugh in horror.

"Jane Anastasia Hutchins!" Mom barks, scandalized.

"Just sayin'." Unapologetic, the sassy woman shrugs. "The man is fine as hell. But look at that grumpy scowl on his face. He is in dire need of some stress relief, if you know what I mean."

My mother drops a hand to my shoulder. "Don't listen to her, Meghan. You and Cash have a beautiful friendship. Don't mess it up by involving romance. Be realistic. You know what happens every time us Hutchins women fall in love."

I feel a boulder drop into my stomach. "I know, Mom..."

Jane and Mom begin arguing. Mom insists that the Hutchins curse is proven fact. Jane insists that it's fiction. Mom says that love isn't available to the women in our family. Jane says that she's single and ready to mingle by choice.

I want no part of this conversation. I'm here to celebrate my birthday and I just want to have fun.

I excuse myself when I spot Alana, Emma and Ziggy standing at one of the high top tables off to the side. I gravitate toward my friends.

Emma works part-time at my mom's baby clothing shop and Ziggy owns the metaphysical shop right next door.

I hug the girls and thank them for coming as they gush over my dress, reminding me that it's been a while since they've seen me in something other than my work scrubs or my beloved yoga pants. I love getting dolled up but I haven't been going out very much lately.

Some appetizers and a round of drinks are placed in front of us in a flash.

"Girl, we're so sorry we didn't hang out with you yesterday." Ziggy over-pouts. Her long wavy hair is turquoise this week and she wears a floor-length flowy skirt with a yellow T-shirt knotted above her bejewelled belly button.

Emma cuts in. "We totally had plans to drag you to one of those male strip clubs in Sin Valley and get a hot, naked, oiled-up man to wiggle his sausage in your face. But Cash—"

"Yeah, I heard all about what Cash did," I cut in, rolling my eyes despite the smile I feel on my lips. "He's a teensy bit over the top, isn't he?"

Ziggy shakes her hips and grins. "Who doesn't love a possessive man?"

"A possessive man who has the hots for you. H-O-T-S."

A glassy-eyed Emma grabs the fabric of her slouchy, off the shoulder top and yanks it up her shoulder.

I feel my cheeks flaming. "Emma, I'm starting to think you got here a little too early and tapped into the open bar a few too many times already." Girl can never hold her liquor.

She giggles without a care in the world. "I may be tipsy but definitely not too tipsy to notice that delicious man undressing you with his eyes."

I roll my eyes. "Alana, are you gonna back me up here? Or are you just gonna stand here and let this girl keep talking crazy to me?" I nudge my bestie in the ribs and get no response.

When I throw a glance at her, I see her staring across the room with a faraway look on her face.

She jolts. "Oh, um, what did you say?"

I follow her gaze to see what has her so enthralled. On the other side of the bar, Davis is huddled on a cozy couch by the back wall in deep conversation with some power suit-wearing woman I've never seen before. Shit.

Alana clears her throat then grabs her purse. "I should... I just...I'm gonna go outside and get some fresh air." Without waiting for a reply, she gets up and hurries her way to the exit.

Although I'm dying to follow her, I know that her ex-husband is a major sore spot for her. When she gets this way, she just needs her space.

My insides hurt for my best friend. I suspect that she's not quite over her ex-husband just yet, and that's definitely nothing to be ashamed of. I just wish she weren't so completely in denial about it because as long as she won't admit her feelings to herself, there's only so much anyone can do to help her.

Ziggy shoves a basket of fries in front of Emma and I

sneak a gaze across the restaurant where I see Cash chatting with Mason and his hoard of uproarious younger sisters. Cash looks my way and our eyes catch and he gives me a small smile nobody else would probably notice. Between us, it feels like a little secret and it makes my belly flutter.

Logically, I know my girlfriends are crazy saying Cash has the hots for me, but when he picked me up tonight, I couldn't help but notice the way his stare lingered on my cleavage. *Thank you, pushup bra.*

Now I'm all mixed up and can't figure out what's reality and where my overeager imagination is blowing up my nice and easy friend-zone relationship with Cash.

Once the girls and I have worked our way through our drinks, a fresh round of alcohol appears on our table. Two or three guys from around town stop by and ask me to dance but I politely turn them all down.

Fuck it. I've given up on romance and I'm not interested in getting my hopes up at this point. All I want to do is have a little fun with my friends.

"Oh come on. Don't be a bore," Ziggy chides when my latest rejected dance partner walks away. Her lips go thin like she's carefully working something out in her head. "Now that I think about it, Venus is aspecting your natal sun in your seventh house. I'm thinking it's a very auspicious time for you to make a love connection, missy."

Ziggy and her astrological predictions. I subtly shake my head.

"I don't even know what that means..." I laugh.

My bohemian friend reaches into her crossbody leather satchel and I already know what's about to happen. But before she can break out her tarot deck, a large, warm hand lands on my shoulder.

"You having a good time?" Cash asks, his fingertips brushing over my skin, making my heart—and brain—stall. His eyes drop momentarily to my chest.

Wait—what was that look that just flashed across his face?

I'm imagining it. I've just got to keep telling myself that I'm imagining it. I can't let myself believe that my best friend has anything but platonic feelings for me.

"Yeah. I'm having a great time." I smile brightly at him.

His jaw hardens and he glances around. "You sure? I see how many guys have been sniffing around you."

I lift a brow. "You have a problem with that?" I challenge, straightening my back.

"I don't like a bunch of assholes getting all in your face," he says in that growly tone he does so well.

It may be the alcohol working its magic in my blood, but suddenly, I feel bold. "Well, there's an easy solution to that." I grin. "Dance with me."

At his momentary silence, I wonder if I've made things weird between us—again—by asking him to dance, but then the corner of his mouth curls faintly. "I can get a dance with you? I thought there was a signup sheet somewhere that I should add my name to, Ms. Popular..." He starts looking around like he's searching for something, making my girlfriends giggle.

Before he can say something else to make my cheeks burn hotter than they already are, I shove my hand into his. "I'll let you cut the line."

With a gentle tug, he pulls me to my feet. "You're far too kind."

"You're welcome."

I flash him a little grin and let him lead me to the dance

floor. He's the only guy I want to dance with anyway. Not because I've got any romantic notions about us in my head. But because he's the only person I feel safe with. In Cash's familiar arms, there's no pressure, no expectations.

Under the muted bar lights overhead, he reels me into his arms. There are only a couple other people dancing around us, the majority of the crowd being far more interested in the free food and booze.

My friend's glinting grey eyes intently peer down at me, and I'd pay good money to know what he's thinking now. Because *I'm* thinking that he's impossibly handsome with the day-old stubble that's sprouted up on his chin. And I can barely restrain myself from sliding my fingers into his messy brown hair. And all I can imagine is how easy it would be to rise onto my tiptoes and steal a taste of those soft-looking lips.

Slowly, his hand rises toward my face. My heart rate picks up as my body gets ready. I *know* he's going to cup my cheek. I *know* he's going to lower his face to mine. I *know* he's going to claim the kiss I've been dreaming about all day.

Instead, he plucks something from my hair.

"Ouch!" I blink.

"Fur ball..." He explains, squinting at the clump of Captain Ginger's hair pinched between his fingers.

"Oh my gosh," I whisper, embarrassed as I steal the fur from him and drop it to the dance floor. "Those cats are ruining my life. I must look ridiculous covered in cat fur all the time!"

He just laughs and pulls my body closer. "Impossible! You're a sexy cat lady and you know it."

My pulse rate triples when he calls me 'sexy'.

My brain completely blanks out on the fact that he *also* called me a 'cat lady'. Selective hearing at its finest.

"Why are you staring at me like that?" he questions, a playfulness in his expression.

Before my brain can filter through my drunken thoughts and determine which ones are safe to share and which ones I should keep to myself, I feel my big mouth yapping away. "Why can't I find a guy who treats me half as good as you do?" *Oh gawd.* Did I really just say that out loud?

Cash's brow goes rigid and his fingers flex on my lower back. "I may be a totally selfish asshole for saying this but—fuck finding a boyfriend. I love that I get to have you all to myself."

My breath catches when he utters those words. I know he didn't mean it in a romantic way but I sort of like being his, too. He's so good to me.

I want to kiss him so bad. But that would ruin everything. And losing Cash's friendship is a risk I can't take.

With nowhere to hide from all these new and scary feelings, I tuck my head against his chest. Bad idea. Now, I'm drowning in the heat and spicy musk of his skin.

Less than a minute into our slow dance, the beat picks up on a new song that appears to be a crowd favorite. A wave of gyrating bodies moves toward the dance floor.

"Oh, no you don't," I chide when Cash tries to backtrack out of my hold. I grab both his hands, holding him hostage. "Where do you think you're going?"

He chuffs. "You know as well as I do that me and rhythm don't mix."

"Too bad." I grin at him, waving his arms around to the music. I look like a drunken puppet master, one who's not even close to matching the quick paced beat. I don't care. "You asked me to dance."

He makes a feeble attempt to fight me, desperate to wrestle back control of his noodly arms. He guffaws. "*You* asked me to dance." Both his eyebrows lift. "Wait. Let me rephrased that. You *ordered* me to dance."

I shrug. "And now, we're dancing," I state simply. "So spin me around, Westbrook." When he hesitates, I pout. "Oh come on. Is that how you treat the birthday girl?"

Cash is great. Obviously. But he's a little strait-laced, if I'm being honest. That's why I like to push his buttons. Get him a little riled up.

He rolls his eyes. But before I know it, he's twirling me around on my toes. My laughter bursts out, mixing with the music, and just like that, all the tension between us is gone and our usual goofy energy comes back.

The crowd is gradually getting wilder. Harry is by the bar, showing off his best dance moves for my laughing mom and aunt. The goofy bastard.

Mason is on the edge of the dance floor, getting twerked on by a couple girls I recognize from around town. From the look on his face, I'm not sure he's sure how to feel about that.

Emma and Ziggy are tearing up the dance floor, too, doing some music video vixen moves. When Jasper takes to the stage, strips out of his shirt and starts doling out lap dances to anybody who wants one, that's when things really get out of control.

Cash is slowly loosening up, too. He actually plays along when I try to get his broken limbs to do the robot. His attention stays pinned on my face as he humors me and my ridiculous dance moves. This is the most fun I've had in ages.

I'm giggling through another dizzying spin when a booming voice breaks through my dance-induced high. "Birthday girls are supposed to get a lap dance!"

I feel a spotlight wash over me from the back. I glance

over to the stage and find Jasper holding a microphone and smirking in our direction.

"Cash, give the girl her lap dance!" someone shouts in the crowd.

"You losers would like that far too much," he yells back.

Cash pulls me deeper into the shadows as I try out some new dance move, and for a minute, I think we're safely off the hook. But then someone on the other side starts chanting, and before I know it, everyone in the tavern has joined in. "Lap! Dance! Lap! Dance!"

"Don't make me come over there," Jasper threatens from the stage where he's now doing a cowboy hip thrust against a red-faced, wide-eyed Emma.

Wait—how'd *she* get up there?!

My heart starts pounding, and my palms grow sweaty. Okay, *sweatier*. Cash waves his brother off and tries to talk his way out of the situation, but Harry appears out of nowhere and slides a chair to the edge of the dance floor.

My gut clenches when someone shouts from somewhere in the crowd. "Enough of all that boring, 'just friends' bullshit. Show the girl your wild side. Show her what she's been missing out on."

Jasper hops off the stage. He's headed in our direction. "If you're not man enough to make the birthday girl happy, you *know* I will." His eyes twinkle with mirth as his gaze bounces between his brother and me.

Cash Westbrook is not a man who backs down from a challenge. "Take one more step over here and you'll regret it," he warns Jasper.

The chanting from the crowd doesn't let up and, ultimately, the mob gets what the mob wants.

With a searing look, Cash grabs my hand and leads me

toward the empty chair. As soon as my ass hits the seat, someone changes the music to Britney Spears.

My face is on fire, and my hands shoot up in a feeble attempt to cover my eyes as my best friend dances around me.

I take the opportunity to peek through my fingers. The determined look on Cash's face sends me into another fit of giggles. But my laughter abruptly stops when he lifts my hands from my face, forcing me to meet his eyes. His fingertips skim my jaw before trailing down my neck, leaving a river of goosebumps in its wake.

My gut spasms. This is not the face of a man who's joking around.

He shimmies around me, while everyone watches and roots for this nonsense to proceed. Before I can figure out how to get out of this without soaking my panties through, Cash has whipped off his shirt. It smacks me in the face, and I quickly inhale his scent before the fabric falls into my lap.

I probably shouldn't stare the way I do but I may never again have the chance to drool over Cash's abs, his muscular V and that sexy little trail. My attention moves to his package and the generous bulge piques my curiosity. I bite my lip, secretly hoping for his pants to slip a little lower.

Hey, it's my birthday. I get a pass for ogling my friend.

He's pumping his arms and rotating his hips. I think he's shooting for slow and seductive, but what I get instead is awkward and off-tune. I wouldn't know because I can't take my eyes off his face. I'm mesmerized.

Everyone is busy hollering and laughing. But this is no game between Cash and me. His dilated pupils and his unflinching eye contact tell me that he's feeling all the unfamiliar things I'm feeling, too.

The song comes to an end and the crowd goes up in

wild applause and laughter. But I can't snap myself out of this trance.

And after the way this man just turned me on, I'm absolutely terrified that I'll never be able to slip Cash Westbrook back into that tidy little box labeled 'just friends'.

SEVEN

CASH

AT THE END of the night, I'm standing outside the gas pump filling up the car. Old time tunes pour softly from the speakers overhead. I'm trying not to stare at the curb across the lot, where Meghan and I made a certain pact that I really shouldn't be thinking about. Especially after what just happened at the bar.

As she sits inside the car waiting for me, I can't help but wonder if she remembers that night. If she's as confused as I am about whether we should do anything about it.

Let me tell you—my rock hard cock definitely has some ideas about how this night should end. But I'm determined to keep my head on straight and not make any more impulsive decisions.

I find myself chuckling under my breath as I picture myself shirtless and dancing around the bar like a low-end, minimum wage male escort.

This night definitely took a wild turn. At least, I managed to get my shirt back.

I stubbornly refuse to be embarrassed about it. I'm Cash Westbrook. I'm good at everything, dammit. I may be a respected corporate executive by day but if I want to be a backwoods go-go dancer for one night, then I'll be a backwoods go-go dancer for one night.

For Meghan.

It would be a lie to say that tonight's strip show wasn't very, very out of character for me. Obviously, I wasn't thinking straight when I took control of the situation, sat Meghan in that chair and I showed her a different side of me she's never seen before.

But as usual, my friend can get me to do anything. And although she didn't ask me to take my shirt off and give her a show, Jasper's challenge to me back at the bar felt like a personal affront. The thought of my idiot brother gyrating all over my best friend nearly made me pop a fuse. It made me mad enough to do something I normally wouldn't do.

Let's just hope I didn't cross any lines Meghan and I can't come back from.

I finish up with the gas and climb back into the driver's seat. Hitting my car's start button, I turn to my gorgeous friend. "You sure you don't want to grab some peanut butter cups? I know you finished that last packet already."

The sound of her laugh fills my soul. "No, I ate so much food at the bar, I can't even think about dessert. And that's saying a lot. Tonight was so much fun. Thank you." Her cheeks redden, and I'd put money down to bet she's thinking about the strip show I gave her earlier.

Christ, I need to make sure none of my idiot brothers recorded that shit.

"Anything for you, Buttercup."

She smiles softly, staring at me from beneath her golden lashes. "When you didn't call on my birthday yesterday, I actually thought you'd forgotten. Honestly, I was a little bummed about that." She gnaws on the inside of her lip, seemingly embarrassed to admit that.

I hate that for even a couple hours, she had to think the worst of me. That I would ever let her down like that.

"Never. You hear me? I never forget anything about you." I brush my knuckles across her blushing cheek, relishing the heat I feel rising in her face.

Meghan has the audacity to roll those pretty eyes. "That's a lie."

I suck in an offended breath. "You wound me, woman." I angle my body toward her and throw an arm across the back of my seat. "Try me," I challenge.

She shifts, lifting her legs up into her seat as she sits sideways to face me. My eyes burn from fighting the painful urge to peak at her bare thighs.

She looks incredible in that little blue dress. I love the way the fabric drips from her curves and the way the gold matches her hair. But it's the thought of completely shredding her out of that scrap of clothing that's been consuming my mind all night.

"Okay," she says, and then gets an evil glint in her eye. "What was my cat's name in high school?"

Now I'm the one rolling my eyes. "You didn't have a cat. You had a guinea pig, and it's name was Rover." I shiver. "I still have a scar on my thumb from when that bastard attacked me."

She tsks. "That was an easy one. And you deserved to be bitten for messing with him. Let's try again...What was my first job?"

"Payroll or under the table?"

"Payroll," she confirms.

"Making pizzas and Italian subs downtown."

"Okay. And what about under the table?"

I smile, amused at how hard she's trying to trip me up. "Babysitting for the Beaufort's toddler twins."

"Ugh. Those monsters were the worst," she laughs. "Fine. Those were all easy. Tell me...the first class I got a B in."

I tap my lip, pretending to be stumped. This girl can throw her little Meghan Trivia at me all damn day. I'll win the champion trophy every time. "Well, Buttercup. That would have to be your eleventh grade computer class. You'd sprained your wrist playing ball in PE, and then Mr. Vesta was a hardass and wouldn't let you be excused from typing."

"Man, that still pisses me off," she growls. "I would have had a 4.0 that year."

"I know. Guy was a douche. But see–" I add smugly. "I told you. I never forget anything about you."

Her gaze drops to her lap. "I...I bet you forgot about the night of your brother's wedding...About that conversation we had..."

A prickle runs down my neck. "Nope," I answer, popping the 'p' as the proverbial elephant finally makes known his presence in the room.

Then, without a second thought, I lean across her lap, open the glove box, and pull out the old gas station receipt. I'm glad she didn't notice the fact that the wrinkled slip of paper was laying right on top. Or ask about how every time I shove new car service receipts in here, I delicately organize this on top of the stack. Or...most troubling, the fact that I still held onto the receipt although I've upgraded cars nearly a dozen times since that fateful night.

I place it on her lap, and she immediately flips it over, reading the messy contract that's written on the back in faded black pen. Out loud.

"You kept it..." she whispers after she reads it.

"Of course I kept it," I say around my strangled throat, my heart thumping ferociously as the air in the car shifts.

"After all this time," she muses, before meeting my stare. "Almost feels like that was just yesterday."

The current in the heated air sizzles around us, and the sweet, familiar scent of her perfume fills my head.

"Guess I should have framed it," I mumble, reaching over and thumbing the frayed corner. My hand brushes over Meghan's fingers, and she sucks in a sharp breath.

Our eyes lock, for longer than would be deemed friend-appropriate. I can hardly breathe when my gaze slips to her mouth and finds her tongue skimming her bottom lip. She shifts closer.

This is it.

The moment I've refused to let myself dream about for...for nearly fourteen years. The moment I'm going to find out exactly what Meghan Hutchins tastes like.

But just as I'm leaning closer, allowing my eagerness to take over from my common sense, Meghan blinks as if emerging from a trance. She laughs softly. "Gosh," she exhales, collapsing back into her seat as her attention returns to the receipt still in her hands. "That sure was silly."

I know she's referring to the contract. But deep down, I can't help but wonder if there's some double meaning there. I mean, holy hell, I almost kissed my best friend in a moment of utter lack of self-control.

I jerk back into my seat. Guilt rockets into my head and I feel downright sick. What the hell is wrong with me? Meghan clearly doesn't want me to kiss her. Of course not. We're nothing but friends. And here I am, trying to put the moves on her. I'm clearly not thinking straight.

I don't know where this sudden onslaught of feelings has come from and I don't have a plan for keeping them in check. I just need to cool my jets and remember what's at stake here.

I can dream about touching her as much as I want, but I can't actually do it. Because that's something you can't come back from. Something you can't fix with a quick *backspace*.

"I...it...yeah. That really was silly," I stutter, trying to excuse my actions, but ultimately falling short. I open the window a crack so we don't suffocate on the sexual tension. Heaven knows I'm generating enough body heat to fog the windows.

She exhales shakily. "We weren't ever serious about the pact. We were practically kids. It was just a joke...right?"

I'm not sure what I see in her eyes in the dim car. But if I had to guess, I'd say there's a whole lot of questioning and not much confidence in the words she's saying.

I'm fucking confused, myself. So I pick the safer option. "We were definitely just goofing around."

Half a second before her gaze leaves mine, an emotion flashes across her face. Was that disappointment? I don't know. Shit. I'm really out of my depth here.

Eyes still on the faded receipt, she chuckles softly to herself. "Do you know how much shit I've gotten from my friends over the years over this stupid contract? I still have my copy of it tucked at the back of an old drawer."

Something sharp and urgent runs through my chest. "You still have your copy?" I remember her snapping a picture of the contract the night we signed it. I'd assumed that photo had gotten lost over the years.

She nods. "The girls stumbled upon it a few years ago when we were searching for something in my room and they never let me live it down."

"Me, too." I laugh under my breath. "Nicky found it once when I let her use my car and I've lived to regret it. Especially since she went blabbing to my brothers."

Meghan looks surprised then she bursts into soft laughter again. "Our friends are some little shits, aren't they?"

"Total assholes," I agree. "They don't know how to mind their own damn business."

"Such gossip-whores, they are." She giggles.

"It's like they can't help themselves." I roll my eyes.

"And they're so judgmental. I hate how much people pressure me about still being single at thirty." She frowns. "They act like it's the scourge of my very existence."

"They need to leave you the hell alone," I bark, instantly feeling protective of her.

A Bonnie Rait song pours in through the crack in the window. I recognize it. *Something to Talk About.* My mom used to love that song.

A mischievous smile covers Meghan's lips and the way her dimples pop causes my stomach to go tight. "Y'know what would be really funny?" That smile widens. "We should just pretend that we *are* together. Pretend that we're totally and completely, over-the-top in love with each other. Just to get them to shut the hell up." She laughs softly.

I want to tell her that I don't want to pretend. I want to tell her that—fuck it—I'd make her my girl in a heartbeat.

But good thing an invisible padlock bolts my throat shut. Because saying shit like that—when she's clearly only joking—would only make things uncomfortable between Meghan and me.

And besides, I'm too busy for this shit. I don't have the time for a girlfriend, let alone a wife.

Suddenly looking embarrassed, she clears her throat

and straightens up in her seat. "Can we just pretend I never brought it up and go back to our regular programming?"

"Definitely." I've never been so thankful for an out.

"I really wish you were staying in town longer," Meghan changes the subject, briefly squeezing my hand.

I nod. These trips never seem long enough. "I've gotta get back to Chicago. Work, y'know."

I need to resume my search for Westbrook Wealth Management's next big client. Time is ticking down to the end of the quarter. My goal of getting the company to a billion-dollar valuation won't accomplish itself.

She giggles, the earlier tension between us long forgotten. "What's the point of being a billionaire—"

"An *almost* billionaire," I correct her.

"—an *almost* billionaire if you can't even take a damn vacation? If you've always gotta run back to work? Doesn't sound like fun to me."

I hesitate, glancing out the window behind her and peering over at the infamous gas station curb and hating how much she makes me want to break all my rules. "Y'know—sometimes I ask myself the same thing."

She clasps her hands in front of her, making a show out of it and batting her big innocent eyes at me. "Stay. What can I do to make you stay just *one* day longer?"

I stare back at her. When I don't answer fast enough, she tugs on the end of my sleeve like an impatient little twit just trying to annoy me. I only pretend like she succeeds.

I narrow my gaze on her. "Give me a reason."

Her lips curve upward, and I already know she's in joke mode. "*Me*. Stay for me." She playfully throws her arms around me, wrapping me up in her ridiculous octopus grip. "Ple-e-e-ease?" Her lips pucker into that sexy pink pout again.

The feel of her warm body against mine does things it shouldn't. Like it or not, I feel a surge of blood rushing to my cock.

Instantly, my brain starts rationalizing.

Tomorrow is Friday. No sense in rushing back to the city when we're on the verge of the weekend anyway.

And I haven't seen Mom yet. If I stay in town another day, I could go visit her. Since the divorce, I haven't been there for her the way my brothers have.

Plus, I don't have any more meetings lined up for the week. And if anything pops up last minute, I can handle it remotely. That's why we have telephones and emails and video calls, after all.

I squeeze her tightly, my voice coming out all deep and strange when I speak. "You think you can make it worth my while?" I ease back just enough to look into her eyes.

Shit—did I just say that? What is happening here?

What I stupidly thought was nerves earlier was well, something a little *lower*. I'm beyond turned on, and if she shifts even an inch, she's going to feel it, too.

Meghan laughs shakily. It's like she can feel the tension, too. "Definitely. I can definitely make it worth your while."

My arms tighten around her, pressing our upper bodies closer together. Even still, the reality of my career resurfaces in my brain. "I can't. I can't miss another day at the office." My words are a complete contradiction to my actions.

She doesn't resist the urge to roll her eyes. "You're my best friend but you can be *such* a bore sometimes." She teasingly tugs on the hem of my shirt again. "It'll be fun, Cash. Fun? Do you know what that is? Do you know how to get a little wild sometimes?"

When she says that, it's like something inside me snaps.

My giant hands grip her small waist and flip her into my lap, right down onto my solid erection.

I don't miss the shiver that runs through her when my lips brush her ear and my low, raspy voice grumbles out. "I'm a Westbrook. Of course I have a wild side."

Suddenly, I can't figure out when the joking ended and the innuendos began. Dammit, she feels way too good in my lap. Between the rattling of her pounding chest, and the throbbing of my damn hard cock, I can't think straight.

And there's so much desire in Meghan's eyes. My best friend wants me.

All I know is, it feels nice—rare—to have someone who genuinely likes me and wants me around. To know that she's here for me and doesn't give a shit about my money. That knowledge does something to my ego. If me being around makes Meghan happy...it makes me wonder what else I could do to make her happy.

My dick could make her happy, too.

"Megs..." I grit out, my jaw clenched. I brush the pad of my thumb over her puckered bottom lip and watch the plump pink flesh fall open.

Gripping the back of my seat, she shifts and her core grazes my erection. The heat in my crotch rises, like it's trying to incinerate every layer of clothing coming between us. I hiss out a breath and I feel Meghan's thigh muscles clench against me.

Suppressing a groan, I look up into her face and brush her wild, blonde hair from her eyes. My gaze hooks on her lips again and she grinds down on me, causing arousal to hit me like an arrow to the groin. I lock my arms behind her back and raise my hips, reciprocating the thrusting movement she makes against me.

All I want is to devour her like a savage. Fuck thinking. I'm done thinking.

In a heartbeat, I'm kissing Meghan. Wildly.

She's not my best friend, in this moment. She's the woman who's been driving me crazy. The woman who's been turning me on for longer than I'd ever admit. The woman who's been awakening part of me that rarely ever comes to life.

And the really crazy part? She's fucking kissing me back.

Lips crushing lips. Tongues and teeth battling. Jerky movements and wandering hands and hair pulling. Suddenly, I can't think of anything other than getting her hot, little body closer to mine.

She continues to grind her hips and undulate her spine, uttering sweet, hungry, desperate sounds that make me lose my head. I grab her waist, grinding her back and forth on my long, throbbing, ruthlessly hard dick.

Lost in this warlike kiss, I've completely forgotten where we are. I slip my hands up under her dress, relishing in the heat and warmth of her soft thighs. My fingertips are right there, at the edge of her soaked panties, ready to slip inside.

And just as I'm about to take things even further, one of us inadvertently bumps into the steering wheel. The car horn honks. Loudly.

The sharp, abrupt sound draws us back into reality. We nervously dart around, remembering where we are. The freaking gas station.

There's an old dude at the neighboring gas pump, staring at us from not ten feet away.

Well, that's not creepy.

Quickly, we fumble around and extract our limbs.

I exhale, but it comes out all wrong and rough. "That came out of—"

Meghan speaks at the same time as me. "Oh my...What the hell—"

"—out of nowhere," I finish.

"—was that?!" Meghan breathes out.

We fall back into our separate seats, Meghan immediately pulling at the hem of her dress, while I'm straightening my tented pants. I mentally say goodbye to her gorgeous thighs, knowing this will be as close as I'll ever be to coming between them.

She swallows heavily when she glances down at my crotch. I may be embarrassed by my actions but my cock is standing tall and proud.

"W-we should probably get out of here," Meghan's lips and tongue stumble over her words. "Before we give people any ideas."

"You're right." I finally find my head again and start the car. "Let me drive you home." *Before I make any other crazy, friendship-altering decisions tonight.*

EIGHT

CASH

"DID you get the chance to read the email I sent you?" Wavy lines wiggle across my screen, distorting Nicky's face.

Shifting in the driver's seat, I snatch my phone out of its dashboard-mounted holder and tilt it left to right. What's a guy got to do to pick up a decent internet connection in this town?

"What email?" I ask my sister as I plop the device back into its holder, giving up on improving the internet connection.

"I finished up the research you asked me to do," she tells me as she's sifting through the papers on the conference table in front of her. "You wanted me to come up with some information on Cannon Kingston, that billionaire tech mogul from Crescent Harbor. Remember?"

"Yeah, I remember. Of course."

When I try to pull up that file on my laptop, I bang my elbow on the door. When I try to adjust the computer to get a better view of the screen, my steering wheel gets in the way. Working remotely isn't all it's cracked up to be. My car is a joy to drive but definitely lacks the perks of my corner office back in Chicago.

After being off for barely a few days, my virtual desk has already piled up. I spent the first hours of the workday fielding calls from the Chicago office, fixing analysis reports, and solving disasters.

It feels good to be needed and to get things done, but it isn't even lunchtime and I already realize that my work doesn't hold my attention like it does when I'm physically at the office, losing myself in the day until late in the evening without even noticing.

"I've been trying to get Kingston on our client roster for months now. But the guy won't even have a meeting with me." I huff.

If I can secure a business deal with him, Westbrook Wealth Management will be unstoppable. He's stinking rich. He probably shits dollar bills. But as things stand, he won't even return my calls.

Dad's grainy image abruptly leans forward in his seat beside Nicky. "Cash, I told you. I don't want you going anywhere near that prospect. I'll handle the Kingstons myself." Despite the shitty reception, I can see the hard lines of his face. He's serious about this.

"Why not?" Nicky asks our father. "Cannon Kingston is definitely the type of client we're looking for at WWM. He'd be a perfect match for us."

Dad nods. "Which is precisely why I don't want your brother messing this up. I'll be the one to reach out to him."

"Well, that's offensive," I snarl at my father over the line. "I thought I'd proven myself to you by now. You don't think I'm capable of bringing him on board?"

"Oh, I know you're *capable*," Dad says. "If you take the time, cultivate a relationship with him, slowly educate him about the benefits of working with our team, you could definitely win him over. But I'm worried that you're too impatient to put in the work. I've watched you burn too many bridges these past months, Cash. We can't afford to lose this one, too."

It's true—over the last little while, I have closed the door on a few deals that *might* have turned out to be lucrative for the firm in the long run. But that's because I'm in a race against the clock.

I want to get the company to the billion-dollar mark. Fast.

I won't achieve that goal if I'm spinning my wheels and investing my time on the wrong people. Even still, I know that Cannon Kingston is exactly the type of client we need.

"*I* will deal with the Kingstons." Dad repeats, wearing a no-nonsense expression. "And since when is client acquisition your department, anyway?"

I shrug. "Fine. On paper, I'm the numbers guy. But in order to meet my revenue goal by the deadline, I'm willing to be the jack of all trades."

"And master of none," Dad responds bitterly. That gets on my nerves.

"I think it's time for you to slow down," I announce. "Let me step in and take some things off your plate." He needs to face it; it's time for him to retire.

Dad doesn't take too kindly to my offer. "And *I* think that *you* should take a few days off when you say you're taking a few days off."

Fuck that. The company needs me. Now more than ever. "I never said I was taking a few days off." I shift again in my seat, still trying to get myself comfortable.

I spent the better part of the morning working from home. And by home, I mean the two bedroom Tudor that I bought in cash, only for my brother to move in and take over.

Heck, Jasper doesn't even have the courtesy to let me enjoy my king-sized bed while I'm in town. Last night, I had to sleep on the tiny bed in the tiny guest bedroom while Jasper was doing god-knows-what-with-god-knows-who in the master bedroom.

Judging from the sounds that were leaking through the thin walls in the wee hours of the morning, I think it might be time to change the mattress. Or drag it to the backyard and scrub it with bleach and holy water before setting it ablaze.

In any case, as I laid there staring up at the ceiling and unable to block out the farm animal sounds coming from down the hallway, all I could think was I didn't want to be in that damn house anyway. I wanted to be next door, with Meghan.

Every time I'd drift into sleep for a few minutes, I'd be transported back to the gas station. She'd be in my lap, working her hips, whispering my name.

Except in my dreams, there'd be no clothes, no inhibitions and not a person around for miles. Thanks to my fatigue and pent-up sexual tension, I'm irritable as shit today.

After what went down between us, I don't know how I'm supposed to get her out of my head. I'm making an effort anyway, throwing myself into work as usual.

It hasn't been easy, though. First thing this morning, I had to call and upgrade the wifi to get a good enough signal to hold a decent teleconference. That shit's embarrassing when you're the boss and you're cutting in and out like a cheesy telecom commercial.

I was going crazy inside that house. I needed to get out

for some fresh air. So now I'm parked on the quiet street outside the elementary school, hoping the cops don't come tap on my window.

Dad speaks and my attention snaps back to the conference call. "I'm serious. Take a few days off, Cassius. Clear your head. You deserve it. I know you're dedicated to your work and I appreciate that but I want you to know that there's more to life than building your career."

"That's rich coming from the guy who's literally watching his health spiral down the drain from how hard he's working," I retort. "Step down as CEO, Dad. Let me take over. So you can focus on you."

"My glory days are behind me," he says theatrically. "I might as well keep myself entertained with whatever time I have left."

Nicky gasps out loud but I just roll my eyes at our father's dramatics. He's not going anywhere any time soon. "Not this shit again..." I mutter scrolling through my laptop like I'm bored of the conversation.

"You need to make the most of your life, son. Or you're gonna regret it one day." He growls.

"Which day is that exactly?" I growl right back.

He slams a fist down on the table. "When you wake up in your multi-million dollar high rise condo on yet another meaningless Tuesday morning and realize that you're alone —again—and you start asking yourself if the relationships you sacrificed were really worth it."

"I'm so sick of everyone making everything about Meghan!" I blurt out.

He furrows his forehead. "I never mentioned Meghan, son," he says calmly. "D'you ever stop to think that I might have some regrets of my own?"

"Oh, Dad..." Nicky softly places a hand on our father's shoulder.

Every now and then, Dad says shit like that. And it makes me wonder if he ever got over my mother. I know they've been divorced for well over a decade but still, sometimes I wonder. And it makes me mad. Why'd they have to go and break up our family just so they could be more miserable apart than they were together? I just feel like, what was the fucking point, y'know?

Dad continues. "And now that you've brought up the topic of Meghan, I just want to say this. If she's the first person that comes to mind when I mention relationships, then you might want to take a minute and *really* explore what that means. Because I'd hate to see you end up like me." On those cryptic words, he rises out of his seat. "See you at the staff meeting at four, Nicky." He squeezes my sister's shoulder and strolls out of the room.

When the door closes behind him, Nicky turns her attention to me. "You really should stop picking fights with him."

"What the hell? I didn't pick a fight with him. He started it," I try to defend myself.

"You, Cassius Westbrook, are a disgrace to five-year-olds everywhere." She grunts. "You *do* realize that you and Dad are virtually the same, exact person, right? No wonder the two of you argue so much."

I scrub a hand down my tired face. "I respect Dad. Deeply. He was a phenomenal business man in his day. But I see now that it's time for him to slow down and focus on other things. Like his health. And to get the point across to him, sometimes I've got to be a little harsh. I've got to compartmentalize, Nicky. I've got to separate my personal respect for him from what's in the best interests of the company."

"Yeah, well, maybe you can compartmentalize with that stupid robot heart of yours but he's my father and I'm worried about him."

The look on her face troubles me. I sit straighter in my seat. "Did something happen?"

There's fear in her eyes as she speaks. "He's been really low energy today and he had this weird dizzy spell earlier. He said something about blood pressure medication and...I don't know what to think."

Suddenly, I wish I were right there to give my little sister a hug because she really looks like she needs some comforting right now. She may be the biggest pain in the ass but deep down, she cares so much about our family, all of us.

I try my best to reassure her. But I don't know how effective I am, seeing as I'm hundreds of miles away. "Look. Don't worry. He's gonna be okay. Everything's gonna be okay."

"I hope you're right, Cash."

In the distance, I hear the school bell ring. In a matter of seconds, children are bursting down the steps of the Honey Hill Elementary School. That's my cue to go.

"Look, Nicks. I'll check in later, okay?"

"Yeah," she nods, pushing a stray tear away from her eye. "Give Mom a kiss for me."

"Will do."

I get out of the car and make my way through the crushing tsunami of tiny humans swarming out the school's front door. I have to get ID'ed by the security guard before being allowed into the building. Every female teacher I pass in the halls gives me a bloodthirsty look as I make my way to my mother's office on the second floor. I avoid all eye contact.

I rap my knuckles against the doorjamb. "So how many little brats are getting detention today, Principal West-brook?" I joke from the doorway.

Laughing, Mom rises from her desk, grey eyes identical to mine twinkling with surprise. "Oh my god, Cassius. Your brothers told me you were in town but I didn't expect that you'd have the time to visit!"

"I didn't expect it either," I say, bundling her up in a hug. "But now that I'm here, I'm so happy to see your beautiful face."

"Oh stop it," she tells me with a laugh as she settles back behind her desk. "My glory days are behind me." My chest aches instantly when Mom echoes Dad's words from only a few moments ago. "At this point, I'm just grateful I was able to pass my good looks to you and your siblings." She winks.

Despite the sting in my chest, I force a smile. "Your contribution to my exceptional genetics is appreciated." I give a fake bow. She guffaws loudly.

My mom is more than just beautiful. She's smart. She's brave. She's a fighter. I wonder if she's happy, too.

"Brought you your favorite sandwich." I hold up the smoked turkey on rye I picked up from Grammy's bakery on the way here.

"My gosh, I'm starving." She peels the sandwich out of its wrapper and takes a messy bite. "I'll never get tired of your grandmother's sandwiches. Thank you."

One thing I admired about the way my parents handled their divorce? They tried their best to not let it hamper with their relationships with the people around them. That's why Mom can stroll into the Wildberry any day of the week and not worry about her ex-husband's mother sprinkling a little something extra into her coffee.

I bite into my own sandwich. "You really missed out on a good time last night. Too bad you couldn't make it to Meghan's party."

I called yesterday to invite her but she had to turn me down because of some school board meeting or other.

"You all had fun?" She watches me intently as I lean back in the seat across from her desk.

I try to sound casual as I bite into my sandwich. "Meghan had a blast."

A little smile comes over Mom's face and her eyes glint knowingly. "Oh, I bet she did. I heard all about the lap dance you gave her."

For a second, my jaw drops open in shock. How the hell did my mother hear about that already? But then I remember—this is Honey Hill. If only I could find an internet connection that works as fast and reliably as the rumor mill in this town...

Mom holds up a hand. "Before you go biting off any of your brothers' heads, just know I didn't hear it from them. At least four of the female staff members asked me to pass their phone numbers to you after seeing your performance." She hides her grin behind her sandwich. "Joe the janitor asked me to pass along his number, too. Depends on what you're into these days."

I glare at her. "Hard pass. On all of them. Joe, included."

Her eyes dance with amusement and she shrugs. "I told them you're already spoken for."

"I'm not dating anyone," I tell her, wondering why she'd assume that I'm in a relationship.

Her brows jump in surprise and a more serious look

comes over her face. "Oh, I just thought...I mean, you're in town for Meghan's thirtieth birthday. So I thought...Y'know, the marriage pact..."

I sigh. "The marriage pact was just a joke, Mom." How many times am I going to have to say this?

She makes an appeasing motion with her hand. "I know, I know. You'd both probably like to act like it was nothing. Still..." she inhales heavily. "I just see that look in your eye whenever you talk about her. That's all."

"What look?" I try to play dumb.

"You know exactly what I'm talking about. It's a look that makes me want to be thirty and feisty again..." She sighs.

I purse my lips to keep from scowling. "You can save me the stories of your 'feisty' thirties, Mom. Please. Sorry to burst your bubble but Meghan and I are just friends." She laughs and I use the distraction to change the subject to her own love life. "How are things going with you? Are you seeing anyone?"

I hate asking the question but I know it's expected. This many years after my parents's divorce, I have to accept that Mom has moved on.

Her face goes earnest. She folds her sandwich up in the wrapper and sets it down. "Yes, I've started seeing someone recently," she announces.

"Oh?" I try to keep my expression neutral. I clear my throat and try to sound happy about this. "Good. Good for you. You've got to do what's best for you. And anybody who judges you is an asshole."

Me. I'm the asshole. It's me.

Because the surly fifteen-year-old inside me still hates the idea of my mom with some guy aside from my dad. Maybe I didn't go through the stages of grief properly.

Maybe I bypassed the acceptance part. The fifteen-year-old inside me needs to grow the hell up.

I push the resentment aside and we continue to chat. We keep the topics light and surface-level. I don't like diving deep with Mom. Things get prickly fast when we dig too far down into the truth.

After long, it's time for me to leave. I rise from my seat.

"Thanks for coming to see me," she whispers, coming around her desk.

I may refer to Honey Hill as my hometown now but Mom knows that moving here wasn't an easy transition for me after my parents split ways.

My siblings and I were actually born and spent our childhood years in Chicago. It wasn't until the divorce that Mom moved my brothers, sister and me to Honey Hill. I hated it here. Couldn't wait to leave. The minute I graduated high school, I moved back to Chicago for college and to start interning at Dad's company. I sometimes wonder if my mother resents me just a little bit for that.

I pull my mother into a hug. "I love you, Mom. I've missed you."

"I love you, too, Cash." She touches my cheek.

Mom walks me to her office door. As I'm strolling out, I notice a dirty-faced little rugrat sitting on the bench in the corner, kicking his feet back and forth like he's waiting to hear his fate after getting himself in trouble.

"Want to tell Principal Westbrook what you did this time, Kenny?" The secretary stationed outside the door makes a pissy face as she stares at the little troublemaker.

"Oh, boy..." Mom whispers under her breath.

The kid's little freckled nose twitches when he dares to look up. "I threw all Emily's pencils on the floor. And then I farted inside her pencil case. But it was an accident. Promise," he hurries to add.

My eyebrows dart up and a laugh gets caught in my throat.

Mom shoots me a scolding look at my outburst but I see the amusement in her own eyes. She wants to laugh as much as I do.

"I'm getting out of here," I announce. I plant a kiss on her cheek. Then another one. "By the way, that second kiss is from Nicky."

She smiles after me as I stroll down the hall. "Tell that girl she owes me more than a kiss. She owes me a visit. I miss her so much."

"Don't tempt me. I might pack her up and ship her back to you," I joke.

"You'd never," Mom dares me just as I jog down the stairs to the main exit with a chuckle.

The second I step back onto the sidewalk, Meghan's on my mind again. As I head back to my car, I feel off-kilter. I have a shit ton of work to do. Still I find myself fighting the urge to blow up Meghan's phone with a thousand thirsty text messages. Or show my face at her place of employment, begging for a second of her time. I've got to keep myself in check, though.

This afternoon's gonna be a tough one.

NINE

MEGHAN

I TAKE A LONG, much-needed sip of my to-go coffee. The hot liquid practically singes off my taste buds but I barely notice. That's how caffeine-deprived I am.

"I needed that," I sigh, strolling out of the Wildberry Bakery with Alana after work.

Every few days, we take a walk through town in the evening instead of rushing straight home from the clinic. Today, it's especially nice to get a break from the constant spring rain so we might as well enjoy it.

"I swear you're not human. That's too freaking hot to drink yet." With a concerned frown, she pops off the lid and blows into her cup.

"I'm too desperate to care." I groan. "I need industrial strength caffeine and a week's worth of sleep to recover from that party last night." I grin as I remember my rowdy guests and all the trouble we made mere hours ago at the Hot Sauce Tavern in celebration of my birthday.

My bestie and I peek through the front windows of a handful of rustic clothing shops as we head toward my mom's store, our usual destination whenever we go for a post-work coffee and stroll. My mother owns Rainbows and Butterflies, a small baby clothing boutique here in town, conveniently located just a couple blocks down from the clinic. It's a cute little shop, enough to give any woman in Honey Hill a bit of baby fever.

A cold spring breeze sweeps across the street. My friend grabs her wool jacket at the collar and hunches up her shoulders to brace against the chill. "You had a good time at the party?"

I smile. "I did. It was so much fun." That's an understatement.

"Good." Alana smiles back at me as we wait to cross at an intersection.

I don't often feel like the center of attention. Frankly, I don't need it. I prefer focusing on bringing sunshine to the people I care about and making sure they're happy. But last night was most definitely about me. Cash made sure of that.

The flutters in my belly are like a tsunami when the thought of Cash storms into my mind.

When I crawled into bed after brushing my teeth and scrubbing off my makeup, that man was all I could think about. Ever since, I've been waging war against the thoughts but I've lost every battle.

That's to be expected. It's not everyday that I find myself playing tongue-hockey with one of my closest friends in the front seat of his luxury car. It's natural I can't get him off my mind.

That kiss was smokin' hot.

As we step into the crosswalk, I feel Alana reading my face. "It was really nice of Cash to surprise you that way." I hear hints of speculation in her intonation.

"It was." Just thinking about him and I don't feel the

cracked concrete of the asphalt beneath my feet. I feel like I'm walking on air.

"Has he left town yet?" my friend asks, still surveying every twitch in my expression.

"Uh, actually, he'll be in town for a little while longer."

Alana keeps her curious stare on me, hiked eyebrows and all. "How much longer?" she questions slowly.

I shrug a shoulder like it means nothing. "I...don't know exactly. One more day? Maybe?"

I see the suspicion swirling on her face as she stares me down. Dammit. Alana always sees everything. "I'm surprised that he hasn't run back to the city already. Usually he can't even spare a few hours away from his big job."

She's not saying anything I don't already know. I clear my throat and adjust my scarf with one hand. "I, um, convinced him to stay longer," I say simply.

"How exactly did you manage to do that?" she asks, her curious eyes giving me a preview of the million other questions floating around in her brain. I know this girl so well.

"I just...he...I guess he's, uh..." The more I stutter, the more suspicious she becomes.

"You two sure looked pretty cozy at the bar last night." It's not a question. It's an accusation.

"We looked cozy because we're friends. Friends get cozy. Stop making this a big deal."

She throws her free hand up innocently. "Sorry. I just find it strange that he randomly decided to stay in town." She sips from her coffee then asks, "Are you sure there's not more going on between the two of you?" From the way she looks at me, I know she knows I'm only telling half the truth.

"No. Of course not. Sheesh! Overactive imagination over there." I take another scalding gulp of my caffeine.

She says nothing. She just clasps her cup in both hands and lifts her coffee to her lips, like she's trying to hide a smile.

It's not long before my guilt takes the wheel and I start rambling to fill the heavy silence. "Maybe he just realized that he missed spending time in Honey Hill. Maybe he misses being with his family." I bite my lip. Shit—I can't keep this from her. "Or maybe it had something to do with the way I jumped his bones at the gas station last night..." I flinch.

"I knew it!" Forgetting all about the cold, Alana squeals and drags me to a roadside bench. "Tell me more," she demands. "Tell me everything."

Gosh—this is embarrassing. But this is the closest thing I've seen to a smile cross Alana's face today, so I'm okay with handing over a piece of my dignity if it means making my friend happy. I plow through the whole thing and share every sordid detail about last night.

Relieved to get this mess off my chest, I give my bestie all the gory details. I start with the barrage of compliments Cash rained down on me the night he arrived in town, then I tell her about the tension that sizzled between us when we slow danced at the bar last night.

And then, the lap dance. I give her *every* detail about the lap dance.

"By the time we got to the gas station, I could barely restrain myself. I don't know what I was thinking, throwing my arms around him and climbing all over him like that in his car. I'm completely embarrassed by the whole thing," I confess to Alana.

"Damn, girl. The gas station really brings out the wild side in the two of you, huh?" She bumps her shoulder teasingly into mine.

I shrug and frown. "There's just something about the warm, neon glow of those gas station fluorescents that seems to go to my head and make me do things I usually wouldn't."

Somewhere in my story—between Cash's hands on my waist and me, tonguing him down while humping the shit out of him in the driver's seat—it hits me.

It's all over for me. I'm ruined.

I don't think I'll ever be able to look at Cash the same way again. And how am I ever supposed to date anyone else when all I can think about is how Cash's lips felt on mine? *Crap.* On the inside, I'm freaking out.

Alana's staring at me, her expression growing uber-concerned as she reads my inner turmoil. I do my best to smooth out my features, and try not to look like a lovesick puppy.

Gotta play it cool, Meghan.

"Wow," she says when I'm done with my story. "Again—what's going on between you two?" she asks when I'm finished rambling.

"Nothing," I reply way too quickly.

Alana narrows her knowing eyes at me, so I add some innocent blinking to bolster my claim. *Damn your coolness, Meghan.*

When I open my mouth, my voice comes out all pitchy and weird. "It was just a momentary brain-fart or something..." *Oh yeah, that'll throw her off.*

"A momentary brain-fart that's been building for more than ten years?" She shakes her head.

Feeling antsy, I pop up to my feet. "Stop making this a big deal," I beg her as we resume our stroll. "It was just a little blip. Triggered by a few of those body tingling shots everyone had."

Alana relents. "Okay, you're getting defensive. I'll drop

the topic. Just be careful? Please? I'd hate to see you get all carried away in your emotions before you know if he's on the same page."

The expression on her face reminds me she's been heartbroken before, and she doesn't want me to experience the same thing.

"Okay." My voice trembles.

My friend gives me a warm smile. Then she gets closer and plucks something out of my hair.

"Ouch!"

She shrugs a shoulder. "Cat hair."

I rake my fingers through my wild curls and smile impishly. "Thanks."

As Alana and I draw closer to Rainbows and Butterflies, I see my mom outside talking to the owner of the building. The landlord has his tape measure out, measuring a large crack in the front glass window, while Mom's standing nearby, with her arms crossed over her chest.

Mr. Jones really is handsome for an older man, probably not more than a year or two older than my mother. He's always been kind to us and didn't bat an eye in those early years when rent was paid on a not-so-consistent basis. Plus, he always gets this cute little twinkle in his eye when Mom's around.

Exactly as he does now while he gazes at her a little too long. He couldn't hide his adoration if he tried.

Mom glances in our direction, giving Alana and me a brisk wave as we approach. But when she turns back to the landlord and notices the way he's looking at her, she freaks out. as per usual. "I...I have to go get back inside to call one of my suppliers," I hear her blurting before she rushes back into the store, disappearing when the glass door swings shut behind her.

I shake my head, knowing she handles all her supplier calls during the day, y'know, when the suppliers' offices are *actually* open.

"Good evening, Meghan and Alana," the landlord greets us when we reach the entrance. He smiles good-naturedly. "When is your mom going to let me take her on a date?" He kneels on the sidewalk to drop his tools back inside a large metal toolbox.

"I'm working on it, Mr. Jones." I give him my usual answer, as though he hasn't already asked me this a dozen times.

"Whenever she's ready, I'll be here waiting patiently."

I suck in a breath. "You're gonna need as much patience as you can muster."

He just chuckles, bidding us good night, as Alana and I head inside the shop.

We step into a jungle of onesies, wash cloths and itty bitty pajamas hanging from the walls and covering every horizontal surface. An instant smile comes to my lips. This store is a second home to me.

Yes, nothing says 'home' like size *three to six months* and handy butt snaps for your convenience. At least in my world.

My mother had to sacrifice a lot to raise me on her own, and she poured her life into this business to support us both. I spent a lot of my evenings working at her store throughout my teenage years, so Mom could save a little on stocking and front desk help. And even though she has a small staff now, I still like to drop by a couple nights a week to make sure everything is going okay.

"Hi, ladies." I pause at the front desk to say hello to Emma and Ziggy.

My mother hired Emma to handle the front of the shop

a few months ago. Though I can't say Emma's getting much work done tonight.

Ziggy flips over another tarot card and gasps dramatically.

"What's the prognosis on my love life today?" Emma side-eyes the cards with a healthy dose of caution. I don't really blame her. With Ziggy's predictions, you never know if it's death or fortune that's headed your way—or an ironic combination of the two.

Ziggy gushes excitedly. "This card here with the cups? It confirms that you're finally going to become one with your soulmate."

"Last time you said the same thing, except it was the empress card." Emma pouts.

"Those cards can have multiple meanings," Ziggy says dismissively. "You just have to know how to interpret them. And it's not my fault you always get the soulmate readings."

Reaching into her purse, Alana sets down a bag of muffins next to the cash register for our friends and laughs. "Let me guess. Jasper?"

For some reason, Ziggy is dead focused on Jasper and Emma being long lost soulmates.

Emma rolls her eyes. "Ha. A man like Jasper does *not* have soulmates. Just bedmates."

"Oh, Jasper's got more than bedmates. Trust me." I laugh. "He's got hallway mates. And kitchen counter mates. And bent-over-the-back-hedges mates."

"My gawd!" Alana gasps. "The back hedges?"

I nod. "It's bad enough that he never closes his blinds or turns off the lights when he's getting down and dirty with his lady friends. But every now and then, he likes to take the action outdoors, too."

Emma's cheeks are as red as fresh-made beet juice by

now. "No need for the visuals, Megs. I've walked in on Jasper and his mates in many a compromising position over my lifetime." I'll take her word for it. Emma and Jasper's sister, Nicky, were besties growing up. I'd bet she's seen lots of things she can't un-see during her time hanging out at the Westbrook home.

"Sorry, girl." With a laugh, I leave my friends behind and enter the back office where I find Mom hunched over her desk, stabbing at her keyboard.

I fall into the ripped chair in front of her old desk. I pull a muffin from my purse and hand it to her. "Whatcha doing?" I keep my tone light, despite the waves of stress and tension that are emanating off my mother.

"Bookkeeping," she mumbles, tapping a few keys and then leaning back to examine her data again.

I watch as she continues working in silence. "No supplier call?"

"Stop giving me that look," she bites, barely glancing at me.

"Mr. Jones is a good guy," I say, trying to reason with her. "He's handsome, and he clearly likes you, Mom. Why won't you just give him a shot?"

"Meghan, why must we keep having this same conversation? You know men only play with my heart. I'm never anyone's first choice. That becomes clearer when you get to be my age." She sighs. "It's time you become more discerning and realistic, darling. We're Hutchins women. We're cursed. Any man who comes sniffing around is only looking for a good time. It's never a man who wants to get serious with us." She swats the air. "I don't have the time for that. I've got more important stuff to deal with."

My heart sinks to the floor when Mom recites the same old story she's been telling me for years.

It was just me and Mom most of my childhood, especially after my father finally stopped stringing her along and got himself a new, improved family. Ever since Dad's betrayal, my mother hasn't been able to open herself up again. I've hated it because she's such a good woman and I hate that she won't share herself with anyone. But as the story goes, no woman in our bloodline was ever able to secure the love of a good man.

According to my mother, the Hutchins women have been playing out the 'all men are dogs' storyline for generations now. For some reason, we just always finish second best. Unfortunately, I have the anecdotal evidence in my dating record to prove her right. Every time I start dating a guy, things start out well enough until he loses interest, things fizzle out and he disappears into thin air.

My stomach is in knots right now because I know that Mom saw me with Cash last night. She witnessed my laughter and dancing and starry-eyes over my friend who is unarguably out of my league. I wonder if she's cryptically reminding me not to get my hopes up. That the Hutchins curse applies to me, too.

That idea terrifies me. Because one thing I've come to learn through my dating history is that relationships are temporary. But my friendship with Cash? That's been one of the only 'forever' things in my life.

Before I can take a ride on that unpleasant train of thought, Mom turns her computer monitor around to face me.

"What's wrong?" I ask.

"This is the store's revenue from the last quarter."

Shit.

"All of it?" I had no idea things at the shop had been so slow lately. "Wow. That's…not good."

She sighs, pinching the bridge of her nose. "I applied for another bank loan. They turned me down."

"Is there any way I can help? Do you need help with the bills? Or maybe I can put in more hours here, if you need."

Mom shakes her head. "No, darling," she says, looking utterly exhausted. "No need. You've already done enough to help me."

I try to ignore the cramp that slashes across my stomach when I'm reminded that I cosigned on her previous bank loan the last time things got bad here.

She reads my face. "Don't you worry about this, Meghan," she warns me. "I just needed to offload a bit."

"I'll try not to," I tell her. I will make an effort, but I refuse to make any promises on that front. I mean, this shop is Mom's whole life. How do I just brush that under the rug?

After I leave Mom's office, there's a sour feeling in my gut. I don't hang around long. I make an excuse about needing to get home to check on my foster cats. I say a quick goodbye to the girls, who are still in deep argument over the legitimacy of Ziggy's tarot readings. Alana is on the chopping block when I make my exit, so there's no telling what Ziggy will uncover there.

I walk the few blocks back to the clinic parking lot to get my car. Cash is on my mind the whole time. But now, so are my mother's cryptic words.

You know men only play with my heart. I'm never anyone's first choice.

Would Cash choose me first? Or, would he just toy with my emotions? Like every guy I've been with in the past? Like every guy who's been with my mother? And the women in my family line before her?

Over the past few days, our whole friendship has been tossed on its head. As much as I'd like to convince myself that Cash and me could be different if we ever tried to explore something new, I can't help but make parallels with my mom's situation.

Being friends with Cash is safe. Knowing that I'm in the friend zone, I don't have to worry about being strung along, about being played, about being tossed aside when all is said and done. And maybe I'm a coward but that feels safer to me.

I'm climbing into my car when my phone rings. It's a familiar number on the screen.

"Hello?" I answer as I slip behind my steering wheel.

"Meghan? Is that you?"

"Yeah." I pull my phone away from my ear to stare at the screen.

"It's me, Shelly from the animal sanctuary. It's about the cats you're fostering. I have some news for you!"

Instantly, my gut knots up.

Really? Today of all days? Really?

Fuck my life.

TEN

CASH

JASPER AND HIS FRIEND, Simon, from the mechanic shop have been shooting hoops on the concrete slab on the side of the house since I got back from the elementary school. Personally, I think they should still be at work, but whatever. I'm not their father.

I'm inside, catching up on a few hours of emails and contract revision. But soon, the aroma of grilled burgers wafts through the house and pulls me away from my makeshift office in the living room. Jasper always manages to burn the first couple when he's in charge of the grill, but even still, I'm eager to call it a day.

Before I know it, I'm outside in the yard with a beer in my hand and the rest of the guys have arrived, too. This is far from my normal weekday routine.

I have to admit that a cookout with the guys is much better than working until ten and crashing alone with take-out. Just one of the perks I traded when I left my brothers here in Honey Hill and moved to Chicago years ago.

Despite being surrounded by laughter, great beer, and good-natured ribbing from my family, I can't help but feel *off.* I chalk it up to having my schedule shot to shit. I'm well-acquainted with a day so jam packed full of meetings and unexpected office drop-ins that I'm lucky to take a piss once during routine business hours.

But today? Today was outside of my norm in every way.

The thought of Meghan played in my head no matter how hard I tried to concentrate. I genuinely tried to get some work done but in retrospect, I don't think I accomplished anything noteworthy.

The guys joke around and I absently listen to them talk about all their latest adventures. Davis is more closed off than usual, though. I keep trying to corner my oldest brother and get him alone, so I can see what's up with him, but I swear he's avoiding me.

He and I have always been close, especially throughout high school when girls suddenly became way cooler than Hot Wheels and video games with our little brothers. Then, our parents got divorced and Mom moved us to Honey Hill. Davis immediately started dating Alana. Then Meghan entered the picture and it became the four of us.

Now, here I go thinking about Meghan again.

The sun starts to duck between the neighboring houses. I find myself walking to the edge of the yard to take a subtle peek over the hedges to the house across the street.

She's still not home. My shoulders sag.

Even though I've kept myself busy since the moment I woke up, it feels like I've spent the whole day just waiting. Waiting for Meghan.

Instead of concentrating on my work, I was watching the clock and wondering what time she gets off from the clinic. Wondering if she takes a lunch break. Wondering if I'm about to lose my cool and do something stupid to screw up my decade-long friendship with the only woman I even trust.

Things took a very unexpected turn last night. I kissed her. I touched her. I acted on the urges I was feeling. And now I've done something stupid and my friendship with Meghan could very well be damaged beyond repair.

"You're looking a little tense, brother," Jasper razzes when I make my way back over to the patio table. He shoves his hand deep inside a chip bag then stuffs his mouth.

"Maybe you need to loosen up. Another lap dance, maybe?" Mason quips and points the neck of his beer bottle at the guys sitting across the table. "I'm sure these assholes wouldn't mind a show."

"Yeah, do you provide in-home services?" Harry gets in on the fun, dropping chip crumbs all over my patio furniture with wild abandon. "You should. That should be part of your new business plan."

I just flip them the bird and take a swig of my beer. *Assholes.*

"Please don't quit your cushy corporate day job. I know you made your best effort out there last night, man, but I don't think you could make a living from those awful dance moves." Jasper offers high-fives to his snickering buddies.

"What's wrong with my dance moves?" I frown. "I think I killed it last night."

Mason cringes. "I don't think anybody, aside from Meghan, appreciated your dance moves."

And there goes that crazy visceral reaction again at the mere mention of her name. What the hell is going on with me?

Harry, being the sensitive one, reads the agony on my face. He scratches his head, then talks with his mouth full of nachos. "Looks like you need to talk to her, bro. It's obvious that you like the girl. Maybe it's time to tell her how you feel?"

I ignore the perfect opportunity to give him shit. The guy who's probably never talked to a girl in his life.

Fine. I can admit that I've had a crush on Meghan for a long time. A little crush. But there was never any point in acting on it. Things are...complicated. She deserves a real relationship and I'm focused solely on my career. Plus, I live in Chicago and she lives here. I could never give her what she needs. So there's no point in stirring up trouble when she and I have a perfectly great friendship as is. Last night's steaming hot makeout session notwithstanding.

At least, that's what I'm trying to tell myself.

Fuck it. I do miss her. I'm trying to act aloof now that I'm with the guys but I miss Meghan so freaking much. I've missed her all day.

This is disorienting. All these years I've known her, and I was fine being just her friend. Where did all these new feelings come from all of a sudden?

"Whatever. Maybe you all should just fuck off," I mumble, stepping away to toss my lukewarm bottle in the trash and grab another from the fridge.

"Grab some ice while you're up?" Jasper calls after me as I enter the kitchen.

I'm inside grabbing another bag of ice for the cooler when I hear an engine out front. My eyes dart straight to the window. The second I spot Meghan's car pulling into her driveway, my heart starts slamming inside my rib cage and I'm tripping all over my feet to get to the back door.

She climbs out of her car, waving when she sees me staring out the open patio door. She self-consciously yanks at her scrubs. This pair has tiny cats and dogs printed on them, and she looks downright adorable.

For a second, I'm frozen, just staring at her. Trying to compute all the beauty standing in front of me. Trying to make it make sense.

I'm used to city women, the kind who never show up to work unless they're donning heels, designer suits, and an inch thick of goop on their face. Still I can say, hands down, Meghan Hutchins, coming home from a long day's work in her faded medical scrubs and blonde ponytail whipping back and forth, is more beautiful than any city woman I've ever seen.

Like an eager little kid under a spell, I rush down the cobblestone steps and jog across the street to greet her.

"Bro! Where's our ice?" Jasper calls out, indignant.

I ignore the guys yelling from the yard, still giving me shit.

I catch up to Meghan before she steps onto her porch. "Hey."

"Hey, yourself." A blush creeps up her face. The way she's fiddling with her keys and struggling to meet my gaze confirms she hasn't forgotten about last night either.

"We're having a little cookout." I tilt my head, nodding over to my house. "I'm sure it's been a long day. You should join us. Unwind. We've got burgers. Beer, too."

I'm rambling. I'm fucking rambling. I need to get it together.

She glances past me across the street, before lifting her hand in a shy, reserved wave. I turn to catch Mason, Harry, Davis, Jasper, and their lame band of dude bros *all* standing at the fence, with canoe-sized grins, staring at us.

"Ugh. Don't mind them. They don't know how to act when they see a pretty girl." Meghan's face reddens even more when I call her pretty. Doesn't she know how gorgeous she is? I touch her hand. "So, what do you say?"

That's when I notice how sad her eyes are. "Sorry, I wish I could. But I'm only here long enough to grab the cats. I have to return them back to the shelter." Her face crumples. "They were adopted, and their new family is picking them up."

"Shit. Really?"

She nods soberly. "I got the call on my way home from work."

Knowing how hard this must be for her, an idea hits me. "You want some company?"

Her brows dip. "I don't want to pull you away from your friends."

"The clowns will hardly know I'm gone." Even though they're still staring at us like we're some damn circus animals.

That pulls a small smile out of her. "I'm not so sure about that. They're looking a little codependent the way they're staring at you."

"Forget them," I say with my own laugh. I go serious. "This must be hard for you. I just want you to know that if you're in need of a little moral support, I've got you."

A slow smile moves across Meghan's face, making my chest pound all over again. I just want to make this burden lighter for her.

"That would be great," she says finally. "Help me round them up?"

ELEVEN

MEGHAN

THE RIDE to the animal rescue was a somber one. The only thing that got me through it without breaking down was having Cash by my side.

Introductions have been made. The paperwork has been dealt with. Now, it's time to hand over my foster cats to their new adopted parents.

We're seated around a rectangular table in a tiny, over-bright meeting room with poor air circulation. It's hot as hell and the scent of wet cat fur lingering in the air sure isn't helping.

The animal rescue's adoption counsellor sits at the head of the table. Across from Cash and me sit a young, bright-eyed couple with a mischief-faced preschooler climbing back and forth between their laps. They're the image of Americana and today, they'll be leaving here with a pair of cat-babies to make their picture perfect family complete. It only sucks that I'll be losing my feline friends in the process.

"So, this is the hard part." The pet adoption counsellor lays a hand on mine, gently coaxing me to release my tight grip on the handle of Captain Ginger's carrier where it sits on the table beside me. "Meghan, it's time to say goodbye." Cotton Ball stares questioningly at me from her own carrier.

My heart feels like it weighs a ton. I'm literally fighting back tears. I want to make this a quick goodbye. I don't want to make a scene in front of everyone. But, shit—I hadn't expected it to be this hard.

I mean, I've fostered cats before. But I sure have grown accustomed to having these two terrors around in the evenings when I get home from work. And having my ankles attacked during the middle of the night bathroom trips.

Still, I know that if I make this difficult, the shelter might not let me stay on the foster list. The last thing I want is to have a *Crazy lady alert* added to my file.

Yes, it's a thing. And yes, it's a code that actually gets added to the paperwork when you show your crazy around here.

I open the door to Cotton Ball's carrier. I give my feline friend a brief snuggle before handing her off to the kind-faced counsellor. Then I nuzzle my face into Captain Ginger's fur and for once, he accepts my affection without looking at me like I've lost my damn mind. I swear, he understands what's going on and he looks so betrayed by my abandonment. "It's going to be okay," I tell him before shooting a smile at the family across the table. "They'll take good care of you."

Putting on a brave face, I release Captain Ginger's carrier. Cash gives Cotton Ball's carrier a little shove toward the family. "There you go, guys. There you go."

"Ohh! I'm getting emotional, too." The young mother blots her eyes and clings to her ornery daughter. "Are you recording this, Jim?" she asks her husband. "Make sure you're recording this."

"I'm recording it," he assures her, his camera aimed to capture the scene.

I don't even realize there's a tear streaking down my face until I feel a warm thumb brushing it away.

Cash grips both my shoulders, squeezing gently. "You good?" he whispers by my ear.

Having Cash here with me, lending me support and keeping me company, is something I could get used to.

I try not to dwell on that.

"Of course I'm good," I answer quickly, but it's not enough to convince the guy who knows me best. I pause. "But...I'm really going to miss those two temperamental felines keeping me company and making sure I don't talk to myself. Too much." Cash smiles softly.

Fostering animals is never an easy job, but I had this pair of cats longer than most. I'm attached, dammit.

When Jim sees how downtrodden I am, he gives me a kind smile. "Don't worry. We'll take good care of them," he assures me.

I nod. "Please do. They're amazing cats."

I make eye contact with the little girl. She gives me this wild-eyed grin. Sort of like Chucky.

I'm not fooled by the frilly pink dress and the pretty bows in her pigtails. You know those kids that are just *evil*? That's the vibe I'm getting from this kid.

The thought falls away when I feel Cash's arm slip around the back of my chair. His fingertips brush back and forth along my shoulder and I sink into the comfort offered by his touch as the counsellor attempts to hand Cotton Ball to her new family.

But the cat isn't having it. Especially when the little demon child bops her in the face with a juice box.

"Eleanor. We don't hit the cat," her mother scolds softly.

The cat squirms and tussles in the shelter worker's hold. When Cotton Ball finally breaks free, her bushy white tail pops up rod straight. She slowly, slowly backtracks into her cage, never taking her eyes off that trouble-making little girl.

"We'll give her a minute. Sometimes, it takes a little while for them to warm up to strangers," the woman explains. "Sometimes cats just need a few moments to feel safe around new people."

The counsellor aims her focus on Captain Ginger. She scoops him off the table. But just as she's handing him off to his new family, the bratty child grabs the cat's tail in her fist and pulls.

Big mistake.

I see the *Bitch, do you know who you're dealing with?!* look that comes across the cat's grumpy face before he leaps up, takes the little girl in a headlock and hits her with a savage one-two punch combo no-one saw coming.

Dad lunges. Mom shrieks. Kid starts bawling.

It's pure chaos.

Everybody's on their feet, springing into action. I hurry around the table and try to help the counsellor and the parents separate the child from the cat's ninja grip without anyone getting hurt.

Cotton Ball burrows deeper into her plastic cave, content to stay far away from the commotion.

By the time all is said and done, I have Captain Ginger restrained in my arms. The mother is a panting mess clinging protectively to her little girl, the father's phone is on the floor with a cracked screen. The smiles and excitement from before have given way to horror.

The counsellor does her best to smooth out the situation but the terrible first impression has been made.

Jim stands between his distraught family and the cats

like a human shield. "I think my wife and I need a minute to reconsider. Before things proceed," he announces.

"Reconsider?!" his wife spits out. "There's nothing to reconsider. I don't want those feral creatures anywhere near my child." She stomps out of the room and her husband is hot on her heels, trying to calm her down.

"I'll go check on them," the counsellor says. She walks out with a cringe on her face and her shoulders up to her ears. The door closes behind her.

I turn to Cash. His shoulders rock. He's barely containing his laughter.

"Stop laughing. That was horrible. Horrible," I scold the naughty feline.

"That evil kid had it coming to her," Cash says unapologetically.

"Oh my god, it's true." I give Captain Ginger's fur a soothing stroke. "But it's not socially acceptable to say things like that out loud."

Cash huffs. "Societal rules are a drag."

Voices from the hallway drift into the meeting room as I sit there, comforting the spooked out cats. I catch pieces of the conversation as they speak.

"...no way I'm having those terrors in my house..." the wife's voice comes.

"...too late to back out?" the husband asks.

"...canceling the paperwork..." The counsellor replies.

I may be a terrible person but with each word they exchange my hope soars a little higher.

Finally, the counsellor enters the room solo and explains to us that the couple has changed their mind about adopting the cats.

I can barely restrain myself from fist-pumping the air.

"Hey, Meghan. You good to keep an eye on these two

for a little while longer?" she asks me warily. "I know you weren't planning on it, but—"

I nuzzle both balls of fur close to my chest. "I'd love to," I tell the woman, unable to hide my relief. These two are becoming like family to me. "I wasn't quite ready to let them go anyway."

Later, I'm still floating on a cloud when Cash and I step out of the animal rescue admin office, each of us carrying one caged feline. I had to sign even more paperwork to keep the cats but I'm cool with that as long as they get to come home with me.

Cash is walking ahead of me and I'm momentarily distracted by his body. Even from behind, the man is beautiful.

Those wide shoulders. That strong back. That squeezable ass. Oh my!

No wonder I was all over him at the gas station less than twenty-four hours ago. He's fine as hell. I suddenly experience humper's remorse—I really should have squeezed that ass last night when I had the chance.

My head's in the gutter, trying to not think about the hot and heavy moment we shared. The one neither of us has mentioned. The one that still lingers in this new air between me and my best friend.

He glances over his back abruptly and catches me gawking. His nostrils twitch and his lips curl into a faint, knowing smile.

It's killing me to wonder what he's thinking. If he's already forgotten about it. Or worse, if he regrets the whole thing ever happened.

But I push all that aside and focus on the matter at hand. I give my friend a sidelong glimpse and I can't help the gratitude overflowing in my heart. Having him here with me today has meant so much to me. And this is precisely why I'd choose our friendship over any romantic affair between us. Because I know that if we ever got involved and things didn't work out, I'd miss out on moments like this—him, being here for me when I need someone beside me, being a friend.

I direct Cash toward the front of the shelter. We lazily stroll through the long aisles, passing large cages and small rooms filled with barking and yowling animals in need of fostering or adoption.

I sigh as we pass an enclosed room with glass walls, dedicated to a new litter of kittens. "If I had enough room, I'd house all these homeless pets myself."

A volunteer is hard at work, filling bowls with milk. He glances over his shoulder and gives us a wave. Taking advantage of the perfect opportunity, the tiniest of the baby cats darts between the worker's feet and sneaks out the door. He immediately skitters over to Cash.

"Aw. Someone has a new friend." The volunteer winks at Cash then turns, already headed to the next room to continue his feeding rounds.

"We'll get him back inside." I offer helpfully, setting Cotton Ball's carrier on the ground. But when I turn back to Cash, I'm shocked to find him now kneeling down, studying the gray, tiger striped kitten mewling around his ankles.

My heart brightens. I can literally feel it.

"He's sure taken a liking to you," I comment.

Cash chuckles, reaching down and scratching the top of the kitten's tiny head. "Huh, he is kind of cute..."

I gnaw on my bottom lip, watching the two of them. "Gah! A man playing with a kitten shouldn't be this hot." Cash checks me out over his back. My cheeks instantly flame. I try to take the heat off myself. "Maybe *you* should foster this one."

He reels back, almost falling on his butt as he gawks at me quizzingly. "What?! No. Hell no. I don't have time for *a cat.*"

I laugh. "It's just a kitten. An adorable baby kitten."

"I'm hardly ever home," he argues.

"Well, I have news for you, buddy. Cats basically take care of themselves, making them the perfect pet for a workaholic like you." I flash him a grin.

"I don't know," he hedges. But I can see that he's considering it. Especially when the kitten starts purring and rubbing his head against the back of Cash's hand.

I kneel down beside them, reaching out and giving the adorable little guy a scratch under his chin. "How about a deal? If you foster this kitten, I'll spend the weekend showing you the ropes. Our cats can get together and have a play date. And I'll teach you all about being the best cat dad ever."

A wary look comes over Cash's features. "I'm leaving town first thing in the morning."

"Why?" I say nonchalantly, like it's no big deal that he's already extended his initial stay in Honey Hill. Twice. "It's the weekend. No need to run back to the office until Monday."

Cash's eyes darken as he stares at me. "Now you're asking me to stay the entire weekend?"

I nod meekly. "Sure...It'd be fun." I straighten to my full height. "Don't forget. You're in town to hang out. Cut loose. Take a break. So, we should be having fun. Right?"

He eyeballs me closely—no doubt, trying to determine my definition of fun—but honestly, I don't have any agenda. I just want to enjoy this time with my friend before he runs back to Chicago. With us living and working in different cities over five hundred miles apart, I know we won't be getting another chance to spend time together like this any time soon.

He rises to his feet, too, towering above me. "I'm always fun, Buttercup. Don't know about you though," he teases.

Why do my nipples tingle when he says those words? In that tone? "Depends on your definition of fun, I guess." I'm using my bedroom voice all of a sudden. My words sound slow, husky and tinged with innuendo. "I know that board meetings and shareholder reports really get your engine going, but maybe I can show you a different kind of fun, Mr. Westbrook?"

His eyes skim down my legs. "Oh, you've already shown me plenty of things today that get my engine going, Ms. Hutchins."

Even though I know he's only joking, that grin does things to my insides. It's worrying.

I return our focus to the matter at hand. "So, will you stay?"

I mentally brace myself for him to turn me down. But in a shocking twist of events, he just furrows his forehead and emits a growly, "Fine."

Well, that took considerably less convincing than I expected. I'm understandably in shock. And less than an hour later, we're walking out of the animal shelter with completed paperwork and a band of *three* mismatched cats.

Captain Ginger yowls and makes a fuss inside his cage as I carry him out the door. As we stroll across the parking lot to the car, I sneak a peek in Cash's direction. I'm literally melting over the way he carries Cotton Ball's carrier in hand while his new kitten is safely cradled in the crook of his arm.

I might be on my way to becoming a cat lady, but if

Cash is right there with me becoming a crazy cat man, then I'm more than okay with that.

I hear Mom's words replay in my head. *You know men only play with my heart. I'm never anyone's first choice.*

In that moment, my hopelessly pounding heart suddenly doesn't give two craps about what Cash would do with it.

Play with it. Steal it. Snuggle it. Dance all over it then smash it to pieces. Whatever. Sign me up.

If he asked, I'd give this man my heart in an instant and he has no idea. Let's just hope he doesn't ask.

Because that's my only hope of making it out of this in one piece.

TWELVE

CASH

"TOLD you we should have kept the shopping cart," Meghan teases again as we walk across the pet store parking lot an hour later.

I peer over my armful of cat supplies to glare at the little know-it-all. But she just nuzzles my brand new kitten to her cheek and gives me a disarming, dimpled smile. That smile nearly makes me drop my entire haul to the ground.

Is she doing this on purpose? Being this beautiful? This addictive? This irresistible? She has to be doing this on purpose.

She's breaking my control. Shattering my rules. Tearing down my walls at an alarming pace.

I've spent nearly three *decades* building these fucking walls, reinforcing them with steel. And this tiny, dimple-faced, sunshine-haired, diamond-eyed woman is tearing them down in a matter of days. If I stay here much longer, I won't even recognize myself. My defences will be gone completely.

Yet, I can't walk away.

She watches me watching her. "What is it?" she asks,

setting the cat into the front seat of my car just long enough to help me unload the supplies into the trunk. "Why are you looking at me like that?"

No way I'm telling her what I'm *really* thinking. So I tear my eyes away from her and stare down into the overloaded trunk. "What am I going to need with all this crap?"

The second we set foot inside that pet shop, what I thought would be a quick run inside for cat food turned into something else entirely. Meghan guided me around the store, stocking our cart with a bunch of ridiculous cat accessories, claiming that each one was a 'cat dad' musthave.

I'm a 'cat dad', y'all.

She actually didn't buy a whole lot for herself, much to my surprise. Apparently she already owns all these absurd supplies and thought I should, too.

"Ha-ha! This is just your 'cat dad' starter pack." She winks at me then rounds the trunk and climbs into the front seat. "There's a whole lot more you're gonna need to get for your little guy."

"God help me," I mutter to myself.

I fall behind the wheel, exhausted and ready to call it a day. I yank open the glovebox and shove the pet store receipt in there, for safe keeping.

Meghan's gaze strays to the marriage contract. Then it travels to me. We hold each other's eyes for a long moment and neither of us say a thing.

Still, I know we're both thinking the same thing. *What the hell are we doing?*

Meghan lets my new kitten crawl all over her lap as I drive. Meanwhile, Captain Ginger and Cotton Ball yowl up a storm from their carriers, snuggly secured in the back seat.

Watching my friend coo over the kitten, I shake my

head. "I'm still not quite sure how you roped me into this," I tell her.

"I fear it may be a little too late for buyer's remorse, good sir," she says in a haughty voice.

"This is crazy. I hope I don't regret it."

"Shush." She covers both of the cat's ears. "He doesn't mean it," she speaks in baby talk. "No, he doesn't. Don't listen to anything the big, grumpy man says about you." Her lips form a pink pout.

"Seriously, woman. This cat is going to take over my whole room. Have you seen how cramped my room is?"

Even in the darkened car, I see the fire that flashes through her eyes. "I haven't seen your room, actually."

Right. Of course she hasn't seen my temporary guest room. But...does she want to? Hell, she's so hard to read.

Afraid to go down that route, I quickly carry on. "I just don't see why I need a big ass cat litter box for an animal the size of my shoe."

"Well," she pauses to grin at me. "Your kitten is going to grow. Plus, this way, you'll have a box that's big enough when you foster an adult next time."

"What? Who said anything about a next time? This is a one-time fluke, Buttercup."

"If you say so," she says too sweetly, turning her eyes away from me as I'm pulling onto our street.

A one-time fluke. Interesting choice of words, asshole. Fostering a living, breathing cat isn't the only one-time fluke I've made over the course of this trip. I seem to be making a whole lot of them. And I could write up a long list of all the other one-time flukes I'm aching to make.

This is getting out of control.

Cutting the engine in my driveway, I turn to face her in

my seat. I take a breath. "Megs...we can't just *not* talk about what happened last night at the gas station," I say softly.

Meghan's chest rises and falls. "I know."

Things are already taking an awkward turn. I'm not quite sure about the protocol for what to say the day after making out with your best friend at the gas station, moments after you promised yourself for the umpteenth time that you wouldn't lose your cool.

I scrub a hand down my face. "I just...I just need to know that we're both on the same page about...about stuff. Between us?" Can I be any more ineloquent than I'm being right now. "What I'm saying is things between us have felt a little different over the past few days. I know you must feel it, too."

"Definitely, yes." Her blonde curls bounce adorably when she bobs her head.

"Look, Meghan, you're my best friend. A lot of the time, you're the only person I even like."

"I know I am." Smirking playfully, she lifts her chin snobbishly, causing me to chuckle.

I drop my head and shake it. "I don't know what's gotten into me these past few days."

"I feel the same way." She sighs. "It's probably just our friends putting all that pressure on us. And constantly bringing up the marriage pact. And..."

It's my turn to nod. "Yeah. That must be it."

Silence fills the car. The cat hops out of her lap and into mine. He climbs my chest and licks my jaw. Fuck, that tickles. Meghan laughs as I squirm away from the little fucker.

The way her whole face lights up with that laugh, makes me lose my head for a second. "You're absolutely gorgeous, Meghan."

She freezes. She swallows. "You're rather attractive yourself."

I roll my eyes. "Is that a compliment or a clinical evaluation?"

She snorts out through her nose and a blush highlights her cheekbones. "You don't need me telling you how hot you are." *Maybe I do.*

I should resist the urge to reach out and tuck her hair behind her ear but I just can't. I cup her cheek. "You're smart. And so fucking kind. You're literally the best person I know. Every time you smile, you singlehandedly restore my faith in humanity. But...but..."

"But friends is all we can ever be." I see some of the light leave her eyes.

"Right," I say, determined to stick to the script in my head. "Because I don't have time for a relationship."

"And dating each other would probably mess up our friendship anyway," she adds.

"And I'm so focused on work, I know I'd make a terrible boyfriend."

"Plus, we live six hours away from each other." After a short silence, she sucks in a breath. "If things ever went bad between us, we'd lose all this." She motions to the air around us. "And I really, really need you to be *this* for me."

The more justifications we come up with for why we could never work, the more I just want to lean across the console, grab her face in my hands and kiss her until none of those reasons matter anymore.

Meghan absently picks a cat hair off of her jacket. "What we have is good. Let's not change that."

I nod. "Yeah."

I battle against my rising annoyance at myself. Fuck all our excuses. I want her and I hate that I have to deny myself. I'm putting on a good act, but even my new cat sees through my bullshit. He skitters out of my lap and goes back to Meghan.

"I should probably get my cats inside." She glances toward her house where it stands in darkness across the street.

"Right."

We get out of the car and I leave my own feline inside just long enough to help Meghan get to her house with Cotton Ball and Captain Ginger.

The little bastards make a prison break from their plastic jail cells the second Meghan opens the doors. Now, she and I are standing face to face in the middle of the living room. The balloon bouquet I bought her is still floating in one corner. That old picture of us that I gifted her sits on the mantle now. I can't help but wonder if I belong here, too.

"Let me get them some dinner," she tells me. "Then I'll come over and help you get all your new accessories and supplies organized."

"Sounds good," I tell her.

With Cotton Ball in her arms, she walks me to the front door and watches as I grab some stuff from my trunk.

"You sure you don't need another five-foot cactus shaped scratching post?" I call across the driveway to her.

"I think I'm good." Meghan giggles, pressing her lips to the top of Cotton Ball's head. "I'll be right over, okay?"

"Okay."

With my own furball in tow, I carry as many bags as I can into my house where another of Jasper's get-togethers is in full swing. I'm nearly bowled over by a bunch of girls headed out the door, cigarette packets and lighters in hand.

"Isn't that the guy who was giving his girlfriend a lap

dance at the Hot Sauce last night?" a girl with brown skin and long braided hair whispers loudly to her friends as they pass by me.

A dangerous-looking one with heavy black eye makeup and multiple lip piercings twists her lips into a cunning smile. "Sure is..." She shamelessly takes me in. "Gotta love a man who knows how to take care of a pussy," she mutters to her friends.

I glare at her.

"The cat, I mean." Giggling, she jerks her chin toward the kitten squirming in my hold.

Yeah, whatever.

"He has a girlfriend, you little bloodhound," I hear the girl with the braided hair hiss.

Vampire Girl snickers. "Well, I don't see that 'girlfriend' anywhere around here. Do you? Maybe she should keep a better eye on her man if she wants to keep him." She pushes up her cleavage in her leather and lace corset. "What'd'y say, sexy?"

I look the terrifying girl up and down. "Not in a million lifetimes." *Or past lives. Or afterlives. Or...*

I need to get away from these women. When I march into the living room, hauling in a cat carrier, my giant new cactus, some weird ass toys, and a ten pound bag of food, five grown men stop their poker game to gawk at me.

"Thanks for the help, dumbasses," I mutter as when empty cat dish slips from my arm and hits the floor.

"Dude." Harry squints at me.

"What?" I grumble, allowing my other supplies to slip, but carefully hanging onto the kitten in the crook of my arm for dear life.

"*Dude,*" Mason echoes him.

I'm annoyed. So annoyed. "Is somebody gonna explain what all the dude-ing is about?"

Davis finally puts me out of my misery. "We were all hanging out," he says slowly. "Then you disappear with Meghan and show up three hours later. With a *cat*."

Mason shakes his head in shame. "Who the hell are you anymore?"

"A pussy-whipped fool," Jasper announces. "Literally."

"Shut up. All of you."

I set the cat loose and start trying to figure out what goes where. Not surprisingly, the guys keep ribbing me as I set up the scratching post and some of the other cat stuff.

"Seriously, though, you need to give that whole 'we're just friends' storyline a rest," Mason advises sagely. "You're clearly in love with her."

Harry adjusts his stupid baseball cap. "That's it. Enough of all this 'just friends' bullshit. You'd better shoot your shot with Meghan—right this minute—and hope for the best. Because if Meghan isn't willing to settle for your grumpy ass, it's all over for you, bro."

I'm doing a great job ignoring them as I set up the cat's new handwoven window hammock, until I hear Meghan's voice just over my shoulder. "You guys are mighty presumptuous, you know that?"

My spine goes ramrod straight. I turn and find her standing in the entrance to the living room.

She's there in an oversized slouchy T-shirt and those sexy fucking yoga pants with her hair in a messy knot high on her head. Her makeup has been scrubbed off, drawing my attention to the scattering of freckles on the bridge of her nose. It takes me a second to snap back into the conversation.

In a heartbeat, I'm standing at her side. "Ignore those

assholes. You weren't supposed to hear that, Megs." I angle myself in front of her, covering her body with mine like a shield. "You assholes need to shut up," I tell the guys.

But Meghan doesn't need my protection. In fact, she's perfectly capable of holding her own. When her arm slips around my waist and she wraps her body around mine, causing my whole system to respond, I realize that I'm the one who might need protection. From her.

She addresses the guys with an audacious expression on her face. "Maybe Cash did already shoot his shot...And maybe he *scored*." The suggestive intonation in her voice makes me insta-hard.

I glance at her. *What the hell is she doing?*

Jasper and Mason exchange a look. Harry's eyebrow hikes up high enough to get lost under his hat.

Davis speaks first. "Are you saying...what I think you're saying?"

I examine her features closely. I'm not sure where we're going with this.

Meghan meets my eyes and smiles at me like a woman deep in love. "Your brother has far more charm than you give him credit for." She affectionately sweeps a palm across my chest.

Jasper sticks out a hand. "To be clear, you're saying that you and Cash hooked up?"

There's hopeless adoration in her expression. She looks at me like she just can't tear her eyes away. I almost buy it. I've met some professional actors in my day. But—damn—Meghan's *good*.

"We're so much more than a hook-up." Meghan sighs dreamily. "We agreed that we wouldn't say anything to you guys yet but...we're an item now."

That's when my fritzed-out brain comes back online.

Meghan's words from yesterday replay in my mind. *Y'know what would be really funny? We should just pretend that we are together. Pretend that we're totally and completely, over-the-top in love with each other. Just to get them to shut the hell up.*

"Since when?" Davis's suspicious gaze bounces between us.

Meghan's eyes sweep over her captive audience. "Cash and I had a serious conversation the night he came into town. We both decided that we're tired of beating around the bushes. We're moving forward with the marriage pact."

Harry's eyes bulge. "You're..."

"Engaged." I blurt out.

Jasper jolts forward and grips the edge of the poker table. "You're shitting me, right?" He looks around at the guys. "No. They're shitting us. They're joking." His eyes sweep to Meghan and me and he laughs awkwardly. "Good one."

Meghan just shrugs a shoulder, like she doesn't care whether they believe her or not. "I guess you'll just have to wait for your wedding invite in the mail. You'll believe it then." She gazes into my face, stroking her hand up my chest. "I need a drink, baby." She grins at me. "You know you make me so thirsty."

I turn smugly to my brothers. "Get it? She's thirsty because I'm hot. I make her thirsty because I'm hot."

Jasper makes a vomit-sound.

"If you'll excuse us," I say to my spectators without taking my eyes off of Meghan. "My bride-to-be has needs. And it's my duty to fulfill them."

With my hand at the small of Meghan's back, I guide her into the kitchen, nearly suffocating on the laughter trapped in my throat.

We burst into the kitchen and Meghan collapses against my chest, erupting into giggles.

"Shhh..." I whisper and yank her into the pantry. "We got them good. Don't mess it up now." I close the door and flick on the light hanging overhead.

"Oh my god. Did you see their faces? Especially Harry —oh my god. And J-Jasper—and—" She's cracking up so hard she can hardly breathe.

In the cramped cupboard, I hold her to my chest, burying my own laughs in her freshly-washed hair. "That's what they get for constantly poking their noses into our business."

"They totally deserve it." She laughs some more but I'm distracted by how amazing her body feels against mine.

Alone with her inside this pantry, the walls seem to be closing in around us. Her hands wander distractedly over my shoulders and arms. Lust zaps under my skin like electricity. Damn—her hair smells good, too. I try to block it out but my cock seems highly motivated to burst through the zipper of my pants.

When she's finally calmed down, she grabs me by the wrist. "Okay. Come on. Let's go tell them we were joking." She turns for the living room.

I give her a soft yank that stops her in her tracks. "Let's drag this out."

"Huh?"

"Let's let them keep believing this. At least for tonight," I suggest. "If we come clean right now, they'll just go back to giving us shit. It'll ruin the whole evening. But if we let them go on believing we're together, it'll keep them off our backs for a while. We can tell them the truth tomorrow."

Meghan likes my idea. I see it in her smile. "Okay. Plus, this is sort of fun."

"Yeah." Fun. This is all for fun.

I decide to ignore the fact that I'm still holding her hand. And I definitely refuse to examine why I don't want to let it go.

An idea flashes across her expression. "Y'know what? Let's make things interesting. Let's *really* give them something to talk about."

"What do you have in mind?" I'm down to play along with any scheme she comes up with.

But when her fingers come to the top button of my shirt, my heart almost gives out right then and there. She has no idea of the dirty thoughts going through my head as she proceeds to unbutton my shirt halfway down. Then she deliberately misbuttons it, leaving me looking rumpled and disheveled. Her fingers then delve into my hair, tussling it up a bit.

She messes up her own hair before yanking the neckline of her shirt so it's sloping off her shoulder, leaving her bra strap visible.

Her eyes sweep over me, appraising her handiwork. She slaps a hand over her mouth and laughs. "You look like you just got some *serious* action, mister." She grins like a cartoon mastermind. "How do I look?" She strikes a pin-up girl pose.

Freshly-fucked. Fuckable. Fuckity-fuck. I'm fucked. My tongue gets lost somewhere in my throat. I can't respond.

She sighs in disappointment. "Never mind how I look. I'm sure it'll do," she chirps, grabbing my wrist and pulling me to the doorway. "Come on!"

When we enter the living room, all eyes land on us, putting an abrupt stop to the conversation in progress.

The new kitten is in Harry's lap, sniffing at shit on the poker table. Meghan scoops the cat out of my brother's arms and then proceeds to hook a finger into the belt loop of my pants. "Which way's the bedroom?" she asks like she's requesting directions at the mall.

Mason's jaw drops open. A beer bottle gets knocked over. Somebody gasps.

"T-that way," Jasper points toward the stairwell.

I can't control my ear-to-ear grin. Playing the role of the love-drunk submissive is fun indeed. I let Meghan take the lead. Putting on a show for our audience, she impatiently drags me toward the stairs.

My big-mouth brothers are speechless.

As soon as we turn the corner, Meghan drops the act. She and I are cracking up as we take the stairs up two at a time.

Halfway up the stairs, she turns and whispers excitedly. "Ooh! D'you have a TV in your room? We could have a National Geographic wildlife documentary marathon." She jogs up ahead of me.

Wow—look at that ass.

I'm in the mood for a wildlife documentary, all right. Starring Meghan and me. All night long.

THIRTEEN

MEGHAN

THROUGHOUT MY JOURNEY as a cat lady, there are things I've become accustomed to.

Waking up to a cat breathing directly into my face.

Waking up to a cat licking my ear.

Waking up to a cat sitting on my head.

But nothing I've experienced so far could have prepared me for *this* sight.

My eyes slowly flutter open to early morning sunlight haloing around the silhouette of a very shirtless Cash Westbrook with his tiny new kitten clenched securely under his arm. He's quietly setting a brimming coffee mug on the bedside table by my head.

"Hey." He flashes a tired smile when our eyes meet.

"Hey." I clumsily sit up, causing the quilt to pool around my waist.

"Didn't mean to wake you. I just thought you'd like your coffee here waiting for you when you woke up." He sets the kitten free onto the bed and the little thing scampers over to me, coming to lick my face. What a cutie!

"No worries. My Saturday alarm was set to go off—" I

check my phone on the bedside table "—in five minutes anyway." I disable the alarm.

He regards me earnestly. "I know."

He does. He knows about my Saturday alarm. He knows how I take my coffee. He knows everything about me.

Or almost everything.

He doesn't know that my panties are getting wet just looking at him right now.

I watch him grab the black T-shirt hanging on the back of the closet door. His muscles ripple as he pulls it over his head and tugs it down his torso. The way it molds to his chest is mighty delicious. *Jasper Auto Body*, it reads.

"New day job?" I pick up the coffee mug and jerk my chin toward his outfit.

He chuckles. "I'm officially out of clean clothes. I grabbed this from the laundry room. One of Jasper's shirts. Mason claims I'll get the 'Sin Valley itch' from wearing it but I'm hoping for the best."

I chuckle.

Despite his obvious exhaustion, he's gorgeous. His hair is sticking up all over the place. He has even more stubble than yesterday. In fact, his facial hair is inching toward a beard. I strongly approve.

Resolved not to be a horny weirdo today, I pull my thoughts into the present moment. "Wow—I really passed out, didn't I?" I try brushing a clump of wild curls away but it refuses to cooperate, flopping right back over my eyes.

Cash lands on the edge of the bed, allowing his feet to hang over the side. "Lucky you. I didn't get any sleep last night. That little creature was crawling all over my chest." Lethargically, he strokes his fingers over the kitten's fur.

"You get used to it," I say, "Cats are nocturnal."

"Fuck. They're nocturnal? Didn't realize that."

I try to assuage his doubts. "They're so worth it, though." I pull the little furball back into my lap and kiss his head. "Aren't you, little one? Aren't you? Even if you disturb your daddy during the night?"

"Would have been great to know that *before* I fostered him." Cash tries to glare at me but I know he doesn't mean it. He yawns and strokes that sexy almost-beard of his.

Gosh—I'd love to ride his face right this minute.

Whoa. Where'd that thought come from?

I imagine that beard scraping the insides of my thighs while my fingers claw their way through that messed up hair and he melts me with pleasure from his tongue.

Instantly, I know I need to get out of here.

I spent all of last night instructing Cash on the ins and outs of caring for a cat. We talked and laughed into the wee hours of the morning as the curious kitten acclimatized to his new surroundings. I don't exactly know when we fell asleep. All I know is that I'm wide awake now and I'm very aware of Cash's commanding energy and how much space it takes up in this tiny room. It's a turn on.

Yes, Cash and I have woken up together several times over our friendship. Always on a couch somewhere or on someone's living room floor after a night of hanging out. But this time is different.

This time, we're in his room. Alone. With the door closed. And the sexual tension between us is turning the temperature up to sauna levels.

I can't stay here much longer. Just yesterday, we promised ourselves that we wouldn't let things get out of hand between us again. But my hormones insist on ruining my resolve. I can't let that happen.

"I should get going." I set the cat down and swing my

legs over the side of the bed. "I need to get a start on my Saturday."

I barely manage to rise to my feet before Cash has grabbed me by the waist. "Stay longer." There's a furrow between his brows and his grey eyes shine at me.

There's no way he doesn't notice the shiver that moves beneath my bones. With his hands on me like that, my body can't help but react.

Cash drops his hands and blinks his own arousal away. Then a small, mischievous smile curls his lips. "Jasper will be awake any minute now. Stay and do the walk of shame out of my bedroom."

I chuckle as I remember the prank that Cash and I pulled on his brothers last night. I recall the satisfaction I got seeing those jerks left speechless when we dramatically announced our pretend engagement.

Ha! We're so bad.

But after all the times they've teased us over the past few days, they deserve to be the butt of the joke for a little while.

"I'm definitely staying to do the walk of shame. Just to see the look on Jasper's face." I grin. Cash's wicked grin mirrors mine.

A mechanical ding fills the room, breaking the moment. "Fuuucckk!" He glances at his phone and groans. "First thing on a Saturday morning, man?" His head falls back on the pillows and he unlocks the device.

I pretend to focus on drinking my coffee and petting the cat. But every few seconds, I keep stealing peeks at his handsome profile as he checks whatever unpleasant matters demand his attention on his phone.

He is *so* hot.

Even when he's frowning at his phone like he wants to set it ablaze by the power of telepathy.

We've been friends for ages but sometimes I still can't believe I have this amazing creature in my life. He's smart and successful and kind, even under his grouchy exterior. And *I* get to be in his bubble, hanging out in his uncomfortable bed on a Saturday morning.

"Goddammit," he mutters, the furrow in his brow getting deeper.

"What is it?" I roll onto my side to face him, propping my cheek on my wrist.

His fingers dive into his messy hair. "Client of mine," he tells me. "The guy is rich as hell. Worth a few billion dollars. His wife owns this yoga studio that does really well, too. Apparently, she's launching a clothing line a few weeks from now."

"That's good, no?" I say, perplexed by the displeasure on his face. "Why's that frown-worthy news?"

"The thing is, she's having some fashion show as part of the launch. I just got an invitation."

"You got invited to a fashion show? A fashion show for a line of yoga clothing?" My attention instantly perks up.

"Yeah." His eyes don't leave his screen. He just keeps glaring at the email. He sighs in frustration. "Do they actually expect me to show up at this thing?" He glances my way. "Help me come up with an excuse to get out of it."

"You really should go," I tell him. "I mean this is your client's wife. I'm sure this kind of thing is important for relationship-building."

He gets all growly. Like usual. "I don't see the need to mix business and pleasure. Why can't these people just keep the business aspect of things to the boardroom? I have no desire to see any of my clients in a social setting." He's still frowning at his phone.

I crawl across the mountain of blankets and pillows, and teasingly tug on the sleeve of his T-shirt. "My gosh, Cassius. Who gets mad and offended that they were invited to a prestigious fashion show?"

Crossing all boundaries and respect for privacy, I grab the phone out of his hand. He doesn't stop me. So I skim through the message myself.

Sorry, not sorry.

I'm way too excited by this invitation of his to respect the rules of social etiquette.

When I've read the email, I snap upright in bed. "Are you fucking with me right now? Cash, you got invited to the debut fashion show for the Prasanna Light Oneness yoga collection? Do you even understand how huge that is? And you're trying to get out of it?"

Prasanna is the most popular yoga studio on the outskirts of Chicago. It's more than just a yoga studio, actually. It's a meditation oasis with a spa and massage center, too. It's located in a small town called Reyfield. Alana and I went there for a weekend after her divorce. It was a healing experience.

Cash rolls his eyes. "You may not have noticed but I don't really wear yoga pants anymore." He feigns being self-conscious. "They do nothing for my thighs."

Now, I roll my eyes.

I continue fan-girling for a while. I can't seem to calm my tits as I click on a link in the email and read through Prasanna's electronic brochure.

With a small smile laced across his lips, Cash examines me thoroughly. "You're really into this fashion show thing, huh?"

"Well, yeah."

"You want those tickets?"

"Yes..." I say, although I don't trust the sneaky look on his face. "You'd give them to me?"

That sly expression of his turns into a full-blown smirk. "Make it worth my while."

The alarm bells go off in my head. This man is up to no good. "What do you have in mind?"

"All I want is for you to go into town with me today. I need to pick up a few T-shirts. Some jeans. Just a few things to get me through the weekend. So I'm not stuck wearing my brother's clothes until I leave town."

"You can't go into town by yourself?" I question. Not because I wouldn't gladly go with him. But because there's a strange hesitancy on his face. It makes me suspicious.

"Every time I show my face around town, the women of Honey Hill look at me like I'm easy prey. Fresh meat. With dollar signs all over it."

"Well, the Westbrook sausage goes for a premium around here." I throw my head back and laugh.

"I can't believe you just said that." He does not look amused.

"So you need a bodyguard?" I try to push back my merriment and mimic the seriousness on his face.

"Just for the day," he tells me.

Okay, he's not joking about this...

My reservations start to slither in. Pranking our friends last night to get them off our back was one thing. Now, Cash is talking about involving the whole town.

He explains himself further. "Half of the women around town think that you and I are together anyway. Not that that stops them from throwing themselves at me. And I hate people breathing down my neck. If you're by my side while I go shopping, at least they'll hesitate to approach me. They'll respect my boundaries."

When I fumble with a response, he hits me with a deadpan stare. "Look, woman—the only reason I'm even in this godforsaken town is because you asked me to stay. You owe me. I want you to come shopping with me."

My stomach cramps. "Wow. Shameless about the blackmail, are we?" His expression doesn't budge. I roll my eyes. "Fine. I'll go shopping with you."

He grins victoriously. "So, one more day of playing the role of my smitten bride-to-be. You think you can handle it?"

I shake my head, plaster a grin on my face and aim to brighten this weird mood between us. "Sure." I'm not sure my expression is convincing.

"What's that look on your face?" he asks before swinging his legs off the bed.

I pull in a breath. "I just...we need to make sure this doesn't get out of hand, Cash. That we don't start fooling ourselves into believing this is real." I'm on very shaky ground with Cash. It would be easy for me to slip and fall headfirst into something this was never intended to be.

His lips flatten dismissively. "Don't be dramatic, Buttercup. It's just a little game. And it's just for one day. Weren't you the one teasing me about letting out my wild side?"

I consider his words. It's just a little harmless fun. Right? "Okay, okay. Fine."

I *have* been having a lot of fun with him. I've been enjoying this different side of him. Isn't that what I wanted? To see him let his guard down a bit? To see him veer away from the carefully-dictated script of his life? At least for a little while?

"Cool." Grinning, he offers me a high-five and I slam my

palm into his, feeling some of my tension dissipate. *This will be good. It'll be fine.*

A sudden crash comes from down the hall causing us to startle. The alarmed baby cat scrambles for cover in my arms. Then there's another series of bangs and tumbles. Like somebody tripping down a flight of stairs.

"Damn it all to hell," Jasper groans, his voice scratchy and tired. "I hate mornings."

Cash grins at me. "Come on, Buttercup. Time to do that walk of shame."

FOURTEEN

MEGHAN

"HEY, how are you doing in there?" I ask Cash from just outside the changing room.

We've been here at this menswear store for about half an hour now. Cash has picked up some essentials to get him through the weekend. T-shirts, jeans, underwear.

While he's been trying the jeans on, I've found myself wandering through the aisles and absently picking out a few more options that I know would look amazing on his tall, leanly-muscled body.

I hear him grunt from behind the thick curtain. There's a bang and I imagine Cash bumping himself into the changing room wall. "I hate shopping, dammit."

I bite on my bottom lip to keep from giggling. He's going to hate me even more for this. "I picked up a few more options for you to try on."

If it were up to Cash, this shopping trip of ours would have been a five-minute deal. He was ready to just pay for the first few items he grabbed on his way into the store.

I had to practically drag him around like a whiny child

as I picked out a few additional articles of clothing that I feel will really compliment his gorgeous body.

Actually, Cash has the kind of body that would look amazing in anything. But over the course of this shopping trip, I've noticed that light brown fitted sweaters really make his grey eyes pop and dark wash slim taper jeans make me want to take a bite out of his muscular ass. I probably shouldn't tell him that, though.

All in all, I've been having a great time experimenting clothing options with my best friend today. As an added bonus, it's been the perfect excuse to ogle him without raising suspicion.

Cash has been serious about using me as his human shield, though. Any time a woman looks at him for too long or makes an inappropriate comment, he just loops an arm around my waist, pulls my torso flush against his and looks at me with the face of a man completely smitten.

It's been excellent acting on his part. But my body has been having a hard time adjusting to the role. The hair on my neck stands on end every time he holds my hand. My words get caught in my throat every time he kisses my cheek. And if I have to hold my breath one more time to keep from drowning in the scent of his shower gel, I'm likely to suffer permanent brain damage.

Thank god I'm wearing a leather jacket over my thin button-down blouse today. My nipples must be harder than little push-pins under there.

"I'm not buying an entire wardrobe, woman." Cash groans from his changing room when I toss three more pairs of jeans over the curtain rod. "I just need a few pieces to get me through the next two days."

"Just *consider* these jeans," I tell him. "I'm sure they'd

look great on you." Then I throw another few pairs of cargo pants over the curtain rod for good measure.

He growls.

I turn to quickly tiptoe away and avoid Cash's wrath, but before I can make my escape something unexpected happens.

I hear the sound of wood cracking. Over my shoulder, I see the curtain rod bending under the weight of all those clothes. I spin on my heels just in time to witness the curtain rod dramatically snap in two and drop to the floor, exposing Cash's goodies to the world.

And my, some fine goodies they are.

He's standing in the middle of the brightly-lit, two-walled cubicle, arms lifted above his head and face concealed by the fabric of the white T-shirt he's in the middle of pulling off. His torso is entirely exposed, the over-head lights highlighting his tight, tanned six-pack. A thin trail of hair and some thick, sexy veins snake along the V of muscle, leading into the waistband of his white boxer-briefs.

My hands leap to my mouth. A harsh gasp leaves my lips and the inner walls of my pussy give a hard, watery throb.

His jeans hang dangerously low off his hips and the fly stands wide open, giving me an unobstructed view of my friend's semi-erection. I swear I see the long, thick shaft jump when I gasp like that.

I'm suspended in time as I stare.

When Cash finally yanks his shirt off, he frowns at the wide open doorway. "Shit," he grumbles as he stares at the mess of clothes on the floor.

Our eyes lock. And the shock settles. And we both break out laughing. Loudly. Hysterically.

"Shut up!" he hisses at me. "This is your fault."

"I...I...Oh my...I..." I can't stop laughing.

Amusement dancing in his eyes, Cash pokes his chiseled shoulders out of the cubicle and looks around. "Does anybody even work here?"

Then his hand leaps to his chest and slowly trails down his abs and over his package. The movement seems like pure reflex. And it makes my insides turn liquid all over again. The mood in the room morphs once more, turning five-alarm sexy.

Damn. This man is fine.

Cash's eyes land on me and he examines my strange expression. "You okay?" he asks, concerned.

I can't answer. I search my mouth for my tongue, y'know, to form words and basic sounds. I don't find it.

I stumble and bump a shoulder into the concrete pillar behind me. "I'm great. Yes, great. Thanks for asking."

He furrows his brows.

I'm being weird. I need to get out of here.

I smile tightly, trying to recover my bearings. "Um, I... I'll get out of your hair and let you finish up. I'm going to walk over to my mom's boutique across the street. She was supposed to finally be getting that front window replaced today, and I'm excited to see how it's turned out."

Cash nods, his dilated pupils tracking my every move. "I'll meet you over there when I'm done here."

"Okay." After flashing him an awkward smile, I break free of our eyelock and stalk out of the dressing area, back into the store.

On my way out, I inform the well-dressed man near the checkout counter that Cash might need some help. Then, I practically burst out onto the sidewalk into the sunny mid-spring Honey Hill afternoon, chest heaving.

Whoa. That was fucking intense.

My breathing starts to steady when I spot my crew of girlfriends huddled together on the sidewalk outside of Rainbows and Butterflies.

As I approach, Mom's landlord is just packing up, while my mother and the girls inspect his handiwork. I sidle up alongside them. "Hard at work, I see," I bump Emma with my shoulder.

"You know it." She grins back, slurping her smoothie through a straw.

"That looks great, Mr. Jones," I say, watching as he wipes the last of the window cleaner off the glass with an old rag. "But you might want to smudge it up a bit, so we don't murder another bird."

"Poor, innocent thing." Emma frowns, mourning the oblivious winged creature who plunged into the window a few weeks ago to his untimely death, leaving behind a cracked glass.

"It won't be the last," Ziggy tells us ominously, her stare shadowy and foreboding. Her hair is tied in a colorful head-wrap today and her long flowy tie-dye dress swishes around her ankles. Ziggy's a mega-hottie in all her beads and bangles and bohemian get-ups.

"Ugh. You and your fortunes," Mom grouses. "I think *you* might be bad luck."

My friend, the mystic, gasps in offense. "Maybe *you* need to sage and clear your karma."

The landlord chuckles. "Now we're talking about sage and karma. I'm out of here. Good day, ladies," he says to all of us, although his parting stare only lingers on my mother.

I watch the way her cheeks pinken. She likes him. I know it. Too bad she won't allow herself to indulge in his affection.

The man turns and walks toward his old pickup truck

where it's parked down the street.

"My God," Emma exclaims, fanning herself. "Did you see that smoldering Harlequin romance eye contact? Good thing there were no children around. I need a glass of ice water. Stat."

"I know, right? I'm going to run a synastry chart on those two," Ziggy decides. "I'm just going to need to double-check the landlord's date, time and location of birth, as well as his birth name and—"

"I think breaktime is over," Mom scolds, turning her stink eye on Emma. "Unless you're good with your next paycheck being docked."

With a squeak, Emma scrambles back inside the store. Ziggy follows at a leisurely pace, cackling as she pulls up a free astrology app on her phone. I'm tempted to ask where she plans to find out the landlord's personal information, but I know that Ziggy is as resourceful as they come. It wouldn't surprise me if that woman has a secret file on everyone in Honey Hill, just waiting to hook them up with their love match.

I wait until the store's door swings shut to turn to my mother. "Has business picked up any?"

Mom's shoulders heave with her loaded sigh. "No. Not yet. But don't count me out yet. I've got a meeting with Sherry from the bank."

Oh, I don't like Sherry from the bank. Nobody likes Sherry from the bank.

That woman is the epitome of unpleasant with the way she looks down her nose at everyone with that stern superiority in her eyes. Like she's silently judging you for every bill paid past its due date and every dollar withdrawn prematurely from your 401k and every ill-advised debit from your bank statement.

She's a human kill-joy. But she may be Mom's only hope of getting herself out of this sticky situation.

"When?" I ask her, worried. I don't know what will happen if Mom doesn't get her hands on some money by the time the next payroll comes around.

Her eyes drift over my shoulder and a concrete smile hardens her features. "Now..."

I turn around to find the middle aged woman approaching with her neatly-combed bun, a proper cardigan and soft blue kitten heels that match her pastel pencil skirt. It's like she didn't get the memo that today is Saturday and she's allowed to pull the stick out of her ass for the next two days or so.

"Hello, Sherry," I say, trying on an amicable smile.

She looks at me from above her glasses. "Meghan."

"Thank you so much for meeting with me today. Especially outside of business hours," Mom addresses the stern woman.

"Let's get down to it." Sherry leads the way to the baby boutique. "I'd like to make the most of my Saturday."

"Of course." My mother follows after her.

Good luck, I mouth after her as she goes.

I glance toward the men's store across the street. Still no sign of Cash. With some extra time on my hands, I hold the door open for a pregnant woman who's exiting Rainbows and Butterflies with her spouse. Then I step across the threshold.

The store is empty now and that adds to my anxiety. *Business really needs to pick up. Business really needs to pick up.* I can't watch this store that my mother worked so hard to build go down the drain.

On the way inside, I straighten up a few clothing racks before finding my way over to the girls both at the front desk. It looks like Emma is supposed to be redesigning the small shelves in front of the cashier, stocking an assortment of organic teething toys, but instead, she's getting a palm reading done by Ziggy, who's behind the counter.

I join their conversation, but idly hang teething neck-laces on the pegs in front of the counter, fighting back giggles every time Emma argues with Ziggy's fortunes.

She yanks her hand back from the fortuneteller and grimaces. "I keep thinking one of these days, you'll finally give me a reading I like."

"It's not about the reading. It's about changing your aura. Aura is everything, Emma." Ziggy taps the counter and brings her eyes to me. "You're up, Meghan."

"Oh, there's nothing interesting on these palms. Trust me."

Ziggy whips her tarot deck out from her purse. "I got you, girl."

I stifle a groan, reluctantly taking Emma's spot and watching as Ziggy slowly flips over my cards, nodding and mumbling to herself. Long minutes tick by before she abruptly slams her hand down on the surface of the desk.

I startle. "What?"

"The seven of swords, the moon, *and* the high priestess." Ziggy narrows her gaze on me. "You're keeping secrets," she announces. "*Sexy* secrets from your friends."

Before I can deny it, Emma joins Ziggy's side of the desk, leaning over to rest her chin in her palms. "I don't need a tarot reading to figure that out. It's written all over that sneaky blush of hers."

"I don't know what you're talking about." I feel said blush growing hotter.

Ziggy closes her eyes, grabbing my hand and flipping it over before I can outrun her. The tip of her fingernail grazes my palm. "I'm envisioning a hot night between you and a smokin' hot businessman...I'm getting some initials here. I'm getting a 'C', a 'W' and also a..."

"Okay, okay. That tickles. Stop it!" Giggling, I yank my palm back, tucking my hands into my armpits for safety. No one is safe around this crazy woman.

"Stop pretending to be a good girl." Emma hops up onto the back counter and swings her feet. "You're a bad, bad girl and you know it."

"You're ridiculous," I retort. "There's nothing romantic going on between Cash and me."

"Tell me you haven't kissed him," Emma dares me.

Instantly, I'm transported back to the gas station. To his mouth on my mouth. To my hips rocking back and forth in his lap.

"Oh my god..." Emma laughs. "It was *that* good?"

I try to straighten out my expression. "It's not...it's not like that..." The girls both stare at me expectantly. I exhale.

I could try to lie, but there's just no hiding from Ziggy. I know it. She knows it. We're at a stalemate.

I give in. "The other night...we got a little carried away. And we...we kissed. Just for a second. Then we snapped back to our senses and it was over," I mutter in one rushed sentence.

Emma squeals, and Ziggy's lips turn upward in an evil grin. "Well, what's stopping you from snapping out of your senses again? Girl, go pick up where you left off."

"Yes," Emma hisses. "Jump his bones already."

I shake my head, not willing to give in to the pressure. "I'm afraid it was just a heat of the moment kind of thing. And that moment's long gone." I try not to let my disappointment shine through.

Emma's head whips left to right. "Ohhh, trust me. It's

not."

"Yeah, we all see the way he looks at you. Believe us. Believe the tarot." Ziggy drums her nails over the cards that are still face up on the counter. "See the two of cups card here? This thing between the two of you is a deep soul connection. You should go for it."

My eyes linger on the fortune-telling deck. I hate to admit it, but the girls are wearing me down here. Making me second guess everything. Maybe Ziggy and Emma are right. I know Cash's been looking at me...*differently* this past week.

And not only did we have that sexy kiss in the car, there was also the hotter-than-sin lap dance. And those heated stares in my living room the night he came to town. One time could be a mishap. A lapse of judgement. A tipsy accident.

But two occasions? Three? That can't be a coincidence.

Cash has to feel something...

"Want me to do another reading on you? I could try another deck?"

A forced smile stretches across my face. "You know....I think I'm good," I reply slowly.

Ziggy keeps flipping cards anyway. She holds up a card featuring a hand gripped around a phallic-looking stick. "Ace of wands."

"Oooh," Emma squeals again. "I don't know anything about tarot but it looks like *someone's* getting lucky tonight!"

"Yes," Ziggy hisses. "Go jump his bones already."

A male voice comes from over my shoulder, the deep, raspy baritone making my stomach tighten. "Whose bones are getting jumped today?"

I whip around. "Cash!" The tall, handsome devil strides into the boutique, two big shopping bags in his hands. He steps up to the counter and his eyes fan across the spread of tarot cards on display.

Silently, I pray that reading tarot cards isn't one of this man's many hidden talents. Because I'd be mortified. I glance at Emma and Ziggy, begging them not to make this weird by saying the wrong thing.

Ziggy gives me an *I've got you, girl* wink. Her eyes turn to Cash. "Want me to do a reading on you? Free of charge."

His smile stretches up to his ears. Those rare smiles of his are becoming less rare as the days go by. "You're serious?"

"Y'know, I think he's good." I grab my friend by the shoulders, trying to guide him for the door. "We should get out of here."

The man is like a concrete pillar. His big, strong body refuses to budge. "Why the hell not?" he says to Ziggy. "A little out of character for me but that seems to be the theme of the weekend."

"Oooh," Emma squeals, clapping her hands together. "Let's see what the cards say!"

Ziggy grins gleefully as she scoops up all the cards into her hand and expertly shuffles them again. She closes her eyes and moves her lips, mumbling in prayer until she's satisfied. A few cards managed to slip out during her shuffling. She gathers them up and slips them back into the deck. Then she fans them out, face down, on the counter in front of Cash. Her eyes twinkle at him. "Pick one," she tells him.

His brows furrow in deep concentration. He's actually taking this seriously. He takes everything he does seriously. So why am I surprised?

"Here." He places a single card in her outstretched hand.

My friend's eyes bulge when she flips the card over. "The emperor." She announces.

"What does that mean?" Emma asks, coming closer to the counter.

"Isn't it obvious?" Ziggy questions, her eyes still wide. "The emperor represents dominance. Unyielding power. He's stable and secure. The ultimate alpha male."

Cash looks at me and smirks. "Obviously." He pops his collar.

I roll my eyes.

Ziggy nods. "He's the paragon of virility. But his power doesn't reach its true potential until he finds his divine counterpart—the empress."

"That almost sounds ominous." Cash laughs.

Ziggy shrugs a shoulder. "It sort of is."

Cash slips an arm around my shoulder and tucks me against his ribs. "I think I'm good without an empress. I've got my Buttercup. That's all I need."

Emma and Ziggy share a bulging-eyed look.

Before he can tell my friends that he's only joking, we hear footsteps approaching from the back office. Sherry and my mother step into the room.

Sherry's eyes sweep across the empty, customer-less showroom floor. At her disapproving expression, my gut tightens. Mom's expression says it all—no deal.

Shit.

When the banker's gaze rises and finds Cash, her expression instantly brightens. "Mr. Westbrook."

He gives her a curt nod. "Sherry."

She watches his arm that's protectively draped around me. She smiles. "Oh, that's right. I did hear that the two of you have happy news." Her eyes twinkle. "Congratulations on your engagement."

Cash and I blink at each other.

I expect him to jump away from me like a pit of hot coal. But he doesn't. Something zaps through me when his arm tightens around my shoulders instead. "Thank you," he tells her. "Meghan and I are very happy about it."

When all eyes shift to me, I smile. "It's been a long time coming."

Sherry grabs my left hand and inspects it. "Where's your diamond, dear? I'm dying to see it."

"Being resized," I say regretfully. "Each passing day without it is torture."

Mom, Emma and Ziggy stand on the sidelines, all wearing the same confused expression that says, *You have some explaining to do, missy.*

Mom opens her mouth.

Uh-oh.

I need to get Sherry out of here. Immediately. "Well, it's been lovely seeing you, Sherry. I'm sure you don't want to waste the rest of your Saturday stuck in here."

"It was lovely to see you again, Cash," the woman says to my so-called fiance. Her eyes turn stern when she looks at me. "Meghan, call me up next week. I want to book an appointment for you with our investment advisor. He'll talk to you about how to maximize the benefits of your Roth IRA." Her eyes stare at my mother. "So you don't find yourself in an unpleasant 'predicament' a few years down the line."

On that, she struts out the door.

The minute she steps outside, Mom turns to Cash and me. "So...care to discuss these congratulations that are supposedly in order?"

Oh, boy. I shouldn't have skipped breakfast this morning. We're gonna be here a while.

FIFTEEN
MEGHAN

"EXCUSE ME, HI? HELLO?" I wave an arm in the air, trying to get the attention of the girl behind the counter.

An older gentleman with a Hawaiian shirt, a cooler bag and a fanny pack around his waist accidentally shoulder-checks me as he unfolds his tourist map and spreads it wide. Before I can open my mouth to demand an apology, his wife grabs the handle of her rolling suitcase and leads him away, giving me the stink-eye from beneath the brim of her visor cap.

It is absolute chaos here at Hot Dog Almighty, probably thanks to the massive tourist bus currently taking up half a block outside this building. This kitschy fast food shack is especially popular among the kids and tourists in these parts.

Management at this establishment closely guard their plastic utensils behind the counter like they're the freaking crown jewels. I've been trying to get a new fork for the past five minutes. But the workers behind the counter have been ignoring me as they're bombarded with orders from their emphatic clientele.

What kind of fast food restaurant is this? Haven't these people ever heard of making a line?

After Sherry left Rainbows and Butterflies, Cash and I had to face down Emma, Ziggy and my mom. It was like a freaking press conference with all the questions they were shooting our way. We told them the truth, that the so-called engagement started out as a prank on the other Westbrook boys last night. We told them that we're only continuing our pretend engagement today in order to keep the town off our backs while Cash shops.

Emma and Ziggy laughed it all off good-naturedly. But I recognized the displeased look on Mom's face. She's worried that I'll get myself in trouble playing this game with this man.

I tried my best to reassure her that it's all innocent but the conversation was exhausting. It left me drained and starving and now, I'm desperate to get some food into my stomach.

Right as I'm about to give up and accept my fate—eating my chilli fries with my fingers—I feel strong hands grip my shoulders and gently move me aside.

"Excuse me." Cash's baritone confidently cuts over all the noise in the establishment. It's like the Red Sea parts and all eyes instantly swing his way.

He flashes an endearing smile at the server who approaches the counter, spellbound.

"Do you mind getting my fiancee here a fork?" he asks, a paragon of good manners.

My tummy flutters. There he goes smiling again. Since when does he smile?

The server gives Cash a reverent nod from beneath the green and yellow store-issued cap. "Of course. Yes, y-yes. Of course." She instantly reaches beneath the counter and places a fistful of plastic forks into Cash's waiting palm. Just like magic.

"Thank you, darling." He winks in gratitude. "Amateur," he mutters to me under his breath a moment later when he passes by me on his way back to our table.

I easily overtake his slow stride. "Some of us follow the rules, line up and wait our turn to get service," I sneer at him. "We don't just go flaunting our good looks to get our way in life."

"Are you saying you think I look good, Ms. Hutchins?" He tosses the forks down on the table next to our overflowing plates and folds his arms across his chest. His new fitted white T-shirt broadcasts his bulging biceps, his tattoos and the prominent veins snaking along his strong forearms. When I assess the way his thighs look long, powerful and strong in his dark jeans, my tummy flutters again.

I narrow my eyes at him. "Using your charm to get what you want in life is kind of...slutty."

"What?" He grips my sides and tickles me before I manage to get away. "I made use of my god-given resources to come to your rescue back there. And you thank me by slut-shaming me?"

We draw a bunch of unwanted attention as I giggle and struggle in the narrow aisle to get out of Cash's hold. I nearly bump into the woman who just pulled open the restaurant door.

When I look up, my eyes land on a familiar face. The joyful smile I've been wearing all afternoon jumps right off my lips. "Excuse me."

It's the same stone-faced mother I saw leaving the pediatric clinic opposite my job with her two young daughters a couple days ago.

She nods curtly. Without another glance my way, the

woman and her girls glide right past me, robotically marching throw the throngs of people crowding the restaurant. The mother seats her children in a booth that's visible from the counter and goes to place her order.

"You okay?" Cash asks, perceiving the shift in my mood.

I muster up a smile for him. "Yeah. Great." I chug from the water bottle I'm holding.

He takes a huge bite out of his hot dog and elbows me in the ribs. "Eat up, Buttercup. We still have the whole afternoon ahead of us and I want to show off my new fiancee for all of Honey Hill to see.

He snaps me a playful wink that should make me smile. But ever since that cruel woman and her daughters walked in here, my mood has taken a sharp nosedive. I recap my water bottle and try not to let the brewing cloud rain on what's been an amazing day.

I try to ignore their presence. I really do. But it's damn-near impossible to ignore those two blonde, curly-haired girls. They're adorable. And their big blue eyes keep shooting shy glances my way.

Cash and I chat about everything and nothing as we refuel after a morning spent strolling the shopping area of town. I do my best to keep my happy face on full display but there's a discomfort under my skin now.

I'm showing him a video of Captain Ginger aggressively shredding a bath towel when I hear a shy, curious voice over my shoulder.

"Is that your cat?"

It's one of those same two girls who have wandered over to our section of the restaurant. The littler one, her stuffed rabbit clutched beneath her arm, as always. She's kneeling on the leather bench of the neighboring booth, peering down on my table.

"What's his name?" she asks.

I swallow the tennis ball in my throat, looking around and seeing their mother still waiting to order. Her absence makes it a little easier to breathe.

"His name?" I motion to my phone.

She gives me a tentative nod with her eyes wide.

"That's Captain Ginger."

"Captain Ginger?!" she giggles.

I find myself giggling softly, too. "Hey, why are you laughing?"

"Captain Ginger's a silly name." She glances at her sister who is shyly approaching at a snail's pace. "Jessica, did you hear that? His name is Captain Ginger." Her blindingly bright eyes turn back to me.

"Does he get along with dogs?"

"How much moneys does a cat cost?"

"Mommy said a cat costs a lot of moneys. Is that true? Do you have a lot of moneys, lady?"

Cash leans back in his seat, enjoying his meal and chuckling as the children chatter away. It strikes me in the chest to realize that this is the first time I've ever seen them smile.

It takes considerable effort to keep my voice steady, to answer each and every one of their questions. To treat them like any other tiny humans to stumble into my path. I deserve an Emmy. Or I'd at the very least settle for a box of wine when I'm done here.

The girls continue to shower me with questions and I share my cat knowledge, partially in disbelief that this whole conversation is even happening. But mostly, my heart just stings.

The mother stomps over to us, her jaw set and her hands full. "What did I tell you two about going off with strangers?!" the woman bites at them.

All the banter cuts off abruptly.

"But she's not a stranger, Mommy," the small, sassy one dares to reason.

The woman's eyes snap to mine. I do my best to keep my expression open and non-threatening but I show her that I won't cower to her.

The girls whine and beg, pulling on the hem of their mother's fashionable blouse, asking if they can *please, pretty please* get a kitten. Or a puppy. Or a hamster.

The woman flashes another look my way. "No pets. Let's go, girls." With her brown takeout bags clutched in her hands, she stalks off toward the exit. My heart hurts, knowing these innocent little girls will probably get in trouble today for sneaking off to talk to me.

The smaller one trails behind her mother, eyeballing the grimy restaurant floor but remaining tight lipped.

This hurts...

My head spins back, surprised to see the older girl still standing beside me. She's a gorgeous child with her loose golden ringlets, her aquamarine eyes and the freckles all over her cheeks. But her skin is strangely pale and her eyes have this hollowness to them that's almost scary. It's unsettling.

Her attention darts to her mother's back, and she pauses a second, seemingly waiting until her mom is completely out of earshot. "I know you're my sister," she tells me, "and I think you're really pretty, and I wish I could get to know you."

My jaw drops. "I..."

I feel Cash's eyes on me, watching from his seat.

But even with the strength I summon from his presence, I'm stunned speechless. I've watched them around this town since the day they were born, but I was always under the impression that my little sisters—my half-sisters—didn't even know I existed.

There's a million things I want to tell her. But before I can sort through my jumbled thoughts, their mother suddenly turns over her shoulder, brown paper bag in one hand and her younger daughter's hand in the other. "I said let's go," she repeats stiffly.

Head hung, the girl walks away. The mother ushers both her girls out of the restaurant, not sparing me even a single glance.

Great running into you, too, step-mother dearest.

SIXTEEN

CASH

THE BARREN TREE branches overhead sway lightly in the breeze. The sun may be out, shining high and bright, but there's a sharp chill to the air.

Meghan sort of moved on autopilot after that weird encounter with that woman and her two little girls. She picked at her meal in silence until finally giving up, tossing her balled up napkin onto her leftovers and pushing the tray away.

When we stepped out of the restaurant, we drifted aimlessly through town until we finally found ourselves here at the edge of the quiet park. As she walks along the dirt path, I follow her lead, knowing she just needs a bit of space from humanity right now.

A perfect white feather twirls down from the sky before landing at our feet. Meghan scoops it up and silently studies it as we walk. It's killing me to see her like this. She seems completely out of it, lost in painful thoughts. So I guide her across the playground, over to the swings.

"So that was them, huh?" I ask, finally, when we're both

seated in side by side swings, with our feet dangling in the sand.

Her eyes snap up to mine, and a flash of surprise swirls in them.

"You...know...about them? My half-sisters?"

I nod.

It's not like she advertised her family drama but I'm aware of Meghan's father having another family. She'd mentioned once or twice that her father had never married her mother. That after years of leading her on, he'd abandoned the both of them and quickly moved on with a new woman. And then he'd never talked to her again.

Not on birthdays. Not at Christmas. Never.

Meghan had never delved into the details but it's difficult to keep secrets here in Honey Hill. Anyone who pays attention to Meghan should have been able to easily connect the dots.

Though judging from her reaction just now, I realize I may be the only one who's been paying attention.

Meghan's eyes drift out across the playground. She purses her lips, gnaws on them, but she doesn't say a word.

This kind of silence is uncharacteristic for her. And while I initially considered just trying to bury it down, change the subject, and cheer her up, I have a niggling suspicion that that's not what my best friend really needs right now.

I stare at her for long moments, considering my words carefully. "You wanna talk about it?" I question softly, never taking my eyes off her face, reading her expression for cues.

Her narrow shoulder pops up before falling dispiritedly.

I press forward with the conversation, careful not too push her further or faster than she's willing to go. "Never seen the three of you together though. The resemblance is..."

"Yeah," she laughs sadly. "Wild, huh?"

"Was that the first time you had contact with them?" That is the only thing that explains the sudden mood shift.

"No. Yes." Her shoulders droop. "I've seen them around. But that was the first time they spoke to me...She *knew* me."

"Wow. That *is* wild."

My siblings are huge pains in the ass. They drive me up the wall ninety-percent of the time. Still, I can't imagine not knowing them.

"How do you feel about that?" I question.

"I feel like a basket case!" she admits softly.

I shake my head. "Buttercup," I scold lightly. "We all deserve to have our moment. To lose our shit. It just makes you...human."

"I don't want to be human. I want to be strong." Before I can argue, before I can tell her that she doesn't need to be strong all the time, the duct tape that's been holding her together cracks. Big tears roll down her cheeks. "He has no idea. No freaking clue. And he wouldn't care even if he did know. It's pathetic. I'm pathetic."

"No clue about what?" I reach across the space between us, squeezing her hand and holding on tight.

"My dad. His abandonment. He has no idea how him leaving us affected me." Her watery eyes meet mine, and my chest aches for her. "It wrecked me. Wrecked my self-worth."

Well, shit. Now she's just gone and ripped out my heart. "Meghan. No. He doesn't deserve your misery. He doesn't even deserve your thoughts. Your happiness. Anything."

I recall more than one occasion where Meghan broke

down in high school, and her father was clearly to blame. But she never wanted to talk about it, and I respected her enough not to pry. Her sadness always seemed to coincide with those big moments in her life, and I put two-and-two together pretty quickly.

Birthdays. Her graduation. The homecoming march, when families lined up to watch. She was all dolled up, with no doting, overprotective father snapping photos. The deadbeat was just never around. But I know now the kind of toll divorce and breakups take on people, and not just on the adults involved.

Meghan aggressively wipes her tears away with balled-up fists. "I tried to tell myself that over the years—that he doesn't deserve my tears. I tried to shut off my feelings. I found ways to make sense of it in my mind but you can't convince your stubborn heart otherwise." She drops her head and shakes it ruefully. "My mom was a mess back then when Dad left her for someone else. So utterly heartbroken. And her grief only poured salt on my wounds. She's just so damn lonely."

"She hasn't moved on? Met anyone new?"

Her lips twist. "I don't think she'll be falling for that trap twice. None of the women in my family can ever get a relationship to work out. At least that's what mom says."

"And what do *you* say?" I ask.

We don't take our eyes off each other. A darkness passes over Meghan's face. The way her eyes lock on mine, deep and piercing, like she's trying to scrape the very bottom of my soul. I want to climb inside her head and know exactly what she's thinking, even the thoughts she'd never admit to me out loud.

She abruptly breaks eye contact. "I...I...don't know." Her breath trembles, almost like she's afraid that she's doomed to the same fate as her mother and her mother's mother and every other woman who came in the Hutchins lineup before them.

Meghan is the sunshine in everybody else's life. Realizing the grim outlook she has on her own destiny, it makes me angry. It makes me sad.

"Damn, Buttercup. I'm so sorry. I wish I could have been there for you."

"You were." She lifts her head. Looks at me with soft diamond-blue eyes swimming in water. Her lips form a small smile. "I know we didn't always talk about that stuff. Most of the time, we didn't talk about anything at all. But just having you there, in the quiet moments, made me feel less alone. Made me feel like I wasn't alone in the world. And even though the situation with your parents was different from what I was going through, I felt like you understood what it was like."

I reach across the space between us and wipe away the last of her tears. The look in her eyes has me wanting to dive across the distance and kiss her senseless. But I put my needs on a leash. I grip the metal ropes of my swing to keep my hands to myself.

"When I look at my little sisters, I can't help but wonder if my father is a good dad to them.

I scoff bitterly in my throat. "If he's any kind of father to those girls, maybe it's just because he's a guilty S-O-B now." I look at her head-on. "You deserved better than that, Buttercup. I hope you realize that."

Her heaving chest shakes tremulously when she inhales deeply. "I just feel this strange sense of protectiveness over those girls, but there's nothing I can do about it." She sweeps her legs forward, giving the swing a bit of momentum. I watch her golden curls fluttering in the wind as she gently sways back and forth.

We've been sitting here so long now, it's basically dinner time. But neither of us are in any hurry to go anywhere. I'll stay here at this playground all night if it gets Meghan to open up to me.

"Have you tried talking to their mother?"

She huffs out a bitter laugh. "Have you seen that woman? She's fucking scary."

I chuckle. "I'd have to agree on that."

"I want those girls to have a better childhood than I did. A real childhood. One that's not bogged down by the real world, adult pressures. One that's not consumed with worrying about whether their mother will be able to get out of bed in the morning or if she'll spend the day with the blankets pulled up to her chin, hating herself too much to even face the world. That kind of life is so hard for a little girl. Because you want to fix it. You want to make your mom happy. So you get good grades and you help around the house and you make a little money from your lemonade stand. But after a while, you run out of ideas. Because you're a kid. And you don't know how to make your broken mother happy."

"And it's not your job to," I tell her firmly. It was her mother's job to provide a stable, loving environment for her. Not the other way around.

Sitting here, listening to her, the pieces of the puzzle are beginning to fall into place. I'm beginning to understand Meghan's good-natured smile, her constant need to keep everyone in her life happy, her obsession with going out of her way to accommodate every person's every need. It must be fucking exhausting.

Dropping one hand to her lap, she angles her body to

face me. The tears are gone, but the melancholy remains. Her words are softer now. "You want to know the really bad part? A small, selfish, insecure part of me wonders...if he's a good father to them, then what does that say about me, Cash? If he can love them and be a dad to them, why couldn't he do the same for me? What did I do wrong?"

I reach out and grab her hand where it's laying on her denim-covered thigh. "You did nothing wrong. Nothing. I can't make excuses for that man and I can't tell you what the fuck he was thinking. But I can promise you that none of that was your fault, Meghan. His inability to be the father you needed, your mother's inability to give you a home where you felt loved and secure, none of that was your fault. You are an amazing person." I cup her cheek in my hand. "You deserve to be surrounded by people who love you, who can hold up the mirror and show you how special you truly are."

Meghan nods into my palm, almost mewling for affection. There's vulnerability splattered across her beautiful features like face paint. "I *so* want you to be right..." she whispers.

"I'm always right, Buttercup."

Her lips curve into a genuine smile. "*Always* arrogant, more like." She straightens and looks at me. "Seriously, Cash. Thank you. Thanks for listening. I can never talk to my mom about this. And my girlfriends, they love me but they expect me to be the problem-solver, the one who's always putting things back together, not the one who's falling apart." She sighs. "What I'm saying is, it's hard to bare my soul like this with anyone but you."

"I'm always here." I lace my fingers through hers and squeeze.

She's strong and I know she could have handled it all on her own, had I not been around. Still, it feels good to be the one she leans on.

I want to lean on her, too.

"Divorce sucks." My gaze drifts out over the playground. The air is quiet. The sky is darkening. We're out in the open but this moment feels so intimate. Safe. "When my parents split, I felt like I'd been torn in two. I loved them both. I was loyal to them both. And then, all of a sudden choosing to love one automatically felt like a betrayal to the other."

"Oh Cash..." The way Meghan sighs my name pulls at something in my chest. It makes me keep talking when normally, I'd shut the hell up.

"And that was especially hard to reconcile for me. Mom didn't want to divorce my father. It broke her heart. She loved him. But she divorced him anyway because she felt like he always put his work before his family." The boulder of guilt sits on my chest, crushing my ribs and constricting my lungs. "So when I chose to leave Honey Hill and go work with Dad in Chicago, it felt like I was betraying my mom. It felt like I was choosing him over her. Like I was abandoning her to walk in the footsteps of the man who had broken her heart." I drag my palm down my face.

Meghan lays a gentle hand on my knee. "Surely she doesn't think that. I'm sure your mother just wants you to be happy. Successful."

"Probably. But the guilt has eaten at me for years. That's why I've worked so hard. It's why I've wanted to make Westbrook Wealth Management the best it could be. To prove to my mom—to my parents—that all the sacrifices we all made as a family were worth it. I want to show them that something good came out of that painful experience.

Like, 'See, we went through all this bullshit, but now we're a billion-dollar company, we're a leader in our industry. It was all worth it.'"

"Oh, Cash..." Meghan gets up from her swing and comes around the back of mine. She loops her short arms around my torso, leaning her chin on my shoulder and smashing her supple breasts against my back in a hug.

It's meant to be a soothing gesture. But that hug rouses parts of me that should never come to life for my best friend.

The two of us have never shied away from the occasional innocent, friendly physical touch. But lately, the touches have become far more frequent. Far less innocent. Friendly in a different kind of way, if you catch my drift. Still, whenever she touches me, it feels natural. It feels right.

"Well, like you just said, you and I need to let go of control and let our parents deal with their own shit."

I huff out a laugh. "Yeah. We need to let our parents deal with their own shit, dammit."

Her sweet smell fills my head when she speaks. "People seem to think that you're some cold, ruthless businessman. But I always knew it wasn't just about the money for you. I knew there was something more to the story."

I smirk. "You knew I had feelings under it all?"

She laughs softly. "Yes. From the first time we met, I could tell that your parents's divorce fucked you up and that you were only trying to make sense of it as best you could."

I think back to my teenaged self. "Gosh. I was such a broody asshole, wasn't I?" I pull her arms tighter around me. This feels good.

She laughs. "You really were."

"I was just so mad that my mom had packed us up and moved us to this damn town." I chuckle.

"You didn't even try to hide it." I hear the pout in her

voice. "Do you remember how hard I had to work to make you my friend?"

"You were persistent." I laugh. "But I'm glad you didn't give up on me." I lift her hand and press my lips to her knuckles.

Her breathing shifts. She squeezes me tighter.

For one hot second, I allow myself to forget that we pledged to only be friends. My arm reaches back. I catch her by the waist and guide her around so she's standing between my legs, facing me.

Reaching up, I brush her hair back from her face. "Feels like you're the only person in the world I could say this to."

Her voice is husky with emotion. "Thank you for trusting me. I like when you share yourself with me."

"The reason I feel safe with you is because you've always shared yourself with me." I touch her face again, trailing my fingers across her cheekbone. "You're the best friend a guy could hope for Meghan. Having you in my life makes me feel like a lucky bastard."

Meghan lowers into my lap. "You *are* a lucky bastard."

Her ass nestles against my erection. I know she feels it. She deliberately pretends to ignore it.

We're playing with fire again.

"You just like being all over me, don't you?" I say it jokingly but on the inside, I'm dying to grab her by the hips and rub her back and forth on my aching cock. Like I did the other night.

Meghan drapes her arms around my neck and grins but I'm not buying the innocence in her smile this time. We both know exactly what we're doing. "I do. You're like a big grumpy teddy bear."

"I don't know how I feel being compared to a teddy bear."

"A very manly teddy bear." She laughs. "With a beard. And with muscles. And with a six-pack." She runs her fingers down my stomach, stopping at the elastic of my boxer-briefs. "Have you been working out, Mr. Bear?"

Aroused to the point of seeing stars, I hiss through my teeth. "Be careful, Goldilocks. This teddy bear has claws and sharp teeth. And I'm not afraid to bite."

Grawr!

Meghan giggles in my face, nearly blinding me with those pretty dimples. "You'd be sexy if you weren't so ridiculous."

"Admit it—I'm sexy anyway. You're sexy too. We're both very, very sexy."

More laughter from her makes me feel like a champion.

"I'm so glad you're here," she says softly. "I'm glad you stayed."

I nod. "I'm glad, too."

Silence pulses between us for a beat.

Might just say, 'fuck it' and kiss her...

Out of nowhere, a crowd of rowdy children come barreling toward the playground. The vibe shifts.

Meghan jolts. She rises from my lap and gives my swing a playful push. My body hardly budges. "Oh my god. What are you? A block of concrete?!"

I force a laugh, wanting the easy mood to return. "No, don't blame me because your arms have the strength of a spaghetti noodle."

"You did *not* just say that to me!"

"I did." I lift a shoulder unapologetically.

And just like that, things are fun between us again. Meghan does her best to push me for a while but only ends up getting sand in her shoes.

When I finally feel sorry for her, I let her sit on the

swing and give her a few pushes. I listen to the sound of my best friend's laughter filling the air as children run and play around us in the darkening park.

Moments later, we're a mess, covered in sweat and sand as we walk arm in arm back toward the center of town. I haven't thought of work once today, or of the sheafs of documents and emails and voice messages that must be piled up on my desk waiting for my attention. All I can think is I'm not ready for the day to be done yet.

"Wanna go grab a drink?" I ask Meghan.

"That would be great." She smiles at me.

"The Hot Sauce?"

She wrinkles up her nose a little. "I'm kind of not in the mood to see the same old faces tonight. There's this new place just past the edge of town I think you might like."

I hook an arm around her neck and pull her close, dropping a kiss on her forehead. Because I feel like it, dammit. "I'm sure I will."

SEVENTEEN

CASH

SEEMS like everybody's out tonight.

We make it to the Snow Moon Brewery on the outskirts of Sin Valley, and we're shown to a secluded table near the back. I motion for Meghan to be seated first, and then I slide into the corner booth beside her. All the heaviness between us—from all those emotions we shared in the park—has dissipated now.

We order drinks and take in the scenery in comfortable silence. The brewery's vibe is laid back but it's packed from wall to wall, and seems to be getting busier by the minute.

We'd had a brief moment where Meghan had toyed with the idea of going home and putting on something dressier but thankfully, she quickly dropped the idea. Everyone is dressed casually in jeans. The decor is like a fancied-up warehouse with an industrial look to it. Exposed pipes, concrete pillars and huge windows overlooking the dock.

Meghan frowns, watching me as I take everything in. "You sure this is good? Or do you want to go somewhere else?"

I glance around again. "It's perfect." Perfect for catching a drink with a friend. Definitely not somewhere I'd take her if we were on a date—especially a first date—but it's perfect for getting a drink with a friend.

Why would that even cross my mind? Of course it's not a date. It's just Meghan and me, hanging out. Like always.

But after everything we shared earlier in the day, and over the course of my entire visit here, if I'm being honest, I must admit that I'm seeing this woman in a whole new light.

I've always appreciated her as a friend. And I could never help but notice her beauty as a woman. Yet now, I'm wondering what she'd be like as a partner, as someone I share my life with. I know we both agreed that the marriage pact was a dumb joke but the *what ifs* keep creeping into my mind.

What if we gave it a shot? What if we took a chance on each other? What if we were crazy enough to try and make it work? We'd be good together...right?

I scrub a hand down my face.

"That frown of yours has me second guessing this venue choice." Meghan reaches across the table to grab my wrist. "You sure you like it? I won't be mad if you want to go somewhere else. We could just go to the Hot Sauce, if that's what you want."

This damn beautiful girl. Always putting everyone ahead of herself.

"It's perfect, Meghan. Because I'm here with you."

"You know how to say all the right things," she teases.

I shrug. "I just like to keep you impressed."

Her eyes go all soft as she props her chin in her elbow and gazes back at me. "Fine, Mr. Charming."

Now, my heart is beating quicker. "Fine, Ms. Beautiful."

Dammit. We're going *there* again.

Our eyes drop simultaneously to our menus on the table before us. Though, I keep taking peeks at her as she browses the menu. Maybe it's because she feels my gaze on her or maybe it's something else, but she keeps stealing peeks at me, too.

God—I like this. I like whatever it is, buzzing in the air between us.

With every heated glance, with every mischievous smile, we're crossing the boundaries of the friend zone. But I can't stop myself.

When the waitress returns, Meghan and I laugh and we chat while we sample the array of brews we received in our beer flight.

Each time she tries a new sample, she takes one sip and crinkles her nose, passing it on to me. "Too hoppy," "Too bitter," "Too heavy," "Too watery." I can't help but make fun of her discerning palate.

"You're picky." I laugh, downing another sample.

She flashes that sexy pink pout I'm addicted to. "I'm not picky." Her gaze flicks to the foam left behind by the beer on my top lip. "I just...I just know what I like. Even when I'm not able to articulate it."

I rub my tongue across my lips to dissipate the foam. My eyes never leave hers. "That's fair. Gotta love a woman who knows what she wants."

Everything is easy, light, and fun, and I realize almost immediately that, even though this evening is strictly platonic, this is exactly what every date I've been on has been missing.

History.

And Meghan.

Being with her is as simple as breathing.

She finally finds a beer she likes, but it's safe to say that most of the beer flight was consumed by me.

We each order a 20 ounce glass of our favorite brew, and when she can't decide on an appetizer, I order one of each off the menu.

"Oh my gosh, Cash. You're going overboard." Meghan is freaking out as the waiter sets out our huge order on our table.

I grin. "Look at it this way, I'm supporting a new local business. I'd say that borderline makes me a philanthropist. Maybe even a superhero."

She laughs. "Your self-importance is endless, isn't it?"

"Endless," I confirm, smirking. "And, it's definitely not the only endless part of me."

Her cheeks flush and she laughs, kicking her head back. "Behave." But from the way her pupils dilate, I'm not sure she means it.

That blush lingers on her skin as we focus our attention on our plates. We share a little off of each dish. I can already tell we'll be stocking up Meghan's fridge with leftovers, because she's got this thing about wasting food. She avoids it at all costs. I don't quite understand it, but it's still endearing to me. Just one more facet of the woman that reels me in.

"Oh my...Cash, is that your brother?" Meghan asks suddenly.

I follow her wide eyes toward the karaoke stage to the right of the restaurant's entrance.

"Fucking Harry..." I groan when my eyes find my brother in the crowd of tall, musclebound, *wasted* Paragons football players currently stumbling about on stage.

I watch the train wreck in horror, as my little brother belts out an awful rendition of a duet with his teammates,

Maxwell Masters and Knox O'Ryan. The guys sound like some tone deaf cats having an orgy in a dark alley. They know they sound awful but they don't care. They're shoving each other around and choking on buffoon-like laughter before they even make it to the chorus.

Wasted, I tell you. Wasted.

Another footballer climbs onto the stage. He steals the microphone away and bumps the other guys out of the spotlight. "Good night, party people," he addresses the crowd. "My name is Jason Bellino and I just wanted to serenade my beautiful wife, Sera—baby girl, stand up let them see you—with a rendition of *I Will Always Love You*."

The music starts and the football player begins to torture the restaurant with his nails-on-chalkboard singing voice. Meanwhile, his poor wife sits at a table with the rest of their party, looking like she can't decide whether to be flattered or embarrassed.

And, oh my god—Harry is singing background vocals now, painfully missing each and every high note.

"Cash, should we do something?" Meghan asks, in complete alarm. She sticks a finger into her ear.

"Nope." I turn my attention back to my food. "If anyone asks, I don't know him."

"Savage." Meghan kicks her head back and laughs.

The crowd won't even let the drunken footballers finish their song. The diners collectively boo them off the small stage and beg them not to come back.

The guys stumble off the stage and Harry catches sight of me with Meghan. Dammit. I curse up a storm, while Meghan laughs uneasily.

Too soon, he's stumbling across the restaurant in our direction. His drunken grin is practically as big as the equator, nearly going the whole way around his face.

He slams both palms to our table, shaking all the glasses. "Hey, man!" Forgetting his friends, my brother tries to slip into the booth on the other side of Meghan. He's still talking too loudly, and people are starting to stare. "Look at the two of you!" he gushes. "You're fucking glowing. God bless this engagement. Love is a beautiful thing. Both of you deserve a happy ending after all these—"

"No fucking way." My hand flies out, stiff-arming Harry as he tries to push in next to my girl.

My brother blinks impishly. "Huh?"

Poor thing looks so dumb. If he weren't being a drunk idiot, I'd maybe have pity for him. He clearly can't comprehend why I won't let him join me and Meghan tonight.

"What's your deal?" He pouts at me. Just like when he was four years old.

"Not tonight, Harry," I say firmly.

His unfocused eyes dart between me and Meghan, before taking in our body language and close proximity. Understanding dawns in his eyes, as sudden and bright as a fluorescent bulb flicking on. If he weren't so goddamn annoying right now, I'd find this cartoon moment amusing.

"Wait—you two are on a date. Right." He nods slowly.

Meghan meets my eyes and bobs her head. She slips back into character as my doting fiancee. She smiles softly, answering Harry with a sweet "Yes," before I can give a smart ass answer.

A big goofy grin stretches across my brother's ugly mug. "Damn. About time." He comes around the table and cups a big hand on my shoulder. "I'm fucking happy for you, man." Damn—he actually means it. A flash of guilt slices through my stomach for making him believe a lie.

Before the guilt really takes hold, he's stumbling away, back to his rambling teammates.

Meghan giggles as we watch him collapse onto a stool at the bar. "Well, that seemed a bit harsh. I don't mind if you want to hang out with him and his friends."

I feel myself frowning even though I have no reason to be territorial. "You want to spend the night hanging out with some annoying, hulking football players?"

She laughs softly. "To be honest, the only man I'm interested in hanging out with right now is the one sitting here in front of me."

I don't think she meant to say it out loud and for a split second, she looks like she might want to take it back, but ultimately, she holds her tongue.

I grasp her hand, thumbing over the soft skin there. "In the past, Meghan, when you and I have hung out around town, it's always been a group thing. But this time, I'm not sharing. Tonight, you're all mine."

Her face turns a beautiful shade of pink, but then she recovers well. We spend the next hour nibbling our way through all the plates and sampling more beers. I can't help but notice that palate of hers becomes considerably less discerning as the night wears on. I'm sure it doesn't help that we've done more drinking than eating, too.

Our night together continues without a hitch. No more idiot younger brothers trying to steal my woman. We laugh, we people-watch and catch up on the last few months.

It's just as great as it always is between me and Meghan, only now there's this crackling energy between us. A promise. An anticipation.

When it's clear neither of us are in any condition to drive, I suggest we ditch my car in the parking lot and get a ride home. I should have been more responsible with the alcohol, but it's been a while since either of us has cut loose, and we needed it.

Meghan climbs into the back seat of the tiny sedan and I follow her inside as she says a friendly hello to the driver. Trying not to crowd her, I leave a decent amount of space between us, leaning an elbow on the edge of the window and allowing my palm to cup the back of my head.

I stifle a yawn. "Damn. I'm so calm right now. I feel like I'm about to fall asleep."

Meghan sets her hand on my chest. Right in the center. She laughs. "Oh my lord. Your heart is beating so slow. Are you even alive?"

Fuck—her hand feels good on me. I instantly feel movement at my groin.

Without thinking, I catch her wrist and bring her hand to my mouth, gently nibbling on her fingertips. "Oh, I'm alive all right."

That's it. There are no more lines to cross. I've officially crossed every last one.

Meghan's breath stutters. But she doesn't pull away. In fact, she scoots across the bench, getting closer to me.

I relax noticeably, draping an arm around her shoulders and pressing a lingering kiss to the spot just behind her ear.

She pants softly, trailing her palm up my chest and around my neck until her fingertips are playing in my hair.

Jesus—friends don't touch each other like this.

I brush my lips down her neck again. "I want you so fucking bad." I hear the words leave my lips but honestly, my voice doesn't even sound like my own.

"I want you, too." She confesses. "It's getting harder and harder to fight."

I take a harsh inhale and her sweet scent fills all my senses. "Remind me again why we're fighting this in the first place."

I'm starved to touch her. Not in a friendly, platonic,

bullshit way. I want to claim her. I want to own her. I want to ravage her.

I don't want to hold myself back anymore.

"Every man I've ever opened myself to has ended up abandoning me in the end." Her words come out as a low, vulnerable whisper.

I drop my forehead so it's touching hers. "You know I'd never do that to you."

She laughs tremulously. "Do I, though?"

"You do," I say firmly. With conviction.

The tips of our noses brush. Her soft, sweet mouth is a breath away.

"Cash, you live hundreds of miles away. And you've repeatedly made it clear that your career is your number one priority..."

As much as I hate it, what she's saying is true. How can I make her promises in good conscience knowing that I can't keep them? This is Meghan. My fucking Buttercup. I can't do that to her.

Her hands softly push at my chest. This time, she's not caressing me. She's pushing me away. "We can't. We shouldn't."

Her words are a splash of cold water over my body. "Shit—you're right." I fall back into my seat next to her. "Dammit. I'm sorry." What is wrong with me? I'm a fucking pig. Disgust crawls through my veins.

"No. No, we both got carried away." She tries to spread the blame around equally, but she has to know this is my fault alone.

"I'm sorry for making you uncomfortable, Buttercup. You mean too much, and I don't want to lose that."

"You, too, Cash. I don't want to lose you."

I try to come up with a joke or a deflection but ultimately, I choose to go with raw honesty. "Yeah, I don't want to lose you, either."

It's not much longer before the tiny sedan drops us off in the middle of the street, between our homes. It's late, and I clasp Meghan's hand in mine as I walk her to her front door. The suburban night envelopes us, a stillness that feels heavy after the events of the day. I wish we were getting a different ending tonight but this is what's best for us.

She unlocks her door, and we linger on the porch. My gaze flitters down to her breasts and she plays with the edge of my shirt. The part that's killing me is I know she wants this as much as I do.

I put us both out of our misery. "Good night, Meghan."

She trembles. "Good night."

I fucking hate leaving her like this.

I watch as she disappears inside her home. Then I head back to my house across the street.

EIGHTEEN

CASH

"SHIT. I SEE THE PROBLEM," I hear Jasper call out with his head under the hood of my car.

I don't like the way he says it. Not when it's early Sunday afternoon and I'm preparing to get my ass back on the road to Chicago in a matter of hours.

This morning when Jasper drove me back across the bridge to retrieve my car from the brewery where I abandoned it in Sin Valley last night, something in the engine started making a funny noise. I really didn't want to have to deal with taking it into the dealership. So I asked Jasper to take a look, promising pizza in return.

"What is it?" I drag my feet across the driveway, getting closer to peek at what's going on. I have no clue what I'm even looking for.

I watch from a distance as he gives my car a thorough diagnostic. My brother peers at me over his shoulder, a worried look on his face. "I...I don't know if I can fix this, man. I don't know if I even have the qualifications." He grabs the hood of my luxury car like he's about to slam it shut.

No. No, no, no. He can't just give up on me. He has to fix it. I need to leave town tonight.

I grunt. "How can you call yourself a mechanic if you just quit without even trying to figure it out?" I whip my arms through the air, adding unnecessary drama to my words. I'm stressed.

"Dude, that thing you drive isn't even a car." He scoffs. "It's a four-thousand pound computer on wheels."

The asshole thinks this is funny. I don't. I've missed how many days of work now? I need to get back to the office.

I fold my arms across my chest. "Well, excuse me for not driving a clunker." I throw a glance at his dinosaur-era monstrosity parked next to my sleek, shiny beauty.

Jasper gasps in utter offence, reaching back to smooth his hand over his classic muscle car behind us in the driveway. "He didn't mean it," he whispers dramatically.

"Seriously. How about signing up for some continuing education classes, bro?" I force my mouth shut and refrain from insulting him further. He is, after all, doing me a favor. Or at least, I'm hoping he can.

I unfold my arms and set my balled up fists on my hips. "What's the problem anyway? Why can't you fix it?" I ask.

Jasper's eyes flip between my car's engine and me. Mirth rises into his expression. "Because if I fix it, I won't get to see the shame-faced look on your face when you realize you could have easily fixed it yourself."

"What?" I lean in close and stare into the engine bay.

"See that cap right here?" He points.

"Yeah?"

"That's your radiator cap."

"Okay?"

"You just need to tighten it," Jasper announces in an amused tone.

I throw up my arms. "How the heck am I supposed to know that?"

"Well, Office Boy, maybe if you'd paid attention for two seconds back when Uncle Eric used to try teaching us about cars..."

"Right..."

Damn car. Making me look like an idiot in front of my brother.

I follow Jasper's instructions on how to remedy the problem. Of course, he shit-talks the whole time, even when I threaten to kick him out of my house and make him sleep in his precious car that he loves so much if he doesn't shut his trap.

Jasper flings me a dirty towel to wipe my hands on. "You love that I live here. Admit it."

He's right. I may put on a big show, complaining that my brother has taken over, conducting himself as man of the house while I'm crashing on a flimsy mattress in the guest room, but to be honest, I wouldn't want anyone outside the family to be living here. I'm not big on strangers. And for the most part, Jasper looks after the property while I'm away.

Not that I'll be telling him that.

"Live it up while you can, asshole." I bare my teeth threateningly. "It's all fun and games until I decide to drop the hustle of the city and move back to Honey Hill for real."

I say it as a joke but—I don't know—after spending all of yesterday with Meghan, the punchline hits a little too high on the serious-as-a-heart-attack spectrum.

"Shit," he mutters, looking slightly terrified. "It's like *that* between you and Meghan? This is really happening? You're serious about this engagement thing? You'd move back here to be with her?"

His downpour of questions feels like an avalanche of boulders falling on my chest all at once. Questions I'm not equipped to answer and I'm too coward to face.

At this point, I should tell Jasper that Meghan and I were pretending to be engaged, as a prank. I'm leaving town in a few hours. There's no reason to not tell my brother the truth. But I don't want to. Because I sort of like the idea of Meghan being mine. Even though it would never happen, could never happen, should never happen.

She and I are best friends. Nothing more.

Still, my imagination keeps toying with the idea of taking things further.

My brother watches me, waiting anxiously for my response. "As much as I love being a guest on *Jasper's Driveway Talk Show* and relishing you with all the envious details of my glittery love life, I have a busy afternoon ahead of me. So stop minding my business and hurry up with finishing your diagnostic."

Snorting, he punches me in the shoulder. "Don't get all full of yourself just because you have a girl now. You know she'll get sick of your ornery ass soon enough, right?" He pops his head back under the hood. "*Jasper's Driveway Talk Show*. Has a nice ring to it."

He's in the middle of educating me on which mechanisms do what, when the door across the street pulls open. My gorgeous neighbor appears on her porch with a watering can.

It's like I'm in a trance. Completely forgetting all about my car, I move toward her like I'm a battery-operated drone on a preprogrammed mission—getting close to her.

I hear my brother huffing behind me. "Don't mind me! I'll just handle things over here on my own!"

I hold a thumb up in his direction, my feet not stopping until I catch up with Meghan.

"Hey, Buttercup." I jog up the drive.

"Hey." She gives me a girly blush that puffs me up with machismo like an action hero. "What are you guys up to?" She points her chin toward my driveway.

I sling the dirty rag over my shoulder and stand a little taller. "Y'know, just fixing cars. Doing manly things."

She giggles, only accentuating the pink hue of her cheeks.

As we speak, I catch sight of Captain Ginger spying on us from his cat hammock hanging in the window, his usual frown in place.

That fucker really freaks me out.

Won't let him deter me, though.

"You hungry?" I ask her. "We're about to order some pizza. Join us?"

An easy smile meets me. "Starved. And I really wasn't up for cooking tonight, so pizza sounds great. As long as I can pitch in and order the breadsticks?"

"Not a chance. You know I'll only go for cheese sticks."

Meghan laughs. "Always so stubborn. Mind if I get changed first?" She smooths a hand down her skin-tight yoga pants that she's paired with a white T-shirt. It says *I prefer sleeping next to a self-absorbed asshole who purrs instead of one who talks.*

Damn, Megs. *I can purr. If you want me to.*

I'm tempted to tell her how hot she looks just as she is. Her curves in those leggings sure do get my imagination going. I keep that bit of information to myself.

"Go for it," I tell her. I glance at Captain Ginger. "And grab your cat, too."

Meghan's stare goes wide. Shit, did I just tell her to grab her cat? That sounded way different in my head.

I fumble. "I mean...I just mean so we can have our final playdate. For the cats. I'm leaving town tonight."

Meghan strokes a hand down her reddened neck like she's trying to sweep her blush away. "Right. Okay."

She disappears back inside the house and less than an hour later, we're all lounging around my living room. Three large boxes of half eaten pizza sit wide open on the coffee table. Meghan's on the leather couch, feet up, nibbling on a peanut butter cup after devouring two slices of pepperoni. Jasper is in the recliner nearby stuffing back his fourth meat lovers' slice, and I'm on the floor, leaning up against the couch washing down a few slices of Hawaiian with some sparkling water. I watch on as my kitten tries to wrestle Cotton Ball, Captain Ginger and my innocent socked feet with wild abandon.

"You still haven't named him?" Meghan asks, laughing as the energetic little guy tries to sneak-attack Captain Ginger, misses, and lands on his head. Cotton Ball hops up and perches regally on the arm of the couch like she's above all that mess.

I grab a cheese stick and dunk it into some sticky sweet and sour concoction. "Do I have to? Can't he wait till he's adopted by his real owners to get a name?"

"Come on, bro." Jasper tosses his half-eaten piece of pizza crust back into the box and grabs a fresh slice. "All pets have to get a name."

I frown. "Well, shit." I stare at the feisty cat, trying to figure out the perfect moniker for him. "I'm going to call him Kitty."

Jasper chokes when he starts to laugh while chewing. "Lame, dude. Might as well call the poor guy Pussy."

Meghan barks out a laugh. She narrows her eyes plaintively at me. "Please don't call him that. He'll get picked on by all the mean kids in school."

"Okay. Fine. I'll name him *Mister* Kitty."

I get an eyeroll in response.

I toss around a few more suggestions. Some of them are pretty great, I think. But they all get shot down.

Giving up, I turn to Meghan. "What would you call him?"

She leans down and scoops him up. Her lips twist to the side as she lifts him in front of her and examines his little face. "How about Braveheart?"

"Damn. That's a good name," Jasper chimes in, nodding slowly.

"It is." I lift a brow. "Braveheart, it is. There's no topping that."

I keep an eye on the time as we laugh and catch up. Meghan doesn't even flinch at Jasper's crude jokes. In fact, she holds her own and puts him in his place in a sweet, sassy way like only Meghan can.

Having this girl hang out with us just feels right. She has always fit in perfectly with my family. And today has been no different. I love everything about having her around.

Everything about this evening feels good. Feels easy. Except for needing to strangle Jasper later, of course.

But my brother needs to get lost.

I want her all to myself. I'm running out of time and I'm anxious to be alone with her one last time. But Jasper's just lounging around, not taking a hint.

I'm getting impatient. I'm eyeballing my younger brother. "Don't you have a booty call lined up for tonight?"

When he catches the way I'm glaring at him, he instantly catches my drift.

"Well, damn, caveman. If you need some space with your girlfriend, why don't you just say so? No need for all the chest-pounding and teeth-baring." He glances at Meghan. "I guess that's my cue to get out of here." He snatches the last cheese stick then grabs the box of half-eaten Hawaiian pizza and heads off toward the stairs. "See ya, Megs."

She chuckles quietly. "Night, Jasper."

Like the asshole I am, I breathe a sigh of relief when Jasper finally makes himself scarce, disappearing upstairs. I move up onto the couch to sit next to Meghan.

The tone in the air shifts instantly when we're alone. This close. I know she feels it, too. Because she doesn't look at me. She just focuses all her attention on Captain Ginger who's now purring contentedly in her lap.

For once, the cat isn't absolutely grumpy. His eyes flutter half-closed as Meghan tenderly strokes the spot behind his ears.

Her eyes drift my way when I wipe peanut butter from her bottom lip with my thumb. "You're really good with them," I say to her. "The cats, I mean."

She seems nervous. I'm right there with her. "Thanks," she says, not lifting her eyes to mine. "They're easy to love. And they love me back. In their own special way."

"Why don't you just adopt them? You clearly like having them around. Why don't you just keep them for yourself?"

Meghan shrugs, her gaze drifts to the far side of the room as she searches for the right words. "Adoption feels so...permanent," she says, like it's a bad thing. "I know it might seem weird but...I'm just used to the relationships in my life being temporary. I'm used to not getting too attached."

Her eyes dare to find mine and her soul seems jagged and torn.

I hate that the things she's loved haven't stuck around. She deserves the stability of knowing that the people and things she cares about won't be taken away. I wish there was a way to give her that. But I can't. Hell—I have one foot outside the door as it is.

Still, I swear, something in her eyes dares me to be different from all the assholes who've let her down before.

She inhales smoothly and glances down at her phone. "Almost eight o'clock. Don't you have to get going now?"

Hell, I should have been on the road hours ago. But I just keep dragging this out. "Yeah. I need to go." I grab a napkin to wipe my hands then I rise up off the couch.

"Weekend's over..." She sighs, glancing out the window where heavy clouds hang in the darkening sky. "I should go get my lunch ready for work tomorrow."

After packing up her cats, she turns for the door and I can't even keep from following her home like a lonely, lost puppy.

I walk her across the street to her door, helping carry the cats. Meghan releases the wild felines inside the house before turning back to me. We stand face to face under her muted porch light.

"Thanks for being here the past few days," she tells me, her voice soft and laden with emotion. "You made my birthday special and you practically forced me to feel good about myself at a time when I was really starting to doubt myself."

I brush a golden coil away from her face. "You should

never have a reason to doubt yourself, Buttercup. Whether or not I'm around."

She smiles wryly. "Logically, I know that...but everything's easier when you're around." After a pause, she throws her arms around me and squeezes herself to my chest.

Letting go of her is so hard. I search my mind for just one more excuse to stay. One more reason to delay my departure.

But I can't.

These past few days have been an awesome escape. But it's time to face reality. And the fact is, she lives here and I live in Chicago.

And even if the distance weren't an issue, there's the fact that she's my best friend. Muddying that connection is a risk I'm not willing to take.

Still, when I ease out of the hug and stare down into her diamond-blue eyes, I can't shut up the voice in my head that's yelling at me. *Kiss her! Kiss her, you fool! Don't let this opportunity slip through your fingers!*

I swear she knows exactly what I'm thinking. Or maybe she hears that silent voice yelling out, too.

All I know is she looks sad.

In a moment of raw, last-minute honesty, I hear myself speak. "It's too bad things couldn't play out differently between you and me, Meghan Hutchins."

The way she stares, I get lost in those diamond-blue eyes. "Yeah, it's too bad, Cassius Westbrook." Her eyes hook on my lips. "Or who knows...maybe we could have this conversation again...in ten years...and things could be totally different then..." Her gaze sweeps back up to mine in a hopeful stare.

I imagine us ten years from now. Could I see myself still

wanting her this ferociously a decade from now? Fuck, yes. Fifty years from now, I'll be hobbling around the nursing home with a walker and my house slippers and I'll still be able to get it up for Meghan Hutchins.

But that's besides the point.

I could never ask her to give up another ten years of her life—her best years—waiting for me. I care about her too much to leave that door even halfway open. I have to close it shut.

"I don't see that happening, Megs. I'm a career man, like my father. I wasn't built to prioritize a family. It's just not in me."

I get flashbacks of the disappointment on Mom's face every time Dad skipped out on Sunday dinner because he had to work all weekend. Or that time Dad had to leave for an emergency business meeting in the middle of a family ski trip and Mom wound up having to wrangle five little hellions on her own. I judged my father so harshly in those moments. So despite the disappointment on her face, I could never put my best friend through that.

Expertly concealing her hurt with a smile, she steps completely out of my hold. "Drive safe, Cash."

The first thick droplets of rain hit my face as I walk backward down the stairs, not wanting to take my eyes off her. "Yeah. Thanks." I wait until she's safely tucked inside, until she's turned out the porch light.

Internally, I'm kicking myself before I've even made it down the final wooden step. *Fuck. I've missed my shot.*

I go back to my place to pack up all my shit. I don't have much of anything to pack up. But I'm procrastinating, thinking about Meghan while rain beats against the bedroom windows.

I want her so fucking bad. I'm fighting against my

desires. Beating myself up, trying to figure out how the hell to just stick with my carefully-laid plan to leave her the fuck alone.

Out of nowhere, a blinding bolt of lightning strikes. In a flash, I drop the pair of dirty boxers I'm refolding for the seventh time. Maybe it's my eyes playing tricks on me, but holy hell, that was close. So fucking close it actually looks like it hit Meghan's house.

Less than a second later, all the lights on the street go out, bathing my room in complete darkness.

Chest pounding, I drop what I'm doing. I dart down the stairs and across the street. My thumping feet hit the sidewalk. I can't get to Meghan's house quick enough.

NINETEEN

MEGHAN

ALMOST THERE...ALMOST there...

My fingernails scratch at the shower tiles while my other hand holds the detachable shower head in place between my thighs.

Almost there. Almost fucking th—

With a startled yelp, I drop the shower head from between my legs and clutch my soapy boobs. That lightning struck so freaking close to my bathroom window.

Clearly an act of god, punishing me for getting myself off to my dirty thoughts about the man I promised was my best friend and nothing more.

Yes. That's exactly what I was doing in the shower half a second ago, with delicious, forbidden visions of Cash flashing through my mind. Bolts of orgasmic pleasure had already begun to zap through my veins.

And then—*bam!*—a different sort of bolt flashed through the bathroom and tried to strike me dead.

I've got a one-way ticket to hell and I know it.

Guilt and shame bubble up as my not-quite-there-yet

orgasm circles my soapy toes and gets washed down the drain.

My mom used to tell me to never shower during a rainstorm. Now, I understand why.

But seriously—it's been raining non-stop this month, and a girl's got to take care of business eventually.

Especially after Cash left me at my front door with a singeing regret in my soul and a throbbing ache in my core. How was I supposed to know there would be a lightning storm from hell?

Thankfully, I wasn't electrocuted on the spot. I'm now dripping wet, hair full of conditioner, tripping over my poor cats as I make my way down my slippery-as-all-get-out stairs in total darkness.

Cash is on his way back to Chicago. Our time together is over. It makes my chest burn. My—ahem—'activities' in the shower earlier was a way to distract myself from this sense of loss.

Somehow I make it to the kitchen without breaking my neck. I rummage around, realizing I have too many junk drawers for my own good. I just need a flashlight. Or matches. Candles. Anything. A 19th-century kerosene lantern would do, at this point.

A loud banging on my backdoor nearly makes me drop my towel. Gripping the flimsy, tattered fabric, my eyes shoot up and find a tall, dark figure looming outside the glass door.

Oh, shit.

Storm.

Power outage.

Dangerous axe murderer.

This is that scene in every horror movie ever made. Right before the slutty female character—in this case, *moi*—gets killed off.

My killer knocks again, instantly sending me into cardiac arrest. A squeak escapes my lips and I prepare for my inevitable fate.

The man steps closer and peers inside. That's when I realize it's only Cash.

Gah. Of course. *Come on, Meghan. What kind of murderer would knock before ruthlessly slaying you?*

Rushing over, I flip the lock and slide the glass door open.

Cash pushes his way inside, chest heaving and rain dripping off his form. His eyes scan me from head to toe. "Are you okay?"

"No!" I laugh bitterly. "You almost gave me a heart attack." I look him over. "I thought you'd be on the road by now."

Agitated energy bounces off him. "I should be." He blows out a heavy breath and finger-combs his wet hair out of his face. "I wanted to come check on you." He peers back over his shoulder, staring into my backyard. "I swear—I saw lightning strike your house."

"*Oh my god*, me too!" I laugh again. "It flashed right outside my bathroom window when I was in the shower. It was so close. I thought it was God trying to strike me down for..." My words abruptly trail off when I realize what I'm about to confess to. Oops!

Cash's gaze squints with confusion. "For what?"

"For...for nothing."

He's standing in the middle of my dark kitchen, with his soaked shirt molded to his sculpted shoulders and chest, like some sexy new superhero who darts into storms to save ditzy, sex-starved women from themselves.

I struggle to not picture all the naughty, naked things I was doing in the shower a short while ago. But Cash is still staring at me in the dark. His grey eyes hold me hostage. And for the first time in my life, I'm terrified that all Ziggy's claims about the existence of mind-reading could be a real thing.

Becoming less sure by the minute about my private thoughts actually being...private, I blurt out the first thing that comes to mind. "I should get you a towel. To dry off."

Because if I continue to stand in the presence of this man, well, I might just drop my damp towel and see exactly how my dirty shower fantasies play out in real life.

Refusing to embarrass myself further, I turn for the stairs. I expect my dripping wet superhero to wait for me in the kitchen, but instead, I feel him following closely behind me up the dark stairs. Suddenly I'm exceedingly aware of every inch of my own wet, naked body, wrapped only in a threadbare scrap of terrycloth.

The overwhelming darkness only seems to heighten the rest of my senses, flooding me with Cash's musky scent and the electricity pinging off his body. Feeling his warm puffs of air on the back of my neck does delicious things to me. Somehow, I'm getting even wetter. Only now, it has nothing to do with the shower.

I'm only a few steps from the top when I stumble on my wobbly legs. I can't say if it's the blackout darkness or Cash's presence that nearly sends me falling facefirst onto the wooden stairs. But right before I land horizontal, a large hand flies out and grabs my hip. I'm simultaneously saved and imprisoned by Cash's arm locked around my middle.

The wind is all but knocked out of me. Our bodies are mashed together. My back to Cash's front.

That's when I feel it. His rock hard erection pressed firmly up against my asscheeks. Well, *between* them to be precise.

Suddenly, I'm panting and a fiery bolt of lightning strikes me between my legs.

I don't know what comes over me. But I don't pull away like I should. Instead, I instinctively arch my back. Push up against his hardness. Moan softly as an overwhelming need threatens to completely take my legs out from under me.

Cash's whole body stiffens. He stands completely still behind me like he's waiting for my next move. Like he needs to make sure he isn't imagining this.

"Meghan, are you...?" A groan vibrates in his throat when I rock my hips again.

Maybe it's the darkness giving me a false sense of courage. But my eyes flutter closed and I push back, rubbing my ass against him. More deliberately this time. So there's no doubt in his mind.

My breath shakes when his hand that's currently banded across my belly moves higher. Higher until his warm palm cups my breast.

"Yes..." I whisper encouragingly, inviting him to take this further.

When I moan again, powerless to hide my arousal, his other hand finds the bottom of my flimsy towel and slides upward along my thigh.

"Fuck, Meghan..." There's a note of pain in his voice when he groans my name.

Shrouded in the shadows of the dark staircase, I spin around and gaze up into Cash's savagely handsome face. His brows are furrowed with a look of deep intensity.

"You need to walk away. Now," he growls huskily.

My stomach clenches with violent need. "Why?" I hardly recognize the breathy voice that comes out of me.

His dark eyes search mine. His fingertips slowly caress the lips of my pussy, coming away drenched. "Because if you don't leave now"—he takes a step, forcing me to take a backward step up one stair—"I'm going to kiss you"—he takes another step and so do I—"Then I'm going to fucking devour your pussy"—he takes another step and when I mirror his, I'm standing at the top of the landing —"And I can't guarantee that we'll even make it to the bedroom."

Struggling to breathe, my hands smooth up the wet fabric of his shirt and lock behind his neck. Pulling him closer, I rasp, "Why the hell would I walk away from that?"

Without another moment of hesitation, Cash grabs my face in his hands. His mouth comes down on mine and my body roars awake as he urgently claims my lips.

He spins me against the wall and I kiss him back with just as much passion, every cell in my being screaming that I want this, that I *need* this. That we've waited too long. That we can't pretend not to want each other this way anymore.

Regardless of what's at stake.

We explore each other with long, hungry strokes of our battling tongues, with bites and licks, with soft nibbles.

"Holy shit, Meghan." There's a raspy quality to his voice when our lips separate.

"Cash..." I whine in response.

His tongue plunges between my lips and tangles with mine again. His kiss is bold. His hands are territorial as they smooth up my back, between my thighs, over my curves, eagerly exploring parts of me they've never touched before.

His attention moves to my neck. He bruises the column of my throat with the softness of his lips and the contrasting roughness of his stubble.

I don't even realize that my towel has fallen to my feet until my bare breasts are in his palms. He cradles the globes in his powerful hands, weighing, squeezing, massaging lightly before bending to sweep his lips over each nipple in turn.

Panting hard, Cash eases back to take a breath. His stare spills over my body, slow and thick like syrup. "Fuck, Meghan. Your body is amazing. You're beautiful, baby."

My stomach scrunches up so tight I'm sure I'll snap my spine in two.

"I need you," I whisper, raking my fingers through his damp hair. My head feels light and airy. All of me feels like I'm floating. I feel like I'm in an elevator in freefall. My feet can't find solid ground.

I eagerly try to peel his wet shirt over his head. When I've tossed the shirt aside, my hands sweep over his strong abs and back. His pelvis pins me to the wall.

Just when I think I've successfully shut down my brain, that I've managed to compartmentalize the friendship that's so dear to me from the raw, explosive chemistry that has led us to this moment, Cash brushes my wet, tangled hair from my eyes and looks at me with genuine concern.

This isn't just some random, horny, naked dude here with me. Cash is my person and the concern in his eyes is born from our deep connection as friends.

"You want this?" he asks me. "You're sure?"

"Keep touching me," I encourage him, my fingernails grating his scalp. "Keep kissing me."

Gripping the wall, Cash lays me down flat on the floor. His chest heaves with his heavy respirations. A breathless grin slides over his mouth. "It would be my absolute pleasure to keep kissing you, Meghan Hutchins. Every inch of you. You're so fucking sexy and you've been driving me crazy for years."

"I have?" I croak out, my hoarse voice barely rising

above the rhythmic sound of the rain beating the windows and the roof.

"You have." He kneels on the top step, his torso between my thighs. "And tonight, I don't want to hear all the fucking reasons why this is 'wrong'. I don't need to be 'right'." His lips sweep over mine. "I need to be inside you."

Before I can formulate another sentence, he gathers my breasts in his hands again. They're hurting for his attention. My core clenches erratically when his tongue flutters over one nipple and then the next.

Pleasure sweeps through me. I surrender control, wrapping my arms around his back.

This is happening. Here. Now.

Between Cash and me.

His hand slides back between my thighs. He caresses my skin with his warm palm and I open up to my desire for him, eagerly spreading my legs.

His finger enters me slow and smooth. My pussy clenches and my arousal slithers down his knuckles. It's been so long since anyone's fingers were inside me. Besides my own. I'm about to embarrass myself with how much it turns me on.

Cash's lips hover over mine. He studies my face with such concentration and intensity. It's like he's trying to solve an equation.

He dips his fingers deeper. "Do you like that?" His whisper sounds like gravel wrapped in silk.

"God, yes," I rasp quietly, my fingertips sinking into his bicep as my body writhes beneath his.

"You'll tell me if it's too much? If you need me to slow down?" His palm cups my mound, grazing over my sensitive clit as his fingers thrust into my opening. Everything is so tender. With every movement of his fingers, my nerve endings deliver delicious jolts of pleasure.

"More, Cash..." I whisper. "Please. Faster. More."

The way his eyes examine mine leaves me feeling vulnerable. Even the act of shedding my wet towel didn't leave me feeling as naked as the experience of Cash's eyes piercing my soul this way.

"What is it?" I dare to ask.

His eyes close briefly and he leans down to sweetly taste my lips. "From the night I showed up in town, I've wanted to touch you this way. And now that we're finally doing this, I've got a million thoughts running through my head."

He knows like I do that there will be consequences for doing this. But I'm willing to put my conscience on pause. Just for a moment, I'm willing to delay the inevitable flood of guilt that will come bursting in the minute all this is over.

In this moment, I don't want to think about all the reasons why this is wrong.

His kisses start moving south. Down over my ribs and over my navel to my hip bone.

By the time his lips are hovering near my pussy, I'm aroused to the point of insanity. "Cash, please..." I beg.

He lowers his face between my thighs. "Your pussy is so pretty. And it smells amazing. I already know you're gonna taste like heaven."

He's done with all hesitation. He parts my walls with his fingers. Then with his tongue.

I'm literally quivering as he tastes me. That beautiful mouth of his is a ravenous monster, hungrily feasting on my pleasure. Responding to my every moan, my every clench, my every, *Please don't stop!*

He fucks me with his mouth and hands, relentless on his mission to satisfy me. My muscles grow ridiculously tight as the orgasm threatens to detonate. My teeth chatter as I try to keep from screaming.

My detachable showerhead is no competition for this man.

My body can't handle any more. The sheer power of the orgasm lifts my head right off the floor. The release of pressure at my core makes me clench Cash's hair at the roots. "Yes-yes-yes-yes-yesssss!!" I chant as I ride his face until there's no more pleasure left to take from his tongue.

I surrender to the orgasm.

Cash crawls up the step and stretches out next to me, propped up on his side. "You okay?" He brushes hair from my face. My wetness is smeared all over his cheeks.

I sweep my palm across his damp skin. Then I kiss his mouth and taste myself there. "I'm...I'm...I...don't even know what to say."

Cash laughs as he rises to his feet. In one smooth movement, he slides his powerful arms under my limp body. He scoops me up against his chest.

He kisses my forehead. "It's okay. You don't have to make conversation tonight, Buttercup. The only thing you have to do is keep moaning my name."

I try to say something sassy that will wipe that smug grin off his face. Once more, I come up wordless.

Cash grins in the wake of my speechlessness. "Shh. Save your strength. It's going to be a long night. I'm not done with you, Meghan. You have no fucking idea."

TWENTY

CASH

MY FINGERS ARE TANGLED in the wet, silky hair at the back of her head. I lift her skull off the pillow and stroke my tongue deeply into her mouth.

Meghan loses herself in the kiss, making sounds that cause my nerve endings to burn with lust. We're stretched out sideways across her mattress. Her arms and legs wrap desperately around my naked body like a vine winding around the trunk of a tree.

My head is so light. I really can't believe this is happening.

She pulls back, panting and smiling breathlessly at me. Her dimples pop and she stares up at me from beneath those golden lashes in the dark room. "Nobody's ever kissed me like that..." she confesses quietly.

"Like what?" I take my time, touching my mouth to her collarbone and chest.

More and more sweet little sounds fall from her lips. "Like...like kissing me matters. Like my pleasure matters. Like *I* matter."

I brush my fingertips down the bridge of her button

nose before letting my touch trace the curves of her mouth. "You matter so much, Meghan. I can't tell you how long I've wanted to kiss these pouty lips. It's a destination I've dreamed of getting lost in more times than you could ever imagine. You matter to me."

On a slight gasp, she hooks an arm around the back of my neck and pulls me in for more kissing. I'm living my number one teenaged fantasy come true—me and her, in her bed, skin to skin, bodies hot and intertwined.

And I'm actively shutting out the voice reminding me how risky this is. Because if things go south—if we can't snap back to normal in the morning when all is said and done—I have more to lose than just my favorite makeout buddy of all time.

I'll lose my Buttercup. And I have no idea how I'd deal with that.

Pushing my hand into the infernal space between her thighs, I sidestep those unpleasant thoughts. I choose to focus on here. Now. Us. Meghan, naked and writhing beneath me and allowing me to touch her like this.

While we make out, I alternate between stroking her clit in a teasing round and round motion, and slowly fingering her opening.

Wetness leaks from her pussy onto my probing fingers. It's the sweet, sticky nectar of forbidden fruit dripping down my hand. Her pussy is pink. The same shade as her lips. And just as sweet. Like I knew it would be.

I'm hovering above her, looking down at her sweet feminine curves and the soft lines of her face. Meghan softly places her hands on my chest and stares up at me. "Is everything okay?" she questions softly. The amount of trust and openness in her eyes nearly makes my knees give out.

"Am I...am I taking advantage of you? That's the last thing I want to do."

Her hand cups the back of my head. She kisses me some more. "To answer your question—no, you're not taking advantage of me. The mere fact that you give a fuck about my feelings is a bigger turn on than you'll ever know."

I growl when her hand takes hold of my red hot erection. She strokes the pulsing staff in her tight fist. Her hand smoothly works up and down my cock, causing precum to leak from the tip.

"You're driving me crazy, Meghan. Everything about you is driving me crazy tonight. Your breasts. Your curves. Your mouth." I lean down and kiss her deeply again.

I'll never get tired of kissing her.

"Fuck me, Cash..." she whispers once I've gotten her worked up and on the edge of losing her damn mind.

I swipe my crown through her folds again and elicit another erotic moan from her.

A lecherous smile covers my lips in the darkness. I pray that she can't see it, that she doesn't know that the mere act of pleasing her is giving me more satisfaction than I've felt in months. Maybe even years.

"You got a condom? I rasp, staring down at her perfectly flushed skin and mussed hair.

"Yes," she says, panting quietly, and I'm relieved to see that I'm not the only one out of breath here.

Meghan stretches over to reach her bedside table and I take advantage of the view. The sexy curves I'm looking at now have been part of my imagination for years. I feel a strong urge to pinch myself and make sure this moment is true.

Opening the top drawer, her arm disappears inside. She

digs around in the back, finally retrieving an unopened box of condoms.

It pleases me to no end that it's unopened. The discovery makes me feel like a conqueror about to lay claim to new territory. And dammit, now I sound like a damn misogynist.

Taking the box off her hands, I make quick work of tearing into it. I struggle to focus on the task at hand as Meghan squeezes, strokes, and traces her soft lips over my skin.

She lies on her back, lust in her eyes, thighs spread wide as I deal with the condom. "Damn. You're sexy."

Her large breasts, her wide hips, her small waist. She's an hourglass come to life. I'm an awestruck fool right now. She giggles at the look on my face.

I really can't believe I'm doing this. That I'm in Meghan's bed. And her sexy curves are damp and bare for me. That her legs are open and her pussy is wet and waiting for me. She's so luscious. So beautiful. Completely willing.

Goddamn. How did I get so fucking lucky?

There will be consequences. I know that. But we'll deal with those consequences tomorrow.

I tear the flimsy condom wrapper open, then I reach down and roll it on with my eyes staying on this beautiful girl.

Only, something doesn't feel right. A strange cracking sound rings out.

Breaking our eye contact, I look down. I find my cock hanging out.

Somehow, my erection has torn a hole clear through the latex.

"What the fuck?"

Meghan's expression is a mix between shock and

amusement. "Try another one." She hands me a new condom.

Chewing on her swollen bottom lip, she watches as I try again with a second condom.

And, I kid you not, this one rips, too. My cock's just hanging out, with shredded condom pieces wrapped around my junk.

Either my dick is the Incredible Hulk all of a sudden, or...

Reaching across the mattress, I grab the torn up condom box. I frown. "They expired a year and a half ago," I deadpan.

Meghan's palms shoot up, covering her blushing face. "Ohmygod," she mumbles through her fingertips. "That's so embarrassing. I knew I hadn't gotten any action in ages. I didn't realize it had been *that* long."

Grinning, I pull her hands away from her eyes. "So what if you haven't? It's better this way."

If she thinks that's going to be a turn-off for me, she's woefully misinformed. Knowing how long she's gone without sex, only makes me more determined to give her the best night of her life.

I inch toward the edge of the bed. "I'll go get some more. The gas station is definitely still open."

She props herself up on both elbows and stares skeptically out the window. "It's a downpour out there, Cash."

I follow her stare. She's right. Shit. The weather is a wreck.

A lightbulb goes off in my head. "Jasper! Jasper definitely has condoms." *I'll do anything, Buttercup. Just let me put my cock inside you.*

"Or..." Her soft hand touches my bicep causing every

hair to stand on end. I read the hunger in her eyes and I try to interpret what she's saying without words.

She gently pulls me back into bed. Then she collapses into the pillows and stares up at me, so much willingness on her face.

Meghan reaches up and guides my hand to the pool of lava between her thighs. My fingers sink inside and my cock whimpers, *That should be me...*

I hover over her. "Are you on the pill?

"Yeah. I'm on the pill. And I'm clean."

"I'm clean, too. And I won't come inside you. I can just pull out."

"Okay," she says nervously. "We can do that."

Our eyes catch. They hold.

Holy shit. I'm about to fuck my best friend. When I promised myself again and again and again that I wouldn't.

But I've never felt this ferocious need for any woman before. Not just because I'm aching to be inside her on a primal level. It's more than that. I have never in my life felt as close to any other person as I feel to Meghan right now.

And still, I want to get closer.

I want to merge with her completely. I want to be buried in her deepest place so there is absolutely no space between us. I don't know what to make of this feeling. And I'll put off psychoanalyzing it for as long as I can. All I know is I can't deny this connection any longer.

She pulls my fingers from inside her and kisses them. "I'm losing my mind, Cash. Don't make me wait any more."

Christ. Did she really just do that? Is she trying to kill me?

I catch her lips with mine and glide the tip of my cock into her hole.

She emits a soft, melodic gasp. "Oh god," she moans, her walls clenching greedily for more.

My teeth grind together as I slowly ease my hips forward, sinking deeper into her wetness and her heat. A jagged breath leaves me. "Fuck, you're tight, Megs."

She snickers breathily. "Eighteen months and counting, Cassius. Eighteen months and counting."

I laugh shakily too. "You're wrong," I tell her, looking deep into her eyes. "I've wanted this for half my fucking life."

An emotion slips over her face. She momentarily purses her lips and closes her eyes. Then she draws me close for another kiss. "Me, too."

I pull my hips back, until my cock is almost out. Together, we watch as I sink all the way inside her again, all the way to the hilt. Fucking erotic. Beautiful. Watching us joined in this way.

Taking a few moments, I savor it, fucking her in long, lazy strokes, trying to control myself so I don't blow my load. Fourteen years of pent up lust have my nuts in a chokehold. I don't want to get carried away and fuck this up.

Meghan grows impatient, her desire cresting as I continue to slowly get her worked up.

She clenches my arm, squeezing my bicep. "Harder, Cash. Please. Make it hurt."

Her words are like a magic spell that break loose the monster in me. When she says that, I grab her by the hips, lift her ass off the mattress and I start pounding her.

I'm an asshole for doing this with her, especially knowing that we're doomed to fail. We're about to blow our friendship to shit. And we're both too caught up in the moment to stop it.

That's why I need this to be good for her. Better than

good. I need it to be fucking explosive. So that in the morning, when things are irreparably changed between us, I can look myself in the mirror and know that it was fucking worth it.

"Yes, like that." She holds my biceps with both hands. "Yes, Cash."

I fuck her deep and mercilessly, not holding anything back.

Every time I thrust into her pussy, her curves shake. When I pound deep to the hilt, her gorgeous breasts sway.

The walls shake and the lamp rattles on the bedside table. I fuck her so hard that the mattress is leaving the bed, half-hanging limp over the side of the bed frame. I don't know if I'll ever get a chance to be with her again so tonight, I'm giving Meghan all of me.

"Is this how you like it, baby?" I lean down and growl by her ear.

Her soft breasts are crushed beneath my damp chest. "Exactly how I like it. Yes, Cash," she cries, clinging onto me, her legs wrapped around my waist.

I lift her ass higher, adjusting the angle. I hesitate to ask, "Is this how you imagined it would be between us?"

She meets my eyes. "It's better," she pants. "This is surreal." She lifts her hips, taking me deeper inside her. "Cash. Oh my god. Having you inside me...it's surreal."

I feel exactly the same sense of awe that she does.

"Your body's like a dream come true, Meghan." My arms quake helplessly as I hold myself above her. "Your pussy is making me weak."

"That's it," she whispers in my ear, her torso sliding against mine as our bodies grind into each other. "That's it. Right there. That's the spot." I reach up and grab one of her breasts, squeezing the fleshy globe.

I pull my hips back and surge forward, giving one final thrust that breaks us both.

I watch Meghan's eyes roll into her skull, revealing the whites of her eyes. She cries out from the depths of her lungs, her voice sounding savage, coarse and wild. Her body convulses as she clings desperately to my arms and the orgasm shakes through her soul.

Meanwhile, I go rigid all over. Pleasure radiates down my spine. Heat and ecstasy consume me. I barely manage to yank my cock from her pussy before I'm shooting ropes and ropes of ejaculate all over her stomach and pussy and thighs.

We collapse on opposite sides of the bed. Before the pleasure has even subsided, a feeling of dread climbs from the tips of my toes, up, up, up, until it's strangling my throat.

Meghan doesn't say a word. She just lies there with a *what the fuck did we just do?* face. She reaches into her bedside drawer for a rag and quickly cleans herself up.

I try not to watch as she hastily covers her nakedness with the blankets that were tangled around the end of the bed.

I feel like a total asshole. Now that the sheet is tucked up around her tits, I tentatively glance her way. "Do...you want me to go? I should go," I hedge.

Meghan's face colors, a rosy blush stretching from her cheeks down to her half covered chest. Her mouth opens and then closes. Whatever she was going to say, she decides against it.

With a heavy sigh, I climb out of bed and find my wet clothes in a heavy clump on the floor. I yank on my cool, damp shirt, and then I fight with my stiff jeans until I finally manage to get them tugged up over my ass. After all that struggling, I don't bother with zipping them.

Meghan is now sitting up, with her blankets now wrapped around her like a robe. "I...it's..." she keeps trying to say something, but it becomes obvious that there's nothing to say in a situation like this.

I did exactly as I figured I would. In the span of twenty minutes, I just threw a decade-plus friendship down the drain, and I feel like absolute scum.

When I'm done shoving my feet into my soggy shoes, I walk toward her bedroom door. With my back to Meghan, I pause and clear my throat. "I'm sorry about all this."

Her lips tighten, and I brace for it. She's going to tell me to go to hell. To stay out of her life. To piss off for ruining what used to be a solid, platonic friendship.

Instead, she swallows hard. "We really got carried away, that's all." She hesitates. "Can we...can we talk about this over breakfast tomorrow?"

"Yeah. Of course. I'll text you." After all that's gone on, what's one more night in Honey Hill?

"Yeah, okay. Text me." Her voice is soft.

I stalk out of her house and back into the rain. I curse up at the sky, at this storm for setting this whole mess into motion.

TWENTY-ONE

MEGHAN

MY KNEE BOUNCES as I sit in the sticky vinyl booth at the Good Morning, Sunshine Diner. I tune out the chatter of early morning patrons and the soft din of the Top 40 hits playing through the speakers. I alternate between fiddling with my plasticized menu and studying the patterns of the chicken and rooster wallpaper.

Cash texted me less than an hour ago, making breakfast plans to meet him here. That didn't give me very long to get ready, but since I half-expected him to ghost me after what happened between us last night, I couldn't turn him down.

The scent of burnt toast lingers in the air. Waitresses in faded uniforms whizz around, delivering orders. I watch as plates of over-crispy bacon and runny eggs pass me by.

This place isn't the best breakfast spot in town but we couldn't exactly have this conversation at the Wildberry Bakery under the watchful eye of Cash's family. So this place will have to do.

I'm nervous as hell, though. Over the years, I've imagined the events of last night a thousand times, and I never pictured myself freaking out afterward. But I ar freaking out because...It. Was. So. Good.

And I really don't know what to do with body is still on fire, humming, tingling, and downright singing. How do I just turn that off?

To say that I need to pull my shit together is an understatement. And I need to do it fast, because Cash is on his way.

My breath catches when I see him waltz through the finger-smudged glass door, making the little bell above it chime.

His gaze finds mine and he immediately stalks toward my table, looking tired, wary and sexy as hell. At the instant knot in my gut, I glance down at my phone. It's already 7:52, and I have to be at work in less than forty minutes. I half-wonder if he's cutting it close on purpose, barely leaving us any time to talk while we eat.

But I force that thought aside. Cash is not one to play games. Considering the weird circumstances between us, he's been mostly straightforward with me. I'm clearly the one overthinking this whole situation. *Again.*

He drops into the squeaky red booth across from me, and I instantly inhale the scent of his fresh, musky shower gel. I discreetly note his freshly-shaven jaw and his still damp hair. "Hey," he mumbles, that unrelenting grey stare of his focused on me like he's trying to x-ray my soul.

"Good morning." Why do those two simple, innocent words feel so darn uncomfortable leaving my mouth?

My eyes drop away from his again, suddenly too interested in the breakfast menu to hold his intense eye contact. *Gah.*

Thankfully, our waitress pops over to our table, entering our awkward bubble. We both order coffee, and while Cash goes all out with a full breakfast platter, I keep things simple with a bagel. I'm afraid I don't have time for much else, and I can't say I'm all that hungry either. With a cheerful smile, the waitress leaves to get our orders to the kitchen.

"D'you sleep well?"

"How's Braveheart?"

We stumble over each other's words, both speaking at the same time.

After a moment of weirdness, I answer his question first. "Uh. Good. Lots of rain, though." *Wow. Brilliant, Meghan. Let's talk about the weather. Like we didn't just fuck my mattress right off the bed frame less than twelve hours ago.*

I hate how awkward this whole situation is with Cash. He's my best friend. Things between us are supposed to be easy. Comfortable. But right now, every word we share is like getting my fingers slammed in a car door.

Cash huffs, glancing out at the overcast skies outside. "Yeah. The weather's been shitty." His frown eases slightly. "The cat's good, by the way. Pain in the ass though."

That brings a genuine smile to my face. "Good thing he's so cute, then."

Our coffees are dropped off at our table, and while Cash adds a spoonful of sugar and a dash of milk, I take the opportunity to stare at him, last night heavy on my mind.

For the record, I did *not* want him to leave me last night. When we were finished climaxing together, all I wanted was for him to stay and hold me. Deep down, I wanted to wake up next to him this morning. Letting him leave in the middle of that rainstorm was torture.

But begging a man to love me has never worked out great for me in the past. My heart has the battle scars to prove it.

I know that if we have any hope of holding on to our friendship, the boundaries we spent the past few days obliterating have to be reestablished quickly. To the best of our abilities.

The painful awkwardness that's thick in the air between us right now doesn't bode well for our chances of regaining normalcy. All those years of restraining my urges and exercising my self-control just for the sake of preserving our friendship. It's like I made all those sacrifices for nothing, and my lady bits are not happy about it.

Cash rubs the back of his neck, after a lengthy silence. "Look, I'm really sorry I let things get out of control last night." He meets my gaze.

The guilt in his eyes has all thought of my selfish sexual desires dissipating. Despite my own internal conflict, I don't like seeing my friend this uncomfortable.

I reach over and gently stroke his hand, ignoring the spark of heat I feel. "Me too."

"We just spent a *lot* of time alone together over the past few days," he rationalizes.

"Yeah. And it'd been a long time since I'd gotten laid." I laugh. "I mean, eighteen months is a long time. I guess it messed with my head."

He chuffs, throwing both palms up. "No judgment here. I lost track of the last time I got any action. A guy can only hold out so long. Plus, all that pressure from our friends about the marriage pact sort of messed with my judgement."

"Pretending to be engaged all weekend didn't help, either," I toss in.

"And it was late. And we weren't thinking straight with the storm and all...We just got carried away. Could have happened to anybody." I shrug.

"The storm definitely had something to do with it," he muses lightly. "That lightning probably hit closer than we realized. You sure you didn't get struck?"

I laugh, pretending to be offended. "Are you saying that a lightning bolt caused me to lose my mind and jump your bones?"

"Maybe. Or maybe it did something to your pheromones," he says with a smirk. "It made you irresistible to me."

I laugh. "Wow. Way to take accountability for our actions."

We share a chuckle.

"Can you blame me?" My heart skips a beat when he reaches over the table and takes one of my hands in both of his. "I'd accept any explanation. Just as long as it means that things can go back to normal for us."

He touches me like that and I'm instantly trying to forget the way his mouth felt against mine, how his tongue felt on my pussy, how his hands felt skimming over my ass. But my brain is repeatedly recreating those everlasting memories in real time.

Cash's voice interrupts my thoughts. "You're my best friend, Buttercup. You mean too much, and I don't want to lose that." There's a seriousness to his tone that's suddenly too much for me.

"You, too, Cash. We're better off as friends anyway," I lie, keeping my tone light. "We know far too much about each other to go down that road. I know all your dirty little secrets and you know mine."

"You wound me, woman. My secrets aren't that dirty."

I laugh and then it peters off. "No, let's be serious for a minute. We just need to be mature about this. Be adults."

After a long moment of staring into my soul, he nods. "Yeah. We've got to be adults."

Our food arrives, and Cash dives right in. As though we haven't been sitting here discussing the fact that we had down and dirty, hot sex with each other and almost smashed our connection to smithereens. What's with this guy always having an appetite? As far as I'm concerned, I need a glass of ice water to cool off before even thinking about enjoying a meal.

The conversation shifts to safer topics while he shovels down his food and I nibble on my bagel.

Discreetly, I breathe a sigh of relief. Considering the last twenty-four hours...things seem good between us. Sort of.

Glancing at my phone again, I see it's time to get my butt to work. I swallow the last of my lukewarm coffee. "Sorry. I've got to get to the clinic. Call me later?" I gather my purse and coat.

"Of course." With a frown, he makes quick work of wrapping up my bagel in a paper napkin and shoving it into my hands. "You still need to eat."

"Okay, bossy." I carefully place it in my purse and pull out a ten dollar bill. Before I can drop the money on the table, Cash snatches it from me and shoves it into the front pants pocket of my scrubs. My face burns at the sudden touch, but I do my best to play it cool, shooting him a glare.

"Your money's no good when I'm around, Buttercup."

I huff. "Pizza's on me next time then."

When I say that, Cash's shoulders visibly loosen in relief. "I'm just glad there'll be a next time." The earnest look of relief in his eyes almost breaks me. "So can we go back to normal?"

"We can go back to normal." I squeeze his shoulder and

try to walk past him, telling myself that it's all good. That everything is back to normal. That Cash and I will be able to completely forget about what happened last night.

We're friends. We agreed. It's for the best.

Before I can get away, Cash grabs my wrist and gently tugs me back toward him. He opens his arms to me. "Can we hug it out?"

Sighing, I step into his embrace. "Duh, bestie."

He chuckles, making his chest vibrate. "Please don't call me that again."

"What...bestie? Bestie, bestie, bestie?"

He growls threateningly. The sound resonates between my thighs.

I shiver. "Okay. Fine."

We step apart and stare at each other.

"Goodbye, Buttercup."

"Goodbye."

I turn for the door. I pretend I'm not hyperaware of his eyes on my ass as I walk out of the diner.

Through the front window, we wave at each other. Then I watch him lower into his seat and pick up his phone. I stand there, frozen for a while.

I remember how those big hands felt on my skin. How his lips felt buried at my core. I want more. More and more and more. I want more of his body. And call me greedy—I now also want his heart.

But we promised we'd be adults about this. We promised we'd stay just friends.

Damn. Being an adult sucks.

TWENTY-TWO

CASH

IT'S THREE-O'-FREAKING-CLOCK on Monday afternoon by the time I drop Braveheart off at my condo and make it back to the office.

I try to slip undetected into the client satisfaction department's weekly meeting. But the second I step into the room, Nicky catches my eye and gives me a conniving grin.

The executives around the table glance at me and whisper among themselves. I'm guessing that my sister has them all up-to-date on the goings on of my hot mess of a private life.

Fabulous.

I don't stay in the meeting long. I make a stealthy escape at my first opportunity. I can't concentrate for shit. Every time I try to tune into the meeting, I hear Meghan's sweet giggles in my head. When I try to read the meeting agenda, my mind drifts off to the way she looked naked beneath me in her bed.

I'm officially losing my mind.

Our night together was more than just sex, dammit. My night with Meghan was a spiritual experience. I swear, I didn't even realize I had a soul until it was dancing and merging with hers.

I don't think I'm gonna be able to get over this.

I want to drop what I'm doing and call her right now. I want to clear the air and tell her what I *really* feel. Because that conversation we had at the diner this morning was bull- shit. Meghan should be mine. Point blank. Period.

Nobody understands me the way she does. Nobody can take care of her the way I can—

Stop deluding yourself, asshole. The last thing you need is another commitment on your plate. Especially a freaking long-distance relationship.

I'm just going to have to narrow my focus, get back into my routine and push Meghan's extended 30th birthday shenanigans to the dark, mothball-scented closet at the back of my mind. It's probably best that I give her some space until I can think clearly again, until I'm not feeling this erratic need for her that I do right now.

Mentally fencing off the gossip-ready eyeballs following my every move, I stride purposefully down the hallway trying to give off the image of a man who's not silently losing his shit.

I hit a slight speedbump when I'm accosted by Agnes, the human resources lady. She comes at me with a plate of fresh cookies and a million questions about my supposed nuptials. She even offers me a handmade body butter she says she prepared specifically for my new bride. Heaven help me. Thankfully, I manage to duck out of the conversa- tion after a minute or two of mumbled responses and deep frowning.

I barricade myself inside my office, and though I can feel eyes on me through the glass walls, everyone knows better than to bug me when the door is shut.

Everybody except Nicky.

"Hey, hey." I ignore her chirpy greeting and her clever smile from the doorway. Or at least I try to.

Right now, I'm silently cursing the contractor who talked me into glass walls when we did those office renovations a year ago. Because I just want to hide out in here and sort through my thoughts in peace.

Tell that to my sister who's got her head poking in through my door.

"What is it, Nicky?" I bellow, already back to my familiar state of constant low-grade annoyance.

"Jeez." She steps fully into the doorway. "I'm just here to brief you on the developments you missed while you were away. Why must I be greeted with such ingratitude and hostility?"

I don't trust that innocent look on her face. I don't trust it one bit.

"Come in," I grouse reluctantly. Against my better judgment. "Close the door."

Nicky does as I ask. She primly lowers herself into a chair across from my desk and diligently combs over the various files that have been updated during my absence. She provides me with meeting notes, data and projections, and thoughtfully answers all my questions.

I'm almost impressed by her professionalism—*almost*—until she slams the final folder shut and grins at me with the pure deviousness I've come to expect from her.

"So..." She leans back in her seat.

"So?" I say bringing my eyes to my iPad.

A beat passes.

"Are we gonna talk about your trip?" She thrusts her phone into my line of vision and my eyeballs are assaulted by that awful video of me and Meghan under the glaring spotlights of the Hot Sauce. "And are we gonna talk about this lap dance?"

Dammit.

"How did you get your hands on that...?" I grumble, already feeling a headache coming on.

She scoffs indignantly. "I don't reveal my sources."

Harry. Her quote-unquote 'sources' are Harry.

"I always knew that the tap dance classes Mom signed you up for when you dropped out of the Boy Scouts would come in handy one day." She smirks.

"I don't have time for this..." I mutter, flipping through a stack of checks I need to sign off on.

"Oh, I'm sorry. I forgot that Meghan is the only person who gets a minute of the ever-busy Cash Westbrook's time."

"I've got shit to do, Nicky." I growl, not bothering to give her the courtesy of eye contact.

She sighs, gathering up her things. "Well, I'm just glad you made it official with Meghan."

"Made what official?"

"Stop playing dumb." She rolls her eyes. "I'm glad you made your relationship official. Congratulations."

"There was never any relationship to make official in the first place."

Her expression collapses like a kid who just discovered the Tooth Fairy is a lie. "But Harry said..."

Ha! Sources revealed, Big Mouth.

"Meghan and I were just pretending. We were pretending to be together for the weekend so everybody would stop breathing down our necks. Like you are now." I glance at the time. "Are you done? I have work to catch up on."

She folds her arms across her chest. "I just want to point something out, in case you haven't noticed."

"What's that?" I ask uninterestedly.

"You were gone for an entire weekend plus nearly *three business days*...and the company didn't go up in a cloud of smoke, the building didn't spontaneously combust into a ball of fire. We were fine. In fact, as of this morning, Dad signed three new clients with hundred million-dollar portfolios for us to manage."

I clear my throat, trying to act indifferent to this hella fantastic news. I choose to be my stubborn self instead. "Well, unless one of them was Cannon Kingston—"

"Cash, you're missing the point!" she snaps out.

My head jerks up so I can stare at her. "What's the point exactly, Nicky?"

She releases an exhale and her features soften noticeably. "You don't have to sacrifice your every living breath for the sake of this company. You don't have to sacrifice your life. Yes, you love Westbrook Wealth Management. But maybe there's space to love something—some*one*—else, too."

She said the L-word. She said the fucking L-word that's been trying to creep into my mind since my drive back to Chicago.

I think I should be freaking out. But somehow, I'm oddly calm. When I think of my big, towering feelings for Meghan, it's not fear I feel. A sense of acceptance washes through my soul.

My attention tunes back in to Nicky. "Cash, you've been building this empire of yours for a long time. Your entire adult life. Would it be such a bad idea to have someone to share it all with?"

"Meghan and I were practically kids when we made that marriage pact," I grouse. "No one should expect us to hold each other to a pact we made when we were kids."

My sister shakes her head like I'm an idiot. "It's not

about the stupid marriage pact. Can't you see? It's about the fact that you're crazy about her. Now. Today. For the past hundred million years that you've known each other. Why can't you see that?"

I don't answer. Because there's a boot on my throat. I know she's right but the truth is a tough pill to swallow.

I know what Meghan said. I know what *I* said back at the diner this morning. We're better as friends. But I also know what it's supposed to be like when two friends hang out together, and that's not what it feels like for me when I'm with her. None of my 'friends' give me a boner the second they walk into the room. None of my 'friends' make me lose my breath with just one smile. Meghan is more than my friend, dammit.

I want to call her. Right this minute. I want to pour my heart out and tell her I refuse to waste one more second, live one more second of my life where she's not my girl.

I'm not calling her. Not yet. I'm giving her space.

Nicky sighs. "I know you think that I stick my nose in your business just for entertainment. And I'll admit it, in large part, I do. But here's the thing—you're my brother, and at the end of the day, I want to see you happy. And in this video"—she holds up the screen—"you're happy."

Eyebrow hiked, I stare at the video replaying on loop on her phone. "I'm scowling," I deadpan.

"That's your happy face." She chokes back a laugh. "Despite the scowl, that's your happy face."

"How the hell do you know so much about my happiness all of a sudden?"

For emphasis, my sister points at the video of Meghan who's blushing and covering her face as she sits hostage in the chair on the dance floor. Nicky gets a twinkle in her eye.

"Because you're only happy when you're with her. Everyone sees it."

As Nicky snatches her things and leaves my office, I know that she's right. About everything.

Now the question that remains is, what the hell am I going to do about it?

TWENTY-THREE

MEGHAN

I CAN'T WAIT to get home and change into my yoga pants. It's been one of those days...

Normally, I stay a little later and prep the exam rooms for the next day's appointments. It's work that's unpaid but usually I don't mind because it gives me a sense of purpose. Under regular circumstances, being at the veterinary clinic always calms me. But it's been three whole days since that weird morning after breakfast with Cash and I'm still feeling out of sorts.

Maxine is in the waiting area watering the plants. I don't stop to chitchat with her on my way out of the clinic. I just wave goodbye and make a beeline for the door.

"Can't spare a minute to talk, huh?" She chuckles. "Don't worry, honey. I'd be in a rush too if I had a fine piece of man meat at home waiting for me."

I scrape together enough energy to give her a smile over my back. "Cash left town," I tell her. "It's just me and the cats tonight." I hate the way my heart sinks when I say that.

"Oh, don't make that sad face. I know that long-distance relationships can be hard, girlie. But Chicago is only a few hours away. And we have video call technology. Plus, reunion sex can be *so* satisfying."

I should correct my coworker then and there. I should tell her that the thing with Cash was just a prank that got out of hand. And that, for better or worse, reunion sex is not one of the perks of whatever it is that's going on between us. But I bite my tongue. For some reason, I don't have it in me to offer an explanation. I just want to go home.

"Have a good night, Max." I offer a final wave before I head out.

On my way through the parking lot, I get a text message from my mother.

Mom: Something strange happened today

Instantly, I'm on high alert. I message her back immediately.

Me: What happened?

Mom: Remember how Shelly decided on Saturday that the bank wouldn't be granting me a loan?

Me: Yes, I remember

Mom: Well, she had a sudden change of heart.

Mom: She just called to set an appointment for me to come in and sign the paperwork

A sense of relief floods me.

Me: Mom, that's great news!! Congratulations

Mom: This might sound weird but...I think I just got a loan because you're dating Cash Westbrook

Oh. Wow. I guess I shouldn't be surprised. That's the kind of weight the Westbrook name carries around town.

There's a pause. Like Mom is waiting for me to respond. Then she messages me again.

Mom: I don't know what's going on with you and Cash but just be careful, Meghan. I hate saying this again but girls like us don't get chosen. Better not to get our hopes up. Because we're never the first choice. We're the ones who get settled for. Temporarily.

I ignore the dagger to my chest reminding me of my inherent unworthiness. I want to text her back. And tell her that Cash and I aren't together. We never were. But what we *did* manage to successfully do was make an irretrievably steaming hot mess out of fourteen years of friendship.

Yay, us!

Not quite ready to explain this all to my mother, I slide my phone into the pocket of my scrubs and slip behind the wheel of my car. With the radio off and the windows up, I drive home.

When I step through the front door, Captain Ginger gives me an apathetic greeting, barely lifting his head to glare at me from his perch on the cactus post. Cotton Ball comes straight at me, bitching and whining until I fill her bowls with cat food and water.

I shower and make dinner for myself but I'm feeling kind of antsy tonight. I don't let my phone out of my sight. Every time it chimes, I jump on it like a maniac. But it's just my old friend, Minka, blowing up my phone with adorable pictures of her baby girl, Melody. I coo and caw over the little cutie pie. But still, my heart is heavy.

Still no word from Cash. A niggling part of me fears that he won't call, that he won't text, that he'll ghost me like everyone else in my life seems to.

"This isn't healthy, Meghan," I whisper to myself.

I hate being this needy. I hate craving validation from outside myself. Especially since it's something I have no control over. But I *do* have control over my own emotions. You'd think that I'd be accustomed to being abandoned by now with all the times that it's happened to me.

I pick up my phone and tap on his name. I debate whether to take the initiative and be the one to reach out first. I want to call him because I'm craving the sound of his voice, his laughter, the heavy vibrations of his breathing. But that wouldn't be healthy.

I can't keep doing this to myself. I have to go back to my old routine, I have to find my normal again. I can't allow myself to sit around missing a man who was never—and never will be—mine.

The last few days I spent with Cash sent my neatly organized emotions into a tailspin. Now that he's gone, I need to rediscover my balance, get my life back on track.

Cash and I need a little bit of space. In a few days, I'll be feeling like myself again and we'll be able to have a conversation like usual, without the emotional charge that was crackling between us the morning he left town.

So I hit the 'back' arrow and scroll to another name in my contacts. It's already 7:30 when I text Alana.

Me: 8:15 show at the TheatreBox?

My friend's response comes a few seconds later.

Alana: There's a new Sandra Bullock I'd love to see

Alana: But we're gonna have to hurry

Because I'm feeling sort of shitty about myself, I allow myself a few minutes to apply some lipgloss and mascara. Mom says it's important to look your best when you're not feeling great about yourself. The makeup and cute outfit lift my spirits a smidgen. They also make me late.

I'm cutting it real close. I'm bustling up Tour Street toward my friend where she's waiting for me beneath the marquee of the local movie theatre.

She waves a long slip of paper at me like a lottery winner. "Already got the tickets! Come on!"

"Awesome. You look so cute!" I squeal, giving her beat-up oversized denim jacket, canvas running shoes and the baseball cap pulled low over her face a once-over as we hustle through the movie theatre's lobby.

She laughs. "You look like a supermodel." She gestures to my leather jacket, floral blouse and jeans. "I'm just a girl who was already tucked in for a Netflix marathon alone when her bestie called her up for an impromptu movie night." Stopped in the lobby, she glances down at our tickets then her eyes sweep around, looking for cinema number four.

"My mood is in the shitter today," I tell her as we head off in that direction. "I had to compensate with makeup and displays of cleavage. You, on the other hand, look cozy. Just so you know, I have every intention of snuggling on you throughout the movie."

She shrugs in acceptance. "Lay it on me. Heaven knows it's the only action I'll be getting for a while."

When we burst through the theatre door, Sandra Bullock is already on the big screen and the movie is in the heat of the action. Heads swing our way.

"No! We missed the beginning," Alana gripes, earning herself a round of *shhhh!*s from the few patrons seated in the theatre.

"It's only a few minutes in," I tell her, keeping my voice low.

She screws up her lips. "Feels like a ripoff watching a movie without the previews, though. I hate missing them."

"Fine," I say, yanking her back into the lobby. "Let's get our tickets exchanged for the later show. Then we can hang out at the Hot Sauce across the street and have some girl talk."

My friend grins. "I like that plan."

I slip my arm through hers and we cross the street to our favorite drinking spot. It's quieter than usual which is to be expected. It's Monday night, after all.

We easily find a pair of high-back stools at the bar. Aunt Jane greets us from behind the counter with a grin.

"Hey girls." She wipes the counter in front of us with a rag. "What are you doing out and about tonight?" She gets right to work making us our usual.

"Too quiet at home." I grin. "We were in need of a little trouble."

"Oh, you know I've got you covered," she assures us, making sure to pour our bourbon lemonades into fancy glasses.

I snatch the glass from her hand and knock back half of it in one gulp, smudging my lipstick and not giving a damn.

Alana's drink dribbles down her chin when she chugs from her own glass. She wipes her mouth with the back of her hand then smiles apologetically at our bartender. "That wasn't very classy, was it?"

Aunt Jane shifts her attention to the wasted group at the end of the bar doing shots and having a burping competition. Her eyes return to Alana. "Trust me, girl—you're classier than most. But not *that* classy."

We all chuckle.

I don't usually resort to middle of the week drinking but today, it's warranted. Alana and I drown our sorrows of the day in booze as we pass the time. Gradually, the chokehold of life begins to loosen as we whine and complain about boys and become one with the alcohol.

At fifteen minutes before showtime, my friend suddenly pops out of her seat. "We've gotta go. Or else we'll miss the beginning of the movie again."

Giggling drunkenly, we wave goodbye to my aunt then stumble across the street. We're sort of sloshed. Luckily, we get to the theatre without getting mowed down in the middle of the street.

"You're buying popcorn," Alana announces as we amble gingerly through the lobby.

"Fine." I grin at her. "But I'm drowning it in melted butter and cheddar powder and there's nothing you can do about it."

She scrunches up her nose. "That stuff tastes amazing but it goes straight to my thighs."

"Then off to your thighs it'll go," I say, nonchalant.

I'm rambling absently to Alana as we head for the concession stand. The lobby of the theatre is virtually empty. Tourist season hasn't started yet and you won't find the locals crowding up the TheatreBox for the late show on a regular Monday night.

But as we're approaching the snack counter, the couple placing their order catches our attention. Alana grabs my wrist to stop me from taking another step. But it's too late.

The tall, dark-haired man turns around, his arms full of popcorn, drinks and candy.

"Davis..." A crack runs right down the center of the word as it leaves Alana's lips.

His eyes widen. "Alana, hi." I see the stutter in his broad chest as his gaze flicks over his ex-wife.

Davis's date approaches, a goodnatured smile on her

face. "Hello..." The bottoms of her high heels are red and the girl boss power suit she's wearing definitely looks designer.

Shit. That's the same woman he was with at the Hot Sauce on my birthday.

"H-hi." I jump in when neither Davis nor Alana move. Or speak. Or blink. "I'm Meghan," I say. "And this is Alana."

The woman's eyes bounce between the formerly married couple. A light blinks on in her eyes. "Oh, Alana... I'm Candace. How nice to finally meet you. What movie are you girls seeing tonight? The Sandra Bullock one looks good, doesn't it?"

Her smile is wide. Her eyes glimmer amicably. This woman actually seems genuine.

But this is my best friend getting her heart re-broken here right before my eyes. I've got my bazooka on standby. Just in case.

Davis finally gets the ball out of his throat. "Uh, Candace and I are just—"

"I forgot my wallet," Alana blurts out. "In the wash-room. At the bar. Across the street."

Before anyone can respond, she barrels off in the direction of the exit, nearly tripping over her sneakers as she hurries out the theatre's wide glass doors.

Candace blinks quizzically.

I smile tightly. "Yeah, silly girl. Always forgetting her wallet in the washroom." I turn my attention to Davis's lady friend. "It was...it was nice meeting you, Candace."

"It was nice meeting you, too." The woman waves, confused as I hustle after my friend.

All my own problems are forgotten. Alana needs me. And at least if I'm keeping my friend from falling apart, that means I don't have time to worry about the way my own life feels like it's crumbling.

I wave goodbye and usher my bestie away from the scene of that train wreck. Davis watches on, his eyes trailing behind his ex-wife. The longing on his face is clear as day.

The second we burst out on the sidewalk, Alana collapses against a wall and grips her chest.

"You okay?" I lay a hand on her shoulder to ground her.

"I handled that like a loser." She buries her face in her hands.

"Al, It was your first time seeing your ex-husband with another woman. You handled it like a rockstar."

"I shouldn't have rushed out of there like that. I looked like a freak." She peels her hands from her face. "And she was so pretty. Why'd she have to be so pretty? Did you see how pretty she was? And why'd I have to be dressed like a college freshman on my way to the laundromat? Oh my god. I'm mortified."

I do my best to comfort her but she's a wreck, rambling her insecurities like she's lost her mind. I love my friend so much but all I keep thinking is, I don't want to end up like that.

What's the use in hoping for love?

Not only does it make me sad for Alana, my heart also breaks for all romance everywhere. Alana and Davis were insufferably in love when they were together. If those two couldn't find their way, there's zero hope for the rest of us.

Maybe I'm a coward but watching my friend try to keep herself from imploding only strengthens my resolve. I can't fall for Cash. Because I'm not willing to let our story end in heartbreak. Seeing the devastated look on Alana's face makes it that much clearer.

TWENTY-FOUR

MEGHAN

"YOU'RE GONNA BE OKAY, BUDDY." I snuggle the adorable baby French bulldog to my chest and stroke my fingers over his fur at the clinic the next day.

He's a little bit banged up from having wandered away from home a few days ago, but with a thorough exam from one of the veterinarians, a round of I.V. fluids and a few extra cuddles prescribed by yours truly, I'm confident that he's on the road to recovery.

His anxious-looking owners smile gratefully at me as I hand him off to them. The little family leaves the exam room and I finish up by making a few notes in his file that the puppy's doctor will review later in the day.

I love my job. Animals hold my heart. But sometimes, it's not enough to be a vet technician. I help with anesthesia, surgeries, and a bunch of other important things we handle in the clinic here. But my credentials don't allow me to actually prescribe meds, diagnose any conditions, or take the lead on a surgery that I've assisted on a hundred times.

What Alana gets to do everyday—working as a veterinarian—that's my dream job. But she's so good at it, and it took way more schooling than just becoming a vet tech, so I'm content with what I have.

But still, I can't help the feeling that I could do more. For the animals. For myself. Hell, even for my mom. If I'd had a better job, maybe I would have been able to help her long before her finances got to this point.

As I stroll out of the exam room with these thoughts heavy on my mind, I realize that I'm only trying to distract myself from what's really bothering me.

Despite my efforts not to, I slip my phone out of the pocket of my scrubs and peek at my screen.

Nothing new there.

Every time I check my phone, I hate myself a little bit. I should be stronger than this. But it hurts that Cash has already forgotten about me.

Walking into the break room, I find Alana there hunched over the table, stabbing at her salad.

I put on my usual cheerful act. "You going to eat that? Or just murder it with your fork?" I ask with a smile.

My girl looks up at me, pushing her food away. When I see her bottom lip tremble, concern washes over me.

"You okay?" I question her.

"Just not hungry. You want it?"

I pull a seat right next to her. "No, sweetie. You need to eat."

Alana shakes her head. "I'm just going to throw it away," she threatens, knowing I hate wasting food.

"Okay. Fine." I pull her uneaten salad toward me. "But you have to tell me what's wrong."

Her shoulders fall and she stares at a wall, likely not even really seeing the cute kitten poster her eyes are fixed on.

"Still bummed out about seeing Davis with that girl last night?" I ask when she doesn't open up willingly.

"No, that's just silly." She shakes her head vigorously but I'm not convinced. "It would be silly for me to be jealous over seeing Davis on a date." There's no confidence in her voice. She sounds like she's trying to convince herself.

But before I can bestow some brilliant advice that I haven't quite come up with yet, Alana changes the subject. "Has Cash called?"

I hesitate, wanting to get to the bottom of Alana's sadness, but also desperate to pull her out of her funk. Perhaps if I get her mind off of Davis, then she'll feel a little better. At least for a moment.

"No, he hasn't called."

Alana's eyes lock on mine. They fill with sympathy. She knows. Of course she knows. I'm putting on a brave face for the rest of the world but Alana knows the hurt and anxiety I'm concealing.

"Now, don't go rushing to any conclusions just because he hasn't called yet, Meghan." She leans forward in her seat and puts a hand on mine. "He spent way longer in Honey Hill than he'd planned to. I'm sure he went back to the office and found a pile-up of work on his desk."

"I know," I say.

But I *don't* know. I mean, how hard is it to pick up the phone and let me know he got back to the city safely? To check in? To see if I'm still duck-waddling after the way he fucked the shit out of me?

Dammit—why are men so hard to decipher?!

Alana speaks again. "If you really want to talk to him, you could be the one to pick up the phone," she tells me. "You could call him."

"No, I can't..." I whisper in response to those terrifying

words. Suddenly, I'm a three-year-old afraid that the Boogey Man will jump out and bite my toes.

"You can," Alana insists. "You are a strong, assertive woman of the twenty-first century. You can pick up the damn phone and call the guy you like. And don't you try to deny that you like him, Meghan."

I shake my head, sitting up straighter. "I know it seems silly. But you don't understand. Being left un-read by a guy I like, getting ghosted. It's practically a way of life for me out in the dating pool. And it's fine. I've gotten used to it. Except this time, we're talking about Cash—my one final hope for a shred of decency from the male species—and I'm terrified to discover that he's just like all the rest of them."

This is exactly why I fought so hard to keep things platonic between us. I didn't want to become this sad, simpering shell of a person over him. Yet, here I am. Sad and simpering.

"Cash isn't like those guys, Meghan." Alana seems mighty confident in her words. "He didn't drive all the way to Honey Hill, spend almost five days pampering you around the clock, give you the night of your dreams and then abandon you, never to be heard from again."

"I know what you're saying makes sense. It's just..." I slump further in my chair.

"Feelings, huh? Yeah, feelings are feelings. They don't always make sense." Alana smiles kindly. I know she gets it.

"The bastards," I chuckle softly.

My friend examines my expression. "You gonna be okay? Or do I have to jump on the next train to Chicago, show up at his office and kick some Cash Westbrook ass?" From the way she says it, I'm half-tempted to believe she's serious.

Seeing how defensive she is of me makes me sort of emotional. Maybe I'm not so alone after all.

Fighting back tears, I give a soggy, little, unconvincing laugh. "I don't think it'll come to that. But thank you."

"Of course, babe." She gets up and throws her arms around me.

"I'm so grateful to have you in my life." I sniffle against her white lab coat, trying to be careful since I've overloaded on makeup to conceal my heartbreak today again.

With a sigh, Alana squeezes me back. Tight. And I feel her appreciation for our friendship. "I'm grateful for you, too, girlie." We ease apart and she checks her watch. "Shit. I've got a patient coming in five."

She wipes her own tears from her eyes and heads for the exit while my butt remains glued to my seat. I'm so tied up in my thoughts.

I really wish I could deny how I feel. I wish I could say that I don't care what happens between Cash and me, either way. But I'm scared to death to find out what will happen next.

I have no clue what I'm doing.

"You coming?" Alana calls from outside one of the patient rooms, where I'm supposed to be setting up for her appointment.

"Yep," I mutter, tossing her uneaten salad back in the company fridge then heading off in her direction.

Work is about the only thing I understand at the moment. I *really* can't screw that up, too.

TWENTY-FIVE

CASH

I'M SITTING in my ergonomic office chair and I should be reading through this fifty page document that landed in my inbox half an hour ago.

Instead, I'm plucking cat hair off my suit jacket. These days, it feels like the more cat hair I pick off my clothes, the more cat hair pops up. It's insane.

Giving up, I shrug the jacket off before rolling it into a ball and flinging it in the direction of the couch.

I miss. Of course. Because *nothing* can go right these days.

The expensive custom-tailored garment falls to the floor. Across the room, I make eye contact with Braveheart. He crouches down and goes perfectly still, narrowed gaze focused on my jacket.

"Don't you dare..." I warn him from where I'm sitting.

The furry bastard ignores me. He promptly leaps off the arm of the couch and pounces on my thousand-dollar-plus article of clothing. His little claws frantically shred through the scrap of fabric like it's his life mission.

Sighing, I fall back in my chair with resignation. This is my life now.

The lights in the hall dim as the building's automated timer kicks in. I push my laptop forward, leaning back to loosen my tie and massage my temples.

Normally, this time of night is when I get my second wind at the office. Working late nights after all the staff have called it quits brings a special kind of peace.

Normally.

Today, all I feel is the tension bunching in my shoulders, the weight of a day of meetings and another couple hours on phone calls trying to untangle almost a week's worth of trouble. It's all bearing down on me.

Four paws and eighteen claws—I can thank Meghan for that fun fact—land in my lap as my troublemaking cat continues to treat my work office as his new playground. I've learned that I can't leave him at my condo alone for long hours. He hasn't been a fan of my busy schedule and lack of play time as I've tried to get work done. And he's paying me back by destroying my life.

Copy paper is strewn around my floor. Cat litter and water bowls are overturned. And the leather couch where I sometimes take my midday cat naps now has ripped claw marks streaked down one side.

I should be driving to the nearest shelter to abandon this evil devil. But honestly, I'm starting to like having him around.

Every time I look at him, I'm reminded of the days I spent with Meghan. How everything was so fun and easy. How I miss her sparkling laughs...her random hugs...her jokes, even though she botched the punchline half the time.

I miss her.

In ways I shouldn't.

I managed to let another business deal slip through my fingers today. Dad was *not* happy about that. The deadline for my billion-dollar goal is quickly approaching and I'm no closer to achieving it than I was before my hometown trip.

I've been struggling to drum up the passion I used to feel during these long days at the office. Over my career, I've made a reputation for being a workaholic—hell, it was even my hobby—but now, it all just feels empty.

I feel empty.

My eyes have darted over to the clock on my wall at least seven times in the past half hour, a clear sign that I'm not engaged. That I'm not productive. I pinch the bridge of my nose and shake my head. How many employees have I fired for less than this?

Pulling the devil cat off my shoulder, I set him on the ground. I lean forward and stare at the document open on my computer. I'm practically forcing myself to not think of Meghan. But every second, my mind wanders to the girl I left behind in Honey Hill. Wondering what she's doing. Wondering if she's even noticed my absence.

Being here now feels like fucking purgatory.

My phone chimes and I find a new email. That client of mine asking me to RSVP to his wife's damn fashion show. I pinch my nose again. I don't have time for this shit.

But the email presents me with the perfect excuse to contact Meghan. I relish the excuse to reach out to her. Fuck it. I need contact with her. Now.

I throw aside my decision to give her space and opt to text message her.

Me: Hey, remember that fashion show thing we talked about? You still interested in going?

She opens the message immediately. An anxious feeling shows up in my belly when the three bouncing dots pop up on the screen, indicating that she's typing a reply. But the little dots disappear abruptly. And my heart stops.

I wait for what feels like an eternity but Meghan's reply doesn't come through. I know she saw my text. Is she ignoring me? What the hell?!

Growing antsy, I pick up the phone again. At first, I consider a regular voice call. But if she has the nerve to ignore me, I'm going all in. I hit the video call button instead.

The phone rings for way too long. A thrill shoots through my bones when Meghan's sweet face appears on my screen and takes a moment to focus.

Holy shit! I'm not sure what she did with her hair or her makeup, but she looks so fucking hot. But also...crazy pissed.

"Hi," I say, holding the phone up so we can see each other. I'm blanketed in shadows here but I'm hoping she can see me well enough.

"Hey." Wary diamond-blue eyes stare back at me.

I realize that she's on her couch with a quilt bundled around her shoulders. There's a bunch of decorative pillows and peanut butter cup wrappers all around her.

Oh, boy.

"You're alive and well, I see..." Her tone is dry.

"Yes, I'm alive. Whether I'm well is up for debate." I sit up straighter, narrowing my eyes at her. "What's wrong?"

She huffs. The camera shifts but she doesn't say anything. I notice Captain Ginger stealthily crawling around atop the back of her couch, his eyes on the screen. Creepy ass cat.

"Meghan. What? Talk to me. What's wrong?"

Her fiery eyes narrow on mine. "I'm great. Perfectly great."

She's wearing that reserved look she gets whenever she's afraid to assert herself and state what she really wants.

That probably means we're going to beat around the bushes for the next half an hour until she finally feels safe enough to circle back to the real issue. Right now, it's making me unreasonably frustrated. Probably because I'm suppressing some wants of my own.

"So I'm getting Passive Aggressive Meghan today, huh?" I smile but it's tight at the corners.

"Quite frankly, you're lucky to be getting any version of Meghan at all."

"What does that mean?"

"Oh, nothing. I've just been sitting around for the past few days, waiting for signs of life from you while you were obviously out living your best life, not even sparing me a second thought."

"What are you talking about?" I question.

Exhausted from tearing up my office, Braveheart decides that now is a perfectly good time to plop down on my lap and curl up for a nap.

"You said you would call me and it's been days and I haven't heard from you. I just can't believe you couldn't even send me a text. I know your car has that voice-to-text bluetooth stuff and...and..." Trying to calm herself down, she sucks in a few heavy breaths. "I know you don't see what the big deal is. It probably *isn't* a big deal. We've never kept tabs on each other. It's just..."

Meghan is being completely hysterical right now. This might be normal behavior for some women but it's totally uncharacteristic for her. She's usually my zen place. But today, she's a hurricane of emotions breaking loose.

And because I know her so damn well, I recognize that it's not the logical side of her brain attacking me. It's her deepest fears steering the ship today. She's drowning in them.

As her best friend, it's my duty to drop the bullshit and tell her the truth. "I was trying to give you space, give things between us some time to settle down. I felt like I was smothering you when I was in town and I didn't want to come across as clingy."

"Clingy? Cash, you're my best friend. I always want to hear from you. And be close to you." Meghan stares back at me, not hiding her wrath, as an angry tear slips down her cheek. She wipes it away with her fist. "I...I'm sorry. I just don't think you understand how fiercely I care about you. And how much I want to protect our friendship at all costs. I didn't even realize the extent of it until now that we've screwed it up."

"We haven't screwed it up, Buttercup. Never. I'd never let that happen." I wish I was there to cup her cheek, to hold her.

"I was hoping things would go back to normal between us after we talked things out over breakfast at the diner. But apparently, I was wrong. Nothing's normal. Nothing's the same. Nothing will ever be the same. Our friendship is ruined, all because we lost control. For one single night."

I snap. "Meghan!"

The commanding tone of my voice catches her attention. Her mouth falls shut.

Silence.

I speak again. Softer this time. "Tell me what's *really* on your mind."

She roughly wipes a tear away with her fist. "First of all...I...I miss you."

"I miss you, too, Buttercup," I tell her without hesitating. When I say these words I've been burying for so long, my heart rattles my ribcage like a prisoner trying to break free of his jail cell. "And second of all?" I question.

"I don't like that I feel this way. I don't like that I feel needy. I don't like..." Cotton Ball is in her lap now, purring and demanding affection. Almost on autopilot, Meghan strokes the cat's white fur.

"You're not the only one who's out of sorts, Meghan. I can't concentrate for shit. All I do is think about you. I'm all fucked up over here."

"You are?"

I nod softly. "One hundred percent."

She breathes tremulously. "Look, I'm sorry for not being straightforward with you. It was immature of me. You're my friend and if I wanted to hear from you, I should have just picked up the phone and called you. But you know my history with men. It's always the same old story for me. I get involved with a guy, we start growing close and then he quickly loses interest in me. I thought that that's what was happening between us and I didn't want to experience rejection from you, the way I've been rejected by everybody else..." She swallows. "I feel super vulnerable right now. When you disappeared on me, it triggered something in me and I freaked out. I'm really sorry, Cash."

Fuck—I should have known. While I was here letting the time pass so I wouldn't come off as desperate for her, she was over there thinking I'd abandoned her, that I'd gone ghost on her like her dickwad exes.

Epic failure in communication.

I scrub a hand down my face. Good god. "I'm sorry I didn't call sooner, Megs. I had no idea that's what was going through your mind."

She lifts a shoulder and lets it fall helplessly. "Well, things have been shaky between us since..."

"Since we had sex," I complete her sentence.

Shit. I finally get it. I finally understand why she tried so hard to fight me on this. Why she didn't want us to cross the line. Why, as good as it felt, she was hellbent on her 'no'.

Things are weird between us now. Everything has changed, just like she warned they would. I'm so mad at myself.

"God—I never wanted you to have to see this side of me," she whispers.

"What side of you?"

"The insecure, desperate, unlikeable side of me."

"There is no side of you that I don't like, Meghan. I like every single part of you."

"Maybe you don't know me as well as you think you do."

"I do know you. I know that you get antsy feeling that the guys you care about don't care about you. I should have been more sensitive to that and called you immediately. But I was too busy battling my own insecurities."

"Your insecurities?"

"I was worrying that I was crossing the line. That I was coming on too strong. That I was being fucking clingy and making things weird between us. I wanted to give you some space. Act like I haven't been obsessing over you. Because I have."

Fuck my ego. Fuck everything.

The genie is out of the bottle, and that fucker's not going back in. Things have inevitably changed between us, whether we like it or not. No hope in returning to the past.

Now, the only question is where do we take things from here?

Suddenly, I'm done playing all games. "I want to be

with you, Meghan. In a relationship. I want you to be my girlfriend."

Her eyes fly wide open. She shivers. "You don't really mean that. That's just the stupid marriage pact talking. And—"

"No more excuses, Megs. This isn't because of the marriage pact. It never was. It's because you're always in my head."

"I am?" she questions, clearly shocked.

A smile tugs across my face as I read her sweet expression. "I can't stop thinking about the way you wear your ponytail and those adorable animal-print scrubs to work. Or the way you sacrifice yourself to pamper your hellish foster cats. Or the way you always get peanut butter and chocolate smeared to the corners of your lips."

She laughs softly and self-consciously blots the edges of her mouth with her knuckles.

"I know that you've been disappointed by a bunch of assholes who didn't value you and who never deserved a minute of your time. But I refuse to let you lump me in with all those losers who hurt your feelings. Because I have always been there for you, Meghan. As your friend." I suck in a strengthening breath. "And now, I want to be there for you as your man."

Her eyes widen. "C-Cash..."

I plow right ahead. "We can make this work. I know it. Despite the distance, despite my schedule, despite everything that you're afraid of. We deserve a shot. So that's why I *demand* a chance." I backpedal. "Well, maybe 'demand' isn't the most romantic choice of words bu—"

"Yes."

I blink at her. "What?"

"Yes, I want to give this a shot with you."

The hopeful ball of muscle in my chest is thumping too fast for it's own good. "You sure?" I frown. "So fast? I have a whole lot more flattery scripted out in my head to convince you."

She laughs. "You've won me over, Cash. I don't know how we're going to do this and I know I'll be scared the whole time but taking a chance beats being sad and broken without you." Her chest rises and lowers slowly. "I want to be with you, too."

I exhale and my throat trembles with relief. "God—I'm so damn happy right now, Buttercup. I don't know why I didn't do this sooner."

Her smile grows wider. "I'm just glad that you're mine now." Those pretty eyes go shy. "You are mine, right?"

"Abso-fucking-lutely." I grin. "Meghan, I'm not a man who plays games. If I tell you I want you in my life, it's because I do. If I tell you you're the most important person in my world, it's because you are."

"Don't make me swoon..." Her eyes flutter.

"I'm telling you the truth, baby. Do with it what you please," I say smugly.

Her girlish giggles make me feel strong and manly like a freaking gladiator.

She goes serious. "Full disclosure—I can be crazy inse-cure and a little bit psychotic sometimes. I need to make sure you know."

I nod resolutely. "Got it. I'm not intimidated by your crazy. And as for your insecurities, I'll do everything in my power to make them disappear."

Her lips purse together and her eyes water up. "I already feel like the luckiest girl in the world."

"That means I'm doing my job." I stroke the corner of

my mouth, trying to keep my grin from getting carried away. "So, the fashion show...Will you be my plus-one?"

Her smile can barely fit on my phone screen, it's so big. "Abso-fucking-lutely."

I'm so happy. Can't remember the last time I was floating this high. Definitely wasn't anything to do with a career achievement or hitting a financial goal. This girl. This girl is everything to me.

After a short comfortable pause, Meghan's brow quirks cheekily on my screen. "So..."

"Yes?" I question.

"I want to hear the rest of that flattery you had all scripted out in your head for me."

I laugh and the throaty sound causes the cat to startle and dart out of my lap. Too bad for him.

I train my attention on my new girlfriend. "Okay, Ms. Hutchins. Settle in. I'm gonna tell you all the things I like about you. We're gonna start from your head and work our way down to your toes. I hope you've got all night."

She sinks deeper into her couch cushions and pulls her quilt up higher. "Lucky for you, I do."

TWENTY-SIX

MEGHAN

I STRUT out of my ensuite bathroom and strike a dramatic catwalk pose. "What'd'ya think?"

"Meh. Not that one." Emma falls across my bed and wrinkles her nose.

Alana sits on the mattress next to Emma, examining my new pair of strappy, wedge heel sandals. "Sorry, girl. I'm not a fan, either." She tries the shoes on.

"Yeah. You look like a nun in that. Definitely not the vibe we're going for." Ziggy digs through the huge box of cheap, trendy clothing that was delivered to my front porch while I was still at work earlier today. She holds up each garment and inspects it in turn before flinging it onto the bed.

Shoulders slumped, I turn toward my full-body mirror and examine the navy blue high-neck dress. I'll admit it looked cuter on the website than it does in real life.

I eyeball my panel of fashion critics over my back. "What exactly is the vibe we're going for?" I ask.

Oh my god. I'm so overwhelmed.

"Ultimate, raw, savage sex goddess queen energy," Ziggy affirms.

"Well, that feels like a tall order." I cringe, not quite sure I can live up to that high bar. "Feel free to lower your standards a bit." I step back into the bathroom and start shimmying out of yet another dress that doesn't make the cut. "I just have to find something decent that's not covered in cat fur and then I'll be all good," I call through the open bathroom door.

I need a new outfit for the fashion show. That's definitely not up for debate. After getting together to hunt through my closet a few days ago, my friends and I failed to find something dazzling. So the girls ganged up on me and coaxed me into some serious online shopping shenanigans.

I'm not proud of it.

I don't hate shopping. In fact, I love it. And I have the jam-packed closet to prove it.

Christmas shopping. Shopping for my foster cats. Even grocery shopping is a thrill, especially if chocolate is on the list.

But all the added pressure to look good on Cash's arm at this fancy event has sucked all the joy out of the shopping experience.

Trying on outfit after outfit, just to reinforce the fact that I'm built like an Amazon woman in a world that's clearly designed for petite little forest fairies? It's left me feeling drained.

Plus, this massive clothing haul has set back my bank account by enough to make me question my sanity. Maybe I shouldn't have insisted on going to the fashion show after all.

Emma performs an eyeroll worthy of daytime soap opera role. "Meghan, you have finally hooked the man you've been pining away for for half your life. So as your girlfriends, we have a job to do. And we take that job seriously."

"What job is that exactly?" I dare to question, poking my head through the doorway.

"To make sure he's head over heels for you. To make sure he's captivated. Mesmerized by your beauty." My friend sure knows how to paint a dramatic picture. "To have that man looking at you with drool hanging from his mouth and a boner so big it'll be dragging on the floor."

Alana cringes and pats Emma on the shoulder. "Maybe not dragging on the floor. Too much lumber can be a little hard on a girl's internal organs."

"You guys are insane." Laughing, I turn away from the girls and tug on a pair of wide-legged black pants. "You should be permanently banned from giving advice to anyone." I strut back into the bedroom in my pants and bra. I do a half-spin and examine the pants in the mirror. *Hmm. A little loose at the waist but not bad overall.*

"We're just excited, babe." Ziggy smiles, her eyes genuinely alight. "We're just so happy to see you *finally* let poor Cash out of the friend zone. You two will be strutting to the altar and making us godmothers in no time."

Her words cause a stutter in my chest. "Guys, guys. Simmer down." I grip my middle to keep my agitated stomach from jumping out of my body. "This isn't a TLC reality show. Cash and I aren't going to just rush off and get married in the next ninety days."

"Why not? Wasn't that the plan? What about the marriage pact?" Emma questions naively.

I vigorously whip my head left to right. "No. We're going to date—like regular people. See where things go. I know we've been in each other's lives as friends for a long time but we still have a lot to figure out as a couple. Especially since we're long distance."

"Boo!" Emma flips onto her back and pouts up at the ceiling.

Alana seems to notice how tied up I am. "Sounds like a solid plan, Megs." She throws Emma and Ziggy a warning look. "No need to rush things. I know all too well that things don't always go according to plan when you let your emotions and your libido lead the way in relationships. Logic and common sense have to play a part, too. You can't just get caught up in your emotions."

"True, but it's also important to envision the highest possible outcome," Ziggy counters, giving Alana a challenging stare of her own. Then she grins at me. "In the meantime, try this." She holds up a citrus-colored blouse with a wrap-tie at the waist. "Maybe with the right jewelry and shoes?"

"No. You need a dress. Trust me," Emma argues. She tosses a colorful, curve-hugging bandeau dress at me.

"Ooh, I like that." Ziggy reconsiders. "Try it on."

Not bothering to return to the bathroom, I chuck off my pants, step into this new dress and pull the slinky fabric up my round hips. Holding my boobs so they don't pop out, I skillfully remove my bra and check myself out in the mirror.

Wow! Really revealing. I wonder if I can pull this off.

Emma and Ziggy start cooing and hollering their approval. I eyeball Alana for the final opinion. She's usually the voice of reason, balancing out our two eccentric friends.

She studies me and nods affirmatively. "Definitely a yes."

Ziggy sways her arms and shoulders in a wave motion, doing a silly dance. "Let all that divine feminine chi flow.

Let the chi flow, girl. Let it flow. Drown that man in the chi."

Alana snorts a laugh. "Okay, weirdo. Aren't you leading a moon gazing session starting in..." she checks my alarm clock on my bedside table. "...twenty minutes?"

Ziggy glances at her phone. "Oh, crap. I'm late." She sighs heavily as she gathers up her satchel and cardigan. "Y'know, I can't wait to transcend the construct of time in this three-dimensional reality."

Emma and Alana share a look.

"Bye, babe." Ziggy blows me a kiss and sweeps out my bedroom door.

Emma is hot on her heels. "I'm coming with you. Remember that hot, barefoot guy with all that chest hair who was there last time? Think he'll be there tonight?" she asks as they hurry down the stairs. "I don't want to go home yet and face my crazy roommate and all her drama."

Alana focuses her attention on me when we're alone. "So, it's really exciting, you and Cash." She smiles, perched on the edge of my bed. "I'm so happy for you, Megs. You truly deserve a good man like him."

"Thank you, girl."

My focus travels to the mirror and I observe the way the deep orange fabric of the dress clings to my breasts and cradles my hips. *Gosh, it really is sexy.*

"I'm so freaking nervous," I admit. "Of course I'm excited to be in a relationship with this incredible man. But there's all this added pressure because of our history. And the marriage pact. And that night of hot sex we had that I want more of."

Alana hops off the bed and comes across the room to brace her hands on my shoulders. "Forget about all that, Meggie. Take the pressure off. Have fun with him, just like you did when he was here for your birthday. Because isn't that what a relationship is about? Finding a person you can be your true authentic self with?"

"Right..." I wonder whether or not she'd had that with Davis. But I decide not to question my friend on her relationship with her ex.

"He's a fine, attentive, considerate man who clearly has the hots for you. Forget about the 'what if's. Enjoy him. You deserve it."

I laugh. *Okay, yeah. When she puts it like that...*

"And do it in *that* dress, because Emma and Ziggy are right. I'd totally take you home in that." Alana shoots me a wink before tossing me the sexy pair of sandals. "Okay. I've got to get out of here. I'm starving and there's a bowl of leftover zucchini noodles in my fridge calling out my name." She laughs as she heads for the door. "I'll see myself out."

"Bye, girl. See you at work tomorrow," I call after her.

"See you tomorrow."

Left standing alone in my room, I leave the dress on a little while longer. I like the way I feel in it. I feel like a new version of Meghan. The Meghan who has a hot boyfriend who makes her feel sexy and special and desired.

"I think I like this dress," I whisper to myself. *Y'know what? I freaking love it.*

I experiment with piling my hair up on top of my head. Then, I allow it to come cascading around my shoulders in pale curls. Then I gather it into a low knot.

I feel beautiful, comfortable in my skin. I'm totally a fan of this feeling.

My phone starts ringing and I hustle over to my dresser to dig it out of the bottom of my purse.

My new boyfriend's name flashes across the screen.

TWENTY-SEVEN

MEGHAN

I'M GRINNING like a grasshopper when I see the name on my phone. Okay—that's not the prettiest visual but it makes the point.

I eagerly hit the green button. When the call connects, I see Cash walking down a familiar hallway, eyes glassy and hair messed up from a long day.

He gives me a tired but happy smile. "Hey beautiful." He pushes open his front door and steps into the expansive modern foyer of his condo. I hear two quick thuds and I imagine him kicking off his shoes.

"Hey handsome. You look tired."

"I am. But I needed to hear your voice before I crash."

Butterflies flutter to life in my belly when he says that. He called me at this same time yesterday. And the day before that. And the day before that, too, as soon as he got home from the office.

Alongside the all day back and forth text messages we exchange, I feel that the nightly calls are becoming a part of our little routine. I like his consistency. I like feeling that I can depend on him. I like to feel that he's making himself available to me.

It's no secret that Cash Westbrook values his time. If he's consistently carving out space for me, it must mean that he values me, too.

"So what are you up to tonight?" He sets down Braveheart's carrier on the kitchen floor and opens the tiny door, allowing the energetic kitten to scamper free.

"Just trying on dresses for the fashion show." I grin, feeling a little silly. "I know it's not for another two weeks. I know. But I'm excited. I want to be ready."

While we speak, he fills the kitten's bowls with food and water.

He's such a good cat dad. It's a turn-on.

"I'm still trying to get half as excited about this thing as you are. The only good part is that you'll be there with me." He scrubs his fingers through his hair and chuckles low.

Gosh, he's so sweet to me. I miss him so much. "I'll make it worth your while," I promise.

He watches me purposefully. "Every time you're near me it's worth my while."

I grab the edge of my dresser for balance. *Swoon.*

His lips curve upward in the sexiest way humanly possible. "Okay now, let me see the dress." He tilts his chin, motioning toward my outfit.

"You wanna see it?"

"Of course. I want my own private fashion show."

"All right. Here goes." Rising to my feet, I hold the phone in front of me then lift my arm and angle the screen down slightly, trying to give him an eagle's-eye view of my outfit. I slowly test out different angles with the camera.

His eyebrows jump up his forehead and his chest expands on a sharp intake of breath. "Wow."

"You like?" I ask, getting a rush off the way he's looking at me.

"Do a twirl or something. Give me the panoramic experience."

I roll my eyes. But despite myself, I prop my phone against the alarm clock on my dresser and spin around anyway. Then I playfully strike a few poses for good measure. I'd probably look corny to a third party observer, but Cash watches me like he's mesmerized.

"I love it. Your body looks incredible. My bangin' Buttercup."

"Thank you." I blush.

His voice grows raspier. "Seriously, Megs. You look so good. Christ, I wish you were here right now."

I feel a pang of longing in my chest. I really, *really* miss him.

Instead of letting my sadness take over, I decide to take a playful approach. "Oh, yeah? What would you do if I were there with you?"

He doesn't hesitate. "I'd be all over you. I wouldn't be able to get enough. You'd have to beat me off you with a stick."

"Is that so?" My body starts to come awake. I know where this conversation is going.

Cash expertly unknots his tie with one hand as he speaks. "Baby, I'd fuck you all over every inch of this apartment." When the tie disappears, I imagine him dropping it to the floor.

I hardly recognize my own voice when I whisper. "Be more specific..."

His eyes bore into me. His lust is palpable even through the screen. He flips the camera around giving me a view of his open concept kitchen. The camera focuses in on a slab of thick, grey marble. "You see that counter right there?"

"Yes," I reply huskily, my heart beating rapidly at the dangerous lilt in his voice.

"I'd sit you on that counter, spread your legs wide and I'd eat your pussy until your knees would start shaking."

A warm blush prickles my cheeks and I steal a razor-sharp breath into my lungs.

The camera pans to another corner of the spacious bachelor pad. He focuses on a plush leather recliner facing a massive window with a front row view of the Chicago skyline. "Over there? You'd get on your knees and take my cock in your sweet, sexy mouth."

I visualize myself doing just that. Heat races up the insides of my thighs. "Oh, god."

The screen jumps rhythmically as he travels down a long, shadowy hallway flanked by expensive-looking art on the pale grey walls. He pushes open a door to reveal a large room with dark, wooden furniture. He zeroes in on a massive bed with plush, ruffled sheets. "In here? This is where you'd sit on my face—"

"You already did...*that.*" My blush grows hotter.

There's a growl to his voice. "I'd do it again."

Standing in the middle of my bedroom, I listen to his story, hypnotized. I'm getting wet. I can feel it.

"Then I'd make you ride my dick so I could see your beautiful breasts bouncing as you come."

I hiss out a breath.

"After that, I'd lay you on your stomach with your ass in the air and I'd fuck you as deep as your pussy would take me, baby. I'd make you scream. People on the other side of the Chicago River would hear you screaming my name."

"Oh, my god, Cash." I gasp, lust pumping through me like an I.V. drip. "I want you right now."

His bedroom door slams shut, presumably to keep the cat outside. The phone camera flips back to his face. He wears a dark, ravenous expression as he lowers onto his mattress. "Take that fucking dress off, baby. I want to see you."

I feel a tremor move up my chest. I've never shared myself with a man this way, especially not over a video call. But this is Cash. I trust him.

He senses my hesitation. "Shit, Meghan. Am I moving too fast?" He watches me apologetically. "We don't have to do this if you don't want to."

"I want to," I hear myself say. "I want you to see me."

"Are you sure?" He watches me with concerned eyes.

"I am."

"Okay...but we can stop at any point, if ever you change your mind."

"I have no intention of changing my mind, Cash. Now, hush. Let me put on a show for you." We're on the runaway train now. The only destination I have in mind is a toe-curling orgasm.

Anticipation shoots through me as I watch him get comfortable in his bed, his back leaned against his imposing dark wood headboard.

With trembling hands, I return my phone to its makeshift perch on my nightstand. I step back, slowly peeling the stretchy fabric of the dress down my torso. My breasts bounce free.

I'm standing there under the bright overhead lights, with my dress bundled up around my waist, ready to follow his every command. I must look ridiculous but it barely registers. All I care about is my pleasure and his.

"Good god." Cash's eyes devour me as he sets down his own phone somewhere on his bed and begins undoing the buttons of his shirt, exposing his muscular chest.

My stomach lights up with excitement. I imagine myself crawling across that vast landscape of warm flesh and muscles to straddle him. I imagine his hands on my hips, guiding me up and down his erection. I barely swallow back a moan.

"Grab your tits, baby," he rasps. "Give them a squeeze."

Forgetting to feel self-conscious, I hoist my breasts into my palms like he asked me to, gliding my thumbs over my sensitive nipples.

At the burst of pleasure, I hiss, squeezing my thighs together. "Cash..."

My orgasm will be explosive. I can already feel that.

"The dress," he responds urgently, almost impatiently. "Get rid of it. I'm dying to see your pussy."

Wriggling my hips, I pull my dress down the rest of the way and kick it from around my ankles. Then I do the same with my panties.

"I'd bet you're dripping," he says hoarsely. "Lay back on your bed and open your legs. Let me see."

Grabbing my phone, I mount my bed and lean the device against my footboard. I'm shameless, spreading my legs to give him a full view. I want him to see everything as I touch myself intimately and writhe in my bed, his name on my lips.

Nothing about this feels weird or uncomfortable. It feels natural sharing myself with him this way. I would have expected this moment to feel awkward seeing that there's always been an invisible line in the sand between us. Now, the line in the sand is gone. Even with over five hundred miles between us, I feel closer to him than I've ever felt to anyone else.

His hand smooths down his bare chest before disappearing off screen. The sound of his zipper sliding down comes through the air.

I watch his arm move back and forth in a jerky motion. I know he's touching himself and it's sensual as fuck, but I need a visual to work with.

"No fair," I whine as I work my fingers between my legs. "I want to see what you're doing."

"Here." He readjusts his phone and his gorgeous cock comes into view. Long, rigid and curved slightly to one side. At the sight of his fist slowly moving up and down the shaft, my pulse gallops inside my pussy.

I want it in my mouth. I decide here and now that the next time I see this man, I'm not letting him out of my sight until I've sucked him the fuck off.

Cash jerks himself aggressively as he watches my fingers sliding back and forth over my pussy lips. Every time I close my eyes, I can almost feel his hand over mine, guiding my movements as I touch myself.

His eyes are wide open. His expression is focused to the point of scowling. His stare is so intense on me. I almost expect his laser-gaze to crack the screen and for him to jump right through the phone, straight into my bedroom.

"What are you thinking right now?" I ask him.

He licks his lips. "I'm thinking that you're the most beautiful woman I've ever seen. I'm thinking that the next time I get my hands on you, I might never let you go."

I don't know what it is about his words—maybe it's the realness in his tone or maybe it's the idea of being held captive by him indefinitely, but suddenly, the pleasure is cresting inside of me.

"Oh, gosh. Cash. It's happening..."

"Shit, are you coming, baby? Don't stop touching your-self. Keep going." His own movements grow jerkier and his eyes grow more savage.

I don't stop until I'm at the pinnacle of a wave so tall I know it's going to crush me. I have no choice but to submit to the pleasure.

Frantic breaths escape me as I orgasm hard. Half a second later, Cash is right there, too. He grunts hard and fast. The camera shakes as he strokes his thick, long shaft vigorously. His facial features tighten, twisting his expression in a savagely handsome way.

Then his whole body goes still. The sound he makes as he orgasms sends a delicious reverberation down my spine. I feel high, buzzed, so intoxicated by this man.

Through the screen, I witness his explosive eruption and the ropes of ejaculate that shoot across his tight stomach.

"Oh my gosh," I hear myself whimper, still panting from my own climax.

After a second, his head lifts off his pillow and his eyes meet mine through the screen. "You okay, Megs?"

"I'm...I'm amazing." I smile at him.

I watch his movements through a heavy post-climax fog.

"Oh, Cash," I whisper as I watch him fall limp against his pillow.

He's grinning, chest heaving and sweat on his brow. "That was so fucking hot, Buttercup."

I grin, too. "Did we really just do that...? Or was it a dream...? It felt like a dream..."

He lifts his head from the pillow again and props himself on an elbow. "I may have fantasized about that a time or two..."

"What?" I giggle. "Seriously?"

He nods. "I've been having dirty thoughts about you for longer than I care to admit."

I shake my head. "And there I was thinking we were just friends."

"We were never *just* anything, Meghan. You were always everything to me." He smiles happily. "And now, you're mine."

"I'm yours..." I whimper, wishing I were locked up inside his strong arms.

Cash's neck swings left to right before he says, "I made a bit of a mess here. Let me go clean up."

"I'll go clean up, too." I force my noodly limbs to lift me out of bed.

"Meet me back here in five?" he asks.

"Yeah," I promise.

I scoop my new dress off the floor and toss it onto the dresser. Then I rush into the bathroom, clean up between my thighs, brush my teeth and wash my face before hopping into some sleep shorts and a matching camisole. When I get back in bed, Cash's face is already on my screen, waiting for me.

"There you are," he says softly with a tender expression that's just for me.

I pull back my sheets and climb between them. "Hi."

He's comfortably sprawled off in his bed. His eyes blink a few times before they close. "Fuck, I'm so tired," he mutters.

I roll onto my side and stare at his profile. He's so damn handsome. "Cash?"

"Yes, baby..."

"I'm so glad we did this."

He smiles wickedly, his eyes still closed. "The phone sex? Yeah, the phone sex was great."

I belt out a laugh. "Not just the phone sex, silly...Us. I'm glad we decided to be together." My pulse triples when I say that.

His eyes open again and he looks right at me. "I'm glad we did, too. And I promise you, it's only going to get better from here."

My heart squeezes.

His eyes close once more and I prop my phone up against the alarm clock on my dresser. I watch him sleep for a moment, but it isn't long before I drift off as well.

TWENTY-EIGHT

MEGHAN

"WE'RE REALLY BECOMING pros at this phone sex thing..." I whisper, scooping up a handful of bubbles and pouring them over my skin. A few days later, I'm basking in the afterglow of yet another explosive solo orgasm while Cash watches on.

His eyebrow hikes. "Need I remind you that you're the only one who got off? I'm just sitting here, hard as a rock, an innocent bystander while you have all the fun."

I laugh throatily. "It was fun for you, too and you know it. You love when I put on a show for you."

"I do love it," he confesses readily. "It does something to me, seeing you naked and wet and coming all over your hand."

Cash called me tonight just as I was drawing a bath. No surprise, it turned into some long-distance sexy times.

It's a regular Thursday night. He's on his office couch right now, his long legs stretched out in front of him. He has wireless headphones in and he's seated with his back to a wall to ensure that no-one can sneak up on him.

We stare at each other and the playfulness drops from his face. "Seriously, though. I fucking miss you so much."

My heart turns to mush. I swallow. "I miss you, too." I laugh softly. "I don't know how I'll make it the next few days without touching you."

"God. Tell me about it," he gripes.

A message pops up on my screen, notifying me that Cash's battery is low and our call might cut off soon. That causes a fresh wave of disappointment to sweep through me. As if it wasn't bad enough that I can't be near him now our call is about to end, too.

"Being this far away from you has been torture." A rueful half-smile crawls across my face. "I wish you'd just show up at my door right this minute."

"You do?" One corner of his mouth curves upwards, too. I nod. "I do."

He fights back his growing smile, his eyes intently peeled to me as I trail my fingers through the bubbles.

My half-closed eyes feel heavy as I lazily sink deeper into the warm bath. "Come back to Honey Hill," I challenge lazily, halfway asleep.

"Give me a reason," he tosses right back. "And I'll be on the road tonight." He starts haphazardly stacking up the papers spread out around him.

He can't be serious, can he?

I'm not sure. But the idea of him dropping what he's doing and driving all night just to come see me has me getting hot in all the right ways. That's the stuff that fantasies are made of. A girl can dream, right?

"Me," I answer, half kidding, half serious-as-a-heart-attack. "Come back to Honey Hill and fuck me."

He's wearing an expression that says he means business. "Fine," he blurts, leaping up from his chair. Braveheart yowls as he tumbles to the floor but manages to land on his feet.

I give a tight laugh. "Cash, I'm only joking."

He slams the lid to his laptop before looking straight into his phone camera. "Making you happy is never a joke to me, Buttercup."

I sit up, my naked boobs popping above the soapy water. "Wh-what?" I stutter, my jaw slack. "Cash, I was joking."

Cash's eyes dart to my bare chest. His expression roars with lust. "And I'm not. Get ready, Meghan. I'm on my way."

Right then, his battery dies and the video call disconnects. I'm still sitting there with my breasts out and my jaw in my lap. He's not *really* on his way here, is he? He's not really going to drive all this way for my benefit.

He wouldn't come all the way to Honey Hill just to fuck me. A six-hour drive for a booty call seems a bit much. Even for Cash, no?

Fizzing anxiety threatens to overflow from my belly. I mean, the last guy I was interested in thought it was too much to get me a gift certificate to the MovieBox for my birthday. That jerk wouldn't even answer my text messages half the time. And now I have this man who is putting his nearly one billion dollar company on hold to come spend time with me.

This is whiplash of the emotional variety.

Oh my gosh, Meghan. You can't just sit around in shock all night. Get moving.

I start with an emergency grooming session with my razor. On top of getting my legs and armpits cleaned up, I need to make sure my lady bits are ready for some up-close-and-personal action, looking cute and smelling delicious.

While the tub drains, I hurriedly dry off, moisturize from head to toe and change into my cutest sleep set.

I grab an army of cleaning products from beneath the sink and get to work scrubbing and shining every surface. Cotton Ball and Captain Ginger look at me like I've lost my mind when I break out the vacuum cleaner at two o'clock in the morning.

It's nearly four a.m. when I head into the kitchen and whip up something to serve my guest. I don't know if it's nerves or if I'm just trying to be a good hostess. Maybe it's a combination of the two. But the adrenaline is still pumping furiously through me.

I've just finished brewing my third espresso when my doorbell rings. I nearly choke on my coffee. I peek out the front curtains and find Cash standing on my porch. My stomach drops to my toes.

He's actually here. He is *actually* here.

I rear back unseen, setting my coffee on the nearest surface and finding my reflection in the small decorative mirror near the entrance.

Holy hell, I look like I spent the night riding a dive bar mechanical bull. My hair is a wreck and my skin wears a splotchy, unflattering blush. And what's that powdery, blue cleaning product on my cheek? I should have squeezed in a few minutes to paste on some makeup between cleaning my house and cooking up a feast. I frantically tug at my frizzy hair before the doorbell rings again.

Cash seems to be running low on patience this morning.

With one last shaky breath, I swing open the front door. My mouth waters at the sight of him.

My man.

Cash is smoldering in his rumpled suit, the same suit he was wearing last night on the video call. Wow, he's a man of his word. A man of integrity. He was quite literally on his way to me the moment our call ended.

The look in his eyes as he stares back at me makes my knees weak.

Making you happy is never a joke to me, Buttercup. I nearly whimper at the memory of his words.

His overnight bag hits the floor. So does Braveheart's carrier.

Suddenly, the magnetic pull between us breaks me. I'm stepping toward him at the same time that he rushes toward me. I can't even tell you who makes the first move, but his lips are on mine, and mine are on his.

Strong hands shoot into my hair, gripping both sides of my head. I grab his shirt by the collar and tug him as close as he can get. There's no sweet, slow exploration here.

Just hunger. Desperation. Starvation.

"Oh my god, I can't believe you came." I rasp, my lips against his.

He growls wickedly. "Of course I came. And now, you're about to come."

Somewhere in the living room, I push him against a wall and drop to my knees. "No, baby. This time, you get yours first."

"Meghan..." he groans, his fingers sinking into my hair.

I free his erection from his pants and cradle it in my hands, making sure to press slow, sweet kisses up and down the shaft.

Then I wrap my lips around the crown and start to stroke him with my mouth. I run my tongue along the underside while grabbing his muscular ass and powerful thighs. He starts moving on instinct, thrusting.

At first it's a slow, steady rhythm of his hips but when I

cup his balls and tickle my fingernails over the sensitive sack of nerves, he begins to lose his mind a little bit.

"Keep doing that," he orders me, his fingernails practically ripping my wallpaper from the wall. "Do it, baby."

He bunches my hair in his fist and takes his strokes deeper down my throat. I don't relent until his perfect, sculpted body goes rigid and the thick, sweet tang of his cum is pooling on my tongue. I swallow it all.

Wiping the back of my mouth, I rise to my feet. Victory blazes through my veins watching the satisfaction on his face as he recovers from his climax.

Cash leans down and kisses me hard and deep. "You're so incredible, Meghan. I've never met anyone like you."

He scoops me off my feet and before I can yelp in surprise, his mouth covers mine. With my body in his arms, he moves skillfully through the house, maneuvering through the living room and up the stairs with his lips on my neck, shoulders and chest.

When we get to my bedroom, he doesn't waste a second. He tears me out of my clothes as I virtually rip his suit from his body.

We collapse onto the bed and our bodies join. The rising sun peeks through my bedroom curtains as we fuck, our intense emotions welling up in the air around us. Everything feels so beautiful, so raw, so pure.

This is so much more than sex. This is two souls merging. I couldn't keep my heart from this man if I tried.

"You're so good to me, Cash. Almost too good," I say hours later as we bask in the afterglow of too many orgasms to count.

"Nonsense. You deserve the world." He brushes hair from my eyes. "I haven't even started giving you all the things I have in store for you."

I still can't believe he's here. I shouldn't be surprised that he's showed up for me. I know Cash. If he says he'll be here, he'll be here. Now, how to train my brain to rely on that?

"Oh, Cash..." I stroke his prickly cheek. I can't find the words to vocalize my fears.

"What is it, baby?" He stares down into my face and he can see the turmoil there. He sees everything.

"I just can't help the feeling that this is all going to go away," I whisper quietly. "What if you get sick of me?"

"Never." Cash rolls me onto my back. He hovers above me, looking down at me with nothing but sheer reverence in his grey eyes. "I don't know if it's too soon to say this. But I'm gonna say it anyway because it's burning a fucking hole in my chest...I love you, Meghan Hutchins. I am *so* deeply in love with you."

My heart stutters. I pause for a second, half-expecting him to take it back, to say he was joking or that he only means it as friends.

But he doesn't retract his statement. Instead, he looks at me with patient adoration like I'm a great treasure.

Oh my god. He means it.

I stroke his cheek again, my fingers trembling this time. "I...I love you, too, Cash Westbrook. You have no idea how much I love you."

Smiling, he brushes his lips over mine. "This trip was so fucking worth it. I'd drive to the edge of the earth and back again just to hear you say those words."

TWENTY-NINE

CASH

I WAKE SLOWLY, gradually becoming aware that my sweaty body is at least two hundred degrees hot. It's dark out with only the faint shadows of a streetlamp beaming into the room. There's still no trace of the early morning sun in sight.

Meghan is curled up against my body. She's sound asleep—and innocently drooling on my chest.

Suppressing a chuckle, I thread my fingers through her messy hair, relishing in her beauty. The woman has completely and absolutely bewitched me, yet she makes it look so simple, so effortless.

I continue to admire her. The moment is perfect and serene...right up until my fingers catch on a knot in her tangled after-sex hair.

"Umph..." She winces and cracks one eyelid open.

I grin sheepishly at her. "Sorry," I whisper, rubbing her scalp soothingly. "I promise I didn't mean to wake you."

She laughs softly, lifting her head off my chest to look at me. "It's okay. As far as wake up calls go, it's really not so bad, getting your hair pulled by a guy you like."

I chuckle and squeeze her tightly, dropping kisses on the top of her head.

We remain in bed, neither of us in any hurry to leave this space as we talk and tease each other. She's wearing my shirt half-buttoned over her sexy frame. The shirt is three sizes too big and swallows her whole. Somehow that makes her look irresistible. My fingers naturally hone in on the soft, smooth skin under the fabric.

"I could stay like this forever," I mutter into her hair.

She rolls away just enough to catch my stare. "Are you sure it's even okay for you to be here?" She asks me tentatively.

"As long as I make it home before my curfew." I pinch the tip of her nose. "Of course it's okay for me to be here."

Laughing, she bats my hand away. "I just mean, I'm sure you're still catching up on the work that piled up when you were in Honey Hill for my birthday, and you're already back here again. I know you have big goals, Cash. And deadlines. I don't want this relationship to be a distraction."

I'm not sure how to explain it, but those 'big goals' of mine suddenly don't feel so important anymore. Yes, I do want to get Westbrook Wealth Management to a billion dollars—and I will—but the burning hot need to get it done on my self-imposed schedule just isn't there anymore.

"Don't worry about my goals and my deadlines. And being with you is definitely not a distraction."

She twists her lips to the side. "Please don't downplay your dreams, Cash. I know that it's important to you. How can I help? How can I support you?"

I didn't know it was possible for me to fall for her any deeper. But hearing those words out of her mouth, automatically, I do. "Just keep being your sweet, gorgeous self.

You're my inspiration. You motivate me." I angle her mouth to mine for a kiss.

After I showed up here in the wee hours yesterday morning, Meghan and I made love until neither of our bodies could take any more. Sometime in the late afternoon, we stumbled across the street to my house where Jasper was hosting another one of his hangouts. It goes without saying that my boys were shocked to see me back in town so soon. But can they blame me? Now that Meghan's mine, I don't ever want to leave her side.

She and I stayed and had a few beers with the guys in my backyard. But it wasn't long before I was ready to take her back to her bed.

Socializing is overrated. Who needs a whole circle of friends? I have everything I need wrapped up in one person. My best friend, my lover, my biggest cheerleader.

Meghan is my soulmate. There's no doubt about it.

Propped up on her elbow, she frowns at my chin.

"What is it?" I ask.

With precise, deliberate movements, she reaches down and pinches a hair out of my beard. "Oh, thank god. It's cat hair." She laughs softly. "For a second there, I thought it was my hair. I thought I was going grey. I've been bracing myself. Ever since I turned thirty, I've been expecting the grey hairs to start popping up all over my head."

I tsk. "Don't even worry about it. You'll be a wicked sexy old lady. You'll still be my bangin' Buttercup."

She gasps, slapping at me playfully. "Please don't say that. Need I remind you that you're turning thirty soon, too?"

I lift a shoulder aloofly. "We'll be old and sexy together. Sounds perfectly all right to me." I'm not even joking. I want to grow old with Meghan by my side. "Besides, I love that you're older than me," I rasp in her ear, enjoying the tremble that zips through her.

"Three months is hardly older," she harrumphs.

Laughing at her feeble protests, I grab both her wrists and flip us over so I'm hovering over her half naked body.

Her utter indignation leaves me chuckling as she squirms beneath me. I'm a fan of the squirming. Whether she realizes it or not, she's rubbing her warm little body all over my stiff morning wood.

"Admit it, Buttercup. You *like* younger guys." I drop my face to her neck, nipping at the skin there.

She adopts a haughty tone. "Yes, I must confess, I do love younger men. You're clearly too old for me. Harry, though..."

"What?" I scoff.

She shrugs. "Or even Jasper would do in a pinch..."

Fuck that.

"I can say with great certainty that neither Harry nor Jasper could ever make you moan like I do. No other man could make you feel good the way I do." I'm getting defensive. Territorial as fuck.

"I'm only kidding around, babe." Meghan's arms come around my neck and I lower myself until our wanting bodies are pressed flush together. "You know I only like *you*. I love you."

When I look deep into her eyes, I feel like I'm dropping off a cliff. "I love y–"

A ringing phone interrupts my words.

"It's mine," I mutter.

By the time I reach it on Meghan's nightstand, I've missed the call. But then it starts ringing again. It's Mason, my cousin.

"What?" I answer.

"Wow, you're cheery in the morning," Mason deadpans.

"Well, your timing is shit. What is it?" I sit on the edge of the bed in my boxers while Meghan gently rakes her fingernails up and down my back. All I can think about is getting Mason off the phone and climbing back under these sheets.

"Sorry, man. I know you're probably trying to get hot and heavy with Meghan as we speak. But can you cover my shift this morning at the bakery? Someone scheduled an emergency appointment with me at the clinic. I have to get there in a hurry. Grammy says she can handle things on her own but...I, uh, don't feel comfortable having her open up by herself."

I yawn, scraping a palm down my face. Shit. I'd agree with him on that. There's just too much around the bakery for Grammy to manage it on her own. She's not quite as spry as she used to be. Although she'd likely murder anyone who has the balls to say so.

Mason's sisters cover the bakery in the afternoons. We've all tried convincing Grammy to hire some extra help for the mornings, but the woman insists on not letting any outsiders around her coveted recipes. She's so damn stubborn. Us, boys absolutely got our stubborn streak from her.

Anyway, the guys all take turns helping her. Considering that I live out of town, I'm not exactly worked into the shift schedule. So I guess it's only fair that I play backup when I'm in town. As a last resort.

I already know Davis's working today, and Harry's out of town with his football team. "What about Jasper?" I ask.

Mason grunts. "His ass is hung over."

"Of course he is." He overdid the partying last night, as per usual. Now, he's useless this morning.

Dammit.

Mournfully, I let my gaze fall on Meghan, mentally taking pictures of her half nude state. I'll need those images to get me through my shift at the bakery.

"Okay, I'll be there in ten," I grumpily concede.

Mason sounds relieved. "Thanks, sourpuss. I owe ya one."

I cut him zero slack. "You fucking do."

I hang up and lean back, twisting around and giving my girlfriend a hot, wet kiss before forcing myself out of bed.

"You gotta go?" She's trying to suppress her disappointment.

"Yeah, sorry. I've gotta help Grammy at the shop."

I feel Meghan's eyes on me as I rustle through our passionate mess from last night and finally find my pants on the floor tangled up in her lacy blue bra.

I really fucking like that bra.

"Grammy can't run everything by herself, so we all pitch in. I need to cover for Mason, but I should be back in a few hours if things are slow." I fasten my pants and pivot, greedily eyeing my girl who's now climbing out of bed.

She stands on the other side of the bed and slowly unbuttons my dress shirt. "I don't start work until ten-thirty today. I could come with you? Keep you company."

I cross her bedroom in two easy strides, reaching down to help her make quick work of the buttons. "You don't have to do that. Stay in bed. Enjoy your morning off." *Be here waiting for me when I get back,* I want to add.

"But I want to," she says quietly, stroking her lips across my chest. "I...just want to be close to you."

I can't help but smile broadly at her sudden shyness. I move quickly, slipping my shirt off her shoulders and loving the emotion I see in Meghan's eyes.

Fuck—she wants to please me. She wants to make me happy.

I reach around and slap her curvy ass. "Come on. You better get dressed quickly."

THIRTY

MEGHAN

I GIGGLE as Cash pushes me up against the muffin display and nibbles a path down my neck. "We'll never get our chores done if we keep stopping to fool around every few minutes," I tell him.

"I'm sleep-deprived and working on an empty stomach here, Megs. I can't start the day right without my breakfast." His mouth moves lower, sliding down the neckline of my sweater to trail along the lace of my bra.

I may be laughing but this is getting serious. I'm getting aroused. At the most inappropriate time. In the most inappropriate place.

We're at the Westbrook family bakery, helping Cash's grandmother get things set up for opening. She's in the back, baking up something that smells absolutely divine.

She left the two of us up at the front of the shop with a long checklist of tasks to complete. But we haven't been getting very much done.

"Come on." I entice him with a sly smile. "If we finish up fast enough, maybe I'll let you make out with me in your car out back."

He groans erotically. "You're a temptress."

Reluctantly, Cash releases me, grumbling the whole time. I follow him around, helping him with the to-do list. Filling the display cases with freshly baked cookies and pastries, prepping the old school coffee pots, stocking the napkin dispensers.

I leave the heavy lifting to Cash. Partly because I don't want my day to end with a trip to the chiropractor, and partly because I like seeing the way his muscles bulge as he effortlessly moves twenty-five pound sacks of flour around.

It's mind-melting, the way his back muscles and biceps flex, visible even through his dress shirt. Heat rises in my cheeks as I watch, remembering that just an hour ago, I was warmly cocooned against that perfect male specimen.

But even more attractive than his hot body? I've never seen this side of Cash Westbrook. The side that knows his way around a kitchen. The side that drops everything to come to his grandma's aid. I like him like this, and I'm definitely impressed.

Now I see why the Westbrook boys all take shifts helping out their grandmother here. There's more than enough work for the three of us, and I'm even doubtful we'll finish in time to open. I can't imagine how that sweet old woman would have managed this on her own. I have the utmost respect for anyone working in the food industry. After barely an hour, I'm already physically and mentally exhausted.

I'm moving around the small dining area, taking chairs down off the tables, when Cash's hands catch my waist again. He presses up behind me, wrapping his arms around my middle, burying his nose in my unwashed hair and groaning like he's inhaling a batch of fresh-made brownies.

A string of naughty words are right on the tip of my

tongue when I sense a presence observing us from across the room. I turn, jumping when I find Cash's grandma ambling out of the back room. Her knowing eyes glitter.

We're so busted.

"Hi Mrs. Westbrook," I squeak. "Need a hand with something?" Totally self-conscious, I unwrap myself from Cash's arms.

"Yes, over here in the kitchen. Do you mind helping me, dearie?"

"Of course." I follow the old lady past the wall that partitions the customer area from the famous prep table in front of the window overlooking Main Street.

"I'm stealing Meghan for a minute." She smirks at her frowning grandson. I don't catch his grumbled response.

I keep my eyes straight ahead, afraid to look back at Cash and get caught eye-fucking my boyfriend again.

Once in the kitchen, she smiles at me. "Wash up and grab that metal bowl, will you, dearie?"

I do as she commands, too nervous that I'm about to be shamed for fooling around with Cash out in the open like that.

I'm a grown woman and I have no reason to be ashamed of my feelings for Cash. But whatever is going on between us is so new, and I have no idea if Mrs. Westbrook is aware of it. His brothers know about us, of course, but I can't imagine that they've run off to their grandmother, telling her Cash's business.

After washing and drying my hands, I slip on an apron and join the woman at the large workspace facing the front window. She scoots a thick, weathered spiral notebook my way. *Recipes* is written across the cover in faded black marker.

I gulp. These are Maude Westbrook's secret recipes. Her secret, *sacred* recipes.

"Go on. Open it up," she encourages me. "It won't bite."

"Me?" I stab a finger into my chest.

"Yes, you." Her weathered face twinkles with humour.

I pull the notebook closer, gently opening the brittle pages. This homemade recipe book has clearly seen better days, the sheets of paper stained and splattered with oil and other secret ingredients.

"Find the page for my sugar cookies," she tells me. "It's toward the back."

"Are you sure?" I find her eyes.

She gives me a very deliberate eyeroll. "Of course I'm sure. How are you going to make cookies, if you don't open up the recipe?"

I grin. This old lady has enough sass to package it up and sell it by the pound.

"I just mean...Are you sure you want me looking at your recipe book? Everybody in town knows how closely guarded your secret recipes are." Biggest understatement ever.

"I share it with the ones I trust." She gives a one-shoulder shrug. "I trust you."

I feel like there's a solid brick of lard blocking my windpipe when she says that. "T-thank you."

"Now, hurry," she commands.

I carefully flip through the notebook until I land on a handwritten recipe for Grandma's Famous Sugar Cookies. "Found it."

"Good." She squints at the paper for a moment like she's trying to decipher the words. She quickly gives up, frowning. "Now read off each of the ingredients, please."

I do as I'm told, reading through the recipe and only

pausing to go fetch a few odd items so Cash's grandma doesn't have to run around the kitchen more than necessary.

I notice Cash poking his head in a few times to check on us. I get distracted. Our eyes catch and I shamelessly ogle him as he hauls huge, twenty-five pound sacks of flour out of the walk-in fridge across the hall and drops them onto a cart to be rolled into the kitchen, so they're ready whenever his grandma needs them.

"Would you stop being a distraction, Cassius?" the old lady says, concealing her knowing grin.

"I'm not being a distraction. I'm just here, innocently doing my chores. Not my fault if Megs can't keep her eyes off me."

Mrs. Westbrook glances in the direction of the clock on the wall without really seeming to see it. She huffs. "It's almost opening time."

Cash sighs and shakes her head. "Don't worry, Grammy. I've got you. I'll unlock the front door and man the front counter."

When Cash is gone, she huffs under her breath. "That boy is crazy about you. He always has been."

I hardly know what to say. "Really?" I croak out, my heart pounding.

"You're a special girl, Meghan. I'm just glad Cassius can finally admit to himself how important you are to him."

"He's important to me, too," I admit, feeling small and girlish. "I'm crazy about him."

The woman just smiles.

We work side by side. If I'm being honest, she *totally* makes me do most of the work. But it's a learning experience that I'm grateful for. She instructs me on what to measure and on which of her various mixing techniques to use. My earlier worries dissipate and I find that I'm actually enjoying myself. The woman is warm and hilarious in a snarky, unexpected way.

"You're a natural at this," she tells me.

"Thanks. I've always liked baking. Not that my mom had lots of spare time for baking back in the day, but I always enjoyed helping her in the kitchen whenever we got the chance."

I read off the next few ingredients, as the old lady hums and whips the spoon around.

"You don't use your mixer? My arm is tired just watching you."

"Only if I have to make an extra, extra large batch. One of my secrets for the right consistency is hand-stirred batter. What's next?" she asks me, stirring up the dry ingredients.

I tell her the last item. "I sure would think that you'd know each of these ingredients by heart after baking them all these years," I add with a laugh.

"Of course I know my recipes by heart."

My brows dip low with confusion. I thought she needed my help. Is she messing with me? "Then...why have me here reading it?"

Cash's grandma gives a forlorn smile. "I just wanted to share it with you, dearie."

My heart constricts, and suddenly, I'm overwhelmed to the point of tears. I keep blinking, fighting not to let them slip down my face.

For as long as I can remember, Maude Westbrook's famous recipes have been coveted by every bakery owner and homemaker in Honey Hill. This woman makes the best cookies I've ever tasted, and everyone who's ever had one is dying to replicate them at home. With no luck, I might add.

And here she is, just handing over all her trade secrets. To me.

"I don't understand..." I say with a tight throat, when I finally trust myself to speak. "You'd give me your recipe? Just like that?"

She hands me something that looks like an ice cream scooper, then takes a similar utensil for herself. She starts plopping neatly measured spoonfuls of dough onto the cookie sheet. She nods for me to do the same.

"Of course I'd share my recipe with you, dear."

"I feel absolutely honored, Mrs. Westbrook."

"As you should," she says smugly, causing me to laugh. "But in all seriousness, I'm not going to be around forever. I've done well for myself with this business. It always kept food on the table for my family. I don't have lots of money or property to leave behind when I'm gone. But I want to leave this. I want to make sure that these family secrets will be passed down to the next generation of Westbrooks."

My stomach flips and tumbles. "I'm not sure how I can help pass down your family recipes."

Cash and I have only just started dating. I have no idea what the future holds for us.

"Of course you can. You *will*," she confidently rebuts my hesitation. "You're Cash's sweetheart. You're the only woman who has ever gotten my Cash to shift his carefully-laid plans. To stick around. You're the one who will get him to settle down."

I hold the wooden spoon with a mighty grip. I feel overwhelmed by how much I want her to be right about this.

The elderly lady winks at me. "Mark my words, dearie. My grandson's no fool. He won't ever let you get away."

THIRTY-ONE

CASH

I MAKE sure to drop Meghan off at the clinic by 10:15 so that she's on time for work.

That leaves me having to figure out what to do with myself while she's gone. I briefly entertain the idea of hanging around the clinic all day so I can be close to her. But I quickly nix the idea. Braveheart is all up-to-date on his shots and I'd look pretty silly sitting there in the waiting room of the veterinary clinic without a sick animal, just hoping to get a glimpse of my girl between patients.

Driving aimlessly around the main streets of Honey Hill, slowing down each time I pass the medical building is also out of the question. I *do* have some pride left. Not much. But just enough.

I'm simping so hard for this girl.

Although I do have work of my own to get done, I'm not in the mood to spend the day holed up in the guest bedroom at my house sorting through contracts and spreadsheets. My responsibilities are piling up at a troubling rate but, I find it so hard to stay focused when I work from the house.

So, I return to the bakery and spend my day with another leading lady in my life. My grandmother.

Sticking around the Wildberry provides a perfect distraction, and Grammy is grateful for the help. While Mason's younger sisters keep busy baking up what we need in the kitchen, Grammy works at the cash register, and makes me her errand boy. I hustle about, fulfilling orders and fetching stuff out of the back.

In the moments between customers, I answer work emails and messages from my phone. Normally mornings at the bakery are wild, with everyone in town dropping in for their breakfast pastries and coffee. The afternoon usually screeches to a miserable halt. But not today. It seems like quite the opposite, actually. As the day passes, we become even busier.

But I have a sneaking suspicion that the influx of female customers, both young and old, are only dropping by to scope me out.

"Hey Cash, you back for good?"

"I'll take the Cash Westbrook special, please."

"I love a man in an apron."

"Maybe you should swing by my house when you're done here and have a taste of my cookies."

For a weaker man, the attention might be a nice confidence boost, but I'm good on that front. I don't need the validation. There's only one lover I'm giving any of my time.

With the way Meghan was all over me last night, I'm perfectly confident in my manhood, thank you very much. And I can't wait till the day is over and I can get back to her.

So, all these local ladies—divorced moms, ex-classmates, old acquaintances—they can all forget about it. They've got nothing on Meghan. Five minutes in their presence bores me to fucking tears, while I'm sitting here counting down the minutes until I can be with my girl again.

It's crazy how I dropped everything I was doing in Chicago to come and be with her. All she had to do was say the word and I was on the road in a heartbeat.

How the hell does she do that? What's this power she has over me? How is it that I never had time for anything outside of work and now that she's mine, suddenly, my whole world revolves around her? Am I being a dumbass? Maybe. But I'm too caught up in the magic of her to give a fuck.

Taking a break from running around all day, I stand off to the side and watch Grammy amble over to greet the group of customers who just walked in. I recognize this middle-aged woman and the two small girls who trail her inside. Meghan's step-mother and half-sisters.

Smiling and making small chat, Grammy sells them chocolate chip cookies and fresh lemonade. The children laugh and giggle good-naturedly. But their mother doesn't even crack a smile. I observe the crinkle of the woman's fore-head and the hard set of her jaw. Absolutely no joy there. She looks like a miserable human being.

Unlike all the other women who came in today, this lady does not even spare me a glance. My grandmother warmly says goodbye but the woman barely responds. She just wearily guides her children out the door with their treats in hand. Well, that was...*something*.

I get back to work, refilling the coffee beans. Grammy corners me by the espresso maker. She throws her arms around my waist.

"What's that for?" I laugh, hugging her back.

"I just find it funny how for years, you could never allow yourself to slow down and spend a few days in town.

And now, all of a sudden, I get *two* visits from you in the span of just a few short weeks. Plus, you're smiling. Since when does my Cranky Cassius smile?"

"I guess I'm realizing that I sort of had my priorities screwed up this whole time."

She pats me on the shoulder. "I say this to all my granddaughters—pay attention to where a man devotes his time. That's how you'll know what's really important to him."

"Well, as always, you're right. Meghan's important to me, Grammy. Very much so."

Her eyes beam. "I can tell."

With all the weird emotions bubbling inside me, I can't even keep her eye contact. I hunch over the counter and steal another sugar cookie from the clear display case.

Grammy slaps my hand away from the cookie display. "You're gonna pay for that?"

I duck out of her reach like I used to do back when I was a teenager stealing food as I helped around the bakery. "Sheesh, woman! I'm already paying you with the gift of my presence. What more do you want?!"

Our playful exchange is interrupted when a customer walks in the front door. The woman who was just here with her daughters less than five minutes ago.

She approaches the counter and addresses my grandmother. "Hello again. I think you made a mistake with my change," I overhear the woman telling Grammy, as she hands back a crumpled twenty dollar bill. "I got this instead of a five, and I just couldn't keep it."

I'll admit that I'm surprised to hear those words from this woman since she doesn't seem to have a friendly bone in her body.

Grammy's eyes widen before she takes the outstretched money and opens the register, laughing awkwardly. "Oh my. Me and my old lady brain. You're a doll for bringing that back. Anyone else would have just kept it." My grandmother reaches out to me, tapping me on the arm. "Give these adorable angels a few more cookies, will you, Cash?"

When I hand the children their treats, they cheer happily. This time, their mother actually looks at me. "Thank you," she says, her voice low and her smile faint.

I hold her eye contact and nod.

Her little girls lead the way out of the store and the three of them disappear down the sidewalk.

I turn my attention to Grammy. Even though the excitement of the moment is now over, she still seems uneasy, embarrassed. She stares off, looking disturbed by the whole ordeal.

I go over and drape an arm around her petite shoulder. "You okay?"

She hangs her head and steps out of my hold. "I'm fine."

"Are you really beating yourself up that you nearly lost out on fifteen dollars? Everyone makes mistakes. It's really not a big deal. Not with the way business has been booming today."

She doesn't look at me. "Would you take over the cash register for me? I...have some things to take care of in the back."

"You sure? I could take care of whatever you need from the back." Honestly, I'd rather be the errand boy than deal with these sexually-aggressive women here up front.

Grammy shakes her head. "No, no. I need you here. At the cash register."

"Okay, fine." I frown, watching her disappear into the bakery's kitchen.

Is it just me or has Grams been acting a little strange lately? She's always been a woman who's marched to her own drum, but I've noticed during my brief time back home that she's just seemed...off.

Taking over the stool behind the register, I start to text Jasper to ask him about Grams, but a flurry of emails load up on my phone, dragging my attention back to work. While I'm not exactly as engaged as I'd like since I've been telecommuting, I feel I've been doing my best staying on top of things at the office. But now it looks like another one of the deals I've been working on may fall through. Shit. It's got me second-guessing my approach. If I want to have Meghan *and* my career, I'm going to need to do a better job of balancing everything.

Luckily, the flow of customers has dwindled down. I spend much of the afternoon tapping out quick emails and putting out fires at work while continuing to oversee the register and helping Grammy with whatever she needs around the store.

At the end of the afternoon, I give her a hand with closing up for the night. Already, I'm anticipating seeing Meghan. I kiss Grams on the cheek and say my goodbyes to my cousins who are washing up baking sheets and prepping for tomorrow in the back.

I'm walking to my car, parked out in the back parking lot when my phone rings.

It's Meghan.

I smile at my phone. I bring it to my ear. "Hey."

"Hey."

"You done with work?"

"In fifteen minutes."

I get in my car. "Great. I'm on my way to pick you up."

I hear the restrained excitement in her voice. "I have some news."

My brow quirks. "Really? What is it?" I settle in behind the steering wheel.

"Well, I've been feeling bad that you've been playing hookie from work to hang out here with me." She hesitates, suddenly sounding nervous. "So, I asked to use a few of my vacation days. That way I can spend some time with you in Chicago. I can stay until the fashion show."

"You serious?"

"Yes. Is that a good thing or a bad thing."

"Fuck, yes, it's a good thing. When can you leave?"

"Um...now? Tonight? Whenever you're ready."

"I'm ready to leave right this minute." I laugh. "We can swing by your place and pack up your cats. Then we'll grab a quick drive-through dinner and hit the road back to Chicago."

"Sounds like a plan."

"Great. I'm on my way to get you now."

"Okay." She pauses. "I'm really excited about this, Cash."

"I'm excited, too."

THIRTY-TWO

MEGHAN

IT'S some ungodly hour of the night when I carefully peel myself off of Cash's naked chest. I take in his form as he snores softly. After spending hours on the road and then screwing me into oblivion the minute we arrived here at his condo, I'm sure the poor man is bone tired.

I probably would be, too, if it weren't for that second cup of gas station coffee I had during our road trip. Instead, I just really need to pee.

He shifts, grabbing at me as I move away. "Come back," he mumbles.

"I'm going to use the bathroom," I whisper back, climbing out of bed and making my escape down the hall. I clean myself up, splash water over my flushed face, and realize I'm wearing nothing but my underwear.

Feeling too vulnerable in my naked state, but not wanting to tread back to the bedroom just yet, I grab the shirt that's hanging on the hook in Cash's bathroom. I give it the sniff test and I nearly drown in the testosterone clinging to the fabric.

Then I tiptoe to the kitchen. I'm still not ready to face Cash right now, as I try to make sense of my feelings.

Much to my irritation, I can't figure out how to turn my brain off. There's this beautiful, heady, exciting feeling that something significant is growing between Cash and me.

But there's another feeling, too. This one is heavy and persistent, trying to warn me off from getting my hopes up, trying to warn me that it's too good to be true. I hate this whisper in my head saying that it's only a matter of time until Cash has had his fill of me and he's ready to move on.

I need a second—or one thousand—to make sense of the battle taking place in my head.

I turn on the kettle, grab a mug and start making myself some tea. While I wait for the tea to brew, I straighten up around the kitchen. Lost in my thoughts, I flutter around putting away dishes, wiping counters and rummaging through the fridge, with three cats around my ankles, competing for my attention.

"Hey."

I startle, jumping and then juggling the tea spoon that's slipped through my fingers. I really sucked at that two-week course on juggling in freshman P.E. class. The spoon clatters loudly to the kitchen floor.

Cash must have snuck out of bed like a burglar but now, he's standing in the entry to the kitchen, wearing nothing but his boxers. He ignores the spoon on the floor, stepping around it.

"You okay?"

I nod repeatedly like a weirdo. "I came in here to make some tea. Then I got carried away tidying up. Did I wake you?"

"And why exactly are you tidying up?" He swipes two

fingertips over the already-pristine countertop. "My cleaning lady's work isn't up to your standards?"

Leaning my ass against the counter, I smile and feel my cheeks glowing with embarrassment. "I'm sorry," I say meekly. "You know how I get when I start overthinking everything."

Within two large steps, he's upon me, wrapping me up in his warm bare arms. "Lay it on me, baby. What are you overthinking?"

My hands climb his strong chest and drape over his shoulders. "Everything. The way things are...evolving between us. A few weeks ago, I couldn't even imagine you being interested in me this way. And now we're here, like this. It's sort of overwhelming."

He inhales deeply. "Well, Meghan, you're gonna have to start believing it. Because all I want right now is you. More of you. If you want me."

I can't help but blurt out, "Yes, I...I want more of you. *All* of you. But..."

My damn insecurities.

Every time I close my eyes, I hear my mother's warning voice in my head. *Any man who comes sniffing around is only looking for a good time.* I wish there were an easy switch to turn it off.

Easing back slightly, Cash grabs both my hands, interlacing our fingers. "I definitely don't want to rush you. But at the same time, I want you to know that I'm genuinely in love with you. I want this." He pauses, his eyes searching mine, while I try to keep my melting spine upright. Am I hearing him correctly? Is Cash seriously saying all the things I've dreamed of hearing? "I don't know how this is supposed to work. How we're supposed to keep it going, especially long distance. But...all I know is that I'm crazy about you, Meghan. Crazy enough to try."

I want to pinch myself. I might be in an alternate universe right now, where Cash and Meghan really are lovers and not just life-long friends, but I'm deluded enough to go along with this illusion. I'm definitely willing to call this new universe home.

"I want to try, too. But this is so crazy to me. So scary. Even though it's scary in a good way."

Cash smiles and nods like he understands my ramblings perfectly.

"Just tell me the next step," I beg.

He leans in close, and I bask in the heat radiating off his naked chest. His lips consume mine, but unlike earlier when we were going at it like jungle animals, this time it's slow. Sweet. Patient. It appears I'm going to experience all the sides of Cash Westbrook in one day, and I'm so giddy I might just burst. I'm breathless when we pull back.

"If you want to go slow, we can go slow. But I want to make my position clear. I don't think there's anything scary about building a future for us. That's what I want. More than anything." He dots kisses all over my face, but it's the silly grin on his sexy mouth that takes my breath away. I rarely see him so carefree. So happy.

"Really?" I dare to whisper.

He mumbles his affirmative before dropping his lips to the skin where my neck meets my shoulder. It feels amazing.

"I want sex." He growls into my neck, causing me to laugh.

"Oh, that's what you're after?"

His lips curl into a smile against my skin. "Yes, but I also want to take you on dates."

I swallow. "Dates?" I'm struggling to pay attention with the kisses he's gently placing up the length of my neck.

"I want to take you around the world. To all the places you've dreamed of going. I want to sweep you off your feet. I want to share my life with you. Do you accept, Meghan?"

"Yes," I squeak.

If he keeps kissing me like that, he could get me to do just about anything. My heart is pounding so loudly. I wonder if Cash can hear it. I'm not sure he's listening. I only get a "mmm..." out of him every once in a while, as he focuses on weakening me with those lips against my neck and throat. A shiver zips through me.

I struggle to string words together. "Damn these benefits you're offering, they just keep sounding better and better."

"As they should." He touches his lips to mine. "Now, I'll ask you—what do *you* want next?"

He catches me staring at his chest and his abs and those biceps. The grin on Cash's face grows, making me wonder just how talented he is at reading my mind.

I stand on my tiptoes to give him a slow kiss. "Maybe we can go back to the sex part now."

"Mmm, the sex?"

My face burns. I nod.

Cash throws back his head, laughing. "Fuck yeah." His lips cover mine. "Well, I *did* promise that I'd eat you out on this counter right here. And as you're about to find out, I'm a man who keeps my word. So climb on up, cowgirl."

Tittering, I leap up on the table. "Giddy up, Westbrook."

THIRTY-THREE

MEGHAN

CASH CLASPS my hand firmly in his as he navigates us through the throngs of fashion critics, magazine editors and industry insiders crowding the large, white tent.

I jolt when I bump into him from behind. "Oops! Sorry." I bite on the smile trying to spread across my bottom lip.

I've bumped into him at least five times since we arrived here. The place is packed with important-looking people. I'm having a hard time paying attention to where I'm walking. I'm like a kid at Disneyland for the first time. I'm too busy gaping around at the venue of this exclusive, invitation-only fashion show.

Bright spotlights beam down from a steel-reinforced ceiling that must be at least twenty feet high. Three rows of sleek black chairs surround both sides of a long white runway. More than a dozen photographers are already poised at the foot of the catwalk, their cameras ready to capture some magazine-worthy shots.

"You excited?" Cash asks as we lower into our front-row seats.

I grab his arm. "I'm buzzing."

We wait for the show to begin. I whisper in his ear, chattering animatedly about everyone's stylish outfits, as they enter the place. I'm not even sure that he understands what I'm saying above the din of the room because I'm speaking a mile a minute.

Smiling adoringly at me, Cash kisses my cheek. "Let me go grab you a bottle of water. I have a feeling you're going to need it." He rises from his seat.

My eyes are following his movements through the crowd when I feel something bump into my arm. My head snaps to my left and I see an extra-pregnant woman attempting to lower into the seat next to me.

"Oh my gosh, I'm so sorry," she says, brushing her dark chaotic hair from her wild blue eyes.

"No worries." I smile at her.

Her purse drops from her hand and hits the floor. "Jesus. Can I be any bigger of a mess right now?"

I laugh. "Here. Let me get that for you." I gracefully lean over and retrieve her purse, depositing it into her hand.

She expels a heavy breath once she's finally comfortable in her seat. "Thank you so much. This is embarrassing."

"Don't be embarrassed. You're obviously doing an important job right now." I gesture to her belly. "How far along are you?"

She pouts. "Not far enough. This is baby number two, and let me tell you, pregnancy is *not* something that gets easier with practice."

I laugh.

The woman and I fall into an easy conversation. Before long, two of her friends appear, filling the seats beside her.

Looking at me, she slaps her forehead. "Sorry, I haven't introduced myself. I'm Alexia." She points to her friends.

"This is Eliza and that's Sadie. We're here to support the designer, our girl, Isla."

"Nice to meet you," I say to them all. "I'm Meghan."

Sadie eyeballs my bandeau dress. "Wow, I really love your outfit."

"Thank you." I beam. "A lot of work went into finding this dress."

Alexia cradles her belly. "I can't wait to pop this baby out so I can start wearing hot girl dresses like that again." We all laugh.

I compliment them on their own dresses and we discuss fashion for a while.

"So, you're all friends with the designer?" I ask them.

Eliza nods. "Yes, we all became friends when our husbands started working on various investment projects together. Us, girls usually only get the chance to get together when the guys abandon us for their poker nights. But Isla's launch is a special occasion so here we are."

Cash returns right then and I introduce him to the girls. We don't have the chance to chat very much because, before long, the lights go dim. A heavy techno beat starts up and a procession of curvy, long-limbed beauties begin regally parading the Prasanna yoga collection up and down the catwalk.

I look on in awe at the parade of colorful and stylish workout gear that clings to the models' curves like second skin. Camera shutters flash and the crowd hums with delight. I mentally make a list of my favorite pieces so I can follow up and purchase them later on.

The show ends way too soon with the designer appearing on stage to take a bow. After an uproarious standing ovation, people begin making their way to an adjacent room for cocktails.

"So...what's your consensus?" Cash asks by my ear as we move along with the crowd.

"It was incredible. Thank you for making this happen," I say to him, stopping right where we are to clasp his cheeks in my palms and kiss him.

He smiles at me. "Gosh. I get such a dopamine rush from making you happy."

"Well, you're really damn good at it, baby." I beam at him. "You won't hear me complaining about how good you are to me."

We turn to start walking again and I bump straight into someone's back.

I slap a hand to my chest. "Oh, I'm so sorry," I apologize. "It's way too crowded in h—"

"Dad?" Cash says when the man turns around.

"Oh my gosh, Mr. Westbrook!" I squeal.

The man takes the last bite of the salmon and cream cheese appetizer in his hand as his surprised eyes sweep from his son to me and back again. His smile spreads a mile across his face. "Well, *this* makes me happy," he announces wiping his mouth with a paper napkin. "Meghan Hutchins in the flesh. And more beautiful than ever."

I laugh as we share a quick hug. "It's been years since I've seen you!"

Luther Westbrook is a hot older dude. The man may have a few more grey hairs today than the last time I saw him but it makes him look distinguished. He's undeniably a handsome man and the idea that Cash will age as well as his father has thrills me to be quite frank.

He eyeballs Cash again, his eyes sparkle with genuine happiness. "I tried not to get too excited when Nicky told me the two of you were dating—I've learned to take that girl's gossip with a grain of salt—but now that I see you two with my own eyes..." He bumps his shoulder into Cash's. "Congratulations, son. You have a beautiful woman on your arm *and* you actually have a life outside of work? Damn. I might as well just sign the company over to you and take my retirement right this minute."

Cash rolls his eyes. "I'm not holding my breath, control freak."

I don't know what to say in the face of the man's overwhelming happiness but why am I surprised? The entire Westbrook family has gone out of their way to make me feel welcome now that Cash and I are together.

"What are you doing here, anyway?" Cash questions his father, looking perplexed.

The man rears his head back in offence. "I was invited." Mr. Westbrook turns to me. "Cash thinks he's the only cool kid around. The designer's husband is a client of our company. I don't know why he's so surprised I got an invitation, too." He steals another appetizer off the tray of a server passing by.

I titter, patting a hand to the center of Cash's chest.

The group of girls we sat next to during the show are coming toward us now.

"Looks like Ms. Popular made herself some friends." Cash kisses the side of my head as Alexia waves a hand in my direction.

"Meghan, we want you to meet someone," she says excitedly.

I'm beaming as the girls introduce me to the designer, a regal athletic-looking redhead. She gives me a friendly handshake. "I'm Isla. It's great to meet you, Meghan," she says to me before turning to Cash and his dad. "Well, if it isn't the handsome Westbrook men." She speaks to her friends. "These gentlemen are responsible for making my husband ten times richer than he was before. They're legends when it comes to money management."

Four tall, dashing men approach us right then, taking their places beside the women. Before they can even open their mouths, I already know these men are rich. That big money vibe is oozing from them like cologne.

The guy with the dark blond man bun and the wicked smirk drapes his arms around Alexia's baby bump. "Did I hear somebody say 'money'?" He pretends to sniff at the air, causing his wife to chuckle.

"Cannon, these are the Westbrooks," Alexia tells her man. "Isla says they can make us richer," she announces, tongue in cheek, laughter in her voice.

His eyes lift to Cash and his father. He squints like he's trying to recall something. "Westbrook Wealth Management, right? I got a few calls from your company while I was out of town. Shit. Returning your call has been on my to-do list but I'm still catching up on everything that's piled up on my desk while I was on vacation."

The man holding Isla in his arms, presumably her husband, interjects. "They're the only ones I trust with my money. Ever since I transferred my portfolio to them, my bank accounts won't stop growing."

"We're in the business of making our clients filthy rich," Cash says assuredly, chin tilted up proudly. "We're the emerging industry leaders in wealth management."

Oh my god, can he be any sexier the way he says that?

The rest of the businessmen are clearly interested in learning more. Cash has their rapt attention.

Alexia's husband bobs his head slowly. "Well, I definitely need to hear more about this."

"Whatever deal Cannon's getting in on, I want in on it,

too," another of the men says. The rest of the men nod along in agreement.

"So, let's talk business, shall we?" Isla's husband nods toward a private, roped off section of the room.

The men excuse themselves and move to the other side of the room. Meanwhile, I hang out with the girls who are so fun. They're an absolute riot with their snarkiness and anecdotes.

But way too frequently, my eyes search out Cash in the crowd as he and his father work on winning over the group of business men. How is it possible that I miss him even when we're standing on opposite sides of the same room? I've got it bad for this man.

He's so assertive and official-looking as he speaks with the group of men. A real business tycoon. And it makes my tummy jump, knowing that I'm the one who gets the different side of him, the softer side, the vulnerable side, the downright sexy side.

He must feel me looking at him because his eyes swing to mine. He gives me a boyish, sideways smirk that makes me blush. I peel my eyes away from his and my gaze happens to land on his father.

Something's not right.

The older man wears a growing grimace on his face as the conversation continues around him. I don't like that expression of his. Not one bit.

A panicked sound leaves my lips when Mr. Westbrook grips the side of his head. He stumbles to his left.

Cash's eyes follow my line of sight. He notices his father's distress and reacts just in time. Cash manages to catch his father right before the old man hits the floor.

THIRTY-FOUR

MEGHAN

EARLY THE NEXT MORNING, I'm nursing my second mug of coffee. Barefoot and wearing one of Cash's T-shirts, I'm pacing the living room of his Chicago residence.

The cats can probably sense my agitation. All three of them have been on their absolute best behavior, lounging peacefully in the living room all morning.

It's no surprise that I didn't sleep all that great last night. The yo-yo of yesterday left me on a jittery high that lasted through the wee morning hours, and I'm paying for it now. I'm still trying to catch up with yesterday's whiplash.

One minute, I was enjoying the post-fashion show cocktail with my lovely new friends while Cash and his dad were across the room, trying to lure new clients in to their firm. The next minute, Luther Westbrook was flat on his back and paramedics were rushing into the venue to cart him away.

I spent the night tossing and turning in Cash's bed, waiting for an update on his father's condition. I'd wanted to stay at the hospital by my man's side but he'd insisted that he and Nicky could handle it. After the doctor's initial assessment confirming that Mr. Westbrook's condition was not life threatening, Cash had told me to come back here and get some rest.

He'd said that I'd be doing him a favor by sitting tight at his apartment instead of curling up uncomfortably in a chair in the hospital's waiting room where he'd have to worry about me on top of worrying about his dad.

A part of me is wondering if he's really okay. Or is he just putting on a brave face to hide this moment of weakness from me?

I hear the condo's front door swing open. I abandon my coffee on the mantle and I rush off in that direction. I catch a glimpse of myself in a mirror on the wall. It's not a pretty sight. I frantically swipe at my raccoon eyes. I knew I should have scrubbed my face before crawling under the covers, but it's too last minute to get myself pretty at this point.

Cash enters, his shoulders slumped, his feet dragging. He has his tie and suit jacket balled up in one fist.

I throw myself into his arms. "Hi..."

He pulls air deep into his belly as he hugs me back. "Hi..." Allowing himself to close his eyes for a moment, he kisses me tenderly.

"How's your dad?" I ask, stepping back to evaluate his expression.

Cash rubs his eyes and strolls into the kitchen. "Exhausted. Dehydrated. Hooked up to an I.V. at the hospital. His blood pressure is a mess. As are his other stats." He grabs a water bottle from the fridge.

"Oh my gosh..." I whisper.

He slumps against the counter and rubs his eyes again. "He worked himself into this condition. The guy's not as young as he used to be. But he refuses to accept that he can't keep working himself to the bone like this." His fingers close around my wrist and he pulls me toward him.

I collapse against his chest and wrap my arms around him. "I'm just glad it's not something worse."

When Mr. Westbrook had grabbed his head and toppled to the side in the middle of the fashion show's reception event, I'd been thinking it was a stroke or a brain aneurysm or something else just as scary. Fortunately, I was wrong.

"I don't even want to think about that," Cash whispers into my hair.

"And how are *you* doing?" I ask him.

He laughs grimly. "Exhausted. Dehydrated. I should probably be hooked up to an I.V. right alongside my father." He picks up a sad-looking brown paper bag from the counter and sniffs the stale donuts inside.

"Oh, baby." I stroke his cheeks. "You should make time to eat something. I can cook you some breakfast. Scrambled eggs sounds good?"

"Sounds amazing." His lips curl faintly. "I fucking love your cooking."

"I'm on it," I tell him. "Is there anything else I can do to help?"

He thoughtfully chews on the corner of his mouth then shakes his head. "No, just having you here helps so much."

I can feel his heart thumping ferociously against my cheek. He really is scared for his dad. He's just trying to be strong.

He kisses my scalp and eases out of my hold. "I can't stay long. I'm just here to see you and to grab a quick shower. Now that Dad's out of commission, it's like another dump truck of responsibility just unloaded on my desk at the office. So I have to swing by there. Then I'll probably go back to the hospital again to check in. And then...I don't even know what's next." A guilty look covers his face. "I'm not sure how long I'll be gone."

"That's fine," I nod, not wanting him to stress about me. "I'll be here whenever you get back."

Tenderly, he caresses my cheek. "Thank you." A heavy sound escapes his chest. "I'm just sorry this had to happen during your trip. I was looking forward to showing you a good time while you're in Chicago."

"Well, I had fun at the fashion show," I assure him. "And I'm just glad to be here for you now."

I hate the apprehension in his eyes when he asks, "When do you have to be back in Honey Hill?" His penetrating stare makes my knees weak.

"Two days from now. But I'll call my work and get some more time off."

"Don't do that," he tells me. "I don't want this to start affecting your work. I'm fine. I'll be fine."

He's not fine. I can see it on his face.

I rise onto my toes and press my open lips to his neck. "I'm not convinced," I whisper into his collar. "But maybe I can make you feel a little better...if you can give me five minutes."

His arm instantly comes around my back. He moans roughly. "Fuck. Five minutes? God, I want more than five minutes with you."

I trail my tongue along his collarbone as my fingers undo the buttons of his shirt.

His fingers flex on my waist. "Meghan..."

I feel his tension start to come loose.

"That's it, baby..." I whisper. "Let me take some of your stress away."

I whip off his shirt as he unbuttons his pants. Then I drop to my knees and reach for his hips.

I shiver when he brushes the glistening tip of his erection across my lips. "Open up, Megs," he begs quietly.

My lips part and Cash feeds his throbbing cock into my mouth. I seal him into the wetness and bob my head, taking him to the back of my throat, giving him the relief he so clearly needs in this moment.

He whispers again and again how much he loves me as I take my fill of him. When he's right on the brink of exploding, he slips his hands into my armpits and pulls me to my feet.

"I need to be in your pussy right now," he says, his voice rough like cracked concrete.

I spin around, bend over the counter and offer myself to him. "Take it."

He lifts the hem of the T-shirt I'm wearing and he slips my panties down my legs. In a second, he's inside me, rocking his hips in long, slow strokes. He pinches my clit between his fingers and manipulates it till I'm losing my mind.

"You ready?" he asks, low and rough.

Cheek pressed against the cold, hard counter, I nod. "I'm ready."

With one firm tug on my clit, he slams himself as far as my fully primed body will take him.

I scream. His throbbing explosion fills my pussy, overflowing and slipping down the insides of my thighs. The orgasm makes me shake violently.

We stay like that for just long enough to catch our breath.

I straighten up and his shaft slips from inside me. I spin around and his arms wrap around me.

Trailing my fingers down his back, I kiss his warm chest. He rests his chin on my sweaty head.

"D'you feel any better?" I ask quietly.

"A million times better," he confirms. "If I had my way, I'd keep you locked away inside my bed. Have you for breakfast, lunch and dinner with zero distractions. For at least one full week. But..."

I smile ruefully. "But...responsibilities."

He nods once. "Responsibilities."

"I know..."

A chill sweeps over my thighs causing goosebumps to break out. I try not to feel sad because I know Cash has to leave soon. He has his life and his job and a thousand new responsibilities on his plate now that his dad is in the hospital. In a just a while, he'll go take a shower and I'll prepare him something to eat. But for now, he just holds me.

He takes a long moment to squeeze me to his chest. "Y'know, I used to think that all I wanted was to be filthy, fucking rich. But now that I have you, I truly know what it means to be a wealthy man."

THIRTY-FIVE

CASH

I STAND in the doorway to my dad's palatial luxe bedroom and watch Nicky plump the silk and velvet pillows behind our father's back. For the nineteenth time.

"I think I'm good now, Nicks." He huffs a little laugh through his nose. "Come on!" he says, softly batting her hands away.

She glares at him, unconvinced. "Hard to believe you when you're toppling over in the middle of crowded social events." She grabs the opulent duvet at the foot of the bed and spreads it out over his legs.

"Christ, Nicky. You're acting like I'm on life support here." Dad shakes his head. "The doctors have given me a clean bill of health. They've released me from the hospital. I'm fine. You can relax."

I thought that I was having a hard time dealing with Dad being laid up in the hospital. Well, Nicky's handled it far worse than I have. My sister has always been a daddy's girl, but now that she works for the family business, they've become even closer. They're partners in crime, always up to no good and ganging up on me. She's really having a hard time seeing him this way.

I'd expected her to calm down a little when he got released earlier today but I think she's even more anxious now at the prospect of him staying at his large home on his own.

"Grammy's been asking for you to call her." Nicky arranges and rearranges the pill bottles lined up on Dad's lacquered antique bedside table. Then she goes over and starts fiddling with the heavy bedroom drapes. "And Harry will drop by sometime this week when his team is in Chicago. I've been keeping Davis and Jasper up to date as well."

As my sister flutters around the room, rambling, I check the time on my watch. Fuck, another day gone. Another day spent away from Meghan when I promised myself I wouldn't leave her sitting alone in my condo again.

Her trip here to Chicago was supposed to be *our* time. Instead I've done nothing but run from the office to the hospital and back again, only stopping by my condo to crash for a few hours in her arms.

Because Meghan is an absolute angel, she tries not to look let down but I know she's disappointed. She's so damn sweet and supportive, putting on a happy face like she doesn't mind that I'm neglecting her. But I do. This is not the kind of relationship I wanted to give her.

I'm doing a terrible job of juggling all this.

I look at my Dad laid up in that big four poster bed. Everything in this room screams, *I'm rich and I want you to know it,* but under the twinkling light of the gaudy crystal chandelier beaming down on him...he just looks small and sad.

It makes me question everything. It makes me wonder if

I'm prioritizing the wrong things. It makes me wonder if I'm making the same mistakes he did, choosing his career over the love in his life. I don't want to go down that dead end. I'm determined to choose a different path.

"I've got to get out of here," I announce, stepping away from the doorjamb.

"Right." Nicky nods and stifles a yawn.

"Meghan's probably eager to see you." Dad smiles softly. "Go to her." He eyeballs my sister. "You can go, too, Nicks. I'll be fine on my own."

"You sure?" she asks.

He nods. "I'm sure."

She looks skeptically around the room like she's trying to see if there's anything she's forgetting to do. "Okay, fine." She gives him a long hug and kisses his cheek. "I feel so terrible leaving you here by yourself. Call me if you need anything. All right? Don't be a macho man and try to do anything strenuous on your own."

"Fine," he says, grousing.

I step into the room and clap a hand on his shoulder. "Don't worry about the office. I've got everything covered."

He nods. "Just make sure you're taking care of Meghan. I don't want you to fuck this up with her. 'Cause if you do..." He gestures around to his lavish, lonely surroundings.

My chest tightens, hating what he's implying, hating that I know it's true. *I don't want to end up alone.* "I know, I know..." I spin and head for the door. "I'll check in on you in the morning."

Nicky hustles alongside me down the long, echoey hallway full of famous art and stone sculptures no one gives a shit about. "We should have gotten him a nurse. Do you think we should get him a nurse?" She watches me with wide eyes.

"Yeah, maybe. I don't know." I distractedly check my watch. Then I pull out my phone, texting Meghan, apologizing again for keeping her waiting, promising again to make it up to her.

Shit. I'm failing at this boyfriend thing.

"I hate that he doesn't have anyone to look out for him," Nicky is saying now. "I feel like he's sad but he'd never admit it and..."

Just as I'm about to tell her to calm the hell down, the doorbell chimes. My sister and I glance at each other. She hangs back as I pull open the door.

The most unlikely person stands on the front stoop, bundled up in a fleece jacket with hesitation in her eyes and an overnight bag clutched tightly in her hand.

I blink to make sure I'm not imagining this. "Mom?"

THIRTY-SIX

MEGHAN

SCENTED PILLAR CANDLES illuminate the room. There are sticky plates and empty glasses cluttering the bedside table. The sheets are damp and tangled from making love.

Cash lays on the bed, flat on his stomach, with his cheek propped on his forearms. "This is so fucking relaxing." He yawns into his pillow. "Your hands feel so good."

I'm straddling his waist, kneading my fingertips into his ropey shoulder muscles. He groans when I hit a particularly tight spot.

"You're all bunched up, baby. Relax." I squeeze some more oil into my palms and run them from his trapezoids all the way down to his glutes. Then I lean down and press a kiss to the back of his neck.

"You're killing me, Meghan." Cash twists around beneath me so he's lying on his back. He reaches up, his hand cupping the back of my skull. He pulls me close for a sensual kiss. "I fucking missed you today."

I smile hearing him say that. "I missed you, too."

He yawns again. "Were you okay by yourself all day?"

"Of course I was." I furrow my brows at him like his question is silly. "I went walking in the park and then I did some sightseeing. I had lunch at this really cute cafe. It was nice."

My words don't dim the guilt radiating from his eyes. "I'm sorry I haven't been around much. This isn't how I'd wanted things to go."

"It's okay. I understand." I lay my palms on his chest.

I've been worried about him. He has so much to stress over, with his father and the company. I hate that he's been stressing about me, too. I don't want to be a burden on him, just one other responsibility vying for his valuable time.

You know what happens every time us Hutchins women fall in love...

Cash smiles happily, his expression conveying the exact opposite of the fearful thoughts in my mind. "You sure I can't just keep you here forever? I really just want to tie you to this bed and just keep you." He reaches up and gently cups my breast, letting his thumb brush back and forth over my nipple.

I laugh ruefully. "I wish I could but Barbara's on vacation next week and they won't give me any more days off from work." As he continues to touch me like that, my hips begin moving on their own. I'm sliding my naked pussy back and forth along his hot, rigid shaft.

"I'm kidding. I-I'm sorry. I shouldn't have even asked." He grips my waist, sliding me back and forth on his erection. "You've been amazing this whole time, asking anything more from you is just selfish at this point."

God, that feels good. I can't take it anymore. We both need this. I lift off his thighs and ease his ready cock inside of me. We both groan. "It's not selfish. I'm your girlfriend. Asking me to be here for you is normal."

We're both quiet for a while as I slowly undulate my hips. Then he laughs softly and breathlessly. "I'm gonna be so mad driving you home tomorrow. I really don't want you to go."

"Cash, I should take the train back home. I don't need you to drive me. You have so much on your plate."

His eyes freeze over with determination. "I'm driving you home, baby. After disappointing you all week, it's the least I can do."

"You haven't disappointed me. Things came up. Important, unexpected things. I understand."

"Meghan, when you agreed to be with me, I made you promises. I promised I'd be good to you. I plan to live up to those promises." He begins thrusting upward, slamming inside of me, squeezing my breast with his hand.

"You have been good to me, Cash."

The pleasure is growing hot and demanding, urgent. So, so good. And for some reason, I'm beginning to panic.

I love him so much it's dangerous. I'm drowning in my feelings for him. And the longer we keep all this going, the deeper I'll fall and the harder the landing will be.

"This is so hard. Too hard. Especially on you. You're running yourself into the ground trying to cater to me."

Cash's brow furrows instantly. I practically see his guard fly up.

He flips us over so suddenly that I yelp. Now, he's on top. He's in control.

He looks down into my face as he ruts. "What are you saying, Meghan? What are you trying to tell me?"

I feel a breath stutter through my lungs and when I open my mouth, I'm not sure if it's the pleasure or if it's the fear or if it's my pure, raw love for him that's talking. "How much longer can you keep doing this?" I whisper. "How much longer till you just give up?" *How much longer till you see I'm not worth the trouble?*

No. No, no, no. Why am I saying these words? Why are they even leaving my mouth?

I don't want to push him away. I want him closer to me. I know it's hard but I don't want to stop trying. I don't want him to stop trying.

Yet here I am, opening the door and inviting him to walk away from me. Because I'm freaking scared. Because these feelings I feel for him are a behemoth, getting bigger by the day and I'm not brave enough to face them head on. I'm afraid that if I don't take a step back, these feelings of mine will crush me.

I see panic in Cash's face. "Shush. Don't say that." He leans down over me, continuing to pump hard and fast. "Don't you say that. I won't give up on us. I love you." His mouth covers mine in a hot kiss, suffocating all my objections until the pleasure is peaking inside us both at the same time.

We crack open together, orgasming hard and vocalizing it, allowing our frantic cries to fill the air. When it's all over, Cash doesn't stay and hold me. He kisses my forehead and rushes out of bed before I can say something else that will ruin the moment.

"Gotta use the bathroom," he grumbles as he grabs his boxers off the floor and heads out the door.

I try to wait for him to return. So we can finish our conversation. But I hear him rustling around in the living room. When I hear sports highlights blaring from the television, I know he's hiding from me and he's not coming back any time soon.

I drift asleep with cool air rustling over my clammy skin and unsettling thoughts sweeping through my hectic brain.

This is all too good to be true.

Girls like me don't get chosen...Girls like me don't get chosen...Girls like me don't get chosen.

Oh, god.

I know it's not rational. But every time I try to chase that thought away, it just sneaks right back in.

I tried fooling myself, telling myself that I could let Cash love me. But maybe I can't. Maybe it's too much. Maybe I'm not capable of accepting what he wants to offer me.

Maybe I'm too afraid.

THIRTY-SEVEN

CASH

MEGHAN and I spend Sunday morning on the road, heading back to Honey Hill. I can't expect her to take any more days off from work. She's been incredibly supportive of me during this hard time and having her around has made my life easier. But I can't be selfish, she has her own life to return to.

I don't want her to go. It feels dumb.

I'm a very wealthy man. I just want to hand her a duffel bag full of money. Take care of all her bills and responsibilities. Force her to stay with me indefinitely. But she wouldn't take that too kindly. She's an independent woman and I don't want to insult her by being patronizing.

Plus, Meghan loves her life in Honey Hill. Her job and her friends and her home. My money can't compete with that.

We've been mostly silent the entire drive, both of us living inside our heads. This is not how I'd wanted Meghan's trip to Chicago to turn out. I'd wanted to show her a good time. Instead it turned into a clusterfuck the moment my father collapsed at that fashion show. I know it's no-one's fault but still, I'm pissed about it.

My phone has been blowing up the entire drive. All business stuff. I've been ignoring the calls and emails for the most part, grumpily rationalizing with myself. *It's fucking Sunday...I'm saying goodbye to my girl...I deserve a few fucking moments of peace.*

In the past, I never had any boundaries when it came to work. But now, I'm starting to resent all the responsibilities that are encroaching on my private time with my woman. I'm wishing I could carve out more alone time for us.

A few miles away from our exit, my phone rings again. Meghan reaches across the console and lays a hand on my thigh. "Maybe you should get that."

"It can all wait," I reply through a stiff jaw.

She's clutching a huge container of cookies in her lap. She crept into the kitchen and baked up a storm in the wee hours of the morning after I'd fallen asleep on the couch. Yes, instead of returning to bed with her last night, I slept on the couch. It was a coward attempt to avoid having another heavy conversation about the future of our relationship.

The fresh-baked cookies tell me everything I need to know about Meghan's mental state. She's stressed. Meghan goes into full-blown domestic mode whenever she's stressed.

Her brow furrows and her pink lips turn downward. "I told you I could have taken the train back home," she mumbles. "You're busy with everything going on in your life right now. I told you I could have taken the train."

"And I told *you* I'd drive you back myself." I need to be close to her. Can't she see that?" Despite all the demands clamouring for my time, I refuse to put her on the back burner like my father did with my mother.

She sighs. "Cash, I don't like this. I'm starting to feel really guilty about it."

"Guilty about what?"

"Our relationship is costing you too much. I feel like I'm standing in the way of your obligations."

"You're not."

"I don't want you to resent me in the long run, when you see you got derailed from your dreams because you were busy chauffering me around from Honey Hill to Chicago and back."

I glance away from the road to meet her eyes. "Look, after seeing my dad collapse like that, I don't even want to let you out of my sight for a second. Putting you on a train was absolutely out of the question."

Money's great, but my priorities are different right now. For the first time in a long time, I'm noticing the *people* in my life. And I want more time, more moments, more memories with them.

I slide my fingers through hers on the console. "The long distance thing is hard, yes. But it's worth it. For me, at least." I look at her. I hesitate. "Is it not worth it for you?"

Her lips tremble and tears threaten to spill from her eyes. "Yes, it is."

I squeeze her hand. "So don't fight me on this."

She purses her lips momentarily. Finally, she whispers, "Fine."

That conversation between us yesterday put a chill on everything. She's insecure about my feelings for her. When I initially asked her to be mine, she made it clear that she had insecurities but I promised her I'm make them go away. Instead, her fears are growing bigger. Fuck. I'm failing.

I'm trying not to panic.

How do we get back to the part where things were

warm and fuzzy between us? What if she decides she doesn't want to put in the effort to make this long distance relationship work? What will I do then?

I shove those thoughts aside, determined to ignore them. I focus on the highway stretching ahead of us. "I want to swing by my grandmother's house for a little bit. Jasper said she's cooking a family dinner today and everybody will be there. Will you come with me?"

"Of course I will," she promises softly.

I'm flooded with relief. After everything that's happened lately, I'm reminded that life is short. And unpredictable. I just want to lay eyes on my family. As much as they may get under my skin, I'm starting to realize how precious they are.

We arrive at Grammy's cottage and pull up behind the many cars crowding the wide gravel lot in the front yard. We're actually a little late, but Jasper and his buddy Simon just pulled into the driveway half a second ahead of us, so I don't feel too bad.

I help Meghan out of the car. She and I leave the tension of our heated discussion behind. I stroll up the wooden stairs behind her and step inside.

Grammy is over the moon about Meghan's presence today. "Oh, Meghan. It's lovely to see you again so soon." The old lady grabs my girlfriend by the arm and starts toward the kitchen, leaving me in the dust.

What the hell?

"Doesn't this handsome face even deserve a hello anymore?" I call after my grandmother.

She scolds me over her shoulder. "Close the door behind you, Cassius. You'll let the bugs get in."

That's all the acknowledgment I get before the women go back to their conversation.

No one ever told me that as soon as I started bringing someone home, I'd become invisible. Still, I find myself chuckling at Grammy and her new best friend. It's kind of cute so I won't complain.

The second they get into the kitchen, Meghan pulls back the lid on the container of sugar cookies she baked earlier this morning.

"I was terrified to try my hand at the recipe you taught me the other day. But after one failed batch, I *think* I got it right." She stands by, watching for my grandmother's expression.

Grammy takes one cookie and gives it a taste-test. And judging by the joy on my grandmother's face when she takes the first bite, I can tell that Meghan's cookies have earned her approval.

"Oh, dearie. I knew you'd do me proud," Grammy raves and Meghan absolutely preens.

That makes me happy.

"Watch out, Buttercup. She'll have you putting in your notice at the clinic to come work at the bakery before you know it," I tease, as we take our seats around the table.

Meghan laughs softly. "Maybe I'll take it on as a side job."

We say our hellos to the rest of the crew. Alongside my brothers, Mason's side of the family is here, too. His parents, Uncle Eric and Aunt Victoria, together with their four savage daughters, Corri, Ruby, Maya, and Naomi who eagerly pull Meghan into their fold.

Over the meal, everybody wants an update on Dad and his condition. I repeat to them what the doctor told me. Basically, my father has overworked himself and he needs to make his health a priority or else it will continue to deteriorate. It's best to tackle the problem now before it evolves into something much more serious.

The meal is delicious like everything Grammy prepares. The rowdy dinner guests are the same as usual over dinner. The ribbing, the name-calling and Grammy's scolding, all on repeat.

Our table is growing a little crowded, though. Grammy is going to need a bigger dining room. Or on second thought, I'm okay with putting Harry and Jasper at the kids' table if they keep acting like dumbasses.

It's perfect. It's everything I don't have back in Chicago. It's everything that makes me want to stay here and never go back.

No—that's a lie. Meghan is everything that makes me want to stay here and never go back.

More and more I've been comparing the life I live when I'm here to the life I have in the city. I'm wondering how I'll merge the two in the long run. Because if I'm being honest, I know I can't keep this going long-term. It's draining. Meghan makes the inconveniences worth it but I know that in the long-run, I'll have to figure something else out.

I'm in the middle of laughing at something stupid that Harry said when I first smell it. An acrid scent that stings my nose and makes me put down my fork.

"Does...anyone else smell...smoke?" I ask cautiously.

This isn't the scent of a chimney burning or the lingering scent of a burnt cigarette on someone's clothes. This is something else. Something serious.

Around the table, the others pause, sniffing the air and all talking at once.

"I do. I smell something burning."

"The smell is getting stronger."

"God, what is that...?"

Before anyone can grind into action, the smoke alarm starts blaring. People jump out of their seats and others cover their ears.

I hop up and run toward the kitchen, where the smoke smells the strongest. Davis is hot on my heels. Fiery flames glow from behind the oven's glass window. We don't even have to open the door to feel the infernal heat.

Davis darts over and grabs the extinguisher from under the sink. I open the door to Grammy's ancient oven and my brother immediately douses the flames. Half of the family bursts into the kitchen just in time to witness it.

When the fire's completely out, I use Grammy's oven mitts to pull the ruined pie out and drop it on the stovetop. It's burnt to a crisp and covered in frothy white residue from the fire extinguisher.

I cough into my fist. "I didn't even realize that she was making pie, let alone that the stove was still on. On *broil*, no fucking less."

"What the fuck?!" Davis's breaths are still heaving from all the excitement. He pushes some windows open.

I lead the way back into the dining room where the other half of the family is still gathered.

Meghan immediately approaches me, sliding an arm around my back. "You okay?"

I nod, suppressing a cough.

She gives me a concerned smile.

Jasper is pushing some windows open. Harry is standing on a chair, waving a hand towel in front of the smoke detector. No one can even hear each other's nervous ramblings until Harry finally gets the thing to shut up.

With my ears still ringing, my eyes land on Grammy, who is slumped in her chair staring out at nothing.

Jasper lowers into the chair beside her. "Grams? What's going on? Why were you baking a pie on...broil?"

She's quiet for so long I don't think she's going to answer him. When she finally speaks, her tone is embarrassed and guilty. "I wasn't baking it on broil. Everyone knows you don't use the broiler for *baking*."

Of course. Of course Grammy knows that. She's the best baker in town.

"Grams?" Jasper questions, knowing as good as all of us that there's got to be more to the story. She's acting...unusual.

The woman finally gazes around the room at each of us, an apology in her eyes. "I just left the pie in the oven hoping to keep it warm. I thought I'd turned off the stove. I must have hit the wrong button." She drops her gaze.

"Well, how'd you do that?" somebody asks.

She swallows hard. "I...I'm going blind," she confesses softly.

Silence abruptly smacks the room.

"I don't understand," I finally say, breaking the tension in the air.

She speaks again, her voice louder, stronger, more defiant this time. "I didn't tell you all, because I didn't want you to worry but...I'm losing my eyesight."

"No. No way, Grams," my cousin, Corri, bellows.

Davis growls. "Who told you that? That quack doctor you've been seeing?"

Aunt Victoria gasps into her hands as Uncle Eric consoles her, rubbing her shoulders.

My grandmother's lips thin as she shakily rises to her feet, ignoring all the questions being flung her way. "I'm tired. I think I'll go lie down for a bit. Leave the mess. I'll deal with it later." With that, she turns and shuffles away, down the hall.

I wait until her door squeaks shut before I turn to Mason, the only fucking doctor in this family. "Did you know about this? Did she go to see you?"

With a deep frown, Mason stands. "No. I've had my suspicions that something was up with her but she always brushed it off. She refused to talk about it."

"I realized that she was 'off', too," Harry confesses. "But I thought I might be imagining it."

Jasper nods. "Yeah, she was constantly giving out the wrong change and asking for help with counting the cash register. I didn't think it was a big deal. Or at least I didn't want to."

Everyone speaks at once, tripping over each other, trying to pinpoint the hints they've gotten over the months that Grammy—the matriarch of our family—has been slowly losing her eyesight.

I'm burning up with irritation. Every damn body got a clue and nobody bothered to have a conversation about it?!

Mason speaks above the noise. "I'll talk to her, make sure she knows her options. See if she's ready for a second opinion."

Everyone watches, still reeling from Grammy's news.

I fall back in my seat next to Meghan. She grabs my hand and squeezes, telling me in her own way that she's here for me. I'm sure she'd rather be anywhere else, but it means the world to me to have her support.

She leans over and speaks quietly to me. "I'm going to go clean up, so your grandmother doesn't have to worry about it later." She kisses me on the cheek and disappears into the kitchen.

"I should go help Meghan," my cousin, Corri, murmurs. The other girls follow her.

Harry flings a dish cloth onto the table, knocking over someone's water glass. "Fuck. That was fun," he mutters as the liquid spills onto the floor. "Same time next week?"

THIRTY-EIGHT

CASH

DAVIS. Mason. Harry. Jasper. Me.

We all stand around in this tiny exam room the next morning and listen to the town optometrist explain Grammy's options to her. Basically, have a risky surgery that she could potentially wake up blind from. Or take some goddamned eye drops for the rest of her life and go blind anyway.

Utter bullshit.

Grammy's scared. I can see it on her face. And there's nothing I can do to help her. My chest feels like it'll burst with anger. At this point, I need some fresh air.

I glance down at my phone. So many missed calls. Always more missed calls. Including three from Cannon Kingston.

Shit—I've been meaning to get back to him. He's been calling me for days now. I shove my phone in my pocket. He'll have to wait a little longer.

It's funny how the situation got flipped on its head. A few short weeks ago, I was spending my days, trying to figure out how to set up a meeting at my office with this guy.

To no avail. Then, I meet him at a freaking fashion show?! I guess I have my Buttercup to thank for that. My girl is magic in too many ways to count. And now, the tables have turned completely and I'm the one forgetting to return Kingston's calls.

"Excuse me," I grunt. I slip out the exam room door while the guys ask the doctor a million and one questions.

A million and one questions that won't change our grandmother's fate.

It's been one thing after another these past few weeks. It's like everything is in the shitter. Every aspect of my life's on fire. Meghan is the only ray of sunshine I have left. And I've been letting her down at every turn.

I'm no stranger to leading a busy life but it's like the second I decided to rearrange my priorities to make room for Meghan, the universe dropped a dump truck of new shit in my lap for me to figure out. I'm stressed like hell trying to make sure that everything gets the attention it deserves.

Desperate for a moment of reprieve, I steamroll into the quiet hallway between the various offices of the medical building. I find Meghan stepping out of the veterinary clinic with a furrow on her brow and her phone in her hand right at that moment.

"Hey," I say, immediately turning in her direction.

She looks up. "Hey." She comes toward me, wearing her adorable ponytail and her adorable scrubs and her adorable dimpled smile.

It's only been a few hours since we stumbled out of bed together. But damn, it feels good to see her.

She slips her phone into the pocket of her scrubs. "I have a short break. I was trying to text to see if you were still around here but I just realized my phone is dead," she explains.

"I'm still here." My shoulders fall when I exhale.

"How'd everything go at your grandmother's appointment?" Meghan asks.

I jerk my chin to the eye clinic behind me. "She's still in there with the rest of the guys. I needed some air." I drape an arm around her and kiss the top of her head.

Meghan leans into my touch and her stomach rumbles softly. This morning, she skipped breakfast. Again. I hate when she does that.

"How long is your break?" I ask her. "Did you get a second to eat something? I could run into town and grab you a snack if you want." I scrub a hand down my face. So fucking tired.

She closely watches my movement. "I'm fine. Don't worry about me." Her hands come to my shoulders. She trails her soothing touch down my arms. "There's so much going on with your dad. And now your grandmother. And... You have enough on your plate. Cash, I'm getting worried about you." Her eyes brim with concern. "You can't be everywhere at once, doing everything for everybody. This is too much for you. And I feel bad that you're worrying about me."

Dammit. I'm growing sick of her constantly trying to downplay her importance to me. It's like she's pushing me away when all I want is to take care of her. It's like she wants me close but every time I get too close, she shuts down with guilt and tries to put space between us.

"I'm starting to get the feeling that you don't want me around," I grumble.

"What?!" She blinks at me with her blonde lashes.

"If you don't want me hanging around, the least you could do is just say it. I don't need you questioning my decision-making about everything." This has got to be my fatigue talking. Not my logic. Because the words I'm saying aren't making any sense.

Meghan's eyes become defensive. Rightfully so. "Okay, you're obviously misreading what I'm saying to you."

"What are you saying, then?" I challenge.

"I'm saying that I'm concerned. I feel like you're burning yourself out. Taking care of your family. And your job. *And* me. It's too much."

My voice comes out harsher than I intend it to. "Leave it to me to decide what my family needs and what my job needs. All you have to decide is whether you're in this with me or not."

Damn. My fucking inner asshole has taken the wheel. Deep down, I feel like I'm failing Meghan. It's making me lash out. And I'm too fucking exhausted to manage this feeling of being out of control.

I hate to admit it but, more and more, I'm wondering if Meghan's been right all along. What if a relationship between us isn't realistic? What if it's too much work? Especially when we live over five hundred miles apart? What if it was too ambitious of me to think that we could have it all? That prospect terrifies me.

Her eyes go narrow. "Cash, I'm mad that you'd even question whether I want to be with you. I've been pretty clear that I love you."

I'm not being fair to her. She's probably only trying to look out for me. But I'm far too tired to be diplomatic right now. Why won't she just let me take care of her?

I really don't intend to come off as gruff as I'm coming off right now. I need her to understand that.

I tenderly cup her cheek. "Yes, I've got a lot on my plate. But everything on my plate is someone or something that I care deeply about. So what do you expect me to do, Megs?

Abandon the people who rely on me? Just because it's hard? Yes, it's hard but I can handle it. I'm not looking for an easy way out."

A man in a white lab coat walks down the quiet hallway. He gives me a wary look before his attention falls on Meghan. "How are you, Ms. Hutchins?"

"Perfect. Great, Dr. Peterson." She forces a smile.

Fuck. I'm making a scene. At Meghan's place of work. *Not cool, asshole.*

She lowers her voice and eyeballs me. "Look, my break is almost over. Can we talk about this later?"

"Fine."

Meghan rises onto her toes, wraps her arms around my neck and gives me a quick kiss. When she pulls back, she searches my eyes. "We're both sort of emotional right now. Maybe we need a little space to clear our heads."

Her words wring my heart inside my chest. I sigh and speak quietly. "How much space are you asking for, Buttercup?"

Her cheeks pinken with a blush. "I...I...Let's just talk later..." *Before either of us says something stupid in the heat of the moment, or makes a decision we can't undo,* her eyes fill in the blanks.

I fill my lungs on a harsh inhale. "Fine. We'll talk later."

"Yeah." She releases me and drops back to her soles.

I watch her, everything inside me tightening as she disappears inside the veterinary clinic again.

My eyes swing back toward the optometrist's office. But I don't want to go back inside that depressing place. So I saunter through the lobby and head for my car parked on the curb.

I'll wait there until Grammy's appointment is over. As I'm about to sink behind the wheel, I feel my phone vibrating with an incoming call. I dig it out of my pocket and bring it to my ear.

"Nicky? What do you need?" I briskly ask my sister. I've been trading emails with her all morning.

"Cash. Cash, this is bad." Nicky is out of breath, panicked, and I can tell she's hustling down an office hallway.

At the alarming tone of her voice, my movements falter, and I pause next to the open door of my car. "What is it?"

She speaks frantically, reading off the fax that just came through. It's about another huge deal that's going sideways. One that may already be fully capsized by the sound of it.

"Everybody's going ballistic," she tells me. "The board is blowing up the phone lines. And I can't call Dad, for obvious reasons. Only you can fix this, Cash. I don't know what to do."

I lean against the cool metal of my car, letting my head rest on the top.

I can't exactly tell her to deal with this on her own. She's an intern for crying out loud. And if I were to hand this mess off to anyone else at the office and the deal fell through, I'd want their head on a platter. What Nicky said is true—I'm the only one who can fix this.

What the hell am I doing?

In a moment of clarity, I see that I've been an absolute idiot. Bailing on work. Following Meghan around. Shirking all my responsibilities. Letting my family down.

I look at the dumpster fire my life has become.

I'm failing. I'm failing. I'm failing.

I'm failing the woman I love.

Maybe I should keep my distance. Maybe I should leave Meghan the hell alone, so I don't end up hurting her in the long run.

I see now that she was right. A relationship between us is not realistic. Not when I've got spinning plates in every other area of my life, too.

I can't have it all.

It's time to be realistic.

It's time to be a damn adult again.

"Cash? Cash? Are you still there?" I faintly hear Nicky. She's still going into hysterics.

I bring the phone back to my ear. "Yeah. I'll be back at the office by eight tonight. Think you can meet me there?"

Work now occupying my headspace, I speed across town to Meghan's house. I change into some work clothes, pack my bags, and load up the cat, ready to leave Honey Hill behind. Braveheart mewls mournfully as I separate him from the other cats and carry him to the car.

I shake my head. This whole ridiculous scene just underscores my loss of sanity.

Me, in my business suit, a squirming cat under my arm, hauling a shit ton of animal accessories to my trunk.

I try to compartmentalize my feelings like I've always done in the past. But this time, it's just not working. Because this time, my heart is involved. Maybe I should take one last shot.

But a quick call to Meghan's phone sends me straight to voicemail without even ringing. Damn. She was serious about wanting her space. I should just respect her wishes.

The delusion was fun while it lasted. But now it's time to face reality again.

THIRTY-NINE

MEGHAN

INSTEAD OF STAYING LATE like I do most days, after work, I rush home.

All day, it nagged me how poorly I handled that conversation with Cash earlier today. I'm worried about him because he's going out of his way, trying to be everything to everybody. And that makes me genuinely concerned for his wellbeing. But I don't think that's how it came across in our conversation. I think I left him feeling like I'm pushing him away. That's really not my intention.

I see how much he has on his plate. And I hate being just one more responsibility he has to look after.

I feel a strong need to explain myself to him. The minute my phone finished charging, I wanted to call him and have a much-needed conversation. But we did agree to give each other some space to think things through.

By the end of the day, I'm finally seeing things clearly. I rush out of the clinic and speed home with Cash on my mind.

I can't help but notice that his car isn't in his driveway when I arrive. Even though he isn't supposed to leave town until later tonight, a twinge of worry pulls at my chest, telling me that he's already decided to quit on us.

Don't be silly, Meghan. I actively remind myself that it's just my familiar old patterns and insecurities playing out their usual song and dance in my brain, niggling me that I'll be abandoned by someone I care for so much.

I push that aside, knowing Cash's not like that. I can't keep comparing him to all the other jerkwads I've gone out with. If this relationship is going to work, I need to trust him.

Pausing and resting my head on my steering wheel, I rehearse what I'm going to say to Cash, hoping and praying I don't screw this up.

I'm all in for him. All in. Ready to support him in any way necessary. I need to cut all my bullshit and make that clear to him.

When I have my speech just right, I take a deep breath and rush up the walkway to his house.

I ring the doorbell, and give my best attempt at a sultry smirk when the door swings open. But said smirk slides right off my face.

"Jasper?" Crap. "Uh, is Cash here?"

Jasper leans out the doorway, eyeing the driveway and drawing my attention back to the obvious. *Cash's car isn't here. And neither is he.*

"Nope. Sorry, neighbor. Your loverboy's gone."

"Gone where?" I ask, trying not to panic.

He arches an eyebrow, looking confused. "He went back to Chicago. Left hours ago. Didn't he tell you?"

"He did not." I blink back the sting in my eyes.

Jasper shakes his head, sympathy on his face. "He ditched the rest of us at the optometrist's office with Grammy. Then he called later and said he was on his way back to Chicago to deal with some emergency at the office." He shrugs. "I don't know what to tell you, Megs."

"Thanks, Jasper."

My spirits utterly deflated, I do a whole new version of the walk of shame, marching back across the street as Jasper looks on. I enter my house, collapsing on my couch, fighting back stinging tears.

So much for Cash not abandoning me like the jerkwads of my past...

It took me nine years to find my big girl panties, and now I've missed my chance to actually wear them, dammit.

Pulling a throw pillow to my chest, I glare off into nothingness. My frustration quickly shatters into bitterness. Into raw, red anger. *Seriously, Cassius Westbrook?*

Okay, I'll admit it. I had a momentary wobble about our relationship. Normal, given the things I grew up believing about myself when it comes to love.

But how dare he leave town without even saying goodbye to me? I sure as hell didn't deserve that.

I'm not going to just put on a rosy, sunshiney smile and let this slide. Whether he knows it's coming or not, Cash is going to get a piece of my mind.

FORTY

CASH

I SPENT the whole drive back to Chicago on the phone, doing my best to untangle the deal on the verge of collapse. The minute I got to the city, I dropped the cat at my condo. Then I entered a never-ending meeting at the client's office across town. It took four hours and three pots of terrible coffee but finally, I salvaged the deal by the skin of my teeth.

Now it's past midnight and I'm trudging the parking garage of the client's office building, toward my car. The adrenaline of today's events has worn off and I'm already feeling empty again.

I need to call Meghan. Urgently.

Fuck me for thinking I could just walk away from her like nothing.

I'm regretting how I left things between us. I shouldn't have lost my temper. And I definitely shouldn't have left town before smoothing things over with her.

Feeling a sense of urgency and worrying that I really have fucked things up, I take my phone off airplane mode and dial her number. Relief floods through me as I watch her beautiful, sleepy face appear on the screen.

"Hi," I say to her.

"Hi," she responds. She sits up in bed and flicks on the lamp on her bedside table. I note the flatness in her eyes and the lack of emotion in her tone. It makes me uneasy.

"How are you?" *Way to beat around the bushes, asshole.*

She emits a loaded sigh. "Not great, Cash." She pauses. "Your brother told me you left town. What the hell?"

I should have known that hasty decision would come back to bite me in the ass. "I'm sorry. I shouldn't have left without fixing things with you. But an emergency came up at work. And with Dad out of the office, I was the only one who could fix it." I rub my tired eyes.

The truth is, as we stood there in the medical center hallway and Meghan was listing off every one of the obligations on my to-do list, I saw something familiar in her eyes. The look of disappointment that my mom wore each time Dad let her down. It killed me seeing that look on Meghan's face. It made me hate myself a little bit. So, when Nicky called with that emergency, on some level, I was grateful for the excuse to run away.

Meghan sighs, looking downcast. "This just confirms what I've been saying all along, Cash. I can't expect you to stick around, making yourself available to me when you have a long list of pressing things that need your attention. That's not fair to you. Your family needs you. Your business needs you."

"And I need *you*. I love you." I hear my own voice crack. I don't even recognize it.

"Yet, here we are, hurting each other." Meghan's words shake. "Cash, we can't go on like this."

I hate this. I hate that she's hurting because of me. I told myself it was my mission to make her happy. Obviously, I've failed. Miserably.

"So what happens now?" I keep my tone cool but I'm sure my expression betrays my panic through the phone screen.

She purses her lips for a moment. "Looks like we're at a stalemate, huh?"

"Don't give up on us, Megs. Please." I'm begging. I don't care. "I know I'm not perfect at this boyfriend thing. I'm still trying my best to figure it out. But I will. I'll figure out a way to make this work."

"But at what cost?" she questions quietly. "I can't claim that I love you and just sit back, watching you run yourself into the ground." She sighs. "You can't be everything to everybody, Cash. You can't be running a company in Chicago practically on your own and rushing to Honey Hill to spend time with me. You have to worry about your dad. And your grandmother. And...Gosh, I just feel like I'm getting in the way."

I don't want to blow up. I'm trying *really* hard not to blow up. Because that won't help my case. It won't help me convince her that out of everything that matters to me, she matters most.

"You're not getting in the way. There's got to be a solution, Buttercup. Give me some time. Let me find it."

She speaks softly. "We both know what the solution is. We have to be realistic. We have to walk away."

"Don't say that." I feel my desperation rising but I don't know what to say to change things.

Meghan is crying now. She's pushing tears away from her eyes. "It's the inevitable truth, Cash. This is too much for you. All of this is too much. I can't sit by and watch you break. I love you too much."

I make one last feeble attempt to save this. "Don't you turn your back on us. Don't."

But she only gives me a small smile. "I'm sorry, Cash. I love you. I always will. That's why I have to let you go."

My screen goes black.

FORTY-ONE

MEGHAN

I CHEW on my thumbnail as I stare at the Google search bar sitting on the screen of the desktop computer.

Vet technician jobs chicago

I glance over the top of the computer monitor, staring out at the pets and their owners in the waiting room of the veterinary clinic. Then I lower my eyes back to the screen.

Why am I even doing this to myself? I don't really want to move to Chicago, do I? That's not realistic. I have my job here. My house. My friends.

It might be fun to daydream about leaving, but in all reality, I don't have the balls to give up my life here in Honey Hill in the pursuit of love.

That thing between Cash and me was nice while it lasted. But it's done now. And these desperate fantasies of mine aren't going to fix anything. I need to face reality.

The truth is that the distance was only one of our problems. Cash is genuinely too busy for a serious relationship. And I'm genuinely too batshit scared to trust him with my heart anyway. So why waste my time daydreaming about forever for us?

Besides, he probably doesn't even want me after the way I ended things between us. I was cold. I didn't hear him out when he was asking for a chance to find a solution.

At the end of the day, I can come up with as many excuses as I want about why Cash and I fell apart. But the truth is I was scared that eventually, I'd be hopelessly attached to him and he'd start to pull away, leaving me crushed.

I should be happy that things are over between us. But nothing's right now that I don't have Cash anymore. Without his nightly calls and his midday text messages and his impromptu visits to town just to see my face, I just want to cry. Every minute of every day, I want to cry. But I'm forced to keep my shit together.

I hit backspace on my Google inquiry just as Maxine walks into the clinic, back from her lunch.

"Hey, girlie!" she chirps, coming back to her desk with an empty container and water bottle in hand. "Thanks for covering my break. You can go grab your lunch now."

I glance at the search bar on the screen again and that foolish, desperate part of my heart gives one more pleading thump.

"Just one sec," I tell her as my coworker scatters the contents of her makeup kit onto the counter and reapplies her lipstick.

Despite my brain telling me to quit my delusions, I type out *Chicago veterinary clinic* jobs again. I click on a job postings website and hit the 'print' button. As the job listings spew out of the printer, I'm reminding myself just how stupid this is, giving myself false hope. But I can't stop myself.

"See you in forty-five minutes," I tell Maxine as I fold up the warm sheets of paper and slip them into my purse. I round the reception desk and head out the clinic's back exit.

Ignoring the hunger pangs in my stomach, I sit on the low concrete curb. My tears come and I let them fall. I miss him so much...

I let my eyes scan the print-out again. I can't help but wonder what life would be like if I *did* move to Chicago. Cash and I would wake up together every morning. Fall asleep together every night. Work and responsibilities and distractions would fill all the hours in between but at least we'd be in each others' lives. It would be better than what we have now.

But how long before all my ugly insecurities would rear their heads again and ruin everything?

This isn't realistic, Meghan. Be realistic.

I hear the clinic's metal back door pop open. I hurriedly wipe the tears from my cheeks before glancing up. A woman I recognize stumbles outside.

My half-sisters' mother—Darlene, I think her name is— collapses against the brick siding of the building, burying her sobs in her palms.

What the hell?! What the hell is wrong with her?!

Alarmed, I forget my own problems and cautiously move in her direction. Even though my common sense tells me to keep my distance. "Hey," I say to her when only a few feet separate us. "Hey, what's wrong?"

She pulls her hands from her face with a start. "Dammit," she spits out quietly when she sees it's me staring at her.

"Is everything okay?" I press on although she's clearly not excited to see me.

She scrubs her tears away with her fists. "I'm fine.

Everything's fine." She shakes her head like she's trying to brush all her worries away.

Obviously, I'm not convinced. "My...my sisters. Are they okay?"

She looks at me. Her eyes fall closed. Then she breaks down again. "I...I can't have this conversation with you," she whispers, shaking her head some more. "Not with you."

I watch her hustle back for the door. But I'm tired. Tired of tiptoeing around the peripheries of my life. Tired of avoiding the difficult conversations.

Usually, I like being agreeable. Smiling and shooting sunbeams out my ass like a freaking rainbow unicorn. Not making anyone uncomfortable or putting anyone on the spot. But here's the thing—being agreeable and sunshiney has been getting me nowhere lately.

"It's not fair to them," I call out after her as she reaches for the door. "We may not have grown up as some big, happy family. But those girls want to know me. We're sisters. We share blood. That means something."

Her steps freeze when I say that. Her shoulders shake.

Slowly, she turns back to me and her face is a mask of pure misery. "Jessica, the older one, she's sick. She needs a... procedure..." Her whole body shakes now. "And...it's just been so hard. Everything is so hard. The doctors appointments and hospital stays and...It's been so hard. Doing it all on my own." She sobs some more.

I move closer to her. "What do you mean, doing it all on your own? My dad—our dad—"

"Hell if I know where to find that deadbeat bastard." She laughs bitterly. "Haven't seen or heard from him in nearly a year."

"What...?" I whisper. "He abandoned them, too?"

She nods. "You look surprised. Isn't that the way he operates? You should know that. I should have known, too."

She's wrong. I had no idea that he would abandon those precious girls. It never occurred to me that he'd leave them the way he left me.

I feel my jaw go tight. "I...I thought he was different with them..."

"Different how?" Darlene asks.

"I thought he had abandoned me because..." *Because I wasn't good enough. Because I wasn't worthy. Because I was cursed. Like all the women in the Hutchins family.*

The woman drops a palm to my arm. Her touch feels foreign on my skin but I don't shrug it off. "Oh, girl. That man doesn't need a 'because'. He's a bastard. And bastards will be bastards. They don't need a reason."

I shake my head. "I always thought that it was my fault. That he left because something was wrong with me."

Darlene's face transforms. Or maybe the way I see her transforms. In this moment, she loses the harsh, intimidating outer shell that always covers her features. In my eyes, she takes on the air of a fierce, protective mother who has had to be tough to shield her cubs from the world.

"The way that man treated you has nothing to do with you. None of it is your fault. That's what I've been trying to teach my girls." Her nostrils flare as her tears overflow from her eyes again. "But try getting a sick child to understand why her own father isn't there for her. Why he won't even get tested to figure out if he's a genetic match to give her the treatments that could save her life. It's a job I wouldn't wish on any mother."

Her words leave me speechless.

My father didn't leave because I was bad? Because I wasn't deserving of his time and attention? He left because

THE WILD SIDE: A FRIENDS-TO-LOVERS ROMANTI... 365

he was the kind of man who thinks it's okay to quit on his own responsibilities...

That man is a bastard.

This new information is too heavy for me. My chest feels like it's been hacked open by a saw, leaving my poor battered heart with the wires hanging out.

Darlene checks the time on her phone. "Oh, shit. I'm sorry. I have to go. I left my girls with the receptionist at the pediatric clinic. I told her I was going to the washroom for a second."

I nod. "Okay. I understand."

She turns back toward the door. Right before she steps inside, she pauses. Then she dips her hand into her purse, pulls out a tiny notebook and scribbles something in messy handwriting. She hands the sheet of paper to me. "I...I don't know if you'll ever use this or not. It's up to you..."

I stare down at her phone number on the paper sitting in the palm of my hand. "Thank you," I say quietly. "And thank you for speaking to me."

She nods. "Thank you for listening, Meghan."

Her sad eyes tell me that it's just too hard to smile. She opens the door and heads inside.

FORTY-TWO

CASH

"IF SOMEONE HAD TOLD me my life would come to this, I'd have given up the cream cheese a long time ago."

I glance over my back and find Dad wiping sweat from his forehead with his long sleeve. His chest heaves.

Beside me, Nicky slows her jog to let Dad catch up. "Hmm...if only." She laughs softly.

It's early and there's a nip in the air but the sky is clear overhead. Over the past week, the three of us have been meeting every morning for a run. Dad's collapse was the wake up call we needed. It shone a spotlight on the fact that we all could stand to make a few changes in our lives.

The running is a good distraction for me. It helps me clear my head and get my blood flowing, especially after spending another sleepless night with Meghan on my mind. As long as no one expects me to talk too much, it's not all that bad.

Since I lost Meghan, life has been so mechanical. So robotic. Day in, day out, I find myself going through the motions. I've been operating on rote, devoting all my mental energy to keeping my thoughts off the woman who walked away from me as I mindlessly tick my way through my to-do list.

There's no more Meghan...No more of the color and the light and the sunshine she brought to my life. She's not my lover anymore. She's not even my friend. I can't believe I let her slip through my fingers.

"So..." Nicky says in that gossipy way of hers. But her eyes are trained on Dad instead of me. "Is Mom still in town?"

Our father's feet get bungled at the mention of his ex-wife. He catches himself and clears his throat. "Um, she left this morning. Her train was at seven. I thought she'd called you."

Nicky smirks. "She did. I was just looking for a polite opening to work her into the conversation." My sister grins. "So are we getting our hopes up over this or not?"

Dad rolls his eyes with a slight frown on his lips. "It's more complicated than that, Nicky. Don't start getting your hopes up for a reunion." He trudges off toward a wooden bench and takes a seat.

The air is crisp. It smells like spring. I silently drop down beside him, drinking from my water bottle.

Nicky is sprite and chirpy as ever, with the energy of a damn hummingbird as she jogs in place in front of our bench. "Complicated, how?" she whines. "Mom dropped everything she was doing and rushed out here to be at your side the second I called and told her you were in the hospital. You love her. You always have. And she obviously still loves you. Sounds pretty simple to me."

Dad wipes his forehead again, looking sad and rueful. "Your mom only came here to help put *your* mind at ease because you were freaking out so bad. She's moved on with her life. She's dating someone now."

Nicky's eyes spin up to the sky. "You trump that other guy and you know it. All you have to do is say the word and she's all yours again."

"Wishful thinking." He looks out over the other early morning joggers circling the park, his expression pained.

"Quitter." Nicky squeezes herself into the space on the bench between us and pouts.

Shit. My dad is still in love with my mother. And she's moving on with another man.

Is that how things will end up with Meghan and me in the long run? Because no way in hell I'll ever find someone to replace her. But what if she replaces me? Of course she will. She's beautiful, smart, sweet. Of course some other man will sweep her off her feet.

This conversation is hitting a little too close to my own situation and I hate how my sister is oversimplifying everything. "Nicky, stop pushing it," I grumble. "Sometimes relationships don't work out. We just have to accept that."

She throws her face upward to the sky and groans. "What is it with the two of you? If you'd put half as much dedication into your love lives as you do into your careers, you'd be living way happier lives. Look at you, Cash. Just merrily walking along in Dad's footsteps. For your information, you can flip the script. You don't have to act this movie out scene by scene like our parents did."

I feel my chest start to go tight. "Don't bring Meghan into this," I warn her.

My sister sticks her fists on her hips. "Y'know what? *Let's* bring Meghan into this. Help me follow along here. You basically let her break up with you because she cared too much about you and you cared too much about her. Please make it make sense."

She's not being facetious. She genuinely wants to

understand. But trying to explain my situation with Meghan to a third party is impossible. Because I'm still trying to make sense of it myself.

"The breakup was her idea. Not mine. I didn't have a say in it." I think back to Meghan and how adamant she was about ending our relationship. There's a hollow ache inside my chest.

How the hell am I supposed to just be done with her? Just carry on with my life like it's nothing? This woman was my best friend for half my life before she became my lover. I spent half my life fighting feelings for her before finally letting them bloom only a few weeks ago. And now I'm just supposed to walk away? Respect her decision and walk away?

"I can assure *you* that a break up is not what Meghan wants," Nicky says like she's an insider on this situation.

"I have too much going on in my life, too many responsibilities on my plate to give her the kind of relationship she deserves. Forcing her to settle for less was selfish of me. I could already see that we were falling into a cycle of me constantly breaking promises to her and disappointing her while she pretended to be fine and go along with it. It wasn't healthy." I pull in a breath before I say the next part. "We're better off apart."

I'm a damned liar.

She and I were doomed from the start. Because I was always doomed to repeat my father's mistakes. Meghan is better off without me as her boyfriend and I have to accept it.

Nicky throws up her hands. "Newsflash, genius. The reason you have so much responsibility on your plate is because you're a damn control freak. Because you want to be in charge of everything. Even things that are none of your damned business."

Dad pipes up. "That's true, actually."

Wow—I can't even believe he'd throw me under the bus like that! "What are you talking about?" I glare at him.

He doesn't back down. "You're chief *financial* officer of the company, Cash. Yet you stick your nose into the operations of every other department."

"All the departments rely on me," I argue, dragging a palm along the jagged surface of the wooden bench. "They need me."

My father shakes his head. "Because you made it that way. We both did. Over the years, we've built a co-dependent culture within the firm that makes it so that one of us always needs to be around. We've made it so that nothing can function without your input or mine. That was a failure on our part. But it can be undone."

I pinch the bridge of my nose, hating that he's right. "How?" I challenge. "How can we fix it?"

"By giving up some control. By hiring people qualified to run each department. By setting up boundaries and ensuring that they're respected."

"Easier said than done," I complain, unwilling to concede. "I single-handedly saved the company from losing a very significant client just a few days ago. I was the only one who could have done that."

"*Again*, because we built the company that way. But we can rebuild it. To run independently of either one of us. So that we can both take a damn breather every now and then." Dad sets a hand on my shoulder. "Then, you can finally have a life of your own and have time for the things that matter to you." He inhales deeply. "One thing became clear to me when I was hooked up to those machines in the hospital. I wasn't thinking about which clients I could have gotten more money out of or which deals I should have pushed harder. I was thinking about the woman I let walk away from me almost fifteen years ago. I was thinking about the one thing I regret in my life above all else."

"What's that?" Nicky asks, her eyes riveted to our father.

Dad's next words hit me straight in the gut because I get a premonition of myself repeating those same words twenty years from now. "I should have fought for her when I had the chance. There's nothing in my life I regret more."

FORTY-THREE

MEGHAN

ZIGGY RUSHES through the front door of the Hot Sauce. She glances around the room then smiles in relief when she sees me at the bar.

"Phew! I thought I was late but Alana and Emma aren't here yet, are they?" She slides her satchel off her shoulder and gracefully slithers out of her long cardigan.

"You *are* late. Alana and Emma aren't coming." I slam back a shot of tequila. I swing my stool around and lift the empty glass to Aunt Jane. "Another one. Or maybe another-nother one," I slur.

By now, I've lost count of how many *'nother ones* I've had tonight.

Ziggy's eyebrows quirk up like question marks. She throws a sidelong glimpse at Aunt Jane behind the bar. "Is... everything okay?" she asks me.

I grab her by the elbow and frantically plunk her down onto the stool next to me. "I need your help."

Compassion rises to her eyes. She gives me the look all girls reserve for a friend muddling her way through heartbreak. "Oh, sweetie. What can I do to help?"

My eyes are having a hard time focusing. I sway forward into her personal space and loud-whisper in her face. "I need a…" I surreptitiously glance around for spectators before speaking above the soft-rock music. "…a consultation with the spirits."

Ziggy's neck rears back and she scrunches up her nose. "My gosh, Meghan. What's your new perfume called? *Eau de Tequila?*"

I cup a hand around my mouth and sniff. *Ohhhh! That's intense.* "Sorry about that," I say meekly. I may be as drunk as a skunk but the least I can do is hang onto my manners.

Ziggy returns to the issue at hand. "Um…okay…so what's this about you wanting a spiritual consultation?" She sounds suspicious. Usually when she starts going on with her metaphysical talk, I run in the opposite direction. But today, I need to have a little chitchat with my higher self.

My bartender aunt slides a bourbon lemonade across the counter at my friend. "You're going to need this," she warns sagely.

Aunt Jane is not wrong. I've been a mess in the days since Cash and I broke up. I haven't been sleeping. Food doesn't taste right. Every outfit I put on looks drab and colorless.

The world is drab and colorless.

Breaking up with him didn't make my nagging guilt and insecurities fade away. Instead, I feel ten times worse than I did before. Goddamn. I broke *my own* heart. I'm such an idiot.

"I need clarity," I mumble, taking the new tequila shot my aunt sets in front of me. "I need to figure out what the hell is wrong with me."

"Okay, we can…we can look into that." Ziggy takes a

long gulp of her drink then slips a tarot deck out of her purse.

I stop her with a hand on her wrist. "I want to know something very specific, though."

Aunt Jane watches us from the other side of the bar with a concerned expression. I briefly make eye contact with her.

"What do you want to know?" Ziggy asks.

I inhale a steely breath before blurting out, "Is the curse real?"

Ziggy's brow crinkles. "The curse?"

Even through my drunken state, I feel a tiny bit embarrassed by how silly I sound saying this out loud. But Ziggy's the most open-minded person I know. I'm sure she's not judging me.

"The Hutchins curse. My mother says the women in our family are cursed. That we can never find true love. And I need to know if it's real." I feel big, fat, juicy tears streaming down my face. "Because I just broke my own heart walking away from the only man that I've ever truly loved, my best friend in the whole fucking world, and I'm losing my mind now." I wipe my tears with balled-up fists. "So I need to know...do you think the Hutchins curse is real?"

I desperately need an answer, once and for all. Because I grew up believing that love would evade me forever, that finding someone to give my heart to just wasn't in the cards for me. Except, it really feels like I found that with Cash. And it feels like I'm the one who threw it away.

Was it fate? Or is this heartbreak I'm feeling my own damn fault?

I watch helplessly as my friend closes her eyes and gathers her thoughts for a long moment.

But when she opens her eyes, she doesn't pull a card from the tarot deck or whip out a crystal ball. Instead, she reaches across the bar and takes both of my hands in hers. "Let me put it this way, honey. The absolute worst spell that anyone can fall under is the curse of their own limiting beliefs."

"Wh-what?" I ask, clueless.

"As humans, nothing outside of us has the power to keep us trapped the way our own negative mindset can. So if you don't have love in your life, it's because, on some level, you're not letting love in."

"It can't be that simple," I say, ready to defend the beliefs that have bogged me down for so long. They *have to* be true. Otherwise, that means that I fucked my own life up over a lie.

"It is that simple," Ziggy tells me. "But the good news? The remedy is just as simple."

"What is it?" I ask eagerly.

Look, I'll gladly dance naked down by the creek under the full moon if I have to. I'm just *so ready* to be free of the thoughts and fears that have been holding me back my whole life.

"Start by asking yourself why," Ziggy says softly "Why won't you allow yourself to be loved the way you want to. And then, decide. Just make the decision that you won't keep telling yourself that old story anymore. Rewrite your story. You have the power to choose something new. And whether you realize it or not, your belief is stronger than the power of any curse."

My gosh. It feels like my whole world is unraveling before me, one frayed thread at a time. Throughout my relationship with Cash, I always had this niggling feeling at the back of my mind. This itchy feeling beneath my skin that he was going to wake up one day and realize that he had better shit to do with his time than loving me. That he was going to lose all interest and dump me and move on to what was *really* important in his life. After all, it's what my father did.

Now, I see that my father didn't abandon me because I was a shitty kid. He abandoned me because he was a shitty man. And that's not a burden I should be forced to carry my whole life.

That changes everything.

I see Aunt Jane wiping tears from her eyes. "I always told your mother that she should let you choose your own story instead of packing your head with fear and feelings of unworthiness. I know that she was only trying to protect you but in her attempt to keep you safe from the world, she made you afraid of the world. And you got hurt anyway."

Ziggy bobs her head. "You spent your entire relationship with Cash trying to prove to him that he'd be better off without you. Yet for some nutty reason, you're surprised that you actually convinced him to walk away, that he finally gave up on you."

Aunt Jane agrees. "That, my darling niece, is called a self-fulfilling prophecy. It's not some unshakeable curse you can't break free of."

I wince and bite my lip. "Shit."

I was too afraid to really examine the reasons behind my fear of being abandoned by Cash so at the first opportunity that presented itself, I removed myself from the equation.

Yes, the long-distance dating was an obstacle but if I'm being honest, I never made a real effort to work with Cash on solving it. I simply took the easy route and ran away.

Ziggy carefully examines my face as this understanding finally dawns on me. She smiles softly.

"Thank you. Both of you." I miserably wipe my runny

nose on my sleeve and laugh ruefully. "I feel like I've been under water my whole life, holding my breath. And now, it's okay to come up above the surface and take a breath."

"That's good, sweetie." Ziggy rubs my back. She begins slipping her tarot deck back into her purse.

I eyeball the fortune-telling deck. "But maybe you can still pull some tarot cards for me? Just to be sure I'm right."

She tilts her head to the side.

"Please? Just one." I clasp my hands in prayer.

"Fine." Ziggy slowly shuffles her deck. She spreads the cards out, face down on the counter. "Pick one," she instructs.

I do as I'm told, selecting one card. I hand it to my friend, too scared to peek at it myself.

The big, triumphant smile that peels across Ziggy's face makes my limp heart soar hopefully. She flips the card face-up on the bartop. "I knew it. The empress. You're his empress."

A fresh set of tears spring to my eyes. Maybe this whole divination thing is real after all.

By the time I'm ready to leave the bar, I'm good and drunk off my ass. But I'm somewhat more optimistic about my fate.

I do still have a bunch of things to work out—between me and my journal—but I feel like I'll be able to sort through it and I'll be able to have a conversation with Cash sometime soon. Whether he'll want me back isn't guaranteed but at least we'll be able to speak openly about everything and I'll be able to own up to how I created this mess we're in.

But all that is for another day. When I'm not being a bumbling drunk.

I vaguely remember Ziggy dragging me into my house

and tucking me in bed. I pass out before my head even hits the pillow.

In the morning, I wake up, squinting against the sun beaming in through my open curtains. My mother is hovering over my bed with the Hutchins family hangover brew in hand.

Shit.

I lift my thousand-pound body into a sitting position. "Ugh! Don't make me drink that," I groan.

"Drink up," Mom says, tone light and compassionate in the face of my self-imposed misery.

Yes, I did do this to myself. Every last bit of it.

Time to own up to my crap. And time to stop letting it own me. That's why I take the tall glass of sketchy-looking brown liquid from Mom's hand as punishment for my stupidity.

Pinching my nose, I down it in a gulp and feel the exact moment the concoction lands in my acidic stomach with a splash.

"Thanks, Mom."

My mother sits at the foot of my bed and smooths my hair back from my sticky forehead. "You'll feel better soon but maybe call the clinic to let them know you'll be a few minutes late."

I wipe my mouth and clear my throat, already getting out of bed. "No. I'll be fine." I shake my head.

Bad idea. Shaking my head is definitely a bad idea. I grab the dresser for balance.

My mom watches me bumbling around.

"So I'm guessing Aunt Jane called you?" I ask her.

She nods. "I'm sorry about what happened with Cash," she says softly.

Cash. Just the mention of his name and my gut starts bubbling all over again.

"But I told you this would happen," my mother says ruefully. "I told you not to get your hopes up over him because I knew it would end like this. You could have spared yourself so much pain if you'd just listened to me, Meghan." There's no cruelty in her voice when she says it. Her heart is breaking to see mine broken.

She's a good mother. She loves me. But she doesn't always know what's best. And I refuse to spend the rest of my life living by her limitations.

"Yes, Mom. You were right. I fell in love with Cash and now my heart is shattered. I would have spared myself a lot of pain if I'd never gotten involved with him." I pull in a shaky breath. "But what else would I have missed out on?"

I think back to his soft kisses. The feel of his arms around me. The sound of his voice in my ear, telling me he loves me.

I may never be able to get those moments back but I cherish them wholeheartedly. Because my time with Cash may have been brief, but for that short time, I experienced what it was like to be loved. Truly, honestly, genuinely loved. And I'd risk heartbreak all over again just for the sake of those memories.

I lower onto the bed next to her. I take her hands. "I love you, Mom. And I appreciate you looking out for me. And while it's true that my heart is broken, it was worth it. So very worth it."

"Meghan, how could you say it was worth it?" She clutches a hand over her chest. "You don't know what you're saying."

"*You* don't know what I'm saying. Because you've never

allowed yourself to be loved. You've been so busy trying to protect yourself from pain that you didn't even realize that you're the one inflicting it on yourself." I smooth a hand down my roiling belly. "True—my dad was the wrong man for you. But guess what? There are quite literally a few billion other options out there, wandering around the face of this Earth. And maybe if you gave yourself permission to open up, you might just find it. If only for a little while, you might find love."

She shakes her head, like she's terrified of my words. "You're talking crazy, Meghan."

I exhale. "Mom—closing yourself off is a choice. You have the power to change your mind about how you feel about yourself. You have the power to choose yourself. And to be open to letting someone else choose you, too."

I pat her hand softly then give it a squeeze. I limp toward my bathroom, leaving my stunned mother sitting on the edge of my bed.

We've both got a lot to think about.

FORTY-FOUR

CASH

SUNLIGHT POURS in through the massive floor-to-ceiling windows behind me. I lean back in my conference chair and watch with bleary eyes as Cannon Kingston signs his name on the signature line. Then he passes the pen to his billionaire friend beside him. And then the pen gets passed around again. And again.

This is it.

This is the moment I've been working so damn hard toward all these months. In fact, it's better than I imagined.

Cannon Kingston, sitting at the offices of Westbrook Wealth Management, signing the documents to seal the deal. He's onboard, pushing WWM over the one billion dollar mark. Officially.

Over lunch earlier this week, I was able to sell Kingston on Westbrook Wealth Management's qualifications to manage his investments. He was eager to come here and sign the paperwork today so we can begin to put our asset growth plan in action. And not only did this man sign on as a client, but he's brought three more of his billionaire friends into the fold, too.

I look at the filthy rich men sitting across from me.

Liam Kline, Raphael Silver and King freaking Xavier of Ridgeland.

What more can I even ask for?!

I should be celebrating. There should be a marching band. And fireworks. Or confetti, at the very least. I should be over the fucking moon.

But all I feel is...nothing.

Because Meghan's not with me. Not as my woman. Now, we're barely even friends.

I stare down at our text message exchange from earlier in the week.

Cash: Hey. Just checking in. Wanted to say hi
Meghan: Hi. How are you?
Cash: Fine
Cash: You?
Meghan: Pretty good, thanks
The end.

Fuck. I want to pull my hair out.

I want to not care. I want to not love her anymore. Because she hasn't left me another choice. I'm trying my best to logic my way out of this situation. But my heart won't listen to logic. My stupid heart is kicking and screaming and begging for more of her love.

Goddammit. Did I try hard enough? Should I have made a bigger effort? I just accepted her bullshit story that we were doomed for failure. I accepted defeat and walked away. What kind of weak bullshit is that?

Painfully, my attention returns to the group of men flipping through documents across from me. None of this would have even happened if it weren't for her. I spent months trying to get a meeting with Kingston, to no avail.

Then, in comes Meghan, strolling onto the scene with her irresistible, sunshine self. If she hadn't dragged me to that fashion show and struck up a conversation with the woman sitting next to her, I wouldn't be sitting across from these men right now.

That's Meghan. She's magic and everyone knows it. Everyone but her. I should have fought for her. I should have made her see how special she is. I should have refused to accept a life without her. Instead, I left her doubting everything.

God, I'm an asshole.

Once all the documents are signed, the men rise from their seats and so do I. We all shake hands in turn.

"I'll be back in Chicago next week," Kingston tells me as we file out of the conference room, "and my wife can't stop talking about your girlfriend. Meghan, was it? It would be great to set up lunch together, if your schedule permits."

Just hearing her name detonates an explosion of pain in my chest.

I try to keep my expression neutral. "I'm afraid that won't be possible." I clear my throat of the emotion clogging it up. "Meghan and I are no longer together, unfortunately."

He arches an eyebrow at me. "That *is* unfortunate. She seemed like a great person."

"The best." *And I let her slip through my fingers.* I bite my tongue and offer nothing but a tight smile because it would be inappropriate to whip out my failed relationship history for a business associate, a complete stranger.

The other men walk up ahead of us, engrossed in their own conversation. Cannon and I stroll in silence, following them to the elevator.

After a moment, he looks at me. "I know it's none of my business, but Alexia will never stop nagging me if I don't ask you what happened." He smirks. "Gotta do my wife's dirty work and get all the gossip when she's not around."

I huff out a little laugh. "It was a distance thing," I say simply. "I live here. Meghan lives over five hundred miles away. And with all the work I have on my plate, a long distance relationship wasn't a good fit for us. It wasn't realistic."

The words don't even feel like my own. I'm just parroting back what Meghan said to me without even believing it.

Cannon's brow knits. "That's *it*? Really?"

I knit my brows right back at him. "What do you mean 'that's it'?" My explanation may be simple but it's valid...Isn't it?

He shrugs. "Well, I mean, yes, distance is hard. But it's...work-with-able."

"Work-with-able?" I snort. "Cool new word for my vocabulary. But a long distance relationship wasn't realistic for Meghan and me."

Cannon shakes his head at me. "Realistic? Why is 'realistic' even a word in your vocabulary." He glances at the busybody staff milling around the hallways. Then, he lowers his voice. "We're fucking billionaires, bro. How 'realistic' is that? We solve difficult problems. It's what we fucking do. It's how we made our fortunes. And you're gonna let a few hundred miles keep you away from your girl?"

When he says that, the ache renews in my chest. The indescribable ache I've been experiencing ever since Meghan cut me out of her life.

I didn't show up at the office today expecting an impromptu coaching session on my dating life but I'll take it. Because I'm fucking miserable without Meghan and I'd sacrifice just about anything—including my pride—to get her back.

Dad was right. The reason I'm so overworked is because I'm trying to control everything. I'm slaving away, trying to carry this billion-dollar enterprise on my back.

I need to delegate shit. Like a boss.

"Fuck. How did I not see it on my own?" I scrub a hand down my face.

Cannon slaps a hand on my shoulder. "Look, my wife and I had our difficulties at the beginning. The only reason we're together today is because we learned how to work with our differences, work around them instead of just giving up. Trust me, it's been worth it."

The elevator arrives and the other men step inside.

"What I'm saying is, there are ways to work around the distance. If that's what you want." He throws his hands up as he backtracks into the elevator. "Of course, no judgment if it's not what you want. So...what do you *actually* want, dude?"

"To fucking be with her," I blurt out. No hesitation.

He gives me a clever, crooked grin as the elevator doors slowly close in his face. "Then man the fuck up, Westbrook."

And with that, he's gone.

FORTY-FIVE

MEGHAN

HALF THE CONTENTS of my closet are heaped on my bedroom floor.

"I can't believe I ever thought this would look cute on me." I stand in front of the mirror, holding a skin tight military-patterned pleather catsuit to my body.

Alana looks over at me from where she's wiggling into a pair of sequined fuchsia booty shorts I thought was a good idea at some point in my life. "I'm pretty sure that's an action movie stunt suit. Where'd you plan on wearing that to anyway?" She hip-checks me out of the mirror and checks herself out.

"I don't know. I always pictured myself wearing this, strutting into the Hot Sauce one night, in my full feminine power, showing this town what I'm made of." I laugh to myself.

Inwardly, I relive the fantasy, with Cash in the crowd, having a front row seat to the show. I picture myself as a different version of me, a stronger version of me. A Meghan who is willing and ready to accept the love of a good man.

I think I'm ready to be that Meghan.

Hence the spring cleaning. It's time for me to throw out the things that no longer serve me and step fully into becoming who I need to be.

"Then I say keep it." Alana tries to tug the shorts down her hips. Which requires some jumping and some shimmying. When that doesn't work, she drops onto my mattress, sticks her legs up in the air and tries tearing the pants off that way. "Because I am all in favor of you owning your fabulousness, Meggie."

"Well, I don't feel very fabulous now. Or very empowered for that matter. Which brings me to the reason for our meeting." I flop down onto the bed next to Alana. "I think I fucked up, Al. With Cash. Ending our relationship was a huge mistake. Probably the hugest mistake of my life. Huger than the military-patterned pleather catsuit."

She's broken out into a sweat, but at least she's free of the bejewelled shorts from hell. "No shit." She laughs, slipping back into her own jeans. She sits up next to me.

"After nearly two weeks of utter agony without Cash, I finally see everything clearly. I spent our entire relationship terrified that he'd abandon me. Yet, I all but begged him to do just that, constantly trying to convince him that he didn't have time for me. All while he was going out of his way, trying to prove the opposite to me." I shudder with regret. "I sabotaged our relationship because I was afraid he'd find something more important than me and reject me. Yet, I was the one who ultimately pushed him away." I drop my cheek to her shoulder.

She strokes my stubborn head. "So now, you have to try again," she says simply. "You have to fight for your relationship like you've never fought for anything before. And if you lose, you'll have no regrets. You'll know it wasn't because you were too coward to fight for what you want."

She grabs me by the shoulders, forcing me to straighten up and face her. "Stop settling for scraps, Meghan. Stop telling yourself you don't deserve the very best life has to offer. Go after what you *really* want."

She's right. The first time around, I only opened my heart a crack, just enough for Cash to wedge a shoulder inside. But this time, I have to fling the door wide open, take the risk, be willing to completely 'go there', be willing to completely let him in, no matter what the outcome might be.

"Gosh. I've been such an idiot," I whisper.

Alana tilts her head to the side. "You're not an idiot," she says softly. "But it does seem like your belief system could use a bit of a software upgrade, though. Meghan version three-point-oh."

We laugh together.

I like that. Meghan version 3.0.

My friend can't stay for long. She leaves me alone with a mountain of clothes dumped on my bedroom floor to sort through as I simultaneously sort through the thoughts in my head.

I make three piles. One to keep. One to donate. One for the trash.

I wish I could come up with such a simple system for arranging the junk in my head.

I grab some garbage bags from the kitchen and stuff them full of the clothes I'll be throwing out. Right before I leave the room, I open my underwear drawer and shove my hand all the way to the back. I slip my hand under the piles of sensible cotton, delicate lace and silky satin. I feel the smooth texture of a photograph beneath my hand.

I pull out the picture of the marriage contract and tears come to my eyes.

On this twenty-fifth day of May, Cassius Westbrook and Meghan Hutchins hereby agree that if neither of them are married by the time they turn age thirty, they shall marry one another.

My heart throbs hard enough to make my head light. From the moment I signed that gas station receipt, I was his. It's time I stop denying it.

I'm ready to fight for you, Cash. Whatever the outcome may be.

I drag my garbage bags down the stairs and to the front porch.

Across the street, I see Jasper, barefoot and disheveled, tugging his own trash cans to the curb.

He lifts a hand in my direction. "Hey neighbor."

I return his wave. "Hey." The corners of my lips feel like a thousand pounds each when I try to lift them.

He drops what he's doing and jogs across the street. Cash's brother gives me a smile that isn't quite as bright as usual. In fact, he looks downright hesitant to approach me.

"You mind if I sit with you for a second?" His eyes sweep over my expression. He must read the downright misery there. And because he's Confident as Hell Jasper, he corrects himself. "Scratch that. I'm sitting with you."

I chuckle softly as he climbs my porch and lowers into a chair. "I look *that* bad, huh?" I ask.

"Sorry. You do." He winces with an apology on his face.

I lower into a chair, too. "So, what's up, Jasper?" I ask.

He plants his elbows on his knees and lets his hands dangle. "Look, I know I'm overstepping my boundaries and I know you're probably thinking this is none of my business but just in case you're wondering, yes, Cash is just as freaking miserable as you are."

"I...I don't know what to say to that," I mumble.

"You don't have to say anything. I just want you to have all the facts." He glances at me out of the corner of his eye. "When you two were together, my brother was a completely different version of himself. He might have had moments when he struggled to manage everything that was going on with work and our family. But he was happy. He had purpose. He was excited about his life. He was...*alive.* And now that you two are broken up, he's gone back to his old ways. He's back in his little cave where the only thing that matters to him is work." Jasper rises from his seat. "So I just wanted you to know that, just in case you're sitting here thinking that he's all peachy without you, he's not. Know that Cash was a better version of himself when you were together."

There's a lump in my throat that keeps me from saying anything. I just sit there and watch as Jasper rises out of his seat then takes off across the street again.

Slightly shaky, I wander back into my house, my eyes landing on the photo Cash gave me on my birthday. Him, frowning. Me, grinning and making bunny ears over his head.

I try to visualize what he must be doing back in Chicago today. If he's not happier without me than he was when we were together, then that defeats the whole purpose of our breakup. And I know I can't wait another second to fix things between us. I need to talk to him. Now.

I start looking around the house for my phone. Before long, the device starts ringing. I get into the kitchen just in time to find it ringing on the counter.

But everything around me stops when I look down at the phone number on the screen.

Shit.

Because today hasn't been enough of an emotional rollercoaster already...

A chill runs through me and my skin pebbles as I press the green button and bring the phone to my ear. "Hello?"

"Hey Meghan, it's Shelly again from the animal sanctuary." I can hear the smile in her voice. "This time it's not another false alarm. This time I'm sure. We have a new adoptive family for the cats."

My heart sinks to the bottom of the sea of misery in my belly when I hear the news. Gosh, I really don't need this today.

I don't bother to fight my tears as I pack up Cotton Ball and Captain Ginger for the second time. Within the hour, I'm driving them toward the animal sanctuary.

I may have gotten lucky the first time around when the first adoption attempt failed but I know this is goodbye. I'm about to lose my cats for real this time.

I wish Cash were here at my side, holding my hand, making it easier for me like the last time. But now that he's gone, I have to face it alone.

Shelly greets me at the front desk and ushers me toward the smelly meeting room where the almost-adoption took place the last time. Dread fills my gut. Gosh, I hate this.

The adoption counsellor smiles at me over her shoulder as I enter the room. But my eyes stick on the man who is here to adopt the cats.

My heart trips and tumbles all over again.

It's Cash sitting there, with his hard jaw flexing and his grey eyes glinting like swords freshly sharpened for battle.

One look at him with those adoption papers in his

hands and my blood goes from frozen to boiling in a heart beat.

No.

No, no, no.

He already stole my heart and flipped my world upside down. Now, he's going to steal my cats, too?

I don't think so.

FORTY-SIX

CASH

CONFUSION FLASHES across Meghan's face when she sees me sitting at the small rectangular table in the stuffy animal rescue meeting room.

She's standing in the doorway in jeans and a simple white sweater. Looking irresistibly beautiful and fiercely protective, gripping a cat carrier in each hand. Her wrists are white from holding the handles so tight.

"Cash, what are you doing here?" she asks cautiously. Her purse strap is slipping down her shoulder, but she's so guardedly focused on me that she doesn't seem to notice.

I rise, stepping around Braveheart's carrier on the floor and meeting Meghan where she stands by the door. "Hi, baby. Let me help you with that."

Eyes wide and afraid, she jerks her cats out of my reach. "Are you here to take my cats from me? Because if you think this is some sick joke and—"

The adoption counsellor stands abruptly and her chair falls over. "Looks like you two need a moment alone." She picks up her chair and starts backing out the door. "I'll be in my office at the back whenever you're ready."

Sensing the tension in the room, Cotton Ball mewls mournfully from her carrier.

The moment the counsellor leaves the room, I turn to Meghan. "I'm not adopting the cats to take them away from you. I'm adopting them so we can take them home. With us. Once and for all."

"What are you saying?" She eyeballs me warily.

I grip the back of the nearest chair to keep from touching her face. "I know how much you love these cats. But when I asked you why you wouldn't just adopt them, you told me that adoption feels too permanent, that you're used to the relationships in your life being temporary."

"Yes, that's what I said."

I dare to take a step closer. "Well, I'm ready to do what you're too scared to do. I'm ready to give you something permanent. I'm ready to give you a solid commitment. And I'm not just talking about the cats." I breathe in. "I'm talking about us."

Her eyes remain guarded, suspicious. "Us?" she echoes me.

I nod. "Yes. I want you back, Meghan. This time, for good." She opens her mouth, looking less than willing to comply. I cut her off. "I know you've already decided that we're over. But hear me out. Listen to what I have to say."

The way her delicate nostrils flare, I know she won't make this easy. But I don't mind. I may have given up once before but today, I'm not leaving here until I convince her that she's mine.

"You broke up with me because you were convinced that we couldn't do the long-distance thing," I say. "You thought a relationship was too much for me to handle with all the other things I have going on in my life."

She nods solemnly. "I saw how much responsibility you

were juggling and I hated adding anything else to your load."

"Bullshit," I say softly. "That's bullshit, Meghan. You know it and I know it. Your reasons go much deeper than that."

She pauses and purses her lips. "I was terrified," she confesses finally. "The truth is, I was terrified by how much I love you. I was afraid that eventually you'd be overwhelmed and have to kick something to the curb and that something would be me." Her eyes lower to the floor. "I was trying to bow out of the competition for your attention so that you wouldn't eventually toss me away instead."

I drop my head and shake it. I fucking knew it. "I don't know what I was thinking, falling for your excuses. I should have seen that you were just scared. I should have known it was just your insecurities talking. I shouldn't have stopped fighting." I sigh. "I guess I was too busy being scared too."

Her eyes fill with concern. She sets the carriers on the floor and touches my cheek.

I leave my ego behind and just be honest with her. "I was scared that I'd forever be disappointing you, that I'd be letting you down at every turn. That I wouldn't be able to give you the attention and the time you needed. I couldn't stand to look at you and see the disappointment my mom used to wear because of my dad." I grasp her hand in mine.

She vigorously whips her head left to right. "I don't feel disappointed in you when I know you're out there making your dreams come true. I feel proud. I get a thrill, seeing you out there pursuing your goals. That's what it is when you love somebody. You want to support them in becoming who they're meant to be."

God, I love this woman. "For years, I've had my blinders on. I was building, building, building. Nothing mattered more than building my empire. But then I opened my eyes up and realized that you'd been standing here all along. Baby, I never needed that billion dollars. Not the way I need you."

"Cash, baby." Her eyes mist over.

I reel her into my arms. "Do you still want me? Do you still love me? Say you do."

"I do," she whispers. "I always have. I'll never stop."

"I love you, too." I cradle her cheeks. "I'm so sorry I gave up when I should have been looking for a solution for us."

She smiles slightly. "Might I propose a solution?" She pulls a folded up piece of paper out of the purse hanging from her shoulder. I take it from her hand.

My pulse thumps hard enough to burst a vein. It's a list of vet tech jobs in Chicago.

I grab her and pull her to me, kissing her until we're both out of breath.

Meghan is panting and giggling when we pull apart. "Is that good?" She motions to the paper I'm still clutching in my hand.

"It's amazing," I tell her. Because it shows that she's willing to work this out with me. And that's what I want from her. Willingness. "But you know I'm not letting you give up your life here and move to Chicago, right?"

Her expression crumbles. Hard. "What? But you said—"

"I'm not letting you move to Chicago. Because I'm moving here," I announce.

Her eyebrows jump up like bagels popping out of a toaster. It's adorable. "You're what?!"

"I'm moving to Honey Hill. Permanently. So we can be together," I tell her.

She stares at me disbelievingly. "You'd move here? For me?"

"It's an easy decision, Buttercup. I would move to another planet, another milky way to be with you. I just..." I brush my fingertips over her bottom lip. "I just want to be with you."

"What about the company? What about your career? You can't do that."

"I'm a billionaire now." I smirk and lift a shoulder. "I can do whatever the fuck I please."

She hugs me tighter and laughs. "You did it?! I'm so proud of you, Cash!"

"Everything that matters to me is here—you, my family, these mangy cats." The three bastards yowl for attention. I ignore them. I kiss Meghan's head. "I just want to prove to you that I'm committed to making this work. By any means necessary."

She presses a kiss to my chin. "I'm sorry I lied to you about why I broke up with you," she whispers against my chest. "I was so accustomed to lying to myself about what I want and what I'm worth. I actually started to believe it."

"Well, now I'm back and I'm not giving up on you. Meghan, I will fight your demons to the bitter end. I'll fight until you believe how worthy you are. You have never been a distraction to me. You're not an obligation. You're my happiness. My literal happiness. For a second, I lost sight of that because you were so damn insistent that I didn't need you. But you are wrong, Meghan. I do need you."

"I'm so sorry, Cash. I need you, too. I didn't realize it until I'd lost you. I guess I'm not a girl who's used to feeling special. I was so convinced that us being together was unrealistic. It just didn't feel realistic that I'd be able to keep you."

I pull back and look her in the eyes. "Not to get too mushy but there's nothing realistic about the love I feel for you. I would tear down a mountain with my bare hands just to be close to you. I love you, Meghan. I know you're my soulmate. There's no doubt in my mind."

She gasps. "Oh god. I know it, too. I love you, Cash."

We kiss again.

"I won't promise you that this will be easy. But I do promise to put my all into it. And I do promise to make it worth your while. I want to wake up every morning for the rest of my life with your golden head on my chest."

She hugs me, her eyes on the cats. "I can't believe we get to keep them. I can't believe I get to keep you."

"You're worth every single sacrifice. I would make them all over again. Because you give meaning to everything I've been building. You and me, we're forever. I'm not letting you get away from me. Never again."

She laughs. "That sounds kind of kidnappy. Also, strikingly romantic."

I slap her butt, chuckling too. "Come on. Let's get this paperwork signed so we can get out of here." I take her by the hand and go off in search of the adoption lady.

I hear the smile in her voice. "Cotton Ball and Captain Ginger missed Braveheart so much. The cats will be so excited to have a reunion playdate."

Grinning, I glance at her over my back. "I can't wait to lock the felines in one room and have a pussycat play date of our own." I waggle my brows.

Her jaw hits the concrete floor. "Cash!"

"You know you want it." I laugh.

"I do want it," she confesses, squeezing her body against my side. "I want all of you."

"So, good thing I'm all yours."

She pulls me to a halt right there in the middle of the smelly hallway with a dozen rescued cats and dogs, mewing and barking and making a ruckus all around us.

"I love you," she whispers, giddily dotting kisses all over my face. "I love you, I love you, I love you."

FORTY-SEVEN

MEGHAN

"WHY ARE you making me stop here?" I grumble to my car full of girlfriends as we pull into the gas station. "We're going to be late for no reason."

My tank is three-quarters full. Yet they insist on stopping to fill up right this minute. To make matters worse, the place is packed. It seems like everyone in town chose tonight to put gas in their vehicles and air in their tires and windshield washer fluid wherever windshield washer fluid goes.

Alana points to the gas pump where someone is driving away. "That one's free."

I circle around and get to the pump before anyone else steals it.

"Top up while you can," Ziggy encourages me. "According to my predictions, prices will be up for the rest of the week."

I roll my eyes. "The same predictions that made me stock my pantry full of saltine crackers after you predicted we'd have a power outage all winter."

The second I cut the engine, Emma hops out of the

back seat. "Gotta go pee." She shuffles toward the convenience store.

I glance over at Alana who's texting away on her phone from the front passenger seat. "Who have you been so busy texting up a storm with?"

Ziggy waves me off. "Just hurry. Go. Go top up the tank."

"Fine." I grouse, jumping from behind the wheel.

I love my girls but today, they're getting on my nerves. It's Cash's thirtieth birthday and we're having dinner at that brewery in Sin Valley.

I have it all planned out. A huge area at the back corded off just for all our closest friends. The last thing I want is to be late. But my girls have been dragging their feet all evening. Like they're deliberately trying to slow me down.

I stride to the pump, pay with my credit card and select the grade. But before I can start filling up, I notice a sleek Audi pull up right beside me.

An impossibly handsome man grins at me from behind the wheel.

"Cash! Thank god." I hurry over to his door. "I thought you were already at the brewery. I was sure we were late. These girls have been slowing me down all evening."

He doesn't respond to me. He only gets out of his car and approaches me, eyes peeled to my face.

"Is everything okay?" I ask, observing his movements. He's acting very, very strange. And he looks nervous for some reason I don't understand.

Until he sets a weathered, faded gas station receipt into my hand and drops to his knees. Right there on the oil-stained concrete in front of the gas pump.

My hands shoot to my mouth. "Cassius, oh my gosh.

What are you doing? How dare you surprise me like this on *your birthday?!*"

"Maybe I'm trying to make you my birthday present." He reaches for my hand. "Meghan Bangin' Buttercup Hutchins, nine years ago, we sat on that curb right over there and I promised you that if neither of us were married by age thirty, we'd marry each other. Well, baby, today I'm officially thirty. And I want to honor our marriage pact."

My jaw is hanging open and I'm blinded by the tears filling my eyes as he speaks.

"I want you to be my wife. Not because we're thirty—heaven knows I should have claimed you a long time ago. Not because it never worked out with anyone else I've ever dated. Not because you're some last resort I have to settle for now that my best days are behind me. I want to marry you because I'm crazy about you. I was crazy about you on the day we signed this gas station receipt. And I'm crazy about you today. Deep down, I've always known you were the one for me. So tell me, once and for all, will you uphold your end of our pact? Will you be my wife?"

I try to get words out of my mouth, I do. But all that comes out are happy, breathless heaving sounds as I vigorously nod my head.

"Is that a yes?" Cash asks, his eyes hopeful and patient and full of love.

"Yes," I manage to croak out. My man springs to his feet and victoriously gathers me in his arms.

I didn't even realize that we had an audience until the hooting and applause starts.

I glance over my back and—holy shit—everyone I know seems to be here. My mom. My friends. All of Cash's family. The girls from the clinic. Even Minka, Declan and their baby are here. Everybody is hanging out of their vehicles, honking their horns and cheering us on as I accept the proposal I've been wanting for half my life.

Cash reaches into his back pocket and produces a ring. He slips a massive, glistening rock onto my left hand. "Oh, baby," I sigh.

We kiss and kiss and kiss. Then I pull back to admire the beautiful ring.

"Let's see it!" Nicky hollers from the next gas pump over.

Laughing and wiping my tears, I wave my hand around in the air.

More honking and cheering.

Cash reaches back into his pocket again and slips a packet of peanut butter cups into my hand.

I break out laughing. "Well, you for sure got me now."

I haul him into my arms, happy tears blurring my eyes. "Thank you for waiting for me all these years," I whisper against his lips when our mouths finally touch again.

Our friends are running in our direction now to wrap us up in hugs and congratulations.

In all the chaos, Cash kisses me hard and possessive. "Are you serious? I always knew I'd never want anyone else but you. You're mine forever. My happy ever after was always meant to be with you."

EPILOGUE

MEGHAN

Three years later...

I'M TRYING to straighten up the stack of animal adoption forms atop the folding table, when a particularly moody cat grabs my attention by trying to escape the makeshift fencing. Again.

"Oh, no you don't," I mumble trying to quickly maneuver around the table. But the cat is just out of reach. She's already climbed to the top of the fence. "Don't you do it!" I scold in a low voice, trying not to draw the attention of the patrons wandering around.

But I'm too late. I'm still too far away to stop the cat when she makes a desperate leap off the top of the gate...

Right into Cash's arms.

"What...? How...?" I stutter, in awe and shock at my man's ninja super hero abilities. "You're here."

The corner of his lips turn upward as he approaches me and presses a sweet kiss to my lips. "Of course I am. I told you I would be. You know by now that I keep my promises to you."

I wasn't expecting to see Cash here today since he just got back to town from a quick business trip to Chicago. While he's set up a small Westbrook Wealth Management satellite office here in Honey Hill, the company's main operations are still run out of their big city headquarters.

He's still the company's CFO but he works reasonable hours and he never lets me forget that I'm the top priority in his life. Well, me and our six cats.

He makes me so happy, always going out of his way to support my dreams. I still work as a vet tech at the clinic but I have other exciting projects in my life, too.

Over the past two years, I've organized an animal adoption drive once a month. The best way to encourage people to foster or adopt homeless pets is to put those adorable faces on display. It's much harder to turn down one of these animals when their sad puppy eyes are staring at you. Trust me, I'd know.

Manipulative? Maybe. But when these shelter animals only have two choices, death or adoption, we'd do just about anything to find them happy homes.

We are set up just inside the entrance of the local elementary school's gymnasium, with a few animal pens set up to house just a handful of the shelter's cats and dogs.

I love doing this event. It's amazing to see the joy on people's faces when these animals win over their humans.

When I went to Cash with the idea, he promised to do everything in his power to help me bring this idea to life. From the beginning, my man has been instrumental in helping me set this up. He used all his contacts and pulled all his strings to make sure I had the resources and support I need.

I'm so lucky to have a man who supports me the way he does.

"What can I do?"

"Besides haul me to the backroom and have your wicked way with me?" Damn, he's sexy.

He laughs. "Yes, besides that."

I decide to behave myself. "Can you keep an eye on the animals for a bit? While I sort the paperwork and get the table all set up?"

"On it." He pivots back toward the animals, clearly taking his new job seriously.

"Oh, and Cash?"

"Yes, Buttercup?"

"You sure you don't want to adopt that cat?"

He looks down, finally noticing the cat he caught, still in his arms. Though instead of fighting to get away, she's curled up sleeping.

Cash shoots me a grim look. "I told you, Meghan, the six cats we already have are enough. I'm putting my foot down. We need to save some room for our human babies, too."

Yeah, yeah. I'll work on winning him over later.

But in all seriousness, although I love being a cat mom of six, Cash and I have been starting to feel it's time for some babies of our own. Babies with his broody grey eyes and my curly blonde hair. We're ready to make that happen. It's the next step for us.

We're crazy busy as the event goes on. We get almost a dozen adoption applications, in the first hour alone, and while I have an inkling that some of those were just women who wanted an excuse to flirt with Cash, I can't even be mad, if it means an animal will get a real home.

I'm pouring fresh water into the animals' dishes, when three familiar smiling faces amble inside.

"Meghan!" my little sisters shriek as they barrel in my direction, arms spread wide.

"Hi girls!" They attack me with hugs that nearly bowl me over.

Darlene comes up behind them, laughing. "Girls, don't kill your sister please. I don't think Cash would like that very much."

My husband greets the mother of my half-sisters with a kiss to the cheek. "I'd toss them to the crocodiles if they hurt my girl!" He jokes, pointing to the crocodile-shaped bouncy house across the room. The girls laugh, running off.

In a heartbeat, they're sitting on the newspapered floor inside a pen filled with small, energetic dogs. There's a chihuahua and a terrier crawling all over them, the dogs waggling their tails in the girls' faces. It's freaking adorable. My sisters are driving Cash crazy with questions, as usual.

"What's this one named?"

"This one here?"

"How much does a dog cost?"

"Do dogs get along with cats?"

"I know we have a cat but can we get a dog, too?"

Darlene's eyes instantly go misty watching them. She looks at me. "I don't know how many times I'm going to thank you for the sacrifice you made for Jessica. For all of us."

I laugh softly. "You don't have to thank me, Darlene. It was no sacrifice at all. They're my sisters."

It's been nearly two and a half years since I donated my bone marrow to Jessica. The minute the tests came back confirming that I was an eligible donor, it was a no brainer for me. Being able to help save my little sister's life has been a gift that has gone both ways. Although the three of us will always have a tiny crack in our hearts left by our bastard father, getting to know these two angels has been an absolute blessing.

My mom strolls across the room with a grin on her face and adoption papers in hand, her arm looped through Mr. Jones's. As Mr. Jones completes the adoption process, Mom and Darlene exchange friendly small talk.

"I knew today would be the day that I finally wore your mother down and convinced her to get the dog I've been dreaming of," Mr. Jones says to me as he scoops his friendly new golden retriever puppy up into his arms.

"Your persistence definitely paid off. Again." I smile at the man and clap him on the shoulder. It's no secret that Mom has been much more open-minded since she finally opened herself up to love again.

After a long day, Cash and I go back to my house—our home—exhausted but happy. We make love in the shower before my man collapses into bed.

He looks so endearing spread out on the mattress half asleep as a National Geographic documentary he's not watching plays on the television.

I stare at him, my heart overflowing with happiness. I can't believe I get to spend my forever with him.

"Hey," I say, standing in the doorway between the bedroom and the bathroom, feeling nervous but excited.

He peels one tired eye open and peers at me. "Hey..." When he sees my expression, his second eye instantly pops open. He bolts upright in bed. "What...?" he asks and I can see that he's trying to restrain his excitement.

I can barely keep from squealing when I whip the pregnancy test from behind my back.

"Fuck, yes!" He jumps out of bed and he's on me in an instant. "Yes, Buttercup. Yes!"

I laugh and cry as he spins me around.

"We're pregnant, Cash. We're pregnant."

"I'm so happy. You've given me everything, woman. You've given me everything I didn't even know I needed." He kisses me and his own eyes blur with tears. "I'm so happy we took a chance on us, Megs."

"It's been wild, hasn't it?" I brush my own tears away.

He nods. "It has. And I want to spent the rest of my life on the wild side with you."

THANK you so much for reading *The Wild Side*! I hope you fell in love with Meghan and Cash.

THE WESTBROOK BOYS aren't done melting your panties yet...Jasper's story, *The Wild One*, is coming next. I won't spill all the details just yet.

But in the meantime, look out for the *Playboys of Sin Valley Series*. Check out an excerpt on the next page.

Book 1: Playing House

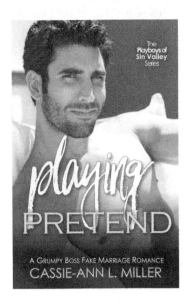

Book 2: Playing Pretend

Book 3: Playing Along

Book 4: Playing Rough

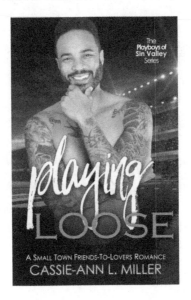

Book 5: Playing Loose (pre-order)

SO WHAT TO READ NOW...?

IN THE MOOD for another steamy, small town friends-to-lovers romance that will melt your Kindle, your panties *and* your heart? Check out an excerpt of ***Playing House***. (Available in Kindle Unlimited)

Excerpt:
Jace

ELECTRIC UNDERCURRENTS FLOOD the glittering Strip. Lights and billboards and flashing things everywhere.

Glitzy casinos. Gorgeous women. Endless booze...A playboy's dream.

I drive past the *Welcome to Sin Valley* sign...

And a giant glob of bird poop splatters my windshield—a pretty accurate representation of my feelings about this day.

"Well, shit... " Declan leans forward from the backseat and braces an arm on my headrest to observe the damage, a sloppy hamburger clutched in his fist.

Next to me, Knox drops his skull against the back of his

seat and groans. The bird crap is further confirmation of what he's been saying all along. "I'm telling you guys—this whole wedding thing is gonna be a drag."

I flip a switch and windshield fluid spritzes the glass as my sleek sportscar coasts down the traffic-jammed Strip under the waning sun.

My face strains into a mile-wide grin that feels like concrete on my lips. "Bird shit is good luck. The wedding's gonna be great." I push the words past the football-sized lump lying sideways across my throat. I tug at the tie strangling my windpipe. "Sera's getting married. It's gonna be great. So wonderful and...great."

My stomach muscles wring hard at the lie.

I'm trying to act like my usual, easygoing self. I'm not sure I'm pulling it off. The truth is, my palms are sweaty against the steering wheel, my scalp is tight, my nervous system is buzzing like I've been doing laps in a swimming pool of extra-strong coffee all day.

Play it cool. Grin and bear it.

I grab my takeout cup from the drink holder and take an icy swallow to wash down my anxiety. Up to this point, I've been playing the role of the bride's supportive friend.

I showed up at her dress fitting for moral support.

I kept her fed while she was running around looking at wedding venues, forgetting to take care of herself.

I made it my job to keep the mood light when the pressure of the wedding planning was weighing her down.

I agreed to walk her down the aisle when her older brother said he wasn't sure he'd be able to make it home in time for the big event.

The courthouse is just around the corner and two streets down. No sense in dropping the nice guy act now.

Suck it up, man. You can do this.

My dashboard lights up, notifying me of an incoming call from Rocky Pfeiffer—the groom. Instantly, my jaw clenches. I casually hit 'decline' on the screen like it's no big deal.

Wordlessly, Declan and Knox share a look. I ignore them, too.

Declan pounds the back of my headrest with finality, causing mayonnaise from his sandwich to drip onto the shoulder of my suit jacket. "That's it! As soon as this wedding is over, I'm dragging your sorry asses to the strip club. You both need a little pick-me-up." In my periphery, I see my idiot half-brother grinning like a baby crocodile and waggling his eyebrows in the creepiest way possible.

Normally, I'd share Declan's enthusiasm. I'm no stick in the mud. I know how to have a good time. And under regular circumstances, a night-out in Sin Valley is fun.

But this is not 'regular circumstances'. This is not business as usual. This day is my personal apocalypse.

I'm just trying to keep it together on the outside, trying to keep the simmering panic from leaking out onto my face. But my stomach is rumbling like I've got a troop of baby elephants mud-wrestling around in there as I drive toward a reality I'm not ready to face.

Keep it together. Hang in there. It'll be over soon. My inner life coach is working overtime today.

I make a right turn off of the Strip, onto Willis Street. It's like driving into a whole different universe. Dull, outdated, unsexy government buildings flanking one side of the quiet road. Crumbling mom and pop storefronts cluttering the other side.

Sin Valley is like any other small town across America.

Quiet, friendly, sleepy. With gossipy neighbors peaking over their hedges and familiar faces in the aisles of the pharmacy. But the Strip is different. The Strip is a playground for debauchery. A place for excessive gambling, spontaneous weddings and other ill-advised life choices. A lot like Las Vegas. But cooler. *Way* cooler. People from all over the country show up here looking for a good time.

"I don't need to go to a strip club," Knox mumbles up at the sunroof.

Declan's not having it. "I beg to freakin' differ. Your divorce is final. At last. You need to stop moping. It's time for you to start living again, man. *At the strip club.*"

"Deck, give the guy a break," I chuckle weakly.

Knox is my teammate on the Iowa Paragons. He's had a rough year. Divorce. Custody battle. That kind of stuff. He's not handling it too well.

Declan turns his attention my way. "And as for you, you must be exhausted from all that fake-ass smiling you've been doing these past few weeks, watching Sera plan this wedding. You deserve a night of fun. *At the strip club.*"

I shrug Declan off my shoulder when another drop of his mayo leaks onto my suit jacket. I unroll that big, ol' grin again. God—my face is gonna need months of physiotherapy by the time this wedding is over. "You don't know what you're talking about." I casually grab my burger from the brown paper bag beside me and take a big bite. My stomach screeches like a race car doing a Formula One circuit. I don't feel that great. I take a sniff of my sandwich. "I think this burger meat is bad. Does yours taste funny?" I glance at my brother.

"The burger meat's fine," he states matter-of-factly. "That's just the sound of your stomach trying to tear itself apart because the woman you love is about to marry some-body else." Declan tosses his empty wrapper at my head. "You did this to yourself. I told you to claim her while you still had the chance. You didn't listen. Now look at you."

Knox lifts an eyebrow at me from beneath the bill of his baseball cap. "He's right, bro. You're not fooling anybody with the Mr. Congeniality shit you've been doing. I know you. I know you've been wanting to rip Rocky's face off with your fingernails this whole time." He shoves a few French fries into his mouth and his big, brown hand brushes salt off the front of his rumpled suit jacket.

I dump the sandwich back in the bag and grab a mozzarella stick. "For the last freaking time—I'm not in love with Sera." I scramble for a logical explanation. "It's just... Rocky. I don't like the guy, okay? There. I said it." Frus-trated, I shove my fingers into my wavy dark hair and pull. "He's a self-centered asshole. And he's all wrong for Sera. He dumped all the wedding planning on her. Forced her to get it all done in just a few weeks so he could focus on the football season. And when the pressure of it almost cracked her, he pressed fast-forward on the whole thing and made her settle for a courthouse wedding when that's clearly the last thing she really wants." I growl. "Selfish. Bastard."

"Well, it's too late to do anything about it now. You missed your shot with Sera. It's very sad...but it's time to move on. *At the strip club.*" Declan displays that goofy, infu-riating grin again. "The one we went to last night for Rocky's bachelor party was awesome. Topless chicks on a merry-go-round. Private dances in blacklight rooms. The dancers even had these payment processor thingies on their ankles so you could tip them with credit or debit if you ran out of dollar bills. And some of the girls had great personali-ties." He nods slowly, a solemn, faraway look on his face. "I met this chick who works part-time as a doula. Another one read my astrology chart for *free*! And I had a really deep conversation with this other dancer—Carrie—about climate change."

Knox picks up his head and swivels his neck to gape into the backseat. "I worry about you, Deck..." He shakes his head and chomps down on another French fry.

Declan keeps rambling on but all I can think about is Rocky hanging out with freaking strippers the night before marrying the most amazing woman on the planet. What a fool!

I glare at my brother over my shoulder. "You realize that your whole stripper fascination is just a distraction from your *real* issues, right?" I wipe my shoulder with a crumpled up napkin, sounding like a resentful old man, grumpy after a Viagra bad-trip. But I'm annoyed—my brother's been in denial about his feelings for his ex-bandmate's sister for a decade. He just refuses to see it. "The party boy life is gonna get old eventually. And then, you're gonna wake up one morning and..."

My words trail off, swallowed up by the grating sound of the windshield wipers still swiping back and forth over the window. I keep my eyes straight ahead on the road but I feel my smile slowly starting to peel off at the corners as the reality of Sera's wedding becomes really, really real. Too real.

"I'm gonna wake up one morning and what?" Declan challenges as he grabs his suit jacket from the seat beside him and tugs it on.

And your favorite person in the world will be marrying some asshat who doesn't deserve her, and it'll be too late for you to do a damn thing about it.

That's what I want to say. But my tongue is dry and

heavy like a plank of lumber as the mental image of Sera silently tortures me.

She's standing at the front of a dreary courtroom, under a blinking fluorescent light. She's floating in a cloud of white silk and lace. She's saying 'I do' to a man who isn't me. I stand by helplessly as some lethargic judge uninterestedly pronounces her another man's wife.

She deserves better than that. Dammit!

Scrubbing a hand down my face, I try to chase away this anxiety. I hate to admit it but I really am a dumbass.

Because this is not some sob story about a guy who's been in love with the same girl since grade school but couldn't work up the guts to tell her.

For years, Sera *really* was just my friend. Nothing more. I was living my life, doing my thing, running around like, 'I'm Jason Bellino, bad boy football player. Look at me running through random women like it's a professional sport.' And then Sera got engaged.

That's when *it* started creeping up.

Feelings. Strange feelings. *Deep* feelings. They jumped out from behind the shower curtain when I was leaned over the toilet taking a piss. These feelings snuck up on me by surprise.

This is a story about an idiot who spent years as friends with a unicorn of a woman and didn't even realize what was standing right in front of him...until she was on someone else's arm.

My dashboard lights up. Rocky calling again. And again, I ignore it. *Why the fuck does this asshole keep calling me?*

Sera's been pressuring him to play nice. She says she wants us to be friends.

Ha! Fat chance.

I never liked the guy. We've played for rival football teams for years. And now that he's about to marry Sera, the possibility of a friendship between us is basically down to zilch.

"You gonna answer that?" Knox asks, both brows lifted.

"Nah. We're almost at the courthouse. Rocky can say whatever he needs to say to me when we're face to face."

Declan and Knox share another telepathic glance.

I chuckle and casually shove more mozzarella in my mouth. "If the two of you keep looking at each other like that, your periods are gonna sync up. Don't say I didn't warn you."

"You're an idiot," Knox mumbles in the seat next to me. He takes a gulp from his heavy takeout cup before dropping it into the drink holder. "You just don't know how good a real, committed relationship can feel. Love. Trust. Devotion."

Declan shakes his head back and forth vigorously. "Don't listen to this guy. He did all the love and kids and marriage crap. Look where it got him..."

I sneak a glance at Knox and cringe. He *does* look pretty rough. Scruffy beard, puffy dark circles around his eyes, he doesn't smell all that great, either. "Yeah, buddy. I don't think you're in any shape to be giving relationship advice," I say with a cringe.

Knox thrusts a middle finger in my general direction. He lays his skull against the headrest and covers his face with his baseball cap. "Fuck you both. I need a nap..."

I chuckle but the sound is hollow. "Would the two of you relax? Sera's just my best friend's bratty kid sister. I'm not secretly in love with her..." That's my official line and I'm sticking to it. Fuck what my stupid heart says.

I'm trying to shed the bad boy image. I'm trying to grow the hell up. I'm trying to not be a shitty human being.

Wrecking my friend's wedding because I'm suddenly 'overcome' by emotions I never bothered to explore in the nearly *two decades* that we've been friends? That is unquestionably some asshole shit. And Sera deserves better from me.

So I'm here to be the nice guy. The guy who'll crack stupid jokes when she gets nervous before the ceremony and tell her she looks gorgeous when she second-guesses her wedding dress and walk her down the aisle because she trusted me enough to ask.

I'm not here to crash the wedding. I'm here to be the bride's friend.

I can do this. With suppression and denial and booze, I can do this.

Because Seraphine Rodriguez is amazing and all I want is to see her happy. Even if it's with another man.

I pull up to the curb outside the courthouse. Sera is standing with her best friends at the top of the wide concrete staircase, her back facing the street.

Her dress is a simple satiny thing that matches the crown of tiny, pale flowers in her dark hair. The hem floats around her knees when she spins around holding a small bouquet in her hands.

And there she is. The Sweetheart of Sin Valley. The nickname really suits her.

She spots me exiting my car and she releases a giant exhale, like she'd been holding her breath for a long time. She adjusts her glasses on her nose and a tiny, genuine, adorable, *terrified* smile slowly pours across her lips.

That's when everything changes.

A switch trips inside my brain. A meteor shower of feelings comes raining down on me. And in this moment, I know I can't do it. I can't watch her marry that douchebag. No way.

Keep it together, man! the reasonable, responsible part of me shrieks. *Keep it together!*

"Nah. Fuck the whole nice guy act."

I might be a selfish asshole. Fine. I can live with that. But I can't live with watching her ride off into the sunset with the wrong man.

I jump out of the car and leap up the courthouse stairs—two at a time—ignoring the warning sounds of Knox and Declan calling my name from the street behind me.

"Don't be *that* guy, Jace!"

"Come on, dude! You're better than that."

"Leave it alone, bro!"

You were doing so well... My inner guidance counsellor wails ruefully. *You were doing so well...*

My heart is beating crazier than it ever has. A stream of sweat is trickling down my neck. But fuck it all. I'm not backing down now.

Because who am I kidding? I've never been the nice guy. I've never been a pushover. I'm the guy who takes what he wants.

And Sera? Maybe, just maybe, she was always supposed to be mine.

FIND OUT WHAT HAPPENS NEXT. **Grab Playing House.**

In the meantime, you can find me here:

Amazon

Newsletter

TikTok

Facebook page

Facebook reader group

Bookbub

DIRTY CAMEOS & EASTER EGGS

I'M an absolute sucker for 'easter eggs' and they're scattered all throughout *The Wild Side*.

If you've read any of my older books, you may have noticed a few familiar faces, quotes and objects making an appearance in *The Wild Side*. If you're new to my universe, here's a little guide to help you figure out who's who and what's what.

THE **DIRTY SUBURBS Series** is a sexy rom-com series set in Reyfield which is a neighboring town to Honey Hill.

Maxwell Masters - Dirty Player
Isla (and Reuben) Barre - Dirty Stranger

THE **BLUE COLLAR Bachelors Series** is a sexy rom-com series set in Copper Heights which is a neighboring town to Honey Hill.

Vivian Hartley, the woman who found a grey hair in her pubes right before her thirtieth birthday - Bad Boy

THE **BAD BOYS in Love Series** is a sexy rom-com series set in Crescent Harbor which is a neighboring town to Honey Hill.

Cannon and Alexia Kingston - Mister Billions

THE **PLAYBOYS OF SIN VALLEY** is a sexy rom-com series set in Sin Valley which is a neighboring town to Honey Hill.

Jason and Sera Bellino - Playing House

Minka and Declan Harris - Playing Rough

Eliza (and Liam) Kline - Playing Pretend

Knox O'Ryan - Playing Loose

Made in the USA
Las Vegas, NV
04 December 2023

82116308R00243